THE
DESERT CONTRACT

A NOVEL

JOHN LATHROP

SCRIBNER

New York   London   Toronto   Sydney

SCRIBNER
A Division of Simon & Schuster, Inc.
1230 Avenue of the Americas
New York, NY 10020

First Scribner hardcover edition September 2008

SCRIBNER and design are trademarks of
The Gale Group, Inc., used under license
by Simon & Schuster, Inc., the publisher of this work.

For information about special discounts for bulk purchases,
please contact Simon & Schuster Special Sales at
1-800-456-6798 or business@simonandschuster.com.

Designed by Kyoko Watanabe
Text set in Original Garamond

Manufactured in the United States of America

10   9   8   7   6   5   4   3   2   1

Library of Congress Control Number: 2008001131

ISBN-13: 978-1-4165-6794-3
ISBN-10: 1-4165-6794-1

to Mariann Elizabeth Befus

. . . he who fears corruption fears life.

—SAUL ALINSKY

THE
DESERT CONTRACT

This novel was written in Dhahran, Los Angeles, Khafji, and Calgary. The author was on the Kuwaiti border at the beginning of the last Gulf war, and in Al Khobar on the day Baghdad fell.

Most of the story takes place in the Eastern Province of Saudi Arabia, in the town of Al Khobar. Strictly, the word "Dhahran" refers to the compounds and installations on the edge of town, adjacent to one another, housing the Arabian American Oil Company, the U.S. Consulate, the International School, and the Royal Saudi Air Force Base. Residents of the province use it generally to refer to the entire community, including the town.

All characters are imaginary.

PART ONE

CHAPTER ONE

A warm breeze from the Gulf blew her hair into my face; can love begin with the smell of a woman's hair? Lust certainly can, but when I tried to kiss her she pushed me away. She called me a ghost, high on the dark balcony of that deserted building where—under different circumstances—we'd first met. She didn't mean me. She meant our old relationship: dead for a decade. I stepped back, and the flash of the explosion far behind me lit her face. Her eyes were hard; the second, more dangerous shock hadn't yet registered. I turned in time to see the fireball vanish like a spent firework over the air base. From that distance the blast wave was only another breeze—from the wrong direction. When I turned back Helen was gripping the balcony railing. She looked suddenly vulnerable, and I felt regret, not for having left, but for having left her.

In memory, past lovers never age. But no one ever stays the same. Earlier that evening I'd awaited Helen's reappearance after thirteen years with anticipation, but also with misgiving. When I'd left her and Saudi Arabia, she was a young Irishwoman—she'd breeze into my apartment with a laugh and a kiss, like a gust of fresh air blown in from the Irish Sea. But I had certainly changed—the gray in my hair was evidence.

She must have changed as well. The southern shore of the Gulf is a poor long-term environment for white women.

The setting for our reunion, the Royal Orient Chinese restaurant, embodied the concept of decay. The street in front had broken and subsided and been repaired inadequately; my spirits began to fall even before I stepped in, carefully, over the uneven tar and concrete. During our affair the Royal Orient had been one of the best restaurants in Al Khobar. Tonight I appeared to be its only customer. Nothing had changed (except the manager—he'd returned to Hong Kong) but everything had deteriorated. Broken plastic vines wound loosely down the room's columns. The pictures of the Swiss Alps on the walls hung flyblown and askew. Wall-mounted air conditioners roared ineffectually; my palms left a watermark of sweat on the plastic tablecloth as I straightened the place mats, the napkins, the silverware—I like things to be in order. A layer of grease lay on every surface, and a heavy grease smell hung on the air.

I wondered why she'd chosen it. Nostalgia? We'd dined there often in the past, but she must have known it had gone downhill. Maybe she saw it as safe. The last terrorist bombing had been months ago, but I'd been warned at an American embassy meeting in Bahrain not to frequent the larger restaurants or hotels in Khobar which catered to a Western clientele. Maybe she had her reputation to consider. Khobar was a very small town. Helen was, after all, now married.

I was considering all this when the door swung open and a tall woman walked into the shadowy foyer. She was without a veil, but like all Western women in public, she wore a black silk *abaya* over her normal clothes. Most wore them like sacks, as if to emphasize the garment's ugliness; hers swept down from her shoulders like a fashion accessory. It was the statement of a woman who had decided she was going to look good in a garment she was forced to adopt.

Her eyes swept the room. She was still in shadow. Maybe I imagined the look of anxiety: like a woman having arrived for a meeting she'd tried to avoid (with her ex-lover? her accountant?), half hoping that a last-minute schedule conflict, perhaps even an emergency, had forced them to stand her up. Then she stepped forward into the light.

My ex-wife used to tell me I was out of touch with my emotions; I'd had reason to keep them under wraps for the past few years. I recognized Helen the moment I saw her face, and the shock immobilized me. She looked like memory come to life—unchanged. I sat stunned as she strode to my table, smiling the fresh-faced smile I'd loved and almost forgotten, leaving the Indian waiter fluttering in her wake. Her walk was the same: impulsive, as if aiming at a target she didn't want to miss.

She held out both hands, happy and welcoming, as if I'd never left her, and greeted me with: "*Dia duit!*" She'd always been proud of her Gaelic. I didn't remember what it meant, but managed to stammer a hello as I rose. It's not safe to indulge in public displays of affection in Saudi, but she kissed me on my cheek, and even the smell of her skin was familiar.

"It's grand to see you again, Steven," she said, sitting down, "and at such short notice. Thanks so much for coming. I'm sorry I'm late but we were stopped twice at checkpoints. It's impossible now to avoid them."

I stared at my past sitting at the table in front of me. Of course it was an illusion. To get a grip I tried to identify the differences that a decade must have made. I tried to see her critically: looking for time's evidence. Her voice, perhaps, was not so strongly Irish. I found my own—I had to say something, she'd mentioned checkpoints—and said, "You're a diplomat's wife. Why would the police stop you?"

Her eyes widened. She said, "You've only been back for a few days?"

"I arrived in Manama a week ago."

"A lot's changed since your day, Steven. But one thing's still the same: this is a very small town. It would have been indiscreet to come to dinner with you in a car with diplomatic plates. I took a cab. The police took their time at the checkpoints. They like to ogle Western women."

Saudi cops ogling Western women. A detail of local culture I'd forgotten. "I'm based in Bahrain," I said, "a civilized Arab country. At least, relatively civilized."

"I'm envious. We used to go there often, to the clubs. Until the

U.S. Navy pulled out, and the bombings started on this side of the bridge, and the state department included Manama on the travel advisory. Now we mostly stay on the compound. This is an outing for me." She glanced around at the stained and faded Chinese restaurant. She said, "I haven't been back here since you left. I'd heard it was getting shabby, but I didn't realize. . . . We'd better order. We don't have much time. The curfew's at nine."

I signaled for the waiter. The Indian shuffled over and handed us two greasy menus and two glasses of Saudi champagne (nonalcoholic), on the house. I wondered if the cuisine would be any more authentic than the decor—or the help. Helen ordered and I followed her lead.

I couldn't take my eyes off her. After the waiter left she slipped off her *abaya*. Underneath it she wore a simple short-sleeved dress. Her figure had changed little. She was slender, with a column-like neck, square shoulders and breasts that were full but not heavy. Her complexion was milk-white Irish. She had sensitive hands, with long, elegant fingers, but with wide wrists. Her features were those that Americans think of as classically Irish, but which in fact represent the peak, not an average, of Irish beauty: the red hair (could it still be that naturally red?), the rectangular, firm-jawed face, the aquiline nose and bold eyes. How old was she? I remembered she was ten years younger than me: she had to be almost forty.

My career's been in finance, in risk assessment. Training took over, and like turning the knurled barrel of a lens the present came into focus. Helen sat before me: Helen in early middle age. The signs of time were there: not quite as slender a figure as I remembered; wrinkles around the eyes; a couple of lines across the forehead and around the neck, a slightly fuller face. They just completed her. She'd arranged an armistice with age. Her look was as unlike as possible the commercial Californian idea of beauty: the blond Hollywood starlet; the cookie-cutter television "personality"; the supermarket magazine cover bimbo. She was womanly. She was real. Her only fault, if it could be called that, was a small, thin-lipped mouth. But, like the rest of her, it was mobile and expressive.

"You look great," I told her. "Stunning."

Her lips rose in a smile her eyes didn't quite agree with. "You were always easy with your compliments. You're looking good yourself. You look as if the wind's been at your back."

With her faded accent the line sounded affected, like stage Irish. But I appreciated the compliment. I have what people call regular features; they hadn't yet started to deform, at least not noticeably. I don't feel older, but I try not to kid myself. During the last couple of years, before I got the job in Bahrain, I'd let things go, and my muscle tone wasn't what it used to be. I had even started smoking again.

I said, "I couldn't believe it when you answered the phone— I couldn't believe I was hearing your voice," and she interrupted: "I couldn't believe it was you—calling from just across the causeway. And on our residence line. The number's supposed to be unlisted."

"Your consulate operator made a mistake. I asked for the commercial officer: Harry Laird. They probably put me through to your home because I asked for him by name."

"And your accent. You and Harry are both Americans."

"I didn't realize he was your husband. I didn't know you were married, or even still here—or that he was out of town."

"Harry's in Washington. A short business trip. He'll be back in a few days."

"I recognized your voice as soon as you said hello."

"As I did yours." She stopped, as if to avoid a conversational road she hadn't intended. She passed her hand through her red hair. "Harry and I got married about a year after you left. I met him on the rebound, in the same place you and I first met: Ayşen's old apartment in Silver Towers."

"Don't tell me she's still here as well."

"She left a couple of years ago, after the first wave of post-9/11 bombings. She's kept the place just in case she ever wants to come back. I'm keeping an eye on it for her."

"So you've been an embassy wife for eleven or twelve years." I meant it to sound congratulatory—I was honestly happy for her—but for some reason the compliment seemed to fall flat.

"Yes," she said. "They've been good years, except for this last."

"You can't have been here since. . . ."

"Since you left me?" She laughed—with the hint of an edge. "Of course not. You mustn't think that. We only stayed for a year after we got married. Then we had assignments in Jordan and Turkey, and finally in Ireland. Harry thought Dublin would be his last station. It was lovely. Harry called it his swan song posting."

"Why swan song?"

"I married an older man. It's such a stock phrase, isn't it? But we were in love. He's much younger than his age. And there were advantages. He has a good position, we've had money, the opportunity to travel. . . ."

The list of advantages ended, like a lonely tune, in a dying fall. It sounded self-consciously pat, as if she'd practiced it too long, like a child who's learned by rote their little story of achievement at school—or their alibi. I asked her, "Why did you come back?"

"Commerce and state are recalling all the old Saudi hands they can still find. The place is such a mess, they don't want to leave it to junior officers. Harry's even put off retirement for a year. They extended his service. We should have been safely back in Ireland by this time."

"You're settling down there?"

"Harry's in love with Ireland. He doesn't want to retire to the States."

"Surely *you* could leave, if you wanted to?"

"In a minute. I'm practically the last spouse left. I had to fight for permission to stay."

It was an admirable example of loyalty. In my years in Los Angeles I'd found a wife, but I'd never found a woman who'd insist on staying in a place like Khobar, just to be with me. Maybe it was envy that made me dig a little deeper: "So it's been a good marriage—no regrets?"

She frowned and for a moment I thought I'd offended her, but we'd been intimate once, and she always was an honest woman. In a soft voice she said, "We have our differences, our problems . . . every couple does, don't they? But no, I don't have any regrets." She wouldn't meet my eye, and we sat in silence, sipping our ersatz champagne. Finally she looked up.

"What about you, Steven? What have you done for the past ten years? What brought you back? Especially now?"

I knew it was coming, but I was temporarily saved by the arrival of dinner. The food was better than I'd expected. What province of China it was meant to represent was debatable, but it was spicy and edible. I was hungry, and after a few mouthfuls I had my equilibrium back. "You remember," I said, "what the boom was like here after the first Gulf war. When we first met. And how short it lasted. I made a lot of money selling mutual funds to expats, especially to Americans. After a year and a half, business began to dry up. In a couple of years it was over." I took a long drink to kill the spice. I'd finished the easy part. The hard part was next.

But I didn't have to tell it immediately. Sitting in sight of the door, I noticed two policemen walk in as if they owned the place (if they'd had a dime between them, they wouldn't have been cops) and call the waiter. Saudi cops, like all Arab police, don't have to look threatening; frequently they look ridiculous. It's not important how they look because everyone knows that what they say, goes, period. The waiter listened to them as he would to a judge handing down a sentence with no possibility of appeal. The police turned and left (not without a lubricious sneer in our direction; my bile rose and I wanted to wipe the sneers off their greasy faces). The waiter shuffled to our table. He gave an obsequious bow—which could only mean bad news—and told us that we had to leave immediately. He'd be happy to pack up our dinner.

Helen argued: it was too early, the curfew wasn't until nine. Until the waiter explained that it was a police order, an unexpected curfew, part of the crackdown on crime, on the remaining nightlife, on terrorism—who knew?

"If it's a curfew," I asked her, "where can we go? Won't everything be closed?"

"Shit," she said, surprising me (she pronounced it in the Irish way, rhyming with "light"). "Yes, even the hotel lobbies will be cleared out."

We stood there, hesitating, while the waiter packed up our dinner in back. The arbitrary orders had come down from above—some colonel?—down the long Arab chain of command to the local cops on the beat, to our Indian waiter and finally to us. The orders were absolute and beyond question. Helen and I were powerless. It was like being the children of a capricious parent: a little taste of everyday Arab adult reality.

Our reunion was about to be truncated. I suspected it would be indiscreet for me to drive her back to her place, and I had nowhere in town for us to go.

Debt had forced me to head back to the Middle East at a time when nobody in their right mind was going there voluntarily. I'd been living since my return in a Manama hotel room. Apart from a couple of potential clients and hotel acquaintances, Helen was the only person I knew on the Gulf.

It's the most successful who take disappointment with the most equanimity, and I hadn't been that successful for a while. I wasn't ready to see the evening end yet.

I said, "Let's cross the bridge. I'll drive us both. We can catch up properly over a drink. I discovered a good bar. You've probably heard of it: the Oasis. Or, we can just go to my hotel's—it's not bad. I'll get you home by eleven, midnight at the latest. There aren't any curfews in Bahrain."

She looked distracted. "It would take us forty minutes to get across the causeway, and another twenty to your hotel. It's too far, Steven, it would take too long."

I wanted to get through to her, to connect; I stepped closer, we were almost touching; I could smell her perfume. Gently as a caress I put my hand on her arm. Her skin was smooth and warm, like a memory of a life I'd almost forgotten. I said, "We've just begun to get reacquainted—after how many years? I want to spend a couple of hours with you. I want to know how you really are, how you've been. Come on. Don't let them win. Come with me."

Different women show openness to intimacy in different ways. Some become wide-eyed and loud. Helen as a young woman would become quiet and conspiratorial. Irishwomen of her generation were not promiscuous (like so much else, that must have changed), and I'd been her first man. Even being taken for the first time she was quiet: holding back her cry, biting her thin lips, digging her nails into my shoulders. I hardly hoped now for her to give in, but she surprised me with a smile, close, almost secretive; she leaned near and said: "I know where we can go."

"Where?"

"Ayşen's apartment. Silver Towers."

She took me off guard, but it was a good idea. The apartment building was just around the corner. The ambience wouldn't be the same as a hotel bar but it would at least be private. It would certainly be more comfortable than the Royal Orient Chinese. "All right," I said, "let's go."

"I still can't stay long," she said, as if flirting with a second thought.

"We'll stay just as long as you like."

So we left the restaurant together in my car.

The sun slanted over the rooftops and the heat beat down on my rented white Toyota, on the garbage littering the potholed roads, and on the concrete and stucco peeling like rot off the shops and apartments. The scene reminded me of a Mexican border town I'd once visited south of Tucson, with its cracked pavements, broken streets and suffocating heat. I turned the car's air conditioner on full, knowing that it would just start kicking in as we arrived at our destination, the oldest high-rise in town.

They'd started building two new towers nearby, but there'd been some contractual or money trouble—or perhaps the right prince hadn't been paid off satisfactorily. In any case they loomed tall and half built, with their cranes standing dejectedly over them. Silver Towers, its sides clad in dusty fake marble, shone in the fading light. I parked in the dirt lot behind. We walked past a gang of skinny Arab kids in flapping *thobes* kicking an old ball, vying to knock over an empty Coca-Cola bottle in the middle of the road.

The two guards who used to sit at a table and record the names of visitors were gone. The foyer was empty. A heavy layer of dust and sand lay over the floor and over the drooping leaves of two potted palms. Palms can survive on very little water—they prefer it dry—but these looked near their end. One of the two elevators was out of service: its doors gaped open to the empty shaft.

"Do you remember the floor?" Helen asked me.

It had been a long time. "No, I don't."

"The eleventh. Near the top—thirteen in all." She pressed the button and a cable shuddered; the lights above the door blinked a descent. Thirteen was an unlucky number, but we would be two beneath it. "Are you certain the elevator's safe?" I said.

She laughed. "As safe as any of the lifts in Khobar. There are stairs, but I'm afraid I'm not up to eleven floors."

"If it's okay with you, it's okay with me."

We creaked slowly upward, then jolted to a halt. We stepped out. The corridor stretched north and south the length of the building, aligned with the coast, apartments on each side. At the far end a door led to a fire escape; there was no point in considering what kind of shape that would be in. A faint light filtered through the door's grimy window, picking out the scarred tile floor and the scabby walls. I began to regret agreeing to come; almost any bar in Manama would be better than this. "The place is falling to pieces," I said.

"It's been nearly empty for years. The last tenants, an Irish couple we knew, finally left a few weeks ago. No one wants to live in an unprotected apartment any longer. But they're cheap, and Ayşen's is still in good shape. Come on." She strode purposefully on, like a girl on an adventure. I felt like a character in a children's novel, a detective story, or a story of hidden treasure: Helen was the brave girl leading me (hanging back and doubtful) through a dim cavern, to . . . what? My own true confessions, presumably. Something I'd rather have kept in the dark.

We walked to the end—I could smell her perfume as I followed her—and she took out a key and opened the door on the left. She entered first; I followed into an even darker hallway. She switched on a light.

An overhead fluorescent flickered, then lit up in garish relief the living room where Helen and I had first met at one of the hundreds of parties after the first Gulf war. Red afghan carpets lay strewn over the floor. A living room set of overstuffed beige furniture sat at convenient angles away from the walls, facing a glass-topped table. Smaller Indian tables of intricately carved dark wood supported Chinese vases and other artistic bric-a-brac. One particularly valued carpet hung from a wall; two bookcases stood against another. There was a slight smell of dust. I recognized nothing from a decade earlier, but everything looked vaguely familiar: a mummified, preserved memory of a certain kind of comfortable, semi-artistic expat lifestyle in Saudi Arabia.

Helen threw her *abaya* over a chair. "I have a woman give it a clean every month. It's not bad, is it? I don't know how much is still here from your—our—day. Ayşen redecorated a lot, but somehow everything always looked pretty much the same." She slipped into the little kitchen, turned on a light and pulled open a cupboard. "Which would you like," she asked me, "some *sid,* or some homemade wine? I'd advise the *sid.*"

Saudi is officially dry; you can't buy liquor in public. It was yet another reason, besides security, for me to stay headquartered across the bridge in wet Bahrain. In Khobar you could, with the right connections, purchase home-brewed wine, or, if you needed something stronger: moonshine—*sid,* short for the Arabic *sidiqi*: friend. *Sid* rotted your guts faster, but it was easier going down. I told her I'd go with her recommendation, and crossed the living room to unlatch the sliding-glass doors leading to the balcony. She joined me, holding a glass in each hand.

We stepped out. The balcony ran the length of the apartment. We had a bird's-eye view of the side of town facing the long desert toward Riyadh; from the far end we could see the northern coast. Seen from above, Khobar looked even smaller: a little, down-at-heel Arab town on the southern shore of the Persian Gulf. None of the flashiness of the capital far inland. But this was where the oil, the wealth of the country, came from.

We walked to the end of the balcony and stared at the Meridien Hotel in the distance, a lonely landmark on the shore. The setting sun flashed on the hotel's sign, and I saw that the giant M was askew, one of its moorings broken.

"Look," I said, "remember how it hung crooked before, and how they fixed it, right after the first Gulf war? Victory brought success. Business was roaring, everyone had a new car, everything got a face-lift. Look at the place now. I don't get it. Oil's been at record highs for years, but except for a couple of new malls outside of town, the place is dilapidated."

"You've been away so long. This isn't Abu Dhabi, or Dubai. The country was on a decline for twenty years, and the good times you remember, after the first war, didn't last. You remember that—it's why you left. In real terms, oil's still lower now than it was twenty years ago. Sure, the royal family's flush, but the average Saudi . . . you don't reverse thirty years of recession overnight." I thought: She's well informed; it's a plausible analysis. But she is the wife of a commerce officer. She continued, "This last war didn't bring us prosperity—it brought us bombs in Riyadh, murders here in town, and hatred on the streets. You said on the phone you were selling investments. Who to?"

"Saudis. Businessmen. They've got the money, I'm sure of it. They're just not investing locally. I don't blame them. I wouldn't either, in their shoes. They're looking for somewhere safe, somewhere offshore." It sounded like a sales pitch, even to me. But I believed it.

The sun was setting and we turned to the east; the last rays lit her red hair like a halo of fire. She saw the way I looked at her, and said, "Let's go in. Tell me about LA." Back inside she took the sofa; I sat on a chair opposite. It felt like an interrogation—but friendly, without harsh lights or thumbscrews.

"You left me and Saudi," she said levelly, "because the boom had run its course. You went back to California. And then?"

I took a drink and a breath. "I'd been good to the company, and it was good to me. The nineties were a great decade once they got started—once Clinton got elected. Pretty soon I was a senior manager. I got married in '97." I looked down at my glass. It was too soon to take another drink.

"The firm got heavily into venture capital funding. I was a lead in opening that line of business, particularly with Silicon Valley start-ups. It was the height of the boom. Then the dot-bomb hit. Within a year our venture capital business collapsed. They brought me back into mutual funds, but by then everything was heading south. We were pretty aggressive trying to keep the company afloat . . . maybe too aggressive. I was one of the last to go before it went under. I'd been out of work for a while when the market finally picked up and I talked myself into this job. I sold them on the idea that there's flight capital here, looking for a safe spot to fly."

Translation: I left you because the job was over; I had a few good years; the dot-bomb washed me up; I'm broke and I came back because it was the only job I could find. It was a summary that left out a lot, but I didn't feel that confessional. By a certain age most of us have periods in our life, and things that we've done, that we'd prefer to forget. I'm an American. I believe in optimism. I believe in looking forward, not back.

Of course, you don't always take all your old friends and acquaintances forward with you. If you confess a failure to a friend, and they look pained or embarrassed, it can be a proof of sincerity. But an attempt to hide a smile is a confession of envy: of your money, your job, your car—maybe even your wife.

Helen looked compassionate. She said so softly I hardly heard her, more to herself than to me: "I remember now—you were always an honest man." She was talking about someone from her past, but it was a compliment and I murmured my thanks. Then she said, "Returning to Saudi, especially now. . . . Didn't you have any doubts? The security situation—you must have kept up on it."

"I did the research. The stats could be worse. The government signed on to the War on Terror. They've rounded up hundreds of suspects. And they're trying to liberalize: the local elections, for instance. Last year about ten Americans were killed or injured. With something like ten thousand of us left in the country that's a point-one percent chance of anything happening—at least to me. There haven't been any bombings on the coast for a couple of years. And I don't even live here. I live in Bahrain; I only drive over for business. So the odds," I finished with a little grin, "aren't bad."

She stared as if trying to discern whether I was serious or just making a bad joke. She said, "You're mad. Completely mad. Steven, do you remember Westvillage—the compound you used to live in?"

I remembered. "Of course."

"They cut the throats of four Americans there. Less than two years ago. How do you convert that to a statistic? The threat's real. And you can't predict when or where the next attack's coming. I wonder how much you really know about this place—or how much it's changed."

"I've kept up. CNN, Fox News, the *LA Times.* . . ."

"CNN, Fox?" Her eyebrows rose, then her voice. "That's entertainment, not news—and vulgar entertainment at that. You'd do better to watch Irish dance. At least that's real. Your American news shows have no idea what's going on here—or they're not interested in reporting it. Or maybe they're afraid to cross your government—it doesn't matter. I don't think you know what's going on here: the hatred, the politics."

"Politics don't interest me. I'm here to make money, that's all."

"Politics is what this place is all about. It's why we're here. America considers this country its great regional ally. What is Saudi Arabia, really? An absolute monarchy. A police state. A police state where probably forty percent of the youth are unemployed—and, most of them, unemployable. The government's pro-American, but the people, certainly the young, hate America. When the news of 9/11 hit the radio, car horns started honking. They loved it! I doubt that made CNN or Fox, did it?"

"Helen, I'm not here to sell investments to the unemployed. I'm dealing with businessmen. Responsible businessmen. Politics doesn't enter into it."

"Would the Arabs want to send their money to your country—a country most of them hate—if they thought it was safe to keep it in their own? We're all involved in politics, whether we like it or not."

"Not me. I'm not involved."

"We all are. We live here."

"I live across the causeway, remember? I'm not here to solve anyone's problems—except their investment problems. I'm interested in local politics insofar as they stay favorable to outgoing investment. Other than that, I don't give a damn."

We'd both become a little intense—over what? Something that wasn't our business, that neither of us could do anything about.

She sat farther back on the deep sofa, farther from me, in silence. After a few moments she asked, "Are you working for an American firm?"

"Yes. Winston Investments, in LA. A mutual fund company."

"How does Harry fit in? You called this morning for him, not for me."

"Your husband's the local U.S. commercial officer: the bishop. I need his imprimatur."

"What do you mean?"

"The federal government's scrutinizing funds leaving the Middle East, particularly funds from Saudi. All part of the War on Terror. I need Harry to vet my Saudi investors, at least the biggest ones. He needs to give them his blessing. And, of course, I'm hoping he'll be able to refer some clients."

She said softly, "I thought it might be something like that." Watching her, I recalled one of her mannerisms: she always looked troubled when giving bad news.

She said, "When you called this morning, I panicked. I asked you to dinner for a reason. I wanted to tell you that we couldn't meet again, after tonight—socially or any other way. It's not that I don't want to see you. It's been wonderful seeing you again. But this is such a tiny town, and the expat community is so very small, much smaller than you remember. There are still a few people here from when we knew each other. We run into them at parties. I'm married now, Steven. It may not be the happiest marriage in the world, but I value it. I don't want anything, even a faint hint of an old rumor, to disturb it. I don't want any rumors, even ancient ones, to reach Harry. You understand, don't you?"

Of course I understood. She'd said she remembered my honesty, but I've never believed in telling everything. Too much truth can be corrosive, even in the best marriage. I'd never mentioned Helen to my wife.

And in any case, what's deader than a dead affair, a dead romance—whatever you like to call it? But with her sitting there, the memory of her taste still in my mind, it was hard not to feel a little disappointment, even resentment—although I'd had plenty of practice in keeping that in check. "I understand completely," I said. "I'll even find someone else to vet my Saudi clients. Someone at the embassy in Riyadh."

Relief spread across her features, a relief so open and simple I could have been again with a girl too young to worry about who knew about an old affair; a girl without the need to keep an older husband in the dark, to know what not to tell. She got up, stepped closer, knelt on one knee and put her hand on my arm. "I thought you'd understand. I don't want there to be any hard feelings—and I'm sure you don't, either. Now do me a favor"—her tone was that of a mother trying to cheer up her child after administering a mild rebuke—"tell me about your wife."

"My wife?" The transition was too sudden. And some failures aren't amenable to the gentle approach. "We divorced shortly after I lost my job."

She recoiled as if I'd sworn at her. She said, "I'm sorry."

Silence fell between us. One can receive too much sympathy. Helen had given me the message for which she had set up our meeting, and I'd given her the reassurance she wanted. Our reunion was over. I got up. "I'd better be going," I said, "and you have to get back to your compound. I can call you a taxi—unless you'd care for me to drive you?"

She hesitated. "I'm not sure you should. . . ."

"Of course not. I'll call you a cab." I looked around for a phone, but she exclaimed, "Oh, Christ, I can call one myself." She took my arm, and said, "Let's try and part friends. Come on, have one more drink. Let's take it outside and get some fresh air."

So I went back out on the balcony, in the dark now, with the lights of Khobar burning beneath. They stretched up the coast to my right, and ahead to the desert's edge, but on my left they stopped halfway to the horizon, as if a chunk had been bitten off the town's perimeter. It was the air base. The Saudis like their security installations dark.

Helen joined me with our drinks, and asked, "Do you remember the parties Ayşen used to have here?"

I thought back. "Yes, I do."

"They were so cosmopolitan. Turks, a smattering of Africans, Greeks . . . do you remember Roberto, the Mexican?"

"Yes," I answered, and we both laughed at the memory. "We had a lot of fun. I met Ayşen through investments. I've forgotten how you got to know her."

"She thought I saved her life. We met on a boat trip—you remember them—the trips out on the Gulf? She almost died of seasickness. I did what I could for her—I was still a nurse, then—and she never forgot."

For a moment the years slipped away, and I was back in another kind of expat community: one of parties, friends, lovers; one without fears, without worries, where a major crisis was—a case of seasickness. "It was a good time," I said.

"It was a grand time." She stood beside me, staring down into the night. "I think I was in love with you. Do you remember?"

"I've never forgotten."

"Why didn't you come back?" She spoke into the night air. "Everyone—including me—thought you were returning."

It was the question that had hovered unspoken all night.

She said, "Did you never think. . . ."

"Of you? Of course I did. Often. But you and this place . . . it seemed like a dream. Like a place from a different planet, a different time." Even in the darkness I could see her face had fallen. I never wanted to hurt her. I thought, There's still time to sweeten it a bit—and there's truth in it, too. "I was a fool," I told her. "I missed you. I had to make myself forget."

"I missed you so much."

She sounded on the verge of tears.

It was an unlikely place for romance. But she was an affair from my past come alive again, and I'd been so long without love. She wore honesty like a child's innocence, without being aware of it. After what I'd gone through in LA—the business illegalities, the failed marriage—

her honesty was as sweet as her perfume, as the taste of her skin. And perhaps the *sid* was having an effect. I set my glass somewhat shakily on the balcony, placed my hands on her waist and drew her to me.

A warm breeze from the Gulf blew her hair into my face; I brushed it aside with one hand, to reach her lips. For a second she yielded, but then pushed me away. She said, "You're like a ghost, Steven. I won't be haunted."

The flash far behind me lit her eyes. I turned in time to see a distant fireball on the edge of town vanish into the air like some piece of trick photography. I turned back to find Helen gripping the balcony railing. She looked vulnerable, and I felt the need to protect someone, to keep them happy—like a pain I never expected to feel again.

The sound of the explosion was as faint as a sigh. A whisper of air from the shock wave ruffled the curtains.

"Jesus," she said, "it's the air base. The Saudi air base."

We looked in its direction, but there was nothing to be seen. It was too far; everything was lost in darkness.

"What was it?" I asked.

"Maybe an accident. Maybe a bomb. I'll call the consulate. The duty officer will have heard something."

We stood staring out at nothing for another minute, then I noticed that traffic at the base of our tower was increasing: cars were speeding toward us and turning in to park in the vacant lot opposite the rear of the building. A police car, with its lights flashing, sped up and joined them. No one was parking in any order. From the eleventh floor they looked as random as dice thrown into a box.

"What do you think's going on?" I said.

"I don't know. They can't live here. The police are probably trying to find out." But as we looked down, more cars, with more police among them, appeared from the west, forming a ragged convoy heading in our direction. In a few minutes the perimeter was clogged with vehicles. We had a confused picture of men moving beneath the streetlights toward the base of the building—and vanishing inside.

"Could we be on fire?" I seemed to be asking all the questions.

She gave a short, mirthless laugh. "That's not the fire department." She slipped past me into the living room and pulled a cell phone out of her purse. I lingered for another minute looking out over the balcony. Cars continued to arrive. Now they were having to park down the road.

"The consulate line's busy," she told me when I walked back in. "Why don't you take a look at the lift."

"What for?"

"To see if anyone's coming up. You can tell from the indicator lights."

Her expression was calm but her posture rigid. We stared at each other for a moment, then I walked out to the corridor. It was empty and almost pitch-black. In order to see, I picked up a small vase and used it to prop open the apartment door. The elevator at the far end seemed very far away.

I saw the lights blinking on the panel on the wall before I was halfway there. The elevator was on its way up; it had already reached the fourth floor. As I watched, the fifth light blinked on. The sixth blinked on, and stayed on. The elevator had stopped.

I looked around. Behind me was a door with a sign indicating a stairway. I pushed it open. In the gloom stairs led up and down from a landing. An obnoxious smell rose from the well. A dead cat, maybe, or a rat that had gotten lost and trapped. I let the door close and heard, faintly, the slap of cables. The lights blinked: the elevator was ascending again. Past the sixth, past the seventh floor, continuing on up.

I started walking back to the apartment, keeping an eye over my shoulder on the indicator.

The eleventh light switched on, then winked off. The twelfth flashed, then the thirteenth.

In the living room Helen stood staring out the window. "Are they coming up?" she asked.

"They've gone past us. Right to the top—the thirteenth floor."

"Whoever 'they' are."

"Did you get through to the consulate?"

"No, the line's still busy."

"Where did I put my drink?"

She reached down and handed it to me. Our fingers touched.

"I'm sorry," I said, "about what happened out there . . . I didn't mean to upset you."

She just shook her head and punched in a number on her cell phone again. This time she got through.

"Bill, it's Helen. I'm stuck in town. What's going on?" She listened for a minute, then told him where we were, and mentioned the crowd below and in the building.

"How should I know," she said, "what the police are doing?" And then, "Do you think it's safe?" A pause. "That's almost certainly impossible. They're all over the place." Her voice fell: "They're bound to see us." After a moment she gave him her cell number, then hung up and turned to me. There was a slight tremor in her voice.

"That was the political officer. He said there's a rumor that something's happening at the air base. One or more explosions. He's trying to find out, but he's swamped with calls. He told me to get out of here and get back to the consulate."

"We're supposed to just walk out?"

"He suggests we avoid the police."

"Why? What's the problem?"

"He said there might be unreliable elements . . . he doesn't know what's going on, Steven. No one knows."

Unreliable elements. It sounded like jargon, a state department term, a euphemism for something. Or for nothing. Two words from a foreign language you needed a code to decipher. "Well," I said, "the police are hardly working for Al Qaeda, are they?"

Her voice was low. "I've no idea. I hope not."

"Oh, come on. . . ."

"Bin Laden's a Saudi, Steven. And there're thousands more just like him out there, in the streets."

A society in which you can't trust the police: it was an equation that didn't add up, like a fraudulent balance sheet. Normally I would have considered the idea alarmist. Now it just froze me, mentally, in my tracks. But it was ridiculous to stand there, immobile. I said, "Let's figure out a way of getting out."

"The lift's no good."

"There's the fire escape."

"Eleven floors down?"

"If it's dark enough. Let's just give it a look." I stepped back out—the corridor was still empty. We were at the end, and the emergency exit door to the fire escape was just to my left. I put both hands on the bar and pushed down, but it wouldn't move; I put my weight on it and it shot down. I pressed my shoulder to the door. It creaked open a few inches; a sprinkle of dust fell from the jamb onto my head.

We heard a faint bell, and turned together. At the far end of the corridor a shaft of light spilled out of the open elevator. A group of men spilled out with it, five in all. Three wore *thobes*; two were in uniforms. I thought I saw one rifle.

They were talking among themselves. In the dark they hadn't spotted us. Helen slipped without a sound back into the apartment's doorway, and holding her finger against her lips, motioned me with her other hand to follow. I'd almost made it when, behind me, the fire exit door gently closed, the bar jerking up as the latch snapped into its socket with a clang.

CHAPTER TWO

Shouts came from the far end of the corridor. I jumped inside and slammed the door.

"Lock it," Helen told me.

I locked it and shot the chain bolt. My hands trembled. I said, "This is pretty damn guilty behavior."

"I know. I'm not sure we're doing the right thing."

"Then why the hell are we doing it?"

"They might suspect us."

"Suspect us? Of what?"

"I don't know. Spying."

"Spying? That's ridiculous. We're just having a drink."

"I know, Steven. We're probably safe. And privacy is sacred in this country, unless. . . ."

"Unless what?"

"Unless they suspect you."

The absurdity of the situation revolted me. "Why don't we just show them our IDs?" I said. "Two of them looked like police."

Her voice almost broke: "We're not sure we can trust them." We jumped back as the door shook under an angry pounding. We retreated to the living room. The pounding stopped. Through the door we heard shouting in Arabic.

Helen said, more calmly, "I'm calling the consulate again. They might have someone to send to fix this. Some Saudi in the secret police."

She got through on the third attempt. As she talked I stepped out to the balcony and looked carefully over the railing. The scene was unchanged. It occurred to me that ours was probably the only apartment in the whole building with a light showing. They would probably have checked out our apartment whether they'd seen us or not. But it was a bit late to turn the lights off now.

When I went back in Helen was stowing the phone in her bag. "He's going to see if they have anyone to send," she told me, "but it's going to take a while. They still don't know what's going on at the air base . . . everything's pretty confused." She looked bleakly toward the door. "He suggested I tell them I'm a diplomat's wife."

"I wonder if they understand that much English."

"I know that much Arabic."

We crept toward the door. Outside in the corridor all was silent again. The lull continued, and I thought: Perhaps that's it, perhaps they aren't interested in us; it's all a mistake anyway. If they're about to go, it might be better to leave well enough alone. I whispered to her: "Don't say anything yet."

The silence lengthened. Helen turned to me with a tentative expression of relief.

Then with a smash the jamb splintered and the door burst open.

We recoiled into the living room as two burly, bearded men in *thobe*s blundered through the doorway. When they caught sight of Helen it was as if they hit a wall. They behaved like two Bedouin who'd burst into the wrong room—not expecting a woman—by mistake. While they hung fire two uniformed policemen pushed past them. They were clean-shaven, one short, wiry, and dim-looking; the other older, heavier and authoritative. They ignored Helen and strode up to me. The older man's brown uniform was as crisp as that of a parade-ground soldier, but the impression of discipline was weakened by a black leather holster belt studded with brass cartridges hanging at an angle over his hips. Despite the incongruity, authority hung on him like the belt: he looked like a man who settled things.

He stopped in front of me and said, in good but heavily accented English: "I am Captain Saad, this is Lieutenant Hassan. Please give me your identification."

I was not brought up to question the police (I'm not inclined, temperamentally, to doubt authority—except perhaps the questionable authority of a broker's buy recommendation), and although alarmed I was relieved to be facing a police officer. I reached into my pocket for my passport, but before I could pull it out Helen produced hers and held it, open, in front of the man's face. "*Ameriki Ana,*" she said. "*Zouwadjat diplomasi.*"

The captain snapped it out of her hand, and without looking at her said, "Please speak English." He held out his palm for mine, and I handed it over.

"This is your apartment?" the captain asked me. He continued to ignore Helen.

"No."

"Where do you live?"

"Bahrain. My office is in the Continental." Having an office sounded somehow legitimate, at least to me.

He turned to Helen. "This is your apartment?"

"Please look at my passport. It's diplomatic. I live on the American consulate."

Her tone was peremptory (if slightly unsteady); her stance hostile. I didn't know if I should admire her or be apprehensive. Was it a good idea? Was it real? Was she really that gutsy? It wasn't one of her qualities I recalled from the past.

The captain thumbed the pages of both our passports—mine standard American, Helen's that of a U.S. diplomatic spouse (in my absence, she'd acquired another nationality, as well as a husband). Presently he looked up again at me. "Steven Kemp. You are not . . . *diplomasi,*" he said. It was a statement.

"No. I'm a businessman."

"What are you doing here?"

"I sell mutual funds."

It was evidently a puzzling answer. "Mutual funds?"

"Investments," I explained.

"I mean," the captain said slowly, "what are you doing in this apartment?"

I was wondering what to say—I could hardly tell him I had come for the view—when Helen broke in: "We came to inspect it. It belongs to a friend of mine. We came to make sure everything was still okay."

"Why now?" the captain asked.

"Why not? I check it every week."

"Where is your husband?"

"At the consulate," she lied. "He is expecting us."

"You and Mr. Kemp."

"Yes."

The balcony curtains waved gently, drawing everyone's eyes to the open glass doors. The captain walked over and looked out through the darkness, in the direction of the air base. When he returned his face was impassive.

"You have a phone," he said to Helen.

"Yes."

"Please call your consulate."

She hesitated for a moment. Then she pulled out the cell phone. "Who do you want to speak to?" she asked him.

"The operator."

"I tried before to get through. I couldn't. The line's busy."

"Try it now."

She dialed the number. As her finger left the last button the captain pulled the phone from her hand and held it to his ear.

I thought: It's a risky lie.

He spoke quickly in Arabic. I know nothing of the language, and the only words I recognized were "Harry Laird." He rolled the Rs of the first name. After a few moments he pressed the button to hang up.

He said something to his subordinate, who was standing like a block of wood, a dim scowl painted on his face. The lieutenant trotted on his thin, bandy legs to the balcony and pulled the curtains closed. The men in *thobes* had stayed in the background. Now the taller of the two, an older man with a long beard, stepped forward impatiently. He exchanged words with the captain; it sounded like an argument. To me he looked like trouble. I preferred the police. A uniform could be threatening but it was also a symbol of discipline, of rules, of limits. The two men in *thobes*, with their beards and disapproving faces, looked like fundamentalists, fanatics—people with unreliable views on limits.

The captain listened and replied calmly. But either his reply or his manner seemed to incense the other. Finally the officer had had enough. He raised his voice and made an abrupt gesture with his hand—the cutoff. He turned to Helen.

"Your husband is not at the consulate. He is in America." He paused. "I do not know what you are doing here, but I do not believe you are just checking this apartment."

He looked at me. His tone was contemptuous rather than interrogatory. "Why are you here, Mr. Kemp? What are you doing with this *Zouwadjat diplomasi*? Why are you both in this empty apartment," he looked toward the curtains, "with a good view of the town, of the air base?"

"We are both Americans," Helen replied, in a controlled, firm tone, pressing her point home as if she were driving a nail through wood. "You can see our nationality from our passports. You know my husband works at the American consulate. There is something going on—we saw the explosion—and the consulate wants us both to leave here immediately and return there, for our own safety. We would appreciate a police escort."

The captain smiled thinly. "The American embassy is full of spies. Now you will move into another room. I must ask Mr. Kemp a few more questions."

Helen didn't say anything, but she stepped closer to me; our shoulders touched. I thought I felt her tremble. Or maybe it was me. I said, "Wait. You can ask me as many questions as you like. But we'll remain together."

"You are not married. There is no reason for you to be together. Mrs. Laird will be more comfortable in another room."

Helen whispered, "I'm not leaving you," and I heard the tremble in her voice. I thought: This has gone far enough.

"You can ask me anything you want," I said. "But Mrs. Laird stays with me." I put my arm around her shoulder.

The captain nodded at his subordinate.

I'd forgotten the wiry little lieutenant. He came up from behind, grabbed Helen's free arm and jerked her away, into the middle of the room. She stumbled on one of the afghan carpets and hit the floor on one knee. The lieutenant pulled her to her feet and started dragging her to the hallway.

I hadn't expected violence. It happened too quickly. I wasn't prepared to react.

Helen staggered after him, then dug in her heels. She shouted something, attempted to stand her ground, and with a twist tried to yank herself out of his grip.

He swung the back of his hand into the side of her face. He was a small man—probably from a Bedouin background, a peasant—but he had a peasant's brute strength. He smacked her exactly as a farmer would move or fell a doltish animal. She dropped in a heap onto the floor.

I've never considered myself a courageous man. My career has been about managing risk, not being brave (especially with other people's money). An American soldier I met in a bar in Manama told me over a drink that bravery is about managing fear; he said he'd been scared shitless almost every time he'd had to advance. But he'd forced himself to do it.

I'd just had enough. I'd had enough of the suspicion, the intimidation, the third world police, the whole third world setup. And there was no way I was going to let Helen be beaten up.

As the lieutenant reached down to pull her up again, I jumped at him and brought both my fists down as hard as I could on his neck. I had a serious weight advantage, and it helped. It caught him unawares. He collapsed like a sack of potatoes.

I knelt by Helen. She lay sprawled on the carpet, legs askew, stunned. She couldn't even raise herself on one arm. The captain and the others looked just as stunned. I don't think anyone had expected things to go that far—to get that out of hand.

While I tried to help her back to her feet, four new men strode into the room. The man in front was dressed incongruously in a three-piece business suit. He took in the picture and spoke sharply to the others. They all replied at once, shouting together. The foreigners were ignored.

I managed to get Helen to the couch; we had to step around the still-fallen and groaning lieutenant. She was shaken, and held her hand to the side of her face where she'd been hit, but she managed to say with a thick voice, "I never knew you were handy with your fists."

"I'm not. I've just put on some weight. I never thought I'd be glad of it."

"I wish you'd killed him."

Coming from her, the words sounded almost obscene. I said, "How are you feeling?"

"I'll survive. What's going on?"

"I don't know. A few more just came in. They're probably arguing about what to do with us."

I wasn't conscious of being more than anxious—until I realized that my shirt was sticking to my back. It was soaked with sweat.

We sat there, some comfort to each other, until the shouting ceased and the man in the three-piece suit detached himself from the others. He looked about fifty, short and somewhat corpulent. He wore a beard, but his was well trimmed. He gave the impression of an academic: one could imagine him at a British university, teaching Middle Eastern studies, or as a long-winded guest on an Al Jazeera political talk show. But, like the captain, he too wore an air of authority—despite the academic appearance. He approached us, smiled reassuringly, and held out his hands in an apologetic gesture.

"I am Dr. Abdullatif Ali," he said. "I am sorry the situation developed as it did, and I hope the lady is not badly hurt. May I sit?" We said nothing, and he lowered himself into an armchair beside the couch. His accent was Arabic with a British overlay. "I have your passports here." He held them up. "And your telephone, I believe." He handed it back to Helen. "You are Mrs. Helen Laird. Your husband has some official position at the U.S. Consulate in Dhahran?"

"He is the chief commercial officer," Helen said, her voice still a little thick but clear.

"And you, Mr. Kemp," Ali said to me, "are a private businessman?"

"I'm an investment counselor. I have an office in Bahrain. Mrs. Laird and I are old acquaintances. We came up here to check on this apartment. Mrs. Laird has been taking care of it for some absent friends. Then this gang burst in. They tried beating up Mrs. Laird—you can see what they did to her—and I was forced to intervene. We're only interested in one thing: getting out of here, back to the American consulate."

"It's a pity I did not arrive sooner. We could have avoided all this unpleasantness. Mrs. Laird, I am truly sorry for this . . . this injury to you. There was no need for it. Neither" (he said like a professor making an additional important point) "was there any need to break open the door. I have master keys for the whole building."

"We have to leave immediately." I wanted to stick to the point. "And I have no intention of letting Mrs. Laird become separated from me."

"No one will separate the two of you."

"They gave it a pretty good try."

"Mr. Kemp, I am the president of our group, the Islamic Arabia Party. I am also in charge of this operation. I can absolutely assure your safety here. And, Mrs. Laird, if you feel you need the attention of a doctor, there are two in our group who can help you. I cannot tell you how sorry I am that this happened."

Helen spoke up: "You're Abdullatif Ali?"

"Yes."

"I thought you were in London."

"Then you have heard of me. Of course, as the wife of an American diplomat, that is not surprising. I was in London—until recently."

"Then . . . what is this all about?"

He smiled like an avuncular cat that had caught the canary. "I think you have guessed, Mrs. Laird. We have mounted a coup d'état. The

Eastern Province is seceding. Both the air base and the oil company compound are falling into our hands as we speak. This is phase one. Phase two is the proclamation of our state." One of the other Arabs spoke from across the room; he uttered a short answer. "I'm sorry that I cannot stay and explain further, but there is much to attend to. I am aware of your position with the U.S. Consulate, Mrs. Laird. No harm will come to either of you."

We heard through the open balcony doors a distant thump, and after a moment the tail end of the blast waved the curtains into the room. A doubt rippled the confidence on Ali's full face. I thought: He may be in charge, but he's not used to this. The other Arabs moved as a man to the balcony.

Helen asked him, "The people who have been blowing up the compounds . . . are you working with them?"

"No, we are not. We are Shia, Mrs. Laird, not Wahhabi terrorists. I personally abhor violence. But this is a coup. The current regime has always used violence against the people of this country, to maintain their grip on the country's income—its oil revenues. I myself was one of their victims. But ours will not be a violent revolution, a bloodbath. A certain amount of intimidation may be needed to achieve our goal, but we are not targeting any civilians, nor foreigners. We are not even attacking soldiers—after all, they are Arabs, like ourselves. I believe what we hear outside are demolition charges. We are rendering the air base and airport runways temporarily useless.

"Now I'm afraid I must go. Mrs. Laird, if you have lived in Saudi Arabia for some time, you are probably familiar with the term *mahram*."

"No," she said, "I'm not."

"It refers to the degree of consanguinity . . . the blood relationship between yourself and Mr. Kemp. In your case, such a relationship does not exist. Because of that some of my stricter colleagues object to your staying together. I have given them their orders and they will not bother either of you, but it would be best not to disturb them unnecessarily. You should both remain here, in this apartment, and try to stay out of their way."

I said, "The best way to stay out of their way is to leave."

"Unfortunately, that is not yet possible." Ali stood up and spoke a command to the others; they turned and started toward the door. "Our command center is on the first floor. Our occupation is only temporary. As soon as key installations are secured our military liaison staff will move to the air base, and I and my personal staff will move to Aramco. That cannot be long now. Meanwhile, both of you, please make this apartment your home. I will station a man by the front door—for your own protection. Please do not try to leave—not yet. I will send word to you when we are successful. You will soon be back in your true homes: Mrs. Laird to the American embassy, and Mr. Kemp . . . to Manama, I presume. If you need anything, write it down and give it to the guard. He'll pass it to me."

He waved, like a university professor in an amateur theatrical playing the part of a magnanimous revolutionary. It was absurd and as a result unreal. But Helen, sitting tense with her hand to her face and a thick voice, was real, and the man still groaning on the floor was real as well—he had to be assisted out by one of his comrades. The door closed behind them. We were alone once more.

I felt a wave of cautious relief. Hope was possible. It was like the second day of steady gains after a market correction: you could imagine the beginning of a trend.

"It's not," I said shakily, "a standard ending to an after-dinner drink." I suppose I was trying to lighten the mood . . . maybe for my own benefit.

Helen ignored the remark. She stood up, went to the door and looked out the peephole. She returned and sat back down next to me, hugging herself as if cold. I put my arm around her, and the tears came; she wept angrily, her body rocking back and forth, her teeth clenched. I held her tighter, and presently she grew calmer. It was shock, of course.

After she came out of it she was more than naturally alert, almost high. She asked me: "What did you think of Ali?"

"He appears more reasonable than the others."

"He's a Shia. So he's probably not going to slit our throats. He's been living in London for years. A political refugee. He was in charge of one of the softer anti-Saudi reform groups. I don't think he's been much in the news lately. As for this 'coup'—the government certainly won't just sit back and let it happen."

"What does that mean, exactly?"

She smiled her slightly high smile. "It means, Steven, they're going to rescue us."

"I wonder how long it will take."

"God knows. It could be days. At least it looks as if they're going to leave us alone." She jumped to her feet. "We'd better do an inventory of our resources. I've no idea how much there is here to live on."

So we checked the place out. She needed the activity, and I needed my mind deflected from the situation. The apartment had two bedrooms, all left fully furnished, with two bathrooms, one with a bath. We tried it out. Water the color of rust spurted intermittently from the tap. "It hasn't been used for months," Helen said, "though it might improve after it runs for a while." But I suggested we turn it off, not knowing how much was in the reservoir, or even whether it was being replenished. In the kitchen she took some ice cubes from the refrigerator, wrapped them in a hand towel, and held it against her cheek. Then we took stock of our larder.

There was a quarter-full water bottle on a dispensing stand. In the freezer there was a still-sealed package of beef bacon and a block of Irish cheddar wrapped in plastic. The refrigerator held a bottle of *sid* and some Cokes, and we found two bottles of Johnny Walker in the cupboard above, one half full, one untouched. "A pity we left our dinner in the car," Helen said, "but at least we don't have to worry about liquor. Ayşen was probably saving it for Christmas. She always threw a big Christmas party."

"I think it's coming early this year. Let's both have a small one."

I poured two over ice, and we took them into the living room. It was only when we caught sight of the remote control for the television set that we realized we'd been left in contact with the outside world. Then Helen remembered her cell phone. Her face lit up.

"I'm calling the consulate," she said.

"I can't believe they didn't think to take it."

"I can. They're just hopping from one crisis to the next. Watch by the door, Steven, just in case."

I took up my post. The jamb by the lock was shattered, but the door still closed. Through the peephole I could make out the guard, one of the Arabs in a *thobe,* smoking a cigarette.

After a few minutes Helen came to get me, and we sat down with our drinks in front of the TV. She was coming down from the reaction. Her shoulders slumped and she looked tired.

"I got through to the duty officer and told him everything. I think he's in a state of shock. You can't imagine how this adds to his problems." She gave a short, unhumorous laugh. "We're to stay as quiet as possible, and not make a move from this apartment if we can help it. They're already aware of the air base. He said that they were making plans to 'defuse' the situation."

"Who's 'they'?"

"The consulate, the embassy in Riyadh, presumably the Saudi authorities. And maybe the U.S. military."

"I didn't know they were here."

"They aren't. They're in Qatar." Qatar's a neighboring state, but only an hour south on the peninsula. The cavalry wasn't next door, but at least it was around the corner.

She continued: "He's putting everyone in the picture about us right now. Everyone will know we're up here. We don't have to worry about that. He said they'd do everything they could to . . . to rescue us."

I hadn't until then considered the fact that we needed rescuing. It seemed melodramatic, unreal—until I remembered the reality of Ali's men. Helen said, "Let's turn on the TV."

We turned the volume down, to make sure the guard wouldn't hear it through the door (the less he knew, the better). We sat beside each other on the couch, and I put my arm around her. She didn't object.

There was evidently a satellite on the roof, and in between the Arab soap operas and the Indian and Hong Kong movie channels, we found CNN and the BBC. CNN was running a Larry King interview—some washed-up movie star talking about her career—but the BBC was already presenting breaking news from Saudi. They'd gotten it from

Al Jazeera. The BBC newscaster was one of those quiet women, ethnic but British to the core, who indicated a serious situation developing by a slight raising of her eyebrows.

She described the Dhahran air base as being "under attack"—by whom wasn't yet clear. Bombs had been heard, but no statement had been issued by either the government or any terrorist organization. It was the middle of the night, and the Saudi government had been taken unawares. She reported speculation that the Saudi military were making plans to relieve the air base.

The U.S. state department had issued a statement saying that they were monitoring the situation closely, in consultation with Saudi authorities. There was as yet only silence from the White House and from Number Ten. The newscaster pointed out that at the end of the last Iraq war, the remaining American troops in the country had been pulled out and moved to Qatar. No statement from the U.S. military there, or from the Pentagon, had yet appeared.

"They don't know any more than we do," Helen said, and switched to the local Aramco channel.

As so often, the oil company's TV channel was showing a nature documentary. It was the safest kind of program, with neither politics nor human sexual content. Tonight a guide resembling the Michelin man—ensconced in parka, hood, gloves, face mask, even mukluks—stood alone in the middle of an icy white waste. From his nasal accent I identified Canada. He was talking about birds, although none appeared in the picture; the sky was clear and frigid blue, and the camera remained stationary on the motionless figure.

"Although we see none at the moment," the Michelin man said, in his homely twang, "in fact both tits and pishers are ubiquitous in the frozen plains north of Edmonton. . . ."

Abruptly the picture deformed, then blinked off. Another picture appeared, wobbled, refocused. The camera steadied and revealed a set for a television news show—a desk and a picture of Riyadh as a background—but behind the desk sat a Saudi dressed in the khaki camouflage fatigues that the U.S. Army has made de rigueur among armies, and liberation forces, around the world.

He shuffled some papers on the desk, straightened up and stared directly into the camera. An expression of perplexity passed across his face, as if the camera's unblinking eye, impervious to commands, had rattled him. He collected himself and began to read. He read his statement first in Arabic—it seemed interminable—then in English:

"Thanks be to God. The Islamic Arabia Party, the IAP, has tonight seized with almost no resistance or casualties, King Abdul-Aziz Air Base and the main Aramco compound at Dhahran.

"The promise of the IAP is to liberate the Arabs of the East, from the Kuwaiti border to Hofuf, from the corruption and tyranny of the Al Saud regime. The IAP pledges to form a new government for the East, an Islamic republic, headed by Abdullatif Ali, with an elected assembly of religious and tribal leaders, academics and businessmen. Exactly one month from the proclamation of the republic, elections for the assembly will be held.

"We call on all the security services in the East, the army, the air force, the navy and the national guard, to free yourselves from the grip of the corrupt royal family. Your jobs, ranks, and responsibilities will be maintained. All political prisoners of the Al Saud regime will be freed immediately.

"We call on the citizens of the Nejd, and of the West, also to rise, and to take control of your own destiny. We are your friends and brothers. We have suffered together. We will support you. The IAP calls on all foreign states and armies, including friendly states, not to interfere by coming to the aid of the Al Saud regime. It will fall.

"Finally, the IAP calls on all Arabs to give us their support. It is time for all of us—all peninsular Arabs—to take responsibility for our own government. Together we can stop the theft by the Al Saud of our national wealth. Together, God willing, we can build the progressive, virtuous, Islamic state that we desire and deserve. God is great."

The speaker looked up from his notes and stared, rather grimly, into the camera. Then the picture was gone.

Helen switched back to CNN. Within a couple of minutes they were playing a tape of the announcement. She turned the volume off.

"Things are moving pretty fast," I said. "Do you think they've really taken Aramco?"

"I can't believe it . . . but Harry could. He's never had any faith in the Saudi army."

"An Islamic republic—at least in this province—with Ali as the president. . . . He didn't look to me like a rebel leader."

"Too academic?"

"Exactly."

"I thought the same. But maybe we're both wrong. Or maybe he has someone behind him."

"Like who?"

"Who knows. Al Qaeda?"

The name was like a bogey: we drew back from it as a young child would from a frightening Halloween mask. I thought it just another equation that didn't add up (I still didn't realize how different Middle Eastern arithmetic is from ours). I purposely said something stupid: "I wonder if they'll still need investment counselors." Helen gave me a long blank look, but then laughed, and I joined her. It lifted our spirits.

After that we discussed possible scenarios, how things might pan out. We didn't plumb the depths—we wanted to stay clear of the dark. We concentrated on how and when we would be released. The more we speculated, the more we realized how little we knew. It was like being reborn into a new life, like the Buddhists, without a clue as to one's talents or aptitudes, or whether fortune would favor you or not. There was almost nothing we could reasonably foretell.

"Another drink?" I asked.

"Sure, you're thinking like an Irishman. But let's break out some of the cheese with it."

We ate and drank, glued to the television, switching from channel to channel, looking for news updates. Little emerged. There were no further updates from Aramco, and the prepared American statement stayed the same. We heard no more explosions, saw no more flashes from outside.

The evening wore on. We sat together, my arm around her as she leaned into me, spent. She'd come to the end of her initiative. I was ready to provide it for her.

Around midnight I thought we should go to bed. She agreed and kissed me on my cheek. She said, "I'll take the far bedroom. Don't let me sleep late. I'll fry up some bacon in the morning for breakfast."

She walked down the hall, but before entering her room she turned and told me: "I'm sorry, Steven—sorry for getting you into this."

"Don't be ridiculous," I said, "it's no one's fault. No one could have foreseen this happening. Good night." So we went to our beds in Ayşen's comfortable old apartment, with her made-up beds and books and night-lights, as prisoners, maybe even hostages. But it's one thing to know, to realize intellectually, with your brain. It's something else entirely to know with your gut. We were in denial. And I hadn't told her what I really wanted to—it sounded too strange, even to me. I wanted to tell her, I'm glad it worked out the way it did: if it had to happen, I'm glad I'm here with you.

CHAPTER THREE

woke the next morning to a strange room and the smell of dust on the sheets. For a moment I was disoriented. Then I remembered where I was and sat up. I fumbled for my watch. Just after six. A yellowish light struggled thinly through a window caked with sand. It occurred to me that anything could have happened while I'd slept. I leapt out of bed, wrapped the blanket around my shoulders, and stepped onto the cold linoleum of the hallway.

The apartment was as we had left it. Was the guard still on duty outside the door? I peered through the peephole, but couldn't see him. Maybe he was curled up on the floor. I decided to leave well enough alone and switched on the television, keeping the volume low. But CNN and the BBC were showing other news; apparently we hadn't yet become a round-the-clock sensation. I shivered. We had neglected to close the sliding-glass doors the night before. It was April, and although the days were already unbearable, the mornings were still cool. I padded across the carpet to the balcony.

Outside, it was still too dark and hazy to make out anything definite in the direction of the air base, but below I could see dozens of vehicles—cars, pickups, vans—parked around the foot of the tower like discarded toys. It was eerily still: I saw no sign of people or traffic.

The morning air was sweet, but when I stepped back inside I realized I stank. It was the stale sweat of the night before. I would have to take a bath. The bathroom was next to Helen's bedroom, and her door was half open; I took a quick look to make sure she was still there. She was lying on her back, with one arm over her head, the elbow bent and above the pillow, as if warding off a blow.

I shut the bathroom door gently so as not to wake her. The icy ceramic tub was set in an icy tiled floor. I squatted and wrestled with the handheld steel showerhead, the coiled metal tube stubbornly twisting in the wrong direction. The water spurted frigid and brown but eventually warmed and cleared to the color of weak tea.

When I finished and stepped out of the bathroom I saw her door still open. I peered carefully in. She was sitting up in bed. She said, "Good morning," and then, "Don't turn on the light"—like a lover who hadn't yet lost her modesty.

I said, "There's nothing new on TV, but there's still hot water in the bathroom—only a little brown—and I'm thinking of making some coffee, if I can find any. Would you like a cup?"

She gave a sleepy laugh. "It's almost like being on holiday in a third world hotel. Of course I'd like some. But don't use the tap water. Only the bottled."

"I'll fry up some of the bacon as well. Care for any?"

"I'd love it. Just let me get up and wash."

A few minutes later, dressed, I had the beef bacon on low while the sound of her bath ran in the background. It seemed the most domestic scene I'd been in since my divorce . . . or long before. I was a prisoner, probably with an armed guard still at the apartment door; Ali and his gang, the "Islamic Arabia Party," were almost certainly still upstairs, plotting the coup d'état; and my job might be about to go up in smoke—not the least of my worries. But I felt strangely happy as the bacon sizzled, the bathwater ran, and the dawn sun shone through the open balcony door.

Helen joined me in the kitchen as I poured the coffee. She had on a different blouse—some of Ayşen's old clothes, she explained. She glanced, frowning, at the harsh fluorescent light on the kitchen ceiling and told me not to look at her too closely: "I'm afraid the left side of my face is black and blue."

I inspected it anyway. There was a little discoloration, a little swelling. "It doesn't look bad," I said, only half lying. "Does it hurt?"

"Not to notice. Put the bacon on a paper towel to drain and let's go out on the balcony."

Outside, the April air was cool and fresh. A faint breeze from the south carried the taste and smell of the desert. Beneath us the sun picked out the sandy, run-down rooftops of a sandy, run-down town. Nothing moved. It looked like the kind of place where nothing ever changed.

I was about to suggest that she call the consulate, to check in, when Helen asked: "Do you hear something?"

Sound travels upward. But the first sounds of the attack were so small and quiet, like the rustles of a nocturnal animal, that it took us a moment to identify them: the muffled ignitions; the dry cough of cold engines; the careful meshing of gears.

Soon vehicles—jeeps and light-armored cars—emerged from alleys and side roads, turning out of the long morning shadows into the light. Beside them ran groups of men in fairly good order.

"Soldiers," I said.

"Yes . . . but they don't look like ours." She sounded like she'd just discovered the horse she'd bet on was coming in dead last. "They're either Saudi army or the national guard. Let's hope it's the national guard."

Perhaps they'd chosen the early morning hoping for the element of surprise. If so, they failed to take advantage of it. They tried to take up positions around the foot of the building, but the jumble of the rebels' cars and trucks hampered them. So it was that the first shots came from the tower, a wild spray of bullets from a lower floor that smashed windshields and holed hoods.

The response from the ground drowned out the opening salvo. The troops—army or national guard, whichever they were—opened up. Semiautomatic fire from dozens of rifles raked the lower half of the building. Instinctively we retreated into the living room, wincing at the clamor. I put my arms around Helen and held her. The firing from both sides continued in waves. It was impossible to tell how much of it was return fire and how much from the ground. I thought: Thank God we're on the eleventh floor.

Soon the shooting slowed, then ceased. We heard the distant clatter and tinkle as bits of walls and windows fell to earth. A curl of acrid, white smoke, tenuous from the long ascent, crept over the balcony into our room.

I became aware that I was holding Helen tight. I relaxed my grip, and said, "We're lucky a bullet didn't hit the balcony doors."

We heard a small ringing sound. Helen said: "My cell! Where is it?" She found it on the table, pressed the button and held it to her ear. She looked at me as she listened, expressing first disbelief then anger.

"Well," she spoke into the phone, "you're a little late, aren't you? It started five minutes ago, you bloody idiot! And what do you expect next? Are you going to fill us in?"

After a moment, she said, "Let's hope it works out that way. Have you heard from Harry?" She listened, and then said more quietly, "When he calls tell him I'm fine. As fine as I can be under the circumstances. They're leaving us alone. And for God's sake, try to be more timely in keeping us informed. If you know something's about to happen, tell us before it does." She pressed the button to hang up.

"He's a junior state department officer. Out of his depth, obviously, but really, it's scandalous. How many members of the consulate do they have stuck in town? One. Me! You'd think they'd be a little more efficient."

"So, what do they think's happening?"

"It's the Saudi army down there. They've told the consulate they're going to try to get Ali's group to surrender. That's literally all they know."

"It's probably a better solution than trying to fight their way in."

"I thought that's what they were trying just now." Hugging herself in a nervous fury, she paced around the room. "Harry always says that the Saudi army couldn't fight their way out of a paper bag. That's his expression."

Harry. I'd never met him, but already I wasn't sure I liked him. I said, "I'm surprised he hasn't called."

Helen stood stock-still. "Maybe he has," she said. "Let me check my messages."

She pressed a couple of buttons, then held the cell phone to her ear. She turned to face the window so I couldn't see her expression.

"Well?" I said, when she'd finished.

"He called twice in the night. I'm going to try to call him back now."

But for some reason he wasn't available. She left him a message, but so quietly I couldn't hear it.

As she turned back to me, a loudspeaker from the ground blared at the tower in distorted Arabic. Someone made an adjustment, and the demand—it sounded like a demand—was repeated more clearly. A couple of minutes passed, but we heard no reply.

"The lower floors must be pretty well shot up," I said. "It may take them a while to respond."

As soon as I said it, we heard a sharp crack, then a blast blew a shock wave up against the side of the building. The whole apartment shook like a California earthquake. Two more followed in close succession. I pulled Helen down to the floor.

Ragged rifle shots broke out, then fell off. We heard shouts, and the sound of vehicles gunning their engines. We remained huddled together for a few minutes, until silence seemed re-established—there was no telling for how long. We got up and moved carefully to the balcony. Crouching below the rail, we peered over.

Three craters, each about the size of a car, lay smoking in the parking lot. The soldiers and most of their vehicles had disappeared.

"They've gone," Helen said.

"Or taken cover. Ali's men must have brought rocket launchers. Round one to the IAP."

We surveyed the scene a little longer, then I started back inside, but Helen grabbed my sleeve and said, "Look!"

Almost directly below, a man was stumbling away from the tower. He was bareheaded, and appeared to be wearing a uniform, but he had to be one of Ali's men. He limped across the street into the parking lot. He held his arms high and his hands open, unarmed, in surrender.

Helen said, "He must be mad."

He stood there, as if uncertain, his hands up, turning one way, then another. I think he was saying something. He looked very alone. A burst of fire erupted from the tower. The man spun around in a puppet's pirouette, his arms flung out. Then he fell over the lip of a crater and slid in a heap to its bottom.

We pulled back from the balcony. I led Helen back to the couch. She sat with her shoulders hunched and her hands clasped tightly together. "I'll get us some more coffee," I said. I picked up our cups and went into the kitchen, making sure on the way that the front door was still closed.

I brought in our coffee and cheese and beef bacon, now cold, and we ate together in silence. I suggested we turn on the TV, but she said, "That's so American, Steven. Like your television news: showing over and over again an insane student's boasting, with his guns in his hands, in between his massacre. . . . What could we learn? Haven't we had enough violence for one morning? Keep it off."

The criticism stung. Was she right? Had my culture made me more inured to violence than hers?

The breakfast had some restorative effect. I wanted to cheer her up, and the only way I could think of was to put an optimistic spin on things: a salesman's pitch, with enough realism to make it plausible. I told her that the attempted attack by the army probably meant that the coup had failed, or been contained. Ali had said that they intended to move to Aramco shortly. The fact that they hadn't—and how could they now, with the army below us?—meant that things had gone badly, or at least not as planned. Helen was less sanguine.

"I'm not sure that most coups do go according to plan," she said. "It may be too early to tell."

"The government clearly still has the army behind it . . . how can Ali hope to hold out against that? The most reasonable thing he can do is try to negotiate terms for a surrender."

"Terms? Reasonable? This isn't a financial deal, Steven. I think you're giving both sides too much credit."

The debate was interrupted by the doorbell—such an unlikely sound that at first we didn't recognize it. We just managed to stand when we heard the door open, and a man in uniform strode into the room.

It was Captain Saad from the night before. He still carried himself erect, but his uniform and face were smeared with what appeared to be concrete dust, and the ammo belt hung a little lower on his hips. His air of authority also hung a little lower, like a flag settling to half-mast.

"Good morning," he said, "I am sorry to disturb you. Dr. Ali wants to know, is there any first aid in this apartment?"

The request stopped us both in our tracks. "You mean," I replied, "are there any bandages, that kind of thing?"

"Yes."

Helen and I looked at each other. She shook her head and said, "There are none in the kitchen."

"There might be a kit in the bathroom," I told him, "let me look." I went to search and the captain went with me. I think he was happier away from Helen.

In a cupboard I found a first-aid kit the size of a shoe box. It had the Red Crescent emblem on the cover, but when we opened it up, the whole kit—bandages, Band-Aids and, for some reason, face masks—turned out to be made in China. Even the instructions were in Chinese. It seemed a very small offering. I handed it to the captain. "I'm afraid that's it," I said. We turned and found Helen standing behind us.

"How many are injured?" she asked him.

"Many on the lower floors. Some bullet wounds, but many cut by glass."

"Do you have any first-aid materials or medicine?"

"Very little. Some of our supplies did not arrive."

"Dr. Ali said you had two doctors."

"Only one. He was on the first floor this morning. He is also wounded."

She hesitated, but only briefly. "I've had medical training," she told him. "I'll try to help if you want me."

If he was surprised he didn't show it, but I'm sure my eyebrows rose. He didn't smile, or look in any way gratified. If anything, his stiffness increased. But he wasn't a fool. "We need help," he said. "Please follow me."

"I want Mr. Kemp to come with us."

"Of course." He handed her the first-aid kit.

The one elevator was still working, and Ali had used it to evacuate his wounded to the top of the building—the thirteenth floor. There they turned two adjoining apartments into a clinic, but a clinic with only four beds and no equipment. There were at least a dozen bloodied men, the worse off on the beds and couches, the rest on chairs or on the floor. A few wore uniforms but most wore *thobes* and as a result the effect was pure carnage: every drop, splash and gout of blood vivid against the white. The men tending the injured used their *gutras*—the Arab head covering—to tie up the wounds.

We found Ali comforting a patient. He rose and greeted his two prisoners courteously. He was without his jacket, but other than that he looked little the worse for wear. There was blood on the palms of his hands, and he was aware of it; he stood with his arms hanging away from his body, the palms outward. A fastidious man.

When Helen explained that she had medical training, he immediately asked her if she would take over the care of the wounded, "as a humanitarian gesture. I am sure that no one, not even the U.S. state department, would object."

She said, "I would be happy to assist you, Doctor."

"I am asking you to take complete charge. Unfortunately my doctorate is in comparative religion, not medicine."

Helen took charge. It had to have been well over ten years since she had been a ward nurse (when I knew her first, she had risen to a supervisor's level), but she was the most capable person there to handle the crisis. Dr. Ali's order ensured cooperation.

I volunteered, of course, to do what I could, but I have no medical training, and Helen saved me from being surplus to requirements by organizing a building-wide hunt for bandages and medicine. It was clear that she wasn't in any danger alone—what wounded man rejects or assaults a nurse? I drew the third floor. Helen found me a master key, and I rode down in a gradually emptying elevator with a group of silent but companionable Arabs. Perhaps by that time they'd accepted me as another shell-shocked survivor. I walked out alone, only three stories from the ground, searching on an empty floor for more first-aid kits, or for anything that could be used as a clean dressing. Even a forgotten bedsheet would have been a find. But every room had been stripped bare. Even the shower and faucet heads were gone.

In the last room I searched I found two useful items in the back of a forgotten cupboard, and selfishness inspired me to stash them in our own apartment on the way back up to the thirteenth floor.

The other scavengers had found little more; some sheets they were busy tearing for bandages I later discovered had come from our own beds. I found Helen pale and bloodstained. She was working with tweezers, picking out shards of glass from a man's leg; the patient, one of the men in *thobes*, lay on his back on the floor, his face drawn and set, but silent, uncomplaining. One of the Arabs brought her a glass of water. She looked almost like a member of the group.

Once again I was a surplus element. I was relieved when Ali showed up and, after consulting Helen, thanked her and made it clear that she'd done enough—at least for the present. He offered us some food—flat Arabic bread and white cheese. I accepted it but insisted we go down and eat it for lunch. It was only just after noon but Helen looked pale; I wanted her to rest. And I wasn't completely comfortable on the thirteenth floor. I no longer saw Ali's men as an immediate threat, but the consulate, and presumably the authorities, thought we were two stories below, and I felt we'd probably be safer there, less of a target.

Our apartment was beginning to feel like home. Helen washed and changed and then together we washed and dried our breakfast dishes, as if we were settling in for an extended stay. Her face was drawn and her manner abstracted. As we put the dishes away, I said, "That was a noble thing to do—volunteering to help them."

"It wasn't much, Steven. Cleaning and dressing a few wounds."

"You didn't have to volunteer."

"We're supposed to help the helpless." The phrase reminded me of a hymn—"hope of the hopeless"? I realized I'd forgotten what her religious convictions were, or if she still had any. I must have known once. As she was Irish, I expected she'd been raised Catholic. She said, "It was good to do something practical again, something worthwhile. It felt good to help them." She put the last dish away. "It's time I checked in with the consulate."

But the line was busy, so we turned on the television to CNN. It was nearing prime time in the States and the news was now full of Saudi Arabia and the coup in the East. Or rather, the attempted coup. Even after several hours, the situation was confused, the outcome unclear. The Aramco headquarters was held by the rebels, but the pumping stations, pipelines and ports were still under the control of the government. The situation at the air base was unsettled. The few Americans attached to the military training mission were confined to quarters but safe. The senior U.S. officer was negotiating with Ali's men; the headquarters in Riyadh was still firmly behind the government. The minister of the interior had issued a statement condemning the insurgents as un-Islamic heretics under the influence and perhaps the pay of foreign interests, but also suggesting an amnesty for members of the military and security services who had defected, should they surrender. Washington was saying that it suspected Iranian involvement, and affirmed its support for the legitimate government. A commentator pointed out that the term "legitimate" in this context could have an ambiguous interpretation.

CNN made no mention of the attack on the rebel headquarters— our building. A background piece filled in time by talking about years of declining living standards, authoritarian rule, the absence of human rights, the enormous oil reserves (almost all just a few miles offshore), and decades of American support for the regime in Riyadh.

The news became repetitive. We turned the TV off and after eating a little of our bread and cheese I suggested we both get some rest. The nursing had improved Helen's morale, but the work had tired her. Not knowing what the rest of the day would bring, I thought it best to conserve our energies. We went to our separate rooms.

Sleep seemed out of the question, but after just a few minutes on the stripped mattress I dropped off.

I seldom dream, or if I do, I seldom remember them. But that afternoon, for whatever reason, I dreamed. I was back in my old office in Los Angeles, with its two desks, one covered by computer monitors. The screens jumped and flickered in front of me with the incontrovertible story of financial meltdown. But I wasn't alarmed. The door to the office opened, and my secretary appeared, but it wasn't my secretary, it was my ex-wife. She asked me if I wanted to sell our house (in reality, she got the house as part of our divorce settlement). I told her, yes, sell everything. I realized I was going to have to liquidate my assets to meet my clients' losses, but the thought didn't disturb me; on the contrary, I was happy as I watched assets, possessions, clients, all flicker, decline and disappear. It was like a release. As the last screen went blank I looked to the door with a vague presentiment of good news, even of happiness; it opened, but no one appeared, and the last thing I remembered was a tiny splinter of doubt . . . then the walls trembled to the sound of a distant explosion and my eyes snapped open to the dusty bedroom and the bed without a sheet.

I heard another thump, almost too low to hear, and swung my legs off the bed. I hurried to Helen's room. She was sitting up on the bed, fully dressed. "It's not us this time," I told her. "It's somewhere else."

We walked through the living room and out to the balcony. It was early afternoon and hot and still. A faint haze of sand obscured the horizon. The sun shone directly on us; with the glass windows behind and the fake marble facade above and below, it was like being in a rotisserie. We saw nothing unusual, yet even as we scanned the scene we heard another thump.

Helen said, "I think it came from the other side." We made our way to the end of the balcony, where we could see part of the coast. The target was immediately apparent.

Less than two miles away, on the corniche, the Meridien Hotel was under attack. It was a midget compared to New York's Twin Towers, but the smoke pouring out of the upper floors shocked and silenced us: it was so close to the television pictures shown over and over on the morning of 9/11.

As we watched we saw a missile trail, a thin streak of white vapor, heading in from the sea, swaying on its course like an arrow on a windy day. It hit its target with a muffled whump. In another minute we saw a jet, perhaps the missile's launcher, wheeling in languidly, as if to observe its handiwork. It turned and headed back out to sea.

"What," I asked, "do you suppose is going on?"

"It's the air force—either ours or the Saudis'. They're hitting the wrong building, that's all."

It might have been amusing, in a dark way, until you considered the implications. And of course the destruction. The implications were that some air force thought they were shooting the hell out of our own tower, concentrating on the upper floors—without warning us beforehand. As for the destruction . . . fortunately business was so poor that the Meridien wasn't anything like full—it was probably more than half empty. One could only hope that the guests were concentrated on the lower floors.

Helen and I stood and watched two more direct hits. Soon the whole upper half of the hotel was wreathed in smoke, with flames licking from the upper windows.

I put my arm around her and she whispered, "There but for the grace of God. Heaven help those inside." I felt her shiver in the heat. She said, "Let's try the consulate again. And I'll try calling Harry."

But her cell phone was dead. Neither of us had thought of the battery. She launched into some unladylike but very Irish profanity. The consulate had done little or nothing for us so far, but it had been a comfort to be able to communicate with them. Losing the phone was a low moment.

"Did you notice," she said, "that it was the upper floors they were attacking?"

"Yes. I hope it was due to a communication breakdown, an intelligence failure."

"Oh, I think we can be sure of that! They attacked the wrong building. I think we can assume it was an intelligence failure."

A faintly positive thought occurred to me: "But at least they were attacking from the seaward side."

Helen gave me a blank look that broke and changed to something like scorn. She wasn't amenable, at that moment, to finding a silver lining. I could hardly blame her. A crisis in which you have no control over events affects different people in different ways. An investment manager is a salesman with an eye on risk management, and at the same time trained for optimism—sometimes when there are few underlying causes for support. Hope, to be effective, needs to be managed like risk. In business I'd been guilty of managing it poorly, of pushing it too hard, even into the realm of illegality. Now, too much hope was just inappropriate. The penalty wasn't indictment, only a withdrawal of sympathy.

The cell phone was gone but we still had the TV. The screen had just come alive when we heard the doorbell for the second time that morning, and I thought irritably, Why won't they let us alone? But it was only Dr. Ali, needing an update. The coup leader looked almost apologetic as he asked me if our television was working. It was one of the things they hadn't brought—like the medical supplies. They'd probably assumed, as I did, that the apartments were still furnished. I invited him in.

Helen and I sat on the couch (a little sandy from the open balcony door), while Ali settled in a nearby armchair. The CNN newscaster in Atlanta announced that the Saudi air force, with planes flown down from an air base at Tabuk, was at that moment pressing home an attack against the rebel headquarters in the town of Al Khobar. Sitting next to the newscaster was a think-tank analyst with the scrubbed, tight-suited earnestness of a Washington neoconservative. He wore a little brass flag in his lapel. When asked what this latest development meant, he replied that it showed the central government was still in charge. The lack of coherent information from Riyadh since the previous day may have been deliberate, he said, a ploy to lead the rebel forces to think that the house of Saud was disintegrating. In fact they'd planned a counterattack. The Saudi army and air force were the best equipped among the Gulf states; they had the benefit of years, decades, of American and British training; they would soon be mopping up what resistance remained.

The presenter abruptly announced they were going to a live feed from Bahrain. So apparently they'd flown in a TV crew. The picture switched to their correspondent in Manama, a young man who announced with excitement that he had actually heard the jets fly in from Tabuk. They were at this moment just across the causeway, less than ten miles away, rocketing the rebel headquarters. The crew had a zoom lens and the picture broke as they attempted to capture the Meridien under attack on the far shore. The heat haze and distance proved too much; the audience saw only a shaky picture of an indistinct building and what may have been a dark smudge of smoke.

Ali seemed to shrink in his chair. His suit looked lived in and too large. He hadn't shaved—perhaps they'd forgotten to bring razors, as well—and the beginnings of stubble blurred the formerly sharp demarcation of his beard. He looked not frightened or worried, but dejected. Helen said, "I should think you'd be happy they're bombing the wrong building."

"I am. Naturally I would rather they bomb the Meridien than us. But it is an embarrassment—as well as a setback. After all, the pilots are Saudis—Sunni, of course—Riyadh has never allowed a Shia in the air force. But we wanted them on our side. Or, at least, not to follow Riyadh's orders."

I said, "There's been no news of a coup in Riyadh, or in Tabuk." But Ali sat up a little straighter. A gleam of assurance reappeared in his eye.

He said, "It may be that this 'mistake' was not a mistake."

"What do you mean?"

"The pilots may have attacked the Meridien on purpose, knowing it was the wrong target."

The surmise, with its typical Arab willingness to clutch at any conspiracy theory, no matter how far-fetched, left me gaping. "If that's the case," I said, "they'll have a lot of explaining to do when they get back to base. They'll certainly send them out again. It will be difficult, even if they want to, to hit the wrong target again."

"They may have done it as a warning," Ali insisted. "A delaying tactic, to give us time. They cannot return immediately. They have to refuel, and reload."

"Do your men still hold the Aramco headquarters and the air base?"

"Yes. And every hour we hold them, the regime in Riyadh will get weaker and weaker. Our job here is to hold out. They calculated, correctly, that we would be on the top floors—that is where they aimed their attack on the Meridien. I do not think they will strike twice at the same place, do you?"

"You mean they'll think you're going to move?"

"Exactly. Where will they aim their next attack? I will redeploy my men throughout the building. Since the top floors are the safest, we will keep the wounded where they are. So that the lights will not give us away, we are turning them all on, every light in every room, as soon as it is dark."

He was a new man. Are coup organizers born optimists? Perhaps they must be, if they expect to succeed, or to remain free—or even to survive. If Ali was any indication, they are certainly enthusiasts.

Helen surprised me by inviting him to dinner later that night, adding that it would be a modest meal. He was pleased, and although he declined—"My place," he said, "is with my men"—he promised to try to visit us briefly afterward, if that would be agreeable.

He departed. Outside, the haze was thickening to an overcast. There was little to do but watch TV and wait. Helen stretched out on the couch with her head on the arm and her feet on my lap. It was a domestic scene, a comfortable scene, but not unduly affectionate. She was withdrawn—not an inappropriate response to the situation. I felt overwhelmed with affection for her, and with a desire to protect. But I remained silent. Sometimes the best comfort is empathy, just being there. I had nothing helpful to say, so I said nothing, and we sat quietly watching the TV turned on low, the talking heads murmuring away and the occasional hazy shot of an indistinguishable building in the distance.

After a while she asked me, "When do you think they'll attack?"

I thought. "It could be as early as this evening, or tomorrow—if they are going to attack. They could just starve us out."

"I think they'll do something a bit more forceful than that."

It wasn't a line I wanted to follow.

She said, "It's foolish of him to keep all of the wounded up there, on the thirteenth floor."

"Why?"

"Who's to say they won't aim there again?"

"He's doing what he thinks best. The next attack could come from the ground again—who knows?"

She said, so serious and low she could have been in a confessional, "I told Bill, the duty officer, where they were last night."

I stared at her. "What do you mean?"

"I told him I thought they'd concentrated their men on the ground floors."

Her admission surprised me. I hadn't realized she'd been thinking strategically. And after our shared experience that day, and her efforts with their wounded, it was almost a confession of betrayal.

"It doesn't matter," I said. "Everyone's in the dark now, the consulate, the military, Ali—all of us. And Ali's plan isn't a bad one."

It didn't mean we were safe. But she seemed more relaxed, and presently she dozed off. I pulled a shawl that lay over the back of the couch down over her as she slept. Someone once told me that everyone has moments of happiness, and the way to lead a happy life is to be conscious of those moments. I hadn't put much faith in the advice at the time; it's my temperament to concentrate on the future more than the present. But I was conscious of a feeling of happiness, strange because it was disconnected from the larger situation, or from any plausible scenario of our near-term future, as Helen lay stretched out, sleeping. My head fell back and I closed my eyes.

The couch jumped backward so suddenly it left me sitting in the same place, but on the edge of the cushion. It was like the parlor trick: the man who whips away the tablecloth so fast he doesn't disturb the plates—even the glasses remain standing.

My eyes snapped open and I saw two pictures that had been hanging on the wall crash to the floor; at the same time Helen fell off the couch onto the carpet. There was hardly time to blink before the shock wave hit me like a two-by-four.

CHAPTER FOUR

I ascended through a perfectly silent world, so silent that although I could see, I wasn't at first convinced I was conscious. The blast had deafened me. I recognized Helen's shirt in front of my face but was too disoriented to understand what it meant; eventually I realized I was on the floor, lying on top of her. I rolled off and propped myself up on one arm. She was breathing and looked unharmed. I called her name and shook her gently. Her lips moved but I couldn't hear her. I got to my knees, crouched down and put my ear against her mouth. She whispered, "We're still alive?"

"Yes, we're still alive."

She opened her eyes. "You're right. You put on weight."

"I expect I'm losing a little every day."

We weren't purposely flippant; it was just shock.

She said, "Where did it hit?"

I looked around the apartment. "Not here . . . not directly. The ceiling and the floor's still intact. But whatever it was, it was close."

She struggled up and said, "I feel sick."

She was Irish and she meant she was going to vomit. Together we staggered to the bathroom. We'd almost made it when another rocket hit the building, this time farther away, lower down.

I pressed her against the hallway wall, bracing us both. The building shook, but the blast wasn't as bad. For a few moments we had silence, then another rocket hit, somewhere above. I was afraid of falling and pulled Helen down to the floor. We cradled each other, and counted five more strikes before the attack stopped. Bizarrely, the first was the closest, but I couldn't make out any pattern. They seemed to be pockmarking the entire building.

By the time it finished we were both shaking uncontrollably. There are reactions in these situations that are automatic, and, I think, practically beyond one's will to stop (I was getting a crash course in combat zone reactions); when shock wears off, intense fear can follow. I wonder if that soldier I met in Manama ever humiliated himself. When the bombardment was over I felt a wetness against my legs. I thought at first it must be blood, and I'd been wounded. But I'd only urinated in my trousers.

We got to our feet and Helen stumbled to the bathroom; through the closed door I could hear her retch. We'd eaten little since breakfast; it was the vomit of fear. While she cleaned herself, I took stock of the apartment.

Everything on the walls had fallen to the floor and there was plaster everywhere. We'd left the sliding-glass balcony doors open and one was off its tracks but both were still intact. The kitchen was a mess: much of the crockery had shot from the cupboards and smashed onto the floor.

Helen stayed in the bathroom for some time; when she emerged she looked shaky but recovered. She'd even managed to brush most of the plaster dust out of her hair. I went in to try to wash out the urine. There was still some water in a hot water tank hung up in a corner, although I doubted if it was still being replenished. When I came out, she asked me, "Do you think they'll try to take the tower now?"

"I don't know. It's nearly dusk. I think it's more likely they'll try at dawn."

"Then let's go upstairs. I want to check on the wounded."

The idea struck me as suicidal, and I tried to dissuade her. I told her that we didn't know when the next attack would come and that we were safer where we were. I even inspected her hands, and pointed out that, like mine, they were trembling uncontrollably. But she insisted. She said that as soon as she'd done what she could, she'd come back down.

There was nothing to do but accompany her. But first I went back into the bathroom and retrieved the flashlight I'd found earlier in the day on the third floor. I left my other find: a small first-aid kit. If the scene upstairs was as I expected, it would prove of little practical use, and there was still a chance that we might need it ourselves later. It was selfish, but I've always believed that charity begins at home.

The hall was empty. Ceiling panels littered the floor. I had no intention of trying the elevator. The interior stairs were still intact and we reached the thirteenth floor easily. But the little window set in the stairwell door showed only black. I put my shoulder to the door and forced it open far enough to get through.

The place was a shambles, the corridor wall opposite a gaping ruin. The twisted rebar told its own story. The wall was reinforced, and only a direct hit on the rooms beyond could have blown it apart. They were the apartments that had housed the two makeshift clinics.

I heard Helen's voice behind me, still in the stairwell: "How bad is it? What's it like?" I told her, "I don't think there's anything we can do." But she pushed her way through.

Against my advice she insisted on entering what was left. I went ahead of her, holding the flashlight—I wasn't sure of the floor. The first room was open to the air with a jagged hole in the outer wall. Small fires burned among the wreckage. In the shattered concrete there were still some combustibles: scattered fragments of furniture; a bit of carpet; several bodies, more body parts. My eyes flicked quickly away. Probably the whole place would have been in flames if there had been enough to burn.

It was the first time I'd seen death outside of a wall-to-wall-carpeted funeral home. If I believed in God, I would have thanked him for the dim light, for the gloom. The darkness obscured the horror. Helen must still have been in denial, otherwise why would she have stopped to search for the pulse of the first two bodies she found? Death was too evident. She gave up and returned to my side. Not one of her patients was left alive.

When she asked in a shaken voice if I thought we should check the rest of the floor, I firmly told her no. We could hardly breathe, and it was too dangerous, especially in the dark: it was difficult to tell where and if the floor, or even the ceilings, were safe. She agreed without an argument.

Halfway back down the stairs she said: "Perhaps we should check the other floors."

"If they need you, they'll come."

We regained our apartment with relief. Even in disarray, it looked infinitely welcoming, secure. It was our bolt-hole; the rest of the building might have been blown up, but we'd survived, we even still had a roof over our heads. Dusk had fallen. The living-room lamps had broken but the fluorescent lights in the kitchen still worked— incredibly, the power was still on.

Helen was depressed and abstracted; I held her briefly but she didn't want to be held. I wanted to give her something to cling to, and said, "It may not be totally by chance that we're alive."

"You must be joking, Steven. You can't seriously think they're that careful, that accurate."

"Why not? The rockets, shells—whatever they were—were probably fired from the ground. Intelligence has to be better here than in Tabuk. We're still in one piece. I don't see why we shouldn't expect to be rescued." Using two negatives to form a positive sounded doubtful even to me. "We could be here another day, maybe two. And we need to eat something." I wasn't hungry but I knew I should be, and we'd have to keep up our strength.

Helen insisted she couldn't eat, but after I made some coffee she admitted she was hungry—ravenous, even. Together we hunted for anything we could find to supplement the remaining bread and cheese and beef bacon. She dug out from the bowels of the refrigerator some forgotten onions—they were too old and soft to eat raw, but could still be thrown in the pan—and I found an unbroken glass bottle of dill pickles. I cooked up bacon and onions while she wiped off and laid the dining room table with what plates we had left. She laid it for three; she reminded me that we'd invited a guest who might appear in time for dinner. I didn't need Ali dropping in, for dinner, for a drink, for anything, but she seemed to look forward to it, as if it were a social visit. I went along with the idea as cheerfully as I could. After what she'd gone through, I was eager for anything that would reinforce an impression of normalcy—that would take her mind, even for a few minutes, off what she had seen.

Our spirits rose as we ate. We were halfway through the meal when we heard a knock at the door. Our guest had arrived.

The doctor's Oxford don suit was a wreck—jacket and pants smeared with concrete and plaster dust. He had lost his tie and with his left hand kept his handkerchief pressed to a cut on his cheek. His face was drawn and haggard, his shoulders slumped. But he greeted us courteously, and asked after our health. Helen told him to come in and sit down, and served him his portion. I poured him a fresh cup of coffee. The minor courtesies seemed to overwhelm him; his hand began to shake and he had to put down his cup. Helen took charge as if he were another patient. She cleaned his cut as best she could; when he tried to thank her, she ordered him to eat, not talk.

Soon he asked if our television still worked. It was an old-fashioned model, and its weight had saved it from being knocked off its shelf onto the floor. To my amazement it actually did work, although the satellite dish had gone and we were down to just two stations: the Saudi TV channel broadcasting from Aramco, and Bahrain.

Aramco TV showed only a written statement in Arabic. Ali read it and informed us it was an announcement of the coup, and a request to the people and the authorities of the previous regime to help the new government.

"That shows," Ali said, in a pause from eating his beef bacon and onions, "that there is still hope. If the authorities had retaken Aramco, we would know it immediately."

"Aren't you in touch with your people there?" I asked.

"Not directly. Our cell phones stopped working this morning. The authorities have probably turned off the base stations."

To me it sounded like another nail in the coffin—the coffin of a failed coup d'état. I asked him: "How many of your men—except for those on the thirteenth floor—survived the last attack?"

"So you know what happened?"

Helen said quietly, "Yes, we went up to offer help."

"They are with Allah," he said, staring her straight in the eye.

"And the others?" I asked again.

"Several wounded, but none lost, thanks be to God. Our doctor, thanks to you, Mrs. Laird, is able to work again, although with very limited supplies."

It seemed that nothing could keep him down for long. All it took was some bacon and onions, a little ambiguous news, a few able-bodied men still left, for his optimism to recover. It was like a desert weed that should have died long ago, but stubbornly remains, showing green at the first hint of moisture.

"According to my men," he said, "the attack came from the ground. That, and the fact that the air attack came from the base in Tabuk, means that the air base here is still in our hands. It has been just a few hours short of a full day and our men are still holding firm. The longer we hold out, the more likely it is that others will join us. Time is on our side."

He was in his dream world. I busied myself with the television, trying to bring in Bahrain more clearly. The picture was snowy but recognizable, the audio only slightly overlaid with static.

They were transmitting the BBC. The presenter was talking about Ali. He was news. He was the acknowledged leader, and the only one among his group known to the outside world.

"... received a doctorate in comparative religion from Cambridge," the presenter said, "and taught there before returning to Riyadh.

"A Shia, his involvement in politics began at the conclusion of the '91 Gulf War, when he formed a group of academics calling for a more Islamic, less corrupt government. He was briefly imprisoned and allegedly tortured. After his release he escaped to Iran and from there made his way to London, where he claimed political asylum. Although much in the news after the '96 Al Khobar bombings, he has been out of the public view since. Indeed, his sudden reappearance surprised most analysts.

"Dr. Ali has been denounced by the British government for being an Islamic extremist, a fundamentalist. He is suspected to have the support of Iran. The communiqué which his group issued calls for democratic elections, along with what they call a 'true' Islamic government."

The picture switched to a poolside terrace in Manama. I recognized one of the better hotels in Bahrain. The BBC correspondent was a young man, painfully thin, wearing an open-necked shirt with a crooked collar. He needed a good dentist—his mouth was overcrowded with teeth. They gave him a liquid lisp as he talked.

"What Ali and his gang have showed us is just how weak, how nonfunctional, the regime in Riyadh has become. As soon as the rebels' initial successes were announced the central government stopped functioning. It was paralyzed. When they finally did act, it was a fiasco.

"There are unconfirmed reports that several Saudia aircraft have left Riyadh within the past few hours, carrying prominent members of the royal family to havens in Europe and America. The king has not made a statement since the coup attempt began. In addition, we have reports, also unconfirmed, that both the Saudi army and the national guard—the latter being the royal family's personal army—are disintegrating.

"The Pentagon has confirmed that the attack earlier this afternoon on the building thought to house Ali himself, an apartment complex known locally as Silver Towers, was made by the U.S. Army at the request of the Saudi government—according to the Pentagon, in support of the war on terror. The big question now is, not what the Saudi government will do next, but what the Americans will do. They're holding the cards."

The scene switched back to London, and an interview began with another expert. I turned the sound back down.

"So it's the U.S. Army out there now," Helen said. For almost the first time that day, she sounded hopeful.

"Yes, and I'm a terrorist," Ali said. "According to the Americans."

"You can," I said, "see their point."

"I forgot, you are an American, aren't you, Mr. Kemp? Yes, I do see their point. In the American worldview anyone who tries to make a revolution, to destabilize one of the U.S.'s allies, is necessarily a terrorist."

Helen deflected the conversation by saying she'd studied in the UK as well, and asked Ali how long he'd lived there.

The doctor smiled. "For seven years—before I became a political refugee. A wonderful country, politically, although the people—most of them—are completely without religion, and of course racist."

Helen said, "I'm neither irreligious nor racist, Doctor. Neither are my friends."

"I apologize, Mrs. Laird. Naturally I didn't include you. My statement was too general. But, if you don't mind my asking, are you really English?"

"No, I'm not. I'm Irish."

"I thought so. There is still some accent left . . . and, of course your red hair. The Irish are not irreligious, quite the contrary. I respect your beliefs."

So he respected her beliefs . . . I don't think it unreasonable that my blood pressure, my irritation, should have risen. The sight of this pompous "leader," this bringer of death and destruction, condescendingly telling Helen that he respected her beliefs. . . . "So you came back," I said, "because you couldn't stand the Brits."

"Not exactly, Mr. Kemp. I came back because, like others, I had been living in an atmosphere of political tolerance for so long I foolishly believed it might be possible to actively push for reforms in my homeland. Of course I was naive. But many of us thought that immediately after the first war, in 1991, it might be possible. After all, there were a quarter of a million American soldiers in this province alone. Certainly if the Americans had wanted political reform, the government would have had no choice but to tolerate it."

I said, "We were both here then, too. Right after the first war. Business was booming, but I don't remember any talk of political reform."

"Sometimes the two go together. They did not at that time."

Helen asked, "Is that when you were imprisoned?"

"Yes. I was jailed for speaking out against corruption. It was not an agreeable period of my life."

"Were you really tortured?"

He looked her in the eyes and nodded. He said, "So were many others. I was not unique." He paused and finished his cup of coffee. "Up until then I had believed that political change in Arabia could be evolutionary. I finally came to realize that the regime, even though rotten inside, would have to be pushed to fall."

"But they released you."

"The report was inaccurate. I escaped. We are a country where tribes are more important than a flag. What can nationality really mean in a country whose very name is that of the biggest thief: Al Saud? Some of my jailers were sympathetic. I was smuggled out. I crossed the Gulf to Iran. From there I traveled to London, and arrived as a political refugee."

I looked at the disheveled figure in his filthy suit, middle-aged and paunchy, but still with an air of the academic—a very down-on-his-luck academic. It was incredible to think of this unlikely figure being spirited out of Arab jails, "crossing the Gulf" into Iran, making his way by God knew what route to London. Don't politicians and men of action generally look the part? Or had I been fooled by too many Hollywood movies? Maybe the real thing doesn't necessarily fit the mold . . . or maybe he was hopelessly miscast.

I said, "It must have cost money, this coup of yours. You must have backers."

"Of course. There is no shortage of people willing, even eager, to fund reform."

"Do those people include Al Qaeda?"

He paused for a moment before replying. "Al Qaeda, Mr. Kemp, as far as I am aware, only funds its own people, or groups closely allied to its cause. It certainly does not fund Shia. I am not anti-Western, only anticorruption, antimonarchy, anti-Saud."

"I hadn't realized there were so many pro-democracy activists with money in Saudi Arabia."

"The people here who are ready to fund my cause may not all fit your idea of democrats, of democracy activists. But they are against the nepotism and despotism of the present regime."

"I thought the Saudi government had shut down the channels—

wire transfers, charitable organizations, and so forth—that funneled money to organizations like yours."

He laughed. "They have. They did. But this is the era of globalization. Who can stop the movement of money? You should know that, Mr. Kemp . . . are you not a man of finance? Let me tell you something: the Arab world is comparatively well regulated, financially, compared to some of the countries on our perimeter. Greece, Turkey, the Mediterranean: these places are porous, poorly regulated. Money flows through them as naturally as the Bosphorus flows into the Sea of Marmara. It will take more than an American government regulation to stop it."

"You still have to get it out," I said.

"America and England have to worry about money *arriving* from certain destinations . . . like this one. They can't cover every third-party transaction in the world. No one can."

He was a politician in his way: he always had the reasonable explanation, the slippery answer, the way out. I said, "The extremists from Afghanistan and Pakistan—they're supporting you, aren't they?"

"Those are Sunni countries, Mr. Kemp. They do not support us."

"Well then, Iran. Syria."

"Politics is the art of the possible. We are in communication with activists in friendly Muslim countries. But we are not under their thumb."

"You're in communication with suicide bombers. With cowards who blow up unarmed civilians all over the world. It sounds to me like a pretty sleazy, a criminal organization."

He looked like I'd finally got under his skin. For a moment the slipperiness slipped away. "Cowards?" he said. "Certainly your administration, your media, even your generals—who should know better—persist in calling them that. Were the British cowards when they massacred tens of thousands of civilians in Bremen? Were the Americans when they did the same in Japan? Did the Algerians lack courage in their fight against the French colonialists, or the Vietnamese in their fight against the same enemies? I don't think these men, and women, lacked courage."

Helen spoke: "Perhaps, Dr. Ali, some of them lacked humanity."

I was about to speak, but Helen placed a warning hand on my knee. She said, "What were you planning to replace the regime with?"

The professor made an effort and recovered his poise. "My plans are not yet in the past tense. You heard the BBC. The government in Riyadh is disintegrating. The royal family is fleeing the country. We still have our chance.

"Most of the oil in this country is here in the east—the Shia's home. But we have never benefited from it. Have you ever been to Riyadh, Mrs. Laird?"

"Yes."

"Compare the palaces, the roads, the government buildings, the hospitals, the infrastructure—compare it to Dammam and Al Khobar! We Shia live in our own Gaza strip, our own West Bank—under occupation by Al Saud. What do we want? The right to govern ourselves, and to enjoy our share of our own wealth. The center and the west of the country may go their own way. Our plans here in the east are detailed and well developed. They include a president with strong executive powers, a *majlis*—a parliament—composed of a mix of appointed and elected figures, and of tribal leaders, and finally, an independent judiciary."

I said, "I presume that you would preside as president."

"Naturally I would hold the post for the first term. After that, it would be open to popular election. I have no wish to be president for life."

It was all I could do to keep from laughing aloud.

For whatever reason—perhaps he read my expression clearly, or perhaps he had a dim idea that he had gone too far, into the realm of the derisory—he fell silent.

Presently Helen said, "I don't know if you drink or not . . . if you'd like it, we can offer you a whiskey."

"Whiskey?"

"We found some here."

"Ha. I could use a drink. Thank you for your offer. But I had better not. The next few hours . . . they may be critical."

She smiled. "Of course. I hope I didn't offend you."

"Not at all. I enjoy the occasional glass of wine or whiskey. A good Muslim can drink—these are matters of interpretation, after all—just not to excess. I am not a hypocrite. And the people who call me a fundamentalist . . . what does the label really mean? An Islamic state is a virtuous state—a state that is organized, as far as we are able, to provide virtuous rulers.

"Believe me, if I fail, then the next revolution will be led by the real fundamentalists. The Sunnis from the Nejd: from Riyadh and Buraydah. It is their followers, not ours, who have been behind the bombings—here, in Iraq, even in Great Britain. The men with money but no scruples. They are ready."

He stood up with some difficulty and walked to the balcony. I wondered what he saw of his dream, as he looked out over the railing, into the night—within it, shrouded in darkness, waiting, the most powerful army in the world. After a moment he turned back and said, "You must excuse me. Thank you for the dinner, and the conversation. I am sorry if I monopolized it. It is a common fault of politicians . . . and professors.

"Now let me tell you where I and my men will be. We will concentrate our forces on the middle floors, to counter what will certainly be an attack from the ground. Tonight we will also attempt to send out a few people, to try to reach our comrades at Aramco and the air base.

"I regret that we had to involve you. It wasn't part of our plan. You could leave now if it was safe, but, as I am sure you realize, it is not. I especially regret having involved you, Mrs. Laird. This is not the place for a woman. Or a representative—even as a spouse—of the American government. I was hoping we could deal with them as friends."

He shook hands with Helen, then offered me his; I took it. I didn't want to be rude in front of her. We walked him to the door. The last thing he said was: "No matter what happens tomorrow, we have accomplished something. We have brought down the house of Saud." Helen shut the door behind him.

CHAPTER FIVE

I was relieved we were alone again. "What did you think?" Helen asked.

"Of him? He's a disaster."

She leaned against the wall, as if drained. "A revolutionary manqué," she said.

"What does that mean?"

"A failure." Her voice expressed no hatred, only sadness. "Why don't I clear up while you make us both a stiff drink."

We had less than half a bottle of whiskey left, so I made her a strong whiskey and Coke and myself a *sid* and Coke . . . close enough, under the circumstances, to the real thing. As long as you didn't smell it. After that we sat on the couch together, watching the snowy picture from Bahrain.

I put my arm around her and we settled back. We might have been a married couple, long past the honeymoon stage, even past the first year's arguments and adjustments, past the anger and despair, with our mutual bitterness under control: the wounded compromise of most married lives. But I was comfortable, and, again, strangely happy. I didn't want to be with anyone else.

After a while, she asked, "How much longer do we have? Where should we be: here, downstairs, on the roof? If we can get onto the roof."

She needed reassurance. I told her, "I doubt they'll attack tonight. With the lights off everybody would be shooting everybody else. They'll wait until dawn, or shortly after. And it is the U.S. Army, not a gang of local yahoos. The consulate knows we're here so the army knows, too. They have to assume we're still alive. Ali told us he's concentrating his men on the middle floors and we're well above them. An attacking force will have to work their way up, so the higher we are, the better. We're only two floors from the top now, and we're pretty comfortable; I see no reason to move. At least, not until things start happening."

Helen said calmly, "In your own mind, Steven, do you think we're going to survive?"

"Yes. We've survived this far. I think there's a good chance we'll make it. I think our greatest danger is getting caught in the cross fire. When it starts, we've got to keep our heads down."

We fell silent. The TV glared its silly scenes in front of us. The rest of the apartment retreated into darkness. The night outside felt near. Then Helen asked me, "Do you believe in the next life?"

It's the kind of question I feel uncomfortable with and normally resent being asked. I didn't resent it from her, but she deserved it plain, not sugarcoated. "No, I don't. Not really. I was raised a Catholic . . . baptized, confirmed, catechized: the works. But I jettisoned the whole thing years ago."

"I remember. You called yourself a lapsed Catholic."

"Very lapsed." She could remember my religious convictions—or the lack of them—from more than ten years before, but I couldn't remember hers. I remembered her hair, her laugh, her figure, the taste of her skin, the way she walked. "What about you?" I asked. "Do you believe in the life to come, and all the rest of it?"

"Yes. I'm Irish, after all. Of course, I don't go to confession and communion here—there aren't any churches, any priests. They aren't allowed. Even in Ireland, with Harry, I only went to Mass now and again, when I felt like it. Harry's like you, not religious. But I still believe. It's in my bones. Even miracles aren't too much for me to believe in . . . and that's certainly what we need now, isn't it? A miracle."

"I don't believe in them."

"What do you believe in, Steven? Everyone has faith in something."

"Not in God. I lost that faith as a teenager."

"Why? How did it happen?"

You have to respect people's faiths; I had no wish to insult hers. I didn't want to tell her that I couldn't swallow the theology: transubstantiation; the Virgin birth; the trinity; Christ dying for our sins. So I told her part of the truth. "Boredom," I said. "Sunday Mass killed me. Every week, every month, every year, the same routine, the same readings in the missal . . . I was so bored I'd read ahead, hoping that there might be something new. But there wasn't. I'd look around the church on Sunday. I was surrounded by old people even older than my parents. The priests were okay, most of the time, but their sermons put me in a coma. And the smell . . . I've never liked incense—or the smell of stale sweat. So when I woke up one day and realized I'd lost my faith, it was a relief. I didn't even miss it."

She smiled. "That's not exactly a picture of a boy in touch with spirituality."

"I don't suppose I was."

She was silent for a while, then said, "I feel that if we survive this, we'll have been given a second chance. Maybe a chance to get some things right that we've gotten wrong; maybe a chance to find things that we've lost."

"To get things right. . . . Yes, I'd like that. I'd like to get one or two things right, to get some things back I've lost."

"What have you lost?"

I thought. "Money. Love. Honesty." I looked at her. "Perhaps not in that order."

"Why do you say 'honesty'?"

I shifted on the couch. Confession, for me, has never come easy. "During the last boom the mutual fund industry exploded. There were regulations, of course—there always have been—but it would have been almost impossible to regulate it thoroughly: there was just too much business. And some of it was fairly sharp, especially toward the end. After-hours trading, commission kickbacks, some pretty fraudulent buy recommendations. Everyone was doing it to some extent— almost everyone. But after the bottom dropped out, companies and individuals were investigated, even indicted.

"I was just a tiny fish in a big pond, but I was involved in my share of . . . illegalities. It's been an anxiety. Every month that goes by the anxiety is a little less. But, you know, I wasn't brought up to it. To breaking the law. I want a life without complexities, without corruption. I want to get back to sticking to the rules."

She said, "And money? Do honesty and money go together?"

"Definitely. They should and do. And I need money. My wife had a great divorce lawyer."

"I'm sorry to hear it." She put her hand on mine. "And where does love come in?"

"Near the top. It's been a hell of a long time, since I had it, since I felt it. After my marriage was over, I tried being a bachelor again in LA . . . bars, clubs, one-night stands. What a waste of time. Hopeless, futureless, mini-involvements. If you're lucky, you'll both get out of it without too much pain, but no matter how little, it still isn't worth it. I finally gave it up. Honesty comes in there, too. I want honest love and honest passion. It's been a long dry period."

She said, so low I hardly heard her, "Me, too."

"You?"

"Oh, I still love Harry. And he loves me. But passion—that disappeared a long time ago."

It was my turn to say, "I'm sorry." I wasn't sure if it was a lie.

"It can be hard to keep passion alive for years. You must know that. And Harry's older, near retirement. It's funny, isn't it? I meant to boast of my marriage to you, when we met in the restaurant."

"To boast?"

"Yes. To show you how well I'd done, after you'd left. Marrying a diplomat. He was like you in some ways. I used to think they were American characteristics: loving, making love—sex—with honesty, maturity. Not like an Irish boy: alcoholic groping on a car bonnet under a dripping tree, outside some pub. And so frozen with shame the next morning they couldn't look you in the eye. Over a grope.

"There was plenty of passion when we first married. But he drinks—I know that sounds funny coming from a girl from Limerick—we're famous for the drink. But it's got a grip on him. Our posting in Ireland wasn't good for him, in that way." She took a sip of her own whiskey. "He was happy when we first met. He even liked this place. Now he's turned hateful—not to me—to his job, to the Arabs, to everything. And his job is all he has. And he hates it. It's hard to live with someone who never sees hope, someone with so little charity." She gave a little sad laugh. "I was so depressed, I even went on Prozac. It's been a great help."

It was a shock; meds were something I associated with my ex-wife's women friends in California. I said, "Are you still on it?"

"Oh, sure, when I feel the need." She leaned forward, her elbows on her knees, her breasts pushing against Ayşen's blouse.

With each count of unhappiness my hopes rose. I felt I was getting closer to her, to a chance of having her, circling in nearer, with her still unaware of my approach. I asked, "What else would you like to have a second chance at?"

"Children. Harry's divorced. He has a grown-up son from his first wife. He doesn't want any more . . . he says he's too old." She looked up at me. "What about you?"

"I never had any."

"It's not too late. You could remarry."

"Who? I married the wrong woman once, and the right one's no longer available."

"And who would the right one be?" She looked away as she spoke, as if she half expected an answer she didn't care for, didn't want to hear. I was determined to give it, but the effort was greater than I thought: it wasn't easy admitting love; it was almost like admitting a crime. The sweat broke out on my palms as I said:

"You."

She sat still as a statue. Then she said, "You can't mean it. How long have you thought that? Two hours, two days?"

"Does it matter? Perhaps it's something I knew all along, but just realized—if that makes any sense."

"It doesn't make sense. I was only a fling for you—I just didn't realize it at the time. I was as naive about love as Ali is about politics. You left me without so much as a call, or a letter. You forgot me."

"I never forgot you."

"Then why didn't you come back?"

"I told you. In LA, all this"—I swept our shattered apartment with my arm—"you, the expat life, this whole place—became unreal. I was on the other side of the world. I wanted to get ahead. I discovered that the work I'd done here didn't really count. Oh, they were happy I'd exceeded my quota. But if you wanted to move up, what mattered was the contacts, the politics, at head office. Al Khobar was the back of beyond. There wasn't even any business here any longer. I never forgot you. But after a while, yes, I did try to forget. There's not much point in dwelling on what you can't have—or on what you didn't choose."

I didn't sound very convincing as a lover, even to myself, but we were adults, and were being honest with each other—as honest as we could. It wasn't the movies. I looked at her. Her expression wasn't one of anger, but of concern: as if she'd heard something that carried the weight of a responsibility she didn't want to face, of decisions that would bring more pain than happiness to everyone.

I never wanted to make her unhappy. "Come on," I told her, "let's have a final drink and get some air." I got up and refreshed our drinks—my *sid* was tasting better—and took them out to the balcony.

The whole town must have been under curfew. The night was utterly silent. The lights below were like the lights of a distant shore just within sight but not listed as a port of call: evidence of life, but out of reach.

Helen joined me, bringing her glass. She looked withdrawn in thought, as distant as the sleeping town. She stood very near. Then she leaned against me, with a light, steady pressure.

She said, quietly, "We're surrounded by wreckage, aren't we? The tower and the apartment's wrecked; your marriage, and maybe mine; maybe soon our lives."

"We'll make it."

"Maybe. But doesn't it give you a feeling of . . . freedom? That, if we survive this, why shouldn't we do anything, anything we want?"

"Why shouldn't we now?"

She didn't answer, but she didn't move away. She felt warm against me and my blood leapt.

A thin scream cut the darkness. A scream dry and tenuous as the desert air. It came not from below, but from somewhere out beyond us. It sounded uncanny. It startled me. If I were an imaginative type, I might say it made my blood run cold. I listened, but it didn't come again. I said, "Did you hear that?"

"Yes." We both faced the night.

"What do you think it was? A night bird of some kind?"

She paused and said, "It sounded like the banshee."

The word didn't register, and then I recollected faintly a world of Irish ghosts and goblins, of little men on a hill. I was incredulous: she must be joking. I repeated the word, as if confirming it was just a laugh, but she told me: "I heard it once before, as a child in Limerick, down on the Shannon, standing on the shore by an old woman's house. It's the warning of present death: you only hear it when death is very near. The next morning she was found cold and lifeless in her bed."

It's easy to forget, in these days of the Irish with higher incomes than the English, it's easy to forget what life must have been like for an Irish child born thirty years before the economic boom. That period and that way of life are history, although most of the participants are still alive; that was Helen's childhood. It's a characteristic of love to find even the loved one's faults dear: a belief in the banshee seemed a very small fault to me.

"We're a long way from Ireland here," I told her. "Whatever it was, I don't think it was a premonition."

But it was for her. She no longer leaned against me.

I looked over the railing and saw that Ali had blacked out the rest of the building. The forces outside must know where we were: our single light showed foolishly—or bravely—high in the tower. In my career I'd become an expert on the positive spin.

I said again, "I think it's likely that the army will attack in the morning, probably around dawn. We should make a plan. I think we should stay in our apartment, at least during the initial attack. We're almost certainly safer here than we would be lower down. They'll have to invade the building sooner or later, and the farther we are from that the better. We don't have to worry much about small-arms fire. We're pretty far up for that. But we should plan where to take cover if they use mortars or missiles.

"The main corridor wall is structural—steel-reinforced concrete— and the entry hallway wall might be as well. But the rest are just hollow concrete block. So, if they use rockets or mortars, as they did today, I think we should try to make it to the corridor outside—if we have time. If not, the hallway."

Helen said, "I'm worried about fire."

"It's going to be hard to make this place burn. The building's concrete. They shot the hell out of the thirteenth floor, and still only started a few small fires. If worse comes to worst, there's the fire escape—or the roof." I put my arm around her. "I think we stand a good chance of getting out of this alive."

For a few moments we were lost in our own thoughts. Then she said, "I'm so sorry for getting you into this mess, Steven. You've been wonderful, you really have. No matter what happens tomorrow, I want you to know how grateful I am for your strength and your kindness. Thank you."

She reached up and kissed me. It took me by surprise. Before I could return it she had turned and gone alone to her bedroom. I stayed for a little while on the balcony, then went to my own room. But neither fatigue nor even the beginning of love could overcome anxiety, and I could not sleep.

The dawn broke without sign of an attack.

I blearily got up, started some coffee, and walked through the wrecked living room out to the balcony.

All was quiet in the early morning light. The haze from the day before had vanished and the sky was crystal clear. The air felt crisp. The detritus of yesterday's failed attack still littered the ground below. There was no sign of further preparations, or a new buildup.

I turned around at a sound behind me. It was Helen, wrapped in a blanket, still half asleep. "So we're still alive," she said. "Let's see if there's any news."

She turned on the TV. Bahrain was transmitting CNN, but Atlanta was only carrying a story about the new government in Indonesia. Helen switched to Aramco. They were showing the same static sign, the call to support the coup, as the night before.

"Well," Helen said, "I hope that whatever happens, it happens before lunch. We've just about run out of provisions."

We were also running out of water. The dispenser in the kitchen had only a liter or two left, and when Helen took a shower a few minutes later, she just had time to rinse off the soap before the flow fell to a trickle, and then to nothing at all. So the hot water heater was empty, and was no longer being replenished.

We sat down and watched the Aramco channel, hoping for a change. Helen sat hunched over, her elbows on her knees. Her posture accentuated the fall of her breasts against her shirt. Watching her, I felt a rush of desire. I was relieved she didn't notice. I thought some distance might be a good idea, and returned to the balcony. I closed my eyes, feeling the sun warm on my face. When I opened them Helen stood by my side.

So we both missed the removal of the sign on the TV. When we heard an American voice we snapped around.

A soldier in early middle age—an American—wearing standard desert camouflage uniform, sat behind a desk talking directly into the camera. His expression was stern. I couldn't make out his rank, but he was definitely an officer. Three times he repeated that viewers were listening to an announcement from the U.S. Army Gulf Command. By the end of the first repeat we were glued to the screen.

The officer cleared his throat, nodded at someone offscreen, then said: "I am General Matthew Grumman. This morning at oh six hundred hours forces from the United States Army, with the cooperation and assistance of forces from the Saudi government, occupied and secured the Aramco headquarters compound in Dhahran, Saudi Arabia.

"Simultaneously, Arab government forces, with the assistance of the United States Army and support from the United States Air Force, secured the Royal Saudi Air Base in Dhahran. Both facilities were secured without any loss of American lives. I repeat, without a single loss of American life.

"My message to all residents of the Aramco compound is this: the situation on the compound is stabilized. You are asked, however, to stay on the compound until further notice. We expect to stabilize the security situation in the Eastern Province today.

"I have a special message to all American Aramco employees and their dependents. You are until further notice under the direct protection and administration of the United States Army. You have never been safer in your lives. Thank you."

He nodded again at someone offscreen, and the picture went momentarily blank, then came up again, this time showing a simple statement in English repeating the gist of the general's announcement.

It was so sudden that for a moment neither of us said a word. Then Helen said, "Thank God."

"It means the U.S. Army has taken over, right?"

"Yes. No doubt about it. I don't know what role the Saudi government's playing, or the Saudi army—if it still exists. But I'm sure the U.S. Army's calling the shots."

"He said the whole Eastern Province would be 'stabilized' today. I assume that includes us." I felt a combination of elation and anxiety. "All we have to do, then, is sit tight and wait."

"Yes. But wait for what?"

The answer wasn't long in coming.

Just a few minutes later, as we watched CNN replay the general's announcement, we heard above the television the distant, jagged roar of a high-speed aircraft. The sound faded quickly—as if the plane had wheeled away.

We both went out on the balcony to look. The sun shone bright out of a clear sky, the buildings below sand-colored and silent. The silence became ominous.

Helen said, "I don't see a thing." Then suddenly we heard it again, faintly: the broken roar of a high-performance jet. I strained to spot it, squinting into the sun's glare.

We stood rooted, transfixed by the distant sound, by the invisibility of its source. Then I recalled the attack on the Meridien. Then the jets had released their missiles at a distance, from far out at sea. Why had they now approached close enough for us to hear? Why had they surrendered the element of surprise? In order to warn us?

We wouldn't be able to hear the missiles, and if we did manage to see them it would certainly be too late to take cover. It was crazy to stay out on the balcony. I grabbed Helen by her arm and pulled her back inside, yelling to make for the corridor.

Panic robbed us of coordination. I tripped on one of the innumerable afghan rugs and Helen ran into the edge of the couch. I got to my feet and, standing there, had a moment of clarity, or perhaps a premonition—although I don't normally believe in such things. We were too late. There was no time to make the outside corridor. But there was still the inside hallway wall. It might provide some protection. In two steps I pulled Helen to the hallway and pushed her roughly into the corner. I wanted her to get down, to lie on the floor, but I didn't have time to get the words out. We were pressed close together in the corner when the first missile struck.

CHAPTER SIX

I was aware of difficulty breathing. The air smelled thick, acrid. I gently opened my eyes.

I seemed to be at an angle: a wall sloped over me. The air was full of gray smoke. Smoke and concrete dust. My hearing had gone again and the smoke and dust swirled silently. It was like waking from anesthesia, discovering one's world bit by bit. Carefully I tried shifting my body and discovered I was lying flat: the hallway wall was at an angle, not me. The concrete had cracked and the rebar had bent, but hadn't broken. The wall still stood, precariously.

Where was Helen? I attempted to turn onto my side and had hardly moved before I felt her next to me. The explosion had flung us both on the floor pressed to each other like two lovers in bed.

A thin coat of plaster and pulverized concrete covered her. She was white and still. I tried calling her name but she didn't answer— I couldn't even hear myself. With one hand I brushed her face and hair. She didn't move. I wondered if she was dead. It would be useless trying to take her pulse—it looked so simple in the movies, but I had never been able to find even my own consistently. She looked unscathed, lying as peacefully as a corpse. I observed her closely and thought I detected the rise and fall of breath.

I examined the wall and became concerned: how stable could it be at that angle? I got to my feet in slow motion, afraid that something might be broken and watching out for pain. The pulverized rubble slid off me. I stepped over Helen, into the living room. The missile must have hit somewhere above us. The ceiling had buckled inward, littering the floor with chunks of concrete, but had not collapsed. The glass doors and curtains were gone. The partition separating the living room from the kitchen was blown into matchwood—the explosion had knocked the two rooms into one.

I searched among the ruins of the kitchen for the kettle, thinking it might still hold some water, but couldn't find it. I did find the big plastic water bottle. By the kind of miracle that only earthquakes and explosions produce, it was still intact, with a little water in the bottom.

Carrying it back to Helen I realized my hearing was returning: I heard my shoes crunching over the floor. I knelt down in the shattered hall—shakily, like an old man unsure of his knees, of his balance—and bathed Helen's face.

Her eyes opened and she recognized me.

"Steven."

"Quiet. Open your mouth. I'm going to give you some water." And I cupped some into my hand, letting it run onto her lips.

She choked, coughed spasmodically, and pushed my hand away. She continued to hack, the plaster and concrete shaking off with every cough.

"Jesus," she said between coughs.

"I'm sorry," I told her, immensely relieved. "How do you feel?"

She coughed some more, then focused. "Like I've been brought back from the dead." She grimaced. "God, my side hurts."

"It looks like the missile hit the floor above. The ceiling held but the apartment's wrecked. That bit of wall saved us."

"You look like a ghost. Are you hurt?"

I put my hand to my face and realized I was as covered in plaster dust as she. "I don't know. I don't think so. Not badly."

She looked up at the wall leaning over her like the slab of a tomb. "Help me out," she said.

I helped her to her feet. She groaned and stifled a cry. There was no place to sit in the living room—rubble covered everything—so I led her back down the hall to the far bedroom, which had escaped the worst of the blast. We sat on the bed and examined ourselves. We both had bruises and minor cuts, and her left forearm had been sliced open above the wrist. She had a sharp pain in her side, probably a bruised or broken rib. I had a gash on my forehead, just at the hairline. My hair was matted and crusted with blood.

The bathroom was still recognizable. I retrieved the first-aid kit I'd hidden in the cupboard. When she saw her white face in the mirror, she said, "I look like Lazarus."

"Lazarus?"

"Christ resurrected him."

"It's only plaster dust."

We cleaned and dressed our wounds as best we could, then crept back to the bedroom and lay down next to each other on the bed. We should have been in a hospital. Neither of us had life-threatening injuries, but we were both shocked, bruised, beat up, bleeding a little and in pain. I was pretty sure the pain was going to increase as the shock wore off.

I told her to stay there while I looked for some aspirin. I found none, and, curious about what, if anything, was happening outside, I returned to the wrecked living room. The smoke had almost cleared.

Without the glass doors the apartment was open to the outside air. I stepped carefully onto the balcony and looked over. The scene below was silent and unchanged under the bright morning sun. There was no evidence of movement. It was a tableau where all hope of action seemed to have vanished. A sliver of glass crunched under my foot. A moment later I ducked and withdrew as the whump of a mortar or missile sounded from the ground. The building trembled and another blast followed and another. They all struck the first floors. Bits of ceiling rained down around me. Silence fell again. I carefully peered out over the edge.

The scene was transformed: troops, unopposed, swarmed like an invasion of ants toward the base of the tower.

Helen called my name from the smashed hall; she'd heard the mortars. "It's the attack," I told her. "The army's invading the building now. This is it."

"What should we do?"

"Stay put. I doubt the air force is going to lob another missile in here. And we can't go down—not yet. When things have calmed down. . . ."

"You mean, when everyone inside is dead."

"Or surrendered." But I didn't think it likely that there would be many surrenders given—or taken.

We went back to bed to wait. There was nothing else to do. We lay side by side with our hands clasped. Helen asked me how long I thought it would take for the army to reach us. I said I had no idea. There would be some resistance, but the main obstacle might be blocked stairwells.

"We're safe," she said.

I didn't understand, but didn't want to question her assurance. She said, "You can't die twice."

"What do you mean?"

"This is our second chance."

I didn't know what to say, so I said nothing. She's shocked, I thought; we both are. When I looked at her, her eyes were closed.

I lay there, trying to regain my strength, trying to get my head together. I heard sporadic firing through the shattered facade. I knew the army was ascending as the firing grew louder. Ali's men must be fighting as they retreated upward. There was no way of telling which floor they were on. There was a long lull, and then shots rang out very near. Was there some way of jamming the door shut? I carried a chair from the bedroom out to the hall, and tried wedging it against the door. I'd seen it done in a dozen films, but Hollywood isn't reality. The back was the wrong height: there was no way to get it securely under the doorknob. While I fiddled with it, cursing, a spray of bullets slammed metallically into something in the corridor—maybe the fire escape. I stumbled back and found Helen standing behind me.

"What is it?" she said.

"Someone's reached our floor—I don't know who. Probably Ali's men. The door won't stop them. We're too exposed."

I started pulling her back to the bedroom, but we'd only made it a few feet when we heard shouting in Arabic and someone kicked the door open. Then a familiar voice: "Mrs. Laird, Mr. Kemp, are you still alive?"

It was Ali. Two of his men helped him in, one under each arm. He'd taken a bullet in his leg and he grimaced in pain. Helen took charge. The sight of someone else wounded, in pain and in need, brought her to life. The men laid him on the bed, then withdrew into the corridor to cover the stairs. With his clothes on I couldn't see the wound, but blood began to soak the mattress. Helen told me to get the first-aid kit and a knife from the kitchen—it took a little time—and then she started cutting away his trouser leg.

"You're lucky," she told him, "I don't think the bullet hit a bone or artery."

"I am happy to hear," Ali said weakly, "that something went right."

Helen put a pad on the hole in his leg and started wrapping it. His face was almost as pale as Helen's. I said, "The game's up. Why don't you surrender? You might still be able to."

"How do you suggest we do that?"

"A white flag . . . do you have a bullhorn?"

He groaned as Helen tightened the bandage. "We lack a loud-hailer, and I don't think the flag would be effective—even if we had one. In any case, my men will never surrender. They really do believe in the paradise spoken of by the Prophet."

Helen asked him, "Do you?"

"I am a Muslim. I believe. But there are levels of belief. These men have a simple, unquestioning faith. Some would call it primitive." He paused, his face contorted. "After what I saw this morning, I have greater respect for the simple believer." He gave a sharp cry.

"I'm sorry," Helen told him, "but I have to stop the bleeding."

"Please ignore me. I have never been a courageous man. . . . I told them everything in Riyadh. They only had to hurt me a little."

I said, "You'll soon be in safer hands than the Saudi police. The U.S.

Army doesn't torture their prisoners." Helen shot me a glance. Then I remembered Abu Ghraib, and Guantánamo, and the secret prisons all over the globe. I had spoken without thinking. The certainties of a earlier age had been first to surface.

"Americans," he said. "You have so many illusions, so much innocence. . . . Violence begets violence. But perhaps you have learned something. I hope you are right. But we must be practical. Your army is why I had my men bring me here. You are both in danger. They are shooting at anything that moves."

"They know we're here. We're unarmed. If we stay put. . . ."

"That is foolish. You must be realistic. It is your only chance." He paused to catch his breath. "You don't have some water?"

Helen got up and fetched the bottle. She cupped some carefully into her hand and dribbled it into his mouth.

"Thank you. Now listen. This floor will be our last stand. What men are left will stay with me. They will fight to the end.

"This is my plan. You will help me back to the stairs. I will keep my men with me as long as I can. You two will climb up, I hope right to the roof. If you can stay above the fighting, and become easily visible, your army may not shoot—they may allow you to surrender. But there is no time. We have to go now."

It sounded better than sitting in the ruins of the apartment. I nodded to Helen.

Ali said, "You will have to help me." We got him off the bed as gently as we could. Helen took one of his arms and I the other. He wasn't a light man. We took him through the shattered apartment—it was my last sight of it—and down the corridor.

A group of his men stood at the stairs opposite the elevators. We'd made it halfway to them when we heard gunfire coming straight up the well. Ali called to them, but they motioned him back.

"Too late," he said. "They're just below."

I looked behind us. "There's the fire escape. It goes up as well as down."

There was no discussion. Helen and I turned Ali around and marched him back to our end. It was difficult; we were too battered to build a rhythm. The corridor was a narrow, confined, dark space, and I wanted to get out of it as quickly as possible.

I slammed down the bar of the fire escape door and pushed. It opened a few inches and jammed. I strained against it until it gave with a crack and swung open.

The sun was dazzling, like stepping out of a dark room onto a beach. But there was no time for careful inspection, or to let our eyes adjust. I stomped down on the metal grille with one foot; it held. I squinted upward. It was impossible to see through the maze of steel stairs and rails, but it looked strong enough to try. We got Ali through the door, and Helen pushed it closed behind her.

The door shut out the sound of the battle inside. We were squeezed together on a steel grille with nothing but a slender railing between us and an eleven-floor fall. We gulped at the fresh air.

There wasn't room to go abreast. Helen told me to lead the way. Ali pulled himself up, one stair at a time, with Helen helping him from behind.

The stairs reversed and we were at the next floor. Ali shouted to me to continue on. We reached the thirteenth and continued past it, but halfway to the roof, at the mid-floor landing, we found trouble. The last stretch of fire escape was gone. The platform was still intact—the stairs had simply disappeared.

I pressed myself against the side of the building, stretching my arms above my head, trying to reach the roof. I thought if I could pull myself up, then I could pull Helen up after me. Ali didn't figure in my emergency escape plan. My fingers reached the top of the roof wall; standing up on my toes I could just put my palms on the wall's upper surface.

If I'd been a younger man, or in better condition—much better condition—I might have tried it. I might have been able to lift myself up. But it was impossible. I didn't have the strength. My arms fell.

"I'm sorry," I said. "I can't manage it. It's too high."

Helen spoke from behind Ali's bulk. "Maybe we can just stay here."

Ali said, "We are safer here than inside, but we would be safer still on the roof. Here, we are trapped. On the roof, we could at least move, find shelter."

"It means," I said, "going back in on the thirteenth floor."

"We should try, Mr. Kemp."

Ali, the least able-bodied among us, seemed to have taken over the leadership position. But he made sense. We went back down to the thirteenth-floor landing. The fire door swung open easily; perhaps it had been blown ajar. Inside it was quiet; the fighting hadn't reached that level. The light from the open door showed the broken corridor, the far end littered with rubble, the former clinic. We tried to prop the fire door open, but there was nothing suitable nearby. As it closed behind us we walked into semidarkness, the way ahead lit by shafts of light where both interior and exterior walls had gone.

We advanced as fast as we could, skirting, stepping, stumbling over the blown-up floor, the blown-in walls, the blown-down ceiling. The smell of smoke hung heavy on the air, as did another, more disagreeable odor. In that hot, humid environment, a day and a night was more than enough time for decomposition to begin.

I went a little ahead and opened the stairwell door. The landing and stairs were empty and silent. But as soon as Helen and Ali caught up, the firing began again, reverberating up from below. I closed the door.

"Did you see anyone?" Ali asked.

"No. But they're down there."

"If we go up," he said, "we must go now. Your army will shoot first and ask questions later. If they ask at all."

"And what about your men?" I said. "Do you think they'll stop and look? Before shooting us?"

He searched in a jacket pocket, his face a rictus of pain. "You are right," he said. "Take this. It may give you some protection. It is probably best to keep it hidden until you need it." He pulled out a small revolver and held it to me. "I don't know how to use it, in any case. There is a safety catch here"—his thumb indicated the base of the barrel—"but I could never remember how to tell whether it is on or off."

I took it. Its weight surprised me. In the gloom I could barely see the safety. The revolver did not impart a sense of confidence or security. I hadn't shot a firearm of any kind for almost thirty years. I did remember enough to know that, completely out of practice and with an unknown weapon, it was doubtful that I would hit anything I aimed at, except at point-blank range.

"Okay," I said. "Let's go. Helen, you and Ali first. I'll bring up the rear."

Ali pulled himself up by the banister with Helen pushing at his side, while I followed, keeping an eye down the stairs. The firing below was intermittent but loud and growing louder. The final stretch rose through the floor of a small room, no bigger than a closet. A door took up most of one wall. Was it locked? Ali turned the handle and pushed.

It swung open. We stepped out onto the roof under a bright morning sun and blue sky.

"Thank God," Helen said, and Ali echoed it with, "*Alhamdilillah.*" I scanned the roof to find someplace to take cover. It could only be a matter of time before what was left of Ali's men emerged from the same door.

But there was nothing. The surface of flat, peeling concrete stretched away on every side to the roof wall, its expanse broken only by knee-high ventilators. We were alone, but there was no place to hide.

I suggested we get as far away as we could from the exit. Helen and I helped the groaning Ali toward the opposite end. We'd made it about halfway when he finally collapsed. His weight was too much for the two of us, and we eased him as gently as we could to the roof. He'd simply come to the end of his strength. Helen bent down to inspect his bandage while I kept a watch on the door.

Helen stood up beside me. "He's semiconscious—he's lost a lot of blood. His trouser leg is soaked." Her voice cracked with exhaustion and she looked ready to collapse herself; I wanted to hold her but we were both so sore I was afraid I'd bring more pain than comfort.

Then we heard the beating of helicopter blades. We looked up.

It came from the south, just a little higher than the tower, so that we saw it over the roof wall, nearly at rooftop level. Not a small attack helicopter, but a large machine—big enough to carry troops, big enough to carry us. The aircraft grew larger and I began to wave, probably hysterically.

The helicopter was nearly upon us when a man stumbled through the door, clearly disoriented by the light and sound.

He wore a uniform, and at first I wondered if he was one of ours. But then he saw us. He was an Arab. He raised his rifle and let off a short burst in our direction. I pushed Helen to the ground and yelled to her to lie flat.

There were only two courses of action. I could try to convince him we were unarmed, not a threat, and hope that he would stop shooting. Or I could shoot back. I don't know Arabic, and he was already shooting at us. I pulled out Ali's revolver.

He didn't see the gun: he had already switched his attention to the helicopter. It had reached the wall. Blotting out the sky, spurting smoke and vapor, it hammered our ears with its rotors and whipped up stinging clouds of dust and sand from the roof.

I have to admit, the Arab showed courage, planting his legs solidly, raising his weapon, and taking careful aim at the machine.

The range was too far for me to have a hope of hitting him, unless by a lucky chance. But I had to try. I didn't want to draw his fire toward Helen, so, crouching, I ran as fast as I could away from her and away from the helicopter, closer to my target. After a few yards I started pulling the trigger. The revolver jumped in my hand.

I doubt I hit him. I'll never know for sure, because after just a few shots the machine gun on the helicopter opened up.

The Arab threw his rifle into the air, then sat down abruptly over a twisted leg, and fell over. His body jumped on the ground, pounded by bullets. The firing ceased and I felt myself kicked in the face by a blast of air. I turned and struggled back to Helen.

Before its skids touched the roof, uniformed troops were jumping out of an open hatch. They splayed out, securing the area. Two made directly for us. Huge and bulky in their uniforms, body armor and munitions, they were more frightening than reassuring until the first to reach us, a giant black man, shouted in a thick Southern accent: "Mrs. Laird, Mr. Kemp?"

"Yes," I replied.

"I'm Major Webster. You're now under the protection of the United States Marines. Please follow me and we'll get you out of here right now."

Never has a Southern accent sounded so beautiful to my ears. The major and I helped Helen to her feet and the three of us ran to the waiting helicopter. At the hatch strong arms waited to pull us in. But Helen hung back. She shouted to the major. I couldn't hear her; he had to put his ear to her mouth. Then he nodded, we were lifted up and inside and as we were buckled into the most comfortless yet most welcoming seats I'd ever sat in, two soldiers appeared in the door carrying the limp body of Ali between them, and he was lifted in as well.

So we exited Silver Towers with the architect of its siege.

The helicopter rose like a theme park ride, pressing us down hard on our hard seats. The rooftop fell away, receded and shrank. Then the machine slipped and slid off to the side, and the whole building came into view. I wouldn't have recognized the smashed and blackened walls.

We picked up speed. My spirits rose with every second we were in the air, I felt delirious with joy, but Helen withdrew. Soon she looked out through the open door and said something lost in the roar and rush of air; I yelled, "What?" and heard her say, "Aramco." I looked down. The curving streets and neat homes of an Arizona or California subdivision passed beneath, then gave way to parking lots and a painted white X. The machine swung round, aligned itself, and settled with a crunch onto the landing pad.

The next few hours were a blur. Helen and I were put on stretchers and carried into the Aramco hospital, but immediately separated. I remember a whirl of hospital rooms, doctors and technicians. I was x-rayed. My wounds were cleaned and bandaged. I was fed. During a lull, still in a hospital gown, I was given a short debriefing by a U.S. intelligence officer. He was only interested in making sure that they had, indeed, picked up Ali. I reassured him on that point.

The afternoon passed and finally they were finished with me. I was handed back my clothes. My last handler, a young Saudi woman doctor, led me to a desk where I was asked to sign some hospital forms. Then I was alone. Just as I was wondering what came next, a door swung open, and Helen walked through.

She wore a new shirt and slacks and a scrubbed look that couldn't hide her exhaustion. But she was happy. She walked straight up to me, smiling with her eyes alight, and I leaned toward her, thinking to kiss her on her mouth. But she turned aside and took my arm to lead me out. "No, not here," she whispered. "People know me. Wait. I'm taking you home."

"Your husband?"

She looked straight ahead. "In Washington. Local airspace is still closed." We exited the air-conditioned building into the afternoon heat. "What do you feel?" she asked me.

I assumed she meant "how." I said, "Exhausted but happy."

She stared at me intently, as if trying to read what was behind my eyes. She said, "I feel exhausted but alive. Like I've been reborn. Do you know what I mean?"

I wasn't sure, but I nodded my head, and said, "Yes."

"Do you have your passport with you?"

"Yes."

"Good. Let me take care of everything."

And she did. For diplomats, Aramco is practically an extension of the consulate. She was comfortably back in her own environment.

We drove in a taxi through the main gate and down a freeway for less than a minute to the U.S. Consulate. It had changed since the glory days of the first Gulf war. The old main building, built of rough-cut stone, was still perched on the same tree-ringed hill, its lonely flag still flying above, but now it was fortified—in the style of all American consulates and embassies in all "friendly" Arab countries. The building huddled behind a high wall, guard towers, snaking concrete barriers and even an earthwork of tar-covered sand.

We passed easily through it all, Helen's face and voice our passport. I only had to show mine once. Inside we drove down a quiet residential street, lined with ranch-style houses. Consulate quarters from a safer, more assured era. We stopped at one and Helen led the way in.

The living room was sunken, with a massive, decorative fireplace and chunky furniture spread out over a roomy floor. The architecture was '40s or '50s American Southwest: Wright-inspired, but diluted enough to be comfortable. Helen turned around and told me: "There's a shower in the guest suite through that door. I'll make you a drink, and lay out some clothes. Go on, get cleaned up."

It was delicious to be ordered around by her. The guest suite was a bedroom, a bathroom, and a dressing room. I made for the shower, stripped and turned on the water as hot as I could stand. It was almost scalding. I twisted at various angles, trying to keep my bandages dry, but soon gave up and just stood under the showerhead. My body ached from a dozen bruises but the water sluiced away pain and tension along with the dirt and dried sweat. It was heavenly. In a daze I lost track of the time.

Finally I stepped out, toweled off and looked at the clothes Helen had laid out on the bed. Fresh underwear, slacks, a shirt and a robe. They must have been Harry's. I pulled on the robe and walked back out into the living room.

It was empty. Another door stood open at the far end. I crossed and walked through.

She was stretched out on her bed, her eyes closed. Reborn she might feel, but fatigue had taken its toll. She had changed into a light cotton kimono, red-and-white striped. I imagined she wore it as a dressing gown. Her long hair was still damp from her shower. A drink sat on the table by the bedside.

I went to her. She breathed peacefully, her breasts rising and falling. Her mouth was slightly open. I sat down on the side of the bed, leaned over, and kissed her parted lips.

She opened her eyes and responded, first gently, then with increasing warmth. I was overwhelmed with lust commingled with compassion; with a desire stronger and a love kinder than I could remember ever feeling before. She untied her kimono and I slipped off my robe. Our lovemaking began slowly but soon accelerated—neither of us had much energy left for foreplay. We ran to the end, exhausting the last vestiges of our strength in a few minutes. Some of our cuts reopened; we left our marks of blood on each other's skin and on the sheets. When she cried out I felt it was her passion completing mine.

Afterward we rolled apart on her big matrimonial bed. We spoke little, and later I tried to recall if either of us had used the word "love" . . . I still can't remember. My last thought before falling asleep was: I've broken one of the biggest rules of all. It didn't bother me. There is no indictment for adultery. No one prosecutes love.

PART TWO

CHAPTER SEVEN

I was back in my dream, but this time I was in my Bahrain office, the one at the Continental Hotel in Manama. And there were other differences: instead of a bank of computer screens, I had only one—as in reality—and the valuations on that were going up, not down. But (also unlike the earlier dream) I wasn't happy. I was nervous: I could feel my palms sweating. My fingers kept slipping on the keys, so that I finally took my hands off the keyboard, and watched the numbers on the screen continue their climb; but the higher they went, the more apprehensive I became.

On my left a window looked out onto a strip of hotel garden and the street, and the bright light of day shone through, but there was something swinging from a lamppost, something that interfered with the sun as it passed to and fro—something that shouldn't have been hanging there. I stole a sidelong glance, but was afraid to linger on what hung: it was black, burned, like an upside-down stick figurine. . . . I would have to change my shirt, I was sweating so much, and then the office door began to open, and I thought: It's the police, the SEC impaneled a jury; they're here to hand me my indictment. But when the person stepped into the doorway, it was only Dr. Ali, in his three-piece suit, looking pressed and academic; he smiled and said something I didn't catch, and I woke up.

———

I *was* sweating, but not with terror: because the air conditioner was turned off. I'd turned it off the night before. Helen found it difficult to sleep with the wall unit's clatter. She was beside me in my bed in my rented room on the seventh floor of the Al Wadi Hotel in Al Khobar, and the morning sun shone through the balcony's glass door. We faced the sea, and the Gulf acted like a huge reflector, bouncing the light up at us. Helen lay on her side, still asleep. In the small hours she had kicked the bedspread onto the floor. Her hips swelled from her waist and her arm hung down over her full breasts. Her mouth was slightly open and her face held only innocence.

We were three months into the post-coup period, and three months into our affair. Harry was three months a cuckold, Helen three months an adulteress, and I—I was three months in love.

I looked at my watch: it was already nine. I flicked the end of the sheet off my legs. I had to get up and turn on the air conditioner. After a night together Helen slept soundly, but the noise would awaken her. The unit stuck out of the wall crookedly; the hotel was forty years old and the rooms wore the shabbiness that a coat of paint was powerless to conceal. But seeing the room in the flood of light from the sea—a light that picked out every flaw—it appeared to me homey, secure, comfortable. Love changes every perception.

I got up carefully, padded over the dusty carpet to the wall, and flicked the switch. The roar and clatter filled the little room. Helen stirred and turned toward the window.

"Draw the curtains," she said, sleepily. "God, for a bit of rain, a soft day."

She meant a cloudy Irish day. It was high summer, and the closest thing we were likely to get was a sandstorm. But I said, "Didn't we have a summer storm once, in Bahrain?" It had been a night of love, over ten years before, in a hotel in Manama. We'd woken to a deluge and hurricane winds, rain pouring through the window and trees knocked flat. We'd leaned into the wind like kids, and returned to bed with renewed passion.

She laughed and said, "My optimistic American. I remember. I love waking up with you here." It was like a cue: I've always been most aroused in the mornings. I forgot the curtains and went back and lay beside her. I caressed the inside of her thighs, and tasted her breasts. She was the kind of woman who meets her lover more than halfway: she sought arousal. In bed she was uninhibited. She was both more experienced and more eager—wilder, even—than I remembered, and I wondered: Was my memory at fault? When one restarts an affair with a woman after so many years, is it really with the same woman? How much of the pent-up desire, as well as the experience, was Harry's legacy?

Afterward I lay back, spent, but Helen got up and, slipping on a nightgown she kept in my apartment, slid open the glass balcony door. She stepped out and leaned over the railing, her gown rippling like a flag in the light breeze. Even several stories above the ground, it was a flagrant act. I put on a robe and joined her.

"Asking for trouble?" I said.

"You're a cautious man at heart."

"Anyone looking up could see you."

"Who'd bother? Look at it down there. A quiet Sabbath morning. A handful of cars. Most people sleeping in. It's as if nothing ever happened. Back to normal." She sounded disappointed.

I said, "I don't know about normal. It's peaceful."

"As peaceful as Prozac."

"You aren't still on that, are you?"

Instead of answering, she said, "Do you ever think of Silver Towers?"

"Not if I can help it." Although you couldn't forget it—the Al Wadi Hotel was on the same street, just a few blocks nearer the coast. I drove past it almost every day.

"I remember waking up the last time, with the apartment smashed and that wall hanging over me, like the lid of a tomb someone just pried open. And you there," she laughed and wrapped her arms tight around me, "trying to pour water down my throat."

It was a hell of a thing to sound wistful about. I looked out at the sand-colored rooftops and the Gulf in the distance, and said, "I'll take this balcony, this scene, any day. It's better than the U.S. Army outside and Dr. Ali's terrorists a few floors below."

"It's quieter."

"Don't you prefer it?"

She straightened up and drew her nightgown tighter. Her husband had spent the weekend in Riyadh, but was due to return that afternoon. She asked the time, and when I told her, said, "I have to get back. When Harry's away he won't call before ten, but I don't want to have to make up an excuse."

I went in and started pulling on my clothes. Her responsible, her loyal self had surfaced again. A familiar resentment started: a chronic, intermittent pain. I believe in keeping track, in keeping count: it's as important in love as it is in the rest of life. We'd had a couple of nights together in May, when Harry had been out of town (he covered the Eastern Province and Kuwait, and the ambassador in Riyadh liked his staff meetings face-to-face). But during June we'd only managed to snatch the occasional evening hour. It was already July, and I didn't foresee a break in the pattern. It wasn't enough.

I tried to keep the resentment out of my voice. I said, as gently as I could, "I'm tired of you always having to get back. This was the first whole night we've had together for weeks."

"I know. It's never enough."

"I love you. I want more of you."

"And you know I want more of you. But for now . . . maybe we should be thankful for what we've got."

It's not my nature to settle for less. Her words reminded me of one of those prayers that suggest we should give thanks to a beneficent deity for what he has deemed fit to grant us. I thought it her Irish Catholicism speaking: a barrier to leaving Harry, to making a commitment to me.

I said, "I think we should try to get all we can out of life. We love each other. I can get rid of my local office." I looked around at the decrepit sticks of furniture, and almost laughed. "These rooms— they've never been much use, except for us. I can move out of my hotel in Manama and get us a decent villa. We could spend every evening there together, every weekend. No more roadblocks, no more surly looks from the locals, no more wondering what's going to happen next, when the next regime is going to fall." She had her back to me, dressing; I put my arms around her from behind and held her tight, pressing her ass into me. "Don't you want that? To be with me, permanently?"

She laid her head back against my shoulder. She said, "Of course I want to be with you. You know how much. But it's not that simple." She pulled away and turned around. "I'm married. I'm not in love with him—sometimes I can't stand him—but he loves me. We've been through a lot together. This is the end of his career, and probably the worst assignment he's ever had. And he's not well . . . it's more than just the drink—he's trying to hide it, but something's wrong. I can't just pack up and leave him." She reached again for her dress. "And you need him, too. What did you call him? Your imprimatur? Your clients' stamp of approval."

It was a like a stone in my shoe, an irritant that got worse with every pace. But it was true: I needed Harry for business.

My face betrayed me. She said, "Don't be jealous, Steven. You haven't cause. You have far more of me than he does. Don't forget that."

She stepped into the same dress she'd worn the night before—she never kept a spare at my place, and hardly ever showered in my bathroom. (When I'd once asked her why, she told me that Harry had lost most of his sense of smell, and she liked taking something of me—even if it was only the smell of sex—home with her.) She was ready to leave before I'd finished buttoning my shirt. It was almost as if she were hurrying from the scene of the crime.

"And don't forget," she told me, "you're coming to dinner tonight. We're having the ambassador over. He wants to meet you." The verve she'd had only a few minutes before, when she'd leapt out of bed and leaned over the balcony, had gone—from her face, her posture, her voice. She said, "It's been three months, but we're both of us still a little bit famous, at least with the embassy crowd."

"I don't want to be famous with anyone, except you. I'd rather be infamous with your husband—I'd rather he knew the truth. Another dinner with Harry. Do you think the presence of the ambassador will keep him sober?"

"No one sets out to become an alcoholic. Harry's got worse since our marriage. I'm probably partly to blame."

"He's only got himself to blame for his drinking. If he's lost you, that's his fault, too."

"I'm a better mistress than a wife."

"I'd better get you home. Before Harry calls."

Looking back, our first two weeks had been the best. They were a gift from the Commerce Department doctors in Washington. It was Harry's blood pressure—that's what he told Helen—and they wanted more tests before clearing him to fly back. Since he'd never been in my mind, it was easy to keep him out; Helen in her own way did the same.

The practicalities of the affair were easier than I thought. The consulate was down to a skeleton staff, and except for Bill, the political officer, Helen had no near neighbors. I spent some nights there, and Helen, inventing a girlfriend at Aramco, spent some with me at the Al Wadi.

It was our honeymoon period, which is synonymous with delusion. But we were both experienced. We both swore to be honest with each other (usually the first promise to be broken) and we even tried to accelerate the process of disillusion: to enjoy the novelty, while seeking out the differences—even those we found uncongenial—so we could try to embrace, or at least tolerate them, in the name of love.

She never spoke much about the elements of my personality which she found uncongenial, or tastes that she didn't share—other than my profession, that amused her: "Drier than a bone," she said, with a smile. I searched for what in her I was afraid I'd find: faults, quirks, lapses of taste: evidences of incompatibility. I'd forgotten so much from our first affair. There was a lot of water under the bridge.

One of her most charming characteristics—it made life so much brighter in that grim environment—was also one that I suspected might be wearing over the long haul: an almost manic gaiety. Trying to cook dinner together at her place—I've never been much good in a kitchen—would reduce her to tears of laughter. She was still Irish to the core, and a letter from home (she read me several old ones, to give me an idea of her family), from one of her sisters, would produce convulsions at someone's "lark" . . . I could see the humor, but it seldom gripped me as it did her. I played along. Laughter's a habit, like anything else. If you keep at it, humor becomes part of your character. I didn't want her to have to laugh alone.

She was an omnivorous reader, so omnivorous it was difficult to discern a specific taste; in music, she was addicted to the modern Irish "musical." I mean the decade-old Irish dance extravaganza, with massed violins sawing in unison, while onstage a chorus line of men in black slacks and women in black tights and short skirts, their torsos rigid as corpses, tap and tap and tap. The expat is always a few years out-of-date. I watched the DVDs with her, while she hummed along. I hid my bemusement. You have to do more than just tolerate the tastes of the woman you love: you have to try to adopt them, even cultivate them, if you can. They're part of her—as much as the smell of her hair.

There are no practicing psychiatrists in Saudi, but she had been seeing a doctor at Aramco, a psychologist, the unemployed wife of one of the oil engineers. Helen had gone to her for depression, and the doctor had prescribed Prozac and a course of therapy. I picked her up one night from a session—her last. She was ecstatic, locking my arm in hers and skipping to the car. She said the doctor told her that she was "cured." It sounded odd to me, and I still wonder if Helen decided to end it herself. I've known so many people in therapy—half the population of LA is on a couch—but I've never known of a therapist pronouncing a cure. A psychologist friend of mine told me once that patients often end therapy when the root of their problem starts to become clear: rather than face it, the patient walks out. Certainly Helen looked and acted cured. I told myself I was her cure—her cure for everything.

I think with most men, sex, in the beginning of a relationship, is more about taking than giving. I don't suppose I'm any different in that regard, but I accelerated that process as well. There was a sense that we didn't have much time to spare, and almost from the first, her happiness, her enjoyment, were more important to me than mine. We'd both gone through a pretty lean spell; we made love as often as we could, and I was happiest when she came. In the mornings, afterward, if we'd spent the night at her place, I'd go into the kitchen and make us both coffee, and bring it in to her in bed (she'd given her Filipina maid, Flerida, an extended paid vacation). She had a passion for Gaelic, and her own country, and after sex she'd try to teach me simple phrases, or quiz me on the names of counties: Cork, Mayo, Limerick. . . . Often we'd go into town in the late afternoons to window-shop in what was left of Al Khobar's expat shopping district, and to have dinner. After that, either back to her place or to mine, and to bed. Her stifled cry, her shudder, were like that old biblical verse: "as a seal upon thine heart." It sealed the day for me, and I believed then in the rest of the stanza, that love is strong as death.

I'm glad we had those weeks, because her gaiety began to decline even before Harry got back. It sank all during the third and last week we had alone together, like a barometer indicating the approach of low pressure. On the last day I moved my clothes and things back to the Al Wadi, and she called Flerida to come and clean the place up. She spent the night with me at the hotel. It was to be our last full night together for a long time, and the sun rose on our first somber morning.

Twelve hours at thirty thousand feet is not pleasant for anyone, but it set her husband back more than most. A week passed before Helen called, to invite me to dinner—Harry wanted to meet the man who had saved her. That was the first of several heavy drinking evenings: they had me over about twice a month. Each visit fueled the frustration and resentment taking over my life. Every now and then Helen and I managed to grab the tail end of one of her shopping afternoons, and hole up for a quick hour at the Al Wadi, with an eye always on the clock. Twice Harry had to stay overnight in Riyadh, on embassy business, and those trips gave us a whole night together.

One evening, at their place, the topic of diving in the Gulf came up.

The two scuba clubs at Aramco had gotten permission to resume their activities, and Harry waxed lyrical over his and Helen's dive trips years earlier in the Gulf. He suggested I take a class. Neither of them had dived since those days, and Harry insisted he didn't need a refresher, but Helen took the two-week class with me. We managed to end three of the sessions with a late-night dinner at my hotel, and then an hour upstairs.

Reading this over, it looks as if we did pretty well: together almost every day for three weeks, and a fair number of snatched hours, even a couple of complete nights, over three months. But it was never enough. The affair was too young, too passionate, and I always wanted more. Not just for myself: Helen was slipping back into depression, punctuated by short-lived highs that were even more manic than before. I wanted her to be happy. That meant cutting the tie to Harry and committing to me. I pressed her, but she hesitated. The more she hesitated, the more my resentment of her husband grew.

I dropped Helen back at the consulate and returned to the Al Wadi. I always left spare clothes at the hotel so I wouldn't have to drive back to Manama to change. That left me with nothing to do until six. There's nothing deader than a Sabbath afternoon in Wahhabi Arabia. My shabby little suite lost its magic without Helen in it. I watched TV until it was time, then put on the lightest-weight cotton jacket I'd been able to find in LA and went back out into the heat to drive to dinner.

It was a small party: just the four of us. The ambassador had come up from Riyadh for two days for an inspection. This wasn't a posting for political appointees: he was tall, elderly, a career officer of the old school with impeccable manners. He wore an out-of-date suit and the air of a man who had happily left the authority of his office at home. He was alone. His wife disliked the humidity of the Gulf, and had stayed in the capital. For company he ate dinner with his senior staff at the station. There were only two left: the consul general and Harry, the senior commercial officer. Tonight was Harry's turn. As Helen had said, we were both still news, and before dinner she and I described, in abbreviated form, our story of the siege—an insider's view. Harry was on his best behavior: he only drank one scotch during our narration.

Helen had prepared hamour, the common local fish. The ambassador was effusive in his praise—it made me wonder about his normal fare. He peered at a fragment on his fork before inserting it in his mouth. "Completely deboned," he said approvingly. "I hate bony fish, don't you?"

"Here's to the chef," Harry said, raising his glass to Helen.

"We eat so much meat," she told the ambassador, "and most of it imported. I thought fish might be a change. You can always find hamour at the Qatif market. So you're eating fresh, contributing to the local economy, and helping the Shia—all with one purchase." She was practiced at consulate small talk: anodyne and politically correct. It didn't take much of it to put me in a coma. But I admired the ease with which she kept up the pretence that there was nothing between us save a shared trauma. She was dressed severely in black, simple and elegant.

"You probably wouldn't eat Qatifi shellfish, though, would you?" the ambassador asked.

"Why not?" Harry said.

"Oh, these native markets. Sanitation. And Gulf oil: contamination."

Harry grinned at his superior's caution. "The Shi'ites don't get sick. And there's no more oil contamination here than in Santa Barbara. Just the occasional bit of tar washed up on the sand." Harry was past sixty and looked, even in a well-tailored suit, like a once-powerful man going to fat. He was of somewhat less than medium height, with a naturally chunky build. His face was full and round, pugilistic, but he wore an amiable expression. He smiled often, but his eyes held an edge. I thought he enjoyed contradiction.

"I'd heard oil contamination on the coast was more serious," the ambassador replied, like a man still unconvinced—Gulf shellfish would stay off his menu. He struck me as temperamentally careful. I doubted that anyone became an ambassador without following the rules, without supporting the party line. It was an attitude toward life that appealed to me.

"Who would have thought," Helen said, "three months ago, that we would have been talking about shellfish as a problem."

The ambassador smiled. "I think we can congratulate ourselves on how we handled the crisis, which is not something we've always been able to do. Saudi, of course, is too important an oil producer for us to have done nothing. We learned something from the Iraq disaster. We kept this government's authority—and their means of exerting that authority—intact. At the same time we've backed reformist elements. The so-called neocons are out of fashion, but wasn't their primary argument for the Iraq war—to bring freedom and democracy to the Middle East—a legitimate foreign policy goal?" His smile faded gently, like a diplomatic indication of disappointment in a favored regime. "To be successful, democracy in the region must be introduced gradually. In this country the first Sharia elections are scheduled for sometime next year."

Coming from anyone else, his peroration might have sounded complacent. Coming from our elderly ambassador, with his authority, it sounded like a legitimate appraisal. I hoped it was accurate. But Harry, like a disgruntled shareholder at the back of a meeting hall, said, "I have trouble admiring a group—the neocons—who knew nothing about the Middle East, but didn't hesitate to use the Big Lie to promote their agenda. They managed to convince the American public that Saddam—a secular dictator under strict UN sanctions—was allied to a group of religious terrorists, had a chemical weapons arsenal, even a nuclear program. Every intelligence agency in the world—even ours—knew it was all bogus."

The ambassador brushed aside Harry's tirade with a wave of his hand. "History. It doesn't negate the fact that promoting freedom and democracy is worthwhile—and practical."

"Freedom? Democracy? This is Arabia: sectarian and tribal. The municipal elections two years ago were frauds—pure window dressing. The government has other things to worry about. They've put down the Shia, but the Saudi terrorists inside Iraq are pouring back across the border. They'll set their sights on Riyadh."

"The government has the situation under control. It took us two hundred years to achieve democracy. We've helped them make a start. We've helped them with much less cost than in Iraq, to make a start."

"Let's hope our half a brigade of troops outside the capital doesn't wind up being part of the cost."

The ambassador stared at Harry with tight lips. Then Helen said, with quiet sincerity, "I should think that Americans would be proud, that all of you here would be proud, that your country is risking the lives of its soldiers for democracy."

The innocence of her statement killed conversation dead: it was like letting the air out of a balloon. The ambassador looked down and fingered his glass. Harry took another drink.

I wanted to believe the ambassador, but I had to admit, outside of the dining room it didn't feel like a country on the verge of a transition to a successful, popularly elected government. The consulate was surrounded by several lines of defense against homegrown terrorists. Just to get in I'd had to pass through three sets of guards. The secret police were rumored to be rounding up thousands.

Harry told his wife, "Our soldiers are here to support the royal family. Not bring democracy to the Arabs."

But she wasn't ready to let go. "Why not? I've talked to lots of Saudi women at our at-homes: academics, professionals, even businesswomen. Sunni and Shia, although separately, not together. Nearly all of them are interested in democracy—in some form. Shouldn't we at least try to encourage it? And wasn't that what Dr. Ali wanted? You remember what he said, Steven. Would it have been such a terrible thing?"

The ambassador smiled as if to a polite and attractive but somewhat slow student. He said, "The professional ladies you entertain are naturally at the forefront, as they usually are in the third world. And certainly we want to encourage their aspirations. But Saudi culture is not yet ready for the kind of full-fledged democracy we enjoy. We are trying to hasten the day when it will be ready. As for Dr. Ali—he never represented anything more than a minority of Shia in the Eastern Province. He wanted to split the country. The peninsula as a whole is conservative and disinclined to revolution. The royals we're working with now are reform-minded, but careful. That's an approach that suits the mentality of the people."

"By 'mentality of the people,'" Harry said, "you mean anti-West, antiwomen, Islamic extremism and violence. I agree: it'd be a mistake to push the democracy card too hard."

Helen said, "Dr. Ali wasn't any of those things."

Harry was dismissive: "He was an academic and he's out of the picture."

"Perhaps," Helen said, "an 'academic' leader might not be such a bad thing."

"He lasted three days. He thought he could secede from Riyadh with popguns. What if he had, through some miracle, brought it off? The central government would have folded. The sheikhs in Buraydah would take over. Sure, they might even hold a vote. But the new government would make the Taliban look like a liberal regime."

It was the first time I'd heard Helen and Harry argue. Maybe it wasn't admirable, but I had to repress a smile of satisfaction.

The ambassador tried to pour oil on the waters. "I don't think we have to expect either a split in the country or a Taliban takeover. Our intervention succeeded. We're working closely with all levels of government. I know it may not be politically correct—outside the embassy—to admire them, but the Saudi secret police, the Mukharabat, are the best in the Arab world."

"And their methods?" Helen asked. "Should we admire those as well?" Her voice held an edge I was unused to hearing in company; I don't think the ambassador noticed. He answered with an avuncular assurance.

"I expect you refer to torture, Mrs. Laird. I can assure you there is far less of that than many of us assume there must be. Generally, the Mukharabat engage in information gathering—spying. They are very successful because the population as a whole is eager to help. Interrogation is seldom necessary. Of course, we deplore their methods when they do get out of control. Fortunately, as I said, it happens seldom, and never—at least since I've been here—to one of our own nationals."

Harry said, "So there were no popular protests, as far as we know, when the U.S. Army turned Ali over to the Saudi secret police?"

The ambassador picked up his wine. Real wine and liquor were allowed on embassies and consulates, and were usually my only consolation (other than seeing Helen) for attending Harry's dinner parties.

"There were none. Dr. Ali's popular following has been exaggerated. It is not even a case of rendition: he is a Saudi national."

Helen asked, too quietly, "Why was he transferred?"

Before the ambassador could reply, Harry answered, "Because the U.S. Army can no longer use the interrogation methods that are so seldom used by the Mukharabat."

Helen jerked her hand up as if to push him away; she hit her wineglass and it spun off the table onto the floor. It didn't break—the floor was carpeted—but we all jumped as if it had. We sat silent for a moment. "I'm sorry," she said, "the stain. . . ."

"Ignore it," her husband said, reaching down to pick up the glass. "The maid will wipe it up."

The ambassador took a breath. "I beg your pardon, Mrs. Laird. I'm afraid the conversation has upset you." He cast a glance devoid of friendliness to Harry. "You and Mr. Kemp were prisoners—although very well treated—of Ali's for almost three days. The consideration he showed you may well have hastened the development of hostage syndrome, which would have been natural in any case."

Helen stared at him, her thin lips slightly open. "Hostage syndrome? What do you mean?"

"I understood . . . well, I believe you did use your medical knowledge, at one point. To provide aid to some of their wounded."

She replied quietly, "Providing aid to the wounded has nothing to do with any 'syndrome.' It's a duty. It's one of the activities that distinguish us from animals. It's more important than politics. It's more important than being a consulate wife. It's even more important than knowing how to prepare hamour."

Harry barked a truncated laugh, then glanced at Helen, and quickly looked down at his plate. She stared over the table, over the remains of dinner, into some private world. I recalled her expression from years before, when, perhaps at a party, she'd been hurt into depression by someone's alcoholic aggression or rudeness to someone she liked. She silenced the rest of us. She was like conscience sitting at the table. The idea of suffering, of pain, had crashed the party like an unwelcome guest of the wrong class. She finally said, "I thought Ali fundamentally a kind man."

The dinner proceeded to its end. Helen recovered herself, and suggested we have brandy in the living room.

I think we all wanted to avoid politics, but it was a subject that didn't want to go away. It hovered on the edge of every topic, waiting an opportunity to pounce. The ambassador asked how morale was keeping up in the expat community.

"Morale's not bad at the consulate," Harry told him. "Of course, most of us are old hands, and there aren't many of us left. We're still at a level-two evacuation. But we're trying to keep things alive, trying to perk life up for the Aramcons, and for our people out in the community—like Steve here. On July Fourth we had the usual beer bash. Later this year we're restarting the international concert program for the highbrows. We've gotten some dive trips arranged for the scuba crowd. The three of us are going out next weekend, from Jubail. Steve and Helen are taking their certification dive." He passed his free hand through his thinning hair. "I don't think that social events in public are such a good idea, frankly—but it's orders."

The ambassador didn't want to go there; he turned to me and asked, "You live in the local community, don't you?"

"I work there. I have an office in town and I get around a lot. But I drive across the bridge nearly every night. My main office and apartment's in Manama."

"And your impressions? Of the community on this side of the bridge?"

I shrugged my shoulders. "It's quiet. There are checkpoints everywhere, but there's no sense of personal fear." Or at least, I thought, not much.

"We in the embassy are somewhat insulated, and we can become isolated very easily. It's good to hear from someone who works in the community. Tell me, how's your business?"

I told him it was good, thanks partly to Harry's referrals. From the point of view of quantity, business was good. Right after the siege I'd had to fight hard with my head office to convince them to let me stay. I'd been vindicated: more clients were coming my way than even I anticipated. The concept of Arab flight capital was a reality.

But from the point of view of quality, business was disappointing. I hadn't factored in the third world economy. Most of my clients owned what we would call medium-size businesses, but they didn't have a lot to salt away. There weren't many big fish, and they were elusive. My salary was modest and my commissions so far were small beer. My living expenses, on the other hand, were high. If you wanted to live like an Arab in the Middle East, your expenses were low. But if you wanted to live like an American—even an American on a tight budget—it cost as much as LA. I wasn't getting ahead.

Business was a safer subject than politics, or maybe the ambassador was just in an interrogatory mood. He asked me, "Are the restrictions on transferring money out of the Kingdom hurting your business?"

"They're why I'm in business. Even the other Arab states in the region—Bahrain, Qatar, the UAE—are wary of Saudi money."

"That's where you come in?"

"I provide a service. My clients give me a check. I deposit it into my company's account in Bahrain, and wire it from there. I'm an American, and the money's going into an American company's account. As far as the Bahrainis are concerned, it's all aboveboard."

The ambassador smiled. "It's almost like a legal form of money laundering."

Harry spoke up. "He'd be an easy mark for the bad guys, if I didn't vet all his clients first."

And that was my position: dependent on the man I was cuckolding every chance I got.

"What a pity," the ambassador said, "that you weren't better established before Ali's attempted coup. If we had a longer trend, it might tell us something about how local businessmen feel now: how their sense of security has gone up, since it was put down."

"The trend line's clear enough," Harry said. "Straight down. The only sectors that've stayed steady are the biggest royals and big business—and that's because they don't depend on operations like Steve's. They've been flying to New York with their checkbooks for years, buying stock in Citibank and Wal-Mart."

The ambassador cleared his throat. "Well, I think we have a better class of royals in charge now." He turned back to me. "You said you were here before, Mr. Kemp, some years ago?"

"Yes. After the first Gulf war."

"Selling investments?"

"That's right. I've been in the game for some time."

"Was it as profitable then as it is now?"

Helen was sitting beside me, also facing the ambassador, but I felt as if she were looking at me. "It was at first. But the postwar boom only lasted a couple of years."

"He left," Harry said, "the same year I arrived on my first tour. We missed each other by just a few months."

The ambassador looked at me curiously. "So few businessmen come here now. Were the prospects that favorable?"

"Favorable enough to get me back," I said, levelly. "But like everyone else here—everyone not connected to the embassy—I'll be out the moment I achieve my savings plan."

"When do you expect that to be?"

I didn't have to answer: a small buzz emanated from his jacket. His cell phone. He put down his glass and pulled out the phone. "Excuse me, I told them I'm not to be disturbed unless it's urgent."

He held it to his ear as an older man would a new gadget he has to live with but doesn't completely approve of. Repose ebbed out of his face, leaving it more lined, somber. He clicked the instrument shut and put it back into his pocket.

"Bad news, I'm afraid. There's an unsubstantiated report . . . the individual we were discussing before may have escaped custody."

"Escaped?" Helen said.

"Sprung," Harry corrected. He leaned forward, his elbows on his knees. His body language suggested he was ready to spring himself— at what?—but his face was as expressionless as a poker player's.

"Sprung?" the ambassador repeated, with a hint of distaste.

"It had to be an inside job. He's only been in Saudi custody a few weeks. It happened once before, remember?"

The ambassador rose. "I should get back and make a call. I'm sorry the evening had to end on an unfortunate note. But I enjoyed myself very much. Mrs. Laird, thank you so much for your hospitality. It was a wonderful dinner. I'm afraid we talked too much politics, but it seems impossible, these days, to avoid it."

I decided to take my leave as well. At the door I kissed Helen's cheek and pressed her hand. I hated leaving her. It was like leaving someone you love in the hands of the enemy.

Ali's escape led to nothing, not even a mention in the government-controlled newspapers. A week later Helen and I sat next to each other at a greasy table in a ship's cabin below deck. A young American airman from Illinois sat facing us, ramrod straight. Even above the diesel engines and the sea crashing against the hull, his voice was loud and clear. He was in his late twenties, perfectly muscled and aggressively clean-cut. He was a living, breathing advertisement for the U.S. Air Force.

He was voluble about his career; I had the impression that he didn't normally have an opportunity to talk to civilians. He'd seen action early in the second Iraq war, but the end of his enlistment coincided with the fall of Baghdad, and he'd left to make more money in the civilian economy. He hadn't much cared for it. "I got back into the service because I couldn't transition to civilian life," he said. "It's difficult for a warrior." (He used the term with a total lack of self-consciousness.) "I was in marketing, and marketing's just another word for sales as far as I could see. I don't regret for a minute joining up again. In fact, I got back in just in time.

"I was on a carrier in the Gulf during the coup. We were the first team off the deck. I flew the 'copter that picked up the American hostages."

The two former hostages sat before him, not saying a word. Like the airman, we wore swimsuits. We'd been training with tanks for weeks, and I was in somewhat better shape than normal: down to five cigarettes a day, and I never smoked around Helen. She wore a two-piece. Her figure was slender but womanly. There were a few other women onboard, most of them younger, but she was by far the loveliest.

Dhahran was not the kind of town where you gained notoriety by pictures in the paper or television interviews. Neither of us was personally known—outside the American diplomatic community and a few discreet friends at Aramco—as one of the two hostages. And now here, by sheer chance, on our first dive trip into the Gulf, was the pilot who had flown us off the roof of Silver Towers.

I thought fast. The airman clearly hadn't recognized us. I threw a glance at Helen, and decided to play dumb.

"I didn't realize," I said, "there were any hostages."

"Sure there were. Two of them. A man and a woman. Both Americans. We had strict instructions to get them out alive, if possible. They were a top priority."

I asked, "What kind of shape were they in when you picked them up?"

"Not bad. They had some fight left in them. The man was trying to shoot one of the terrorists. My gunner took care of that. That's how we recognized them. There wasn't any other way you could tell them apart from the Arabs."

Helen said, "She couldn't have looked like an Arab."

"She didn't look like anything on earth to me. Hell, you couldn't even tell their skin color underneath all the dirt."

I tried not to smile.

"What do you do?" the young man asked me.

"Finance. I work for a management consulting firm." It was my stock reply to people who didn't belong to the potential client category. It sounded like it meant something, and was dull enough to inhibit most from inquiring further.

"And you?" the airman asked Helen. "Are you a nurse?" It was a safe guess. Most of the working women on the Gulf were nurses.

She shook her head. "No, I'm just a dependent spouse." It was the formal state department description.

"Too bad. I've heard that married couples can really bring in the money here, if they're both working, what with housing usually free and no taxes."

It was a blatant mistake that took us both by surprise. Although we'd been together often—at dinner, shopping, at our dive classes—no one had mistaken us to our faces for a married couple.

"We're not married," I corrected him. "Or rather, I'm not—Helen is."

"Okay," the airman said. He looked at us a little more coolly.

The ship rolled and the cabin tilted; Helen slid up to her feet and away from the table. "Let's go up and check on Harry. I'm sure he's getting too much sun."

"Nice talking to you," I told the young man.

"Yeah. See you on deck."

I struggled up the stairs to the cabin door. I pushed it open, stepped out into the glare and reached back to give Helen a hand.

The sun rippled off the choppy blue sea; a cloud of spray came over the side. We were making good time. The coast had long since disappeared.

Our vessel had started its life as an oil company ferry; retired, it found a new career as an excursion boat earning its keep ferrying groups of recreational scuba divers to diving sites in the Gulf. In the cramped engine room aft of the single cabin, two powerful diesels thrust it forward, bow high. On deck, a small wheelhouse contained the helm and engine controls; a carpeted, flat steel roof stretched behind. The roof did double duty: as an upper deck—a sunning platform—for the passengers, and as a shade for the deck below. It was needed, for the summer sun heated exposed metal to the burning point.

Three Pakistanis made up our crew; twelve Westerners our passenger manifest. Almost all were divers. Our destination was the coral reef around Jana Island, two hours out in the Gulf.

Helen and I climbed the ladder to the upper deck. The sun beat down on the swimsuited men and women lolling on the green all-weather carpet. Harry lay on his back in the far corner, thick arms and thick legs splayed out. His barrel chest rose and fell. His belly pushed his swimsuit down almost to his crotch.

"Harry," Helen said, "if you're going to lie out here, please put on some more cream."

He opened his eyes and blinked at the sun's glare. His wide, round face creased into a smile.

He heaved himself up on his elbows while Helen knelt beside him and picked up the bottle of sunscreen. She started to spread it onto his shoulders. Without warning he reached up and grabbed her, his heavy arms squeezing her slender body, and fell back onto the deck, taking her with him. Helen let herself be taken. It was a little game—a little marital game. Harry laughed, said something about not needing sunscreen with her on top; Helen murmured a remonstrance, probably about propriety; his arms relaxed and she rolled off him. He continued to chuckle. She rose to her knees beside him, squeezed out some more lotion from the bottle, and began again to massage it onto his chest and neck.

I turned away. Back down on the main deck, divers crowded the shaded area beneath the roof; tanks and gear cluttered the stern. I slipped around the wheelhouse to the bow. There was a bench there, facing forward. Perhaps there was still space on it.

A space remained—beside Joe and Susan Hamad. I didn't want to intrude, and would have turned back, but they saw me. Joe yelled over the engine, "Steve! Come and sit down! We've been saving this seat for you!" He laughed, his brown, tight face broken by a wide-grinned chuckle. I'd seen him serious, but I'd never seen him down, and he was usually up. He had the likable personality of the born salesman.

He was known as Yousef to his Arab clients. Harry had given me his card. He was a good source of referrals, although so far all of them small fry. Clients of that class preferred to approach me through someone who spoke their language. His parents were Iraqis who'd run into some trouble when Saddam took over, and settled in Jeddah when the Saudi west coast was still open for Arab refugees. Joe emigrated to America years later, and married Susan while in some community college in upstate New York. He'd come back to cash in on the oil boom. A mixer and a fixer, his knowledge of both cultures stood him in good stead. In the States I might have thought him a con man; here he was the real thing—at least, his referrals were real enough.

Joe slid closer to his wife, making room for me on the bench. I sat down. He was a small man and both his wife and I towered over him.

"You met Susan before?" Joe asked.

"When we boarded."

Joe turned to his wife. "Steve's the representative for Winston Investments."

She asked me, "Have you been here long?"

"Only a few months."

She gushed: "Then you'll have to come to our party—you'll meet a lot of people you really should know. Two weeks from today."

"Thanks."

"I didn't know you dove," Joe said.

"I just started. Mrs. Laird and I've been taking a course for the past month. This is our certification dive: open water to ninety feet. How about the two of you?"

"Not on your life. You wouldn't get me down there for anything."

"You're going in for a swim, aren't you?"

"Sure. Man landed on the moon, why shouldn't I visit the Gulf? But I'll observe it from the surface. The bottom of the sea belongs to the fish—and to the dead."

His comment reminded me of our goal: a known wreck site. An Iraqi jet fighter shot down during the '91 Gulf War. Too deep for most casual dives, it sat at the perfect depth for certification. "Something better than just mud to aim at," our instructor had said.

Joe spoke more quietly, so I could hardly hear him over the waves and the engine: "That Iraqi pilot was just a poor schmuck. He should never have taken off. He should have cut off a finger, anything, to stay grounded."

I thought: He's grounded now.

Susan pointed over the bow. "Look—is that the island?"

I squinted. A thin, whitish line bisected the sea and the horizon. As we watched, it grew more distinct—no higher, but clearer and longer.

"It's called Jana," I said.

"I thought it was supposed to be a coral island," Joe said. "It looks like a sandbar."

"The coral will be there all right, but around it, under the water. We'll probably anchor some way off."

On cue the roar of the diesels dropped and the bow sank. Inertia pushed the three of us forward on the bench. I got up and looked over the side, holding on to the rail.

We glided into shallower water. The color of the sea changed from blue to turquoise. Soon we saw the corals sliding by underneath. I left the two of them standing by the rail, staring down into the depths, and headed back to the rear deck.

Coast guard regulations insisted that the boat be in port by sunset. There was just time for two dives, with an hour's rest between, before we would have to raise anchor. The experienced divers wasted no time. They were already suiting up. Deck space was at a premium. I swung onto the ladder and climbed up to the roof.

Helen and Harry stood at the rail with our dive master. I joined them and looked down on the others.

This was no Stateside holiday dive trip. There was no one here to help you don your gear, or slide you gently in the water and pull you gently out. You jumped in from the deck, six feet above the waterline, and at the end of the dive you were expected to climb up a metal ladder let down from the stern. The first of the divers were already suited up. After a last check they walked awkwardly in their fins to the edge of the deck, held their masks tight to their heads, hesitated for a moment, waiting for the downward roll, then took the giant stride off the boat. They strode out into the air. One by one they disappeared in a splash of broken water, then reappeared, heads and shoulders bobbing under a tangle of straps and hoses. They formed up in groups and made a last check of their gear, then vented air from their buoyancy compensators and sank into the choppy sea.

In a few minutes the lower deck was clear, the boat strangely quiet. Our dive master broke the silence: "Okay guys, let's go."

We descended. Helen and I were in practice: we expertly assembled our tanks, buoyancy jackets, regulators and the other paraphernalia. I kept an eye on Harry. He hadn't attended a single evening of our course. Although admitting it had been years since he'd strapped on a tank, he'd insisted on going with us on our certification dive. He had an ancient card to prove he'd been trained, and the dive master reluctantly agreed. It was easy to strap or screw something on wrong and I expected Harry to flub it. But he didn't. He was rough and ready with his gear but accurate.

We helped one another with our tanks, holding the air cylinder up while the other backed into their jacket and strapped in. Harry helped his wife. He was attentive, holding up her gear for her until he was sure she was completely ready. The tanks, full size and full of compressed air, were heavy, and our weight belts were hung for the Gulf— one of the saltiest and most buoyant seas in the world. Finally we inflated our jackets and steadied one another as we stepped into our fins. By the time we were ready, Harry's face was red and glistening with sweat.

"Feeling okay?" I asked him.

"Sure," he grunted. "Just a little hot. This deck's baking. I can't wait to get in the water."

The dive master called for our attention. He was a young man, lean and fit, a former U.S. Navy SEAL, brought in to teach the fledgling Saudi navy. He taught civilian classes in his spare time.

"Our objective," he told us, like an officer briefing his men, "is to reach ninety feet. We're anchored over the coral reef that circles the southern half of the island. It descends gently, and then at thirty feet it drops straight off. We'll follow the wall down until we reach the bottom.

"The bottom of the Gulf is soft black mud. Stay above it. We'll descend slowly toward the south, following a compass heading of one hundred and ninety degrees. Just follow me. Remember: our goal is to reach ninety feet. We're breathing compressed air, not pure oxygen; we can stay at ninety for only ten minutes before starting a controlled ascent. If we find the wreck, great. If we don't, that's okay too. Ten minutes at the bottom, then follow me up. There's a little current. We'll be swimming against it on the way out, but it will make our return that much easier."

He looked over the side. "It's choppy, but it'll be calm once we're under. I'll go in first. Just follow me. Keep an eye on your air gauges, remember your practice sessions, and don't lose sight of your buddy."

He slipped in his mouthpiece and stepped gracefully off the boat. We heard the splash. Then Harry took the lead and flopped in his fins to the side of the deck.

He prepped himself according to the book, lingering for a moment on the edge. The boat rolled and Harry swayed. One leg jerked back as he steadied himself. He waited until his side rolled down, then stepped out into the air and dropped like a stone.

From the sea the dive master signaled to wait; I imagined he was concerned for Harry. But he seemed all right. The two of them joined up several yards from the boat. The dive master signaled Helen and me to proceed. I let her go first, made sure she surfaced, then followed her over. The fall through the air felt over before it had begun: I seemed to hit the water as soon as I stepped off the deck. The sea ejected me like an unwelcome foreign body: I shot to the surface through the foam. Looking up I saw the rust-streaked hull towering above, rising and plunging as it rolled. Helen and I swam awkwardly away from it, hampered by our gear, toward the dive master and Harry.

We formed up, checked everything one last time as we'd been taught, then followed the signal to commence the dive. I held my valve above my head and pressed the button. The air hissed out of my jacket; I sank beneath the waves.

The four of us went under together, feet first. The only sound was my breathing through the regulator. With every foot we sank, we lost buoyancy and descended faster. Soon we had to valve air into our jackets to slow our descent. I looked down. The waves had churned up the seabed, and fine grains of sand swirled in the water around my face mask. But I could still see, as if through a haze, blue parrot fish and fat groupers gliding over the yellow fan and red rock corals.

Five feet above the bottom a brittle fan coral spread out directly beneath; I kicked a little to the side to avoid it, pulling Helen with me by her arm. She wasn't afraid of the sea but she'd never been completely comfortable with the apparatus. We touched down gently in a small sandy clearing.

Thirty feet of water had compressed our bodies; we spent a minute tightening straps and rearranging gear. Then we took our positions. In diving every diver is assigned a buddy. The dive master had teamed the more experienced with the novices, counting Harry, thanks to his certification, among the experienced. At the signal we set off, the instructor and Helen in the lead, Harry and I following. We swam south, parallel to the bottom, finning against the current, away from the boat and the island.

At forty feet, the coral floor dropped away, vanishing into darkness. We had reached the wall. It was as if we had stepped out beyond the edge of a steep and very high cliff—and remained suspended. The water beneath was ink-black, the bottom nowhere to be seen. I felt a rush of irrational panic. Out of the corner of my mask I saw Helen's legs wheeling frantically, air bursting in rapid gasps of silver bubbles from her regulator. I finned toward her but the dive master reached her first. He held her by her jacket and with hand signals asked if she was all right. The sight of him calmed her; she got a grip on herself and answered yes. He took her hand, and motioned to Harry and me to bring up the rear.

We dove straight down, following the wall.

I'm a Californian. I've never been afraid of the water. As a young man I lived my summers on the beach and in the sea. But I'd never swum down into such darkness. A trick of the light filtered from the surface made it seem as if we descended through the center of a cone, its apex vanishing into the blackness below. At one point I slowed and looked up. It gave me a shock: at this depth the sea above was black as well. Only a distant circle of light identified the surface.

At sixty feet we hit a thermocline, a layer of colder water. We swam on. My gear became loose around my chest as I continued to compress. I saw the dive master and Helen level off. In another moment we hovered just above the black mud at eighty feet below the surface of the Persian Gulf.

We set off following the sea floor, heading gently down. The surface had vanished completely, but as our eyes adjusted we saw one another and the black, flat bottom clearly—only the color was gone. I tightened my gear as I swam, and shot enough air in short bursts into my jacket to maintain neutral buoyancy. Against expectation, the current was stronger at depth, tugging at our bulky tanks, trying to pull us back to the wall. It was becoming harder to fin forward, but at least our return would be easy.

We reached our depth goal of ninety feet still without the wreck in sight. But the dive master continued, and we followed. Visibility was less than twenty feet, and we had only ten minutes before we had to return to the surface. The longer we swam the more doubtful I became that we would find the wreck, and I was surprised when the dive master suddenly wheeled and struck out to the east, pulling Helen with him by her hand.

We'd almost swum right past it. Bit by bit the sunken fighter came into view, first the right tail fin, still vertical, then the right wing, jutting up at a broken angle from the sea floor. Immersed in the salt-rich waters of the Gulf, the plane had rusted badly, the thin metal skin of the wings falling from the ribs in patches like flesh from a decaying corpse. But the bulk remained intact. Although most of the fuselage was sunk in the mud, the aircraft still loomed enormous—much bigger than I had imagined. It had come to rest in a slightly nose-down attitude, with the left wing low, as if turning into a last, final approach.

We swam over the wing, dwarfed by the expanse of rusting metal. Coral had not touched it; it was too deep, too dark. The dive master headed toward the cockpit, and we followed, beating against the current. The nose was buried in mud almost to the canopy's forward edge.

The pilot had not ejected. He'd ridden the aircraft down. Why would never be known. He could have been dead before the aircraft hit the water, or just unconscious. Or maybe the escape mechanism had failed. The canopy, as we swam up to it, was covered with a thin, fine layer of silt. The dive master swam a length ahead, and with a single kick of his fins swept the glass clean.

Harry and I swam forward, but Helen stayed behind, clinging by one hand to the right engine intake, the current levitating her parallel to the bottom.

The dive master shone his flashlight through the canopy. The cockpit was drowned, flooded, half buried in silt and mud. We saw clearly the old-fashioned Soviet dials on the instrument panel, and the frame of the ejection seat. The interior was intact. Only the occupant had vanished. There was no sign of the pilot. He was like a ghost you know to be present but can't make out through the gloom. Then, in the flashlight's glimmer, I thought I saw a movement within. I finned a little closer. It was a gray crab, feebly waving a claw in the silt.

Entranced, we ignored the increasing current, even though we all had to fin strongly just to stay in place. In the darkness, encased by so much gear, with almost no peripheral vision, it was impossible to keep everyone in sight at once. And so I was the only one who saw Harry slip backward, his gloved fingers sliding off the still smooth glass canopy. His right hand dug into the soft mud but failed to find a purchase. He slid and slipped and fell backwards, the current grabbing him, pulling him away from the fuselage, where he might still have found a handhold, and sweeping him farther back, his hands grabbing wildly for anything but finding only water, back between the tall tail fins and finally back into the darkness toward the wall.

He disappeared in less time than it takes to tell.

Concerned for Helen, I swung around. She was still safe, clinging like a limpet to the other side of the fuselage.

I wanted to stay with her. But he was my dive buddy—an absurd term, but, in the most important rule of diving, the one person you never desert. I rapped on the dive master's tank to get his attention, and signaled him to stay with Helen. Then I arched myself backward and let the current carry me over the wrecked aircraft, into the dark after Harry.

In a moment the wreck was gone. Swimming with the current I skimmed over the mud, scanning the area in front and above me. But Harry had vanished.

He might have surfaced. If so, had he performed a controlled ascent, or had he panicked? If he ascended too fast he could face nitrogen poisoning, but at least he would be alive and breathing fresh air. And there was a good chance that someone on the boat would see him; the current would sweep him back toward the ferry. Or he could still be underwater, swimming back to the boat. Worse scenarios: panicked, he might have hyperventilated and passed out; he could even have had a heart attack. Unconscious, he could still have a chance if the regulator stayed between his teeth. The current would take him to the wall and sweep him up; with every foot he rose his buoyancy would increase. Unless, of course, he had water in his lungs. In that case he might be at the bottom of the wall, pinned against it, too heavy to rise.

I had no choice: I had to go with the worst-case scenario. The bottom rose slowly and I rose with it, valving air as I went to keep from shooting to the surface. I decided to simply let myself be swept along . . . it was the best strategy I could think of to find him—if he was still underwater.

The wall appeared suddenly out of the gloom. I finned madly to avoid slamming into it. I valved more air and searched the base, twenty fin strokes to the left, twenty back, and twenty to the right. I saw nothing but rock, a little coral, a few fish. I began a gradual ascent, making sure not to rise faster than my own bubbles, zigzagging back and forth as I rose.

I broke through the thermocline into warm water. I hadn't realized how cold I'd become. The light increased but there was more sand in the water than during our descent. Conditions were deteriorating. The current swept me over the top of the wall, and still I saw no sign of Harry.

I thought of surfacing and hailing the boat, to see if he was aboard or had at least been spotted. But there was little to be gained from that course. The other divers would probably still be under and unavailable to offer help. And the chance of finding Harry after diving again would be reduced. So I continued on, sweeping the water around with my eyes, keeping a few feet above the sea floor as it rose gently toward the island.

At about thirty feet corals and marine life became abundant; as I drifted into shallower water the corals grew smaller and fewer, subsiding at last to a seabed of pure white sand. At about a yard's depth I put my fins on the bottom, straightened up and broke the surface. The sun struck me like a blow, the whole world a blinding white glare. I tottered, half out of the water, half in, my tank a dead weight, my harness pulling at my shoulders.

The current had swept me halfway around the island. The shore was near, the sea this close in, calm and without surf. I turned and walked backward on my fins to the water's edge.

On the beach I pulled off my mask, unstrapped and dropped the jacket and tank and weight belt, and stepped out of the fins. I was alone. But in the distance a low black pile smudged the sand. I walked toward it in the shallows.

It was Harry's gear. So he had reached the island, and in good enough shape to climb out of his equipment. Above the beach a scrappy carpet of gray, ankle-high salt-brush covered a mass of low hillocks. The scrub kept the sand cool to the skin, and I found Harry in a sandy hollow: on his back, with his legs drawn up, asleep, his mouth open. I bent down and shook his shoulder.

"Harry, wake up."

He opened his eyes. "Steve." He struggled up onto his elbows, trying to focus. His voice was hoarse and low. "Couldn't hold on any longer. The current grabbed me. Blacked out for a while. How long have I been here?"

"Only a few minutes. I came right after you."

"Where's Helen?"

"With the dive master. I'm sure they've surfaced by now. They're probably on the boat."

Harry lurched to his feet with a groan. "You left her behind?"

"She'll be okay. I left the two of them together."

He panted, blinking, catching his breath. "You left her at depth, with that kid?"

"Harry, she'll be okay. You were my buddy. The buddy system, remember?"

He stared at me with disbelief. His face, already red, grew redder. "The buddy system? What the fuck's that?" He staggered closer, his eyes squinting to focus. "We were over ninety feet down, and you left her with that kid, the navy washout?"

I took a step back. "I was going by the manual, Harry."

He was breathing heavily, his legs straddling the sand. "This is life, not a fucking dive manual. You stay with your own, Steve, you stay with your own."

I wondered if he was going to take a swing at me. I'd searched half a mile of sea floor, I was exhausted, at the end of my rope. I shot back: "She's not my own, Harry. She's not mine."

A hot breeze swept over us, like an air conditioner in reverse. The crisis passed. Harry looked toward the sea. "You're right," he said, "she's my responsibility. I should have hung on. The current was too strong. But I should have hung on." His face glistened with sweat. He passed his hand over his eyes. "Thanks for following me up. I appreciate it."

"Forget it. Come on. Let's get back to the beach."

We walked together to the water's edge. Harry sat down in the shallows while I fetched my gear. When I returned he was standing, his arm outstretched, pointing. "Look, there they are."

It was the ship's inflatable dinghy, propelled forward by an outboard. Helen stood in the middle, waving. I felt a surge of relief. I'd followed the book, I'd followed the rules, I'd done the right thing. So why did I feel as if I'd let her down?

"Thank God," Harry said, "she's okay."

I couldn't be as demonstrative—I had to be careful. I said, "I was sure she would be. I wouldn't have left her if I'd had any doubt."

The dinghy drew nearer. I saw the dive master behind Helen, his hand on the tiller. Harry took a step farther into the water, his face hard. "It was stupid of that kid to insist on finding the wreck. Stupid. We'd already reached the target depth. The current was too strong, the visibility poor. The plane was nothing but a grave."

I thought to deflect him. "What do you suppose happened to the pilot?"

"What hasn't been eaten's still there. Under the silt by the rudder pedals. Right where we put him in '91."

The clatter of the little motor filled the air, then snapped and stopped abruptly. The dinghy's bow pitched down. Helen lost her balance and fell forward to her knees.

"The idiot," Harry said, "he's struck the bottom with the prop." He started wading farther in, his thick legs cleaving the water, unstoppable as a bull.

He met the dinghy and lifted his wife out, clasping her to him. I couldn't hear what they said. The dive master slipped over the other side and began dragging the boat toward the shore. Before he reached the beach Harry had left Helen in the shallows and caught up with him. He grabbed the younger man's arm and pulled him round. I heard him yelling about the depth, the visibility, the current; when he paused to catch his breath I heard the dive master say, very clearly: "If I'd realized how unfit you were for diving, I wouldn't have agreed to take you."

Harry's broad fist landed on the younger man's jaw and lifted him bodily off the sea floor. He collapsed in a heap in two feet of water. Helen shouted, "Harry, lift him out. He'll drown," and tried to rush forward; I waded in deeper to lend a hand.

Harry took charge. He loaded the dive master into the dinghy like a sack of potatoes and helped his wife back in, then we retrieved our gear from the beach. We piled it into the inflatable and climbed aboard, Harry in the stern, Helen tending the dive master stretched out in the middle, myself in the bow.

One tug and the outboard roared to life.

It was an uncomfortable journey back to the ferry. Helen was furious at her husband; Harry was sullen. I almost pitied him. He'd been more solicitous of her than I, and it had turned to dust in his mouth.

Pity might come later. When I was more secure. The affair was still too new, he was still too much a part of the picture. There'd be time for pity when he was safely removed—a figure from the past, in the background. I knew his schedule as well as my own. In two weeks he'd be in Riyadh for a three-day conference. Like a hunter, undercover and in camouflage, I made my plans.

CHAPTER EIGHT

A week later a tall, well-preserved Brit in a well-preserved suit sat in front of me at my table in the Al Wadi's otherwise empty second-floor restaurant. The lines of age on his face gave the impression of probity. They hid his enthusiasms.

He gazed fixedly over my head with a poet's inspiration, declaiming Yeats. The harsh morning light glared through the windows, picking out a bit of egg on his lapel. Not wanting to disturb him, I let my own breakfast grow cold. His style was rapt, with a slightly crazed intensity. The poem was "The Second Coming":

> *Turning and turning in the widening gyre*
> *The falcon cannot hear the falconer;*
> *Things fall apart; the centre cannot hold;*
> *Mere anarchy is loosed upon the world,*
> *The blood-dimmed tide is loosed, and everywhere*
> *The ceremony of innocence is drowned;*
> *The best lack all conviction, while the worst*
> *Are full of passionate intensity.*
>
> *Surely some revelation is at hand;*
> *Surely the Second Coming is at hand.*

The Second Coming! Hardly are those words out
When a vast image out of Spiritus Mundi
Troubles my sight: somewhere in sands of the desert
A shape with lion body and the head of a man,
A gaze blank and pitiless as the sun,
Is moving its slow thighs, while all about it
Reel shadows of the indignant desert birds.
The darkness drops again; but now I know
That twenty centuries of stony sleep
Were vexed to nightmare by a rocking cradle,
And what rough beast, its hour come round at last,
Slouches towards Bethlehem to be born?

His eyes dropped to mine in a triumphant smile. "What do you think of that?"

I'm a creature of habit. It was convenient to eat breakfast at the hotel (it was included in the bill); it was quiet (there was seldom another soul there), and I caught up on the news by reading the *International Herald Tribune*. It was a solitary morning break I enjoyed. But these unwanted interruptions were something I had to put up with.

Arthur Hartley was the hotel manager. Nothing in the little-frequented hotel escaped his eye, and of course he knew about me and Helen. He was a British gentleman, and he was never intrusive—in fact, neither Helen nor I had ever seen him during any of our dinners, or our surreptitious exits from the restaurant, using the elevator to go up to my rooms, instead of back down to the lobby. But he knew. And without ever being direct he'd let me know he knew. As a result, I'd felt obliged to accept his invitation to his home to meet his lonely wife and children over drinks—he managed the little expat compound where Joe also lived—and I felt obliged to listen to his poetry.

He was the picture of an elderly, erect, proper Brit hotel manager, and I could only assume his passion for reciting forgotten poems was a symptom of the same eccentricity that had made him spend the latter half of his career managing a seedy hotel in Al Khobar.

I answered, "I'm afraid the meaning's obscure."

"Obscure? We're living it. He's talking about the end of an era—the Christian era: our era. The beast's waking up. Of course, Yeats wrote it probably a hundred years ago—he couldn't have foreseen the nature of the beast. But we know now what it is." He glanced out the sand-begrimed window overlooking the street; it was one of the town's main streets, nicknamed Pepsi Road for the bottling plant sited at its terminus on the coast road.

"Yes?" I said.

He turned back to me, and said, in a lowered voice, "Islam. Everything this place stands for."

Hartley had lived most of his middle age in Khobar. It had provided fertile ground for the prejudices of his class and generation. He always spoke them in a whisper because one never knew when a Muslim member of his staff, or even a guest, might walk in. His boss—the hotel owner—was a Saudi for whom he'd worked for years; nearly all his staff were Muslim; most of his guests were Arabs. He seldom had a good word for any of them. He was an extremist, and an extremist of whatever stripe is always fundamentally a bore. But I never contradicted him. His acquiescence was essential to my affair.

I looked at my watch. "It's nearly time for me to go. A friend's picking me up at ten."

"Where're you off to?"

"Qatif. A potential client."

"A Shia city. Not quite as fanatical as the Wahhabis, and better workers. But you can't trust them. They have a lot to be resentful about. I'd be careful if I were you."

"I will be."

"Busy this evening? The wife and I thought we might have you over for dinner and a few drinks. She's making shepherd's pie."

I hadn't seen Helen since the dive trip. Harry was taking me to Qatif and there was a chance that he might invite me over afterward. It was a chance to see her at least, even if it was in his company. I said, "I don't think I can tonight. A prior engagement. Can I take a rain check?"

"Of course. I know you spend a lot of time at the consulate. They have their privileges. Real liquor. Although I managed to get a bottle myself, through a British Aerospace connection. Johnny Walker Red. We'll save it for you. But not for too long."

"That's good of you."

"Not at all. The wife likes your company. How is the consulate crowd, by the way? Laird, the commercial fellow, still here?"

The hotel had a sideline in catering, and Hartley had been around long enough to know everyone. He knew my occasional dining companion was Harry's wife. I said, "Laird's the one picking me up."

His eyebrows went up almost imperceptibly. "Really? Taking you to Qatif?"

"He knows the client. An old acquaintance. And apparently there's no city map available."

"Well, he ought to know the lay of the land. I've heard he's quite the Arabist."

I grimaced. "I don't think he'd regard that as a compliment." I got up and said good-bye, picked up my briefcase, and walked down the fake marble stairs to the lobby. Outside, I spotted a double-parked car with diplomatic plates and Harry behind the wheel.

We took the coast road. There was little traffic. On each side we passed rows of half-built houses, started in some past oil boom, now abandoned and slowly filling up with sand. The sky was like a giant, unnatural rainbow: sand-colored over the desert on our left, a white glare overhead, a chemical turquoise over the sea.

Harry and I exchanged pleasantries. Nothing about him—physically, mentally, emotionally—resembled Helen. But he was her husband. His presence was like a catalyst: I could almost imagine her in the backseat. He surprised me by saying, "Helen misses you. We're going to have to invite you over sometime soon." I looked at him out of the corner of my eye, but it was just the usual pugilistic face, the usual amiable expression. I wanted to pursue it, to ask about her, but didn't. It was safer not to appear too interested.

He switched to business. "Hussain's a doctor," he told me, "educated in the States. He had some connection with someone at the consulate, and I used to see him at parties—when Saudis were still invited. He was always pro-American, like everyone in those days, but he was also proud of his hometown. Every little third world town has its leader—now they probably call them 'change agents,' or some jargon like that—who pushes for development. Wants to modernize the place. Wants to see some progress. That was Hussain. He had a private practice, but he opened a clinic for the poor—most of the population—and was involved in a whole shitload of other community projects. A good guy. Now he wants to get his money out. You can't blame him. My guess is he wants to get his family out, too, but that's going to be harder. I'll try to pull a few strings, but there's not much that anyone can do for a Saudi these days—unless they're a royal, of course."

"He'll be my first Shia client."

"He might be your last. There aren't that many with money to send out. And Ali's a Shia. I doubt there was a Sunni in his gang. Riyadh's never trusted them. They're frozen out of government, the military, even business."

I said, "But there were police in Silver Towers, part of Ali's gang."

"Yeah, they've got a few local cops. Just for Qatif. But none of any rank. They'll count for even less now. Especially with Ali on the run."

"Where do you think he is?"

"No idea. In Yemen, on his way to Iran, maybe even here in Qatif, or somewhere else on the coast—some little Shia town."

"Surely he wouldn't come back here."

"He didn't the first time he was on the run. He got out. It'd be safer for him if he got out now. But you can't tell. It's funny that an academic should have that much guts. In my experience they usually don't."

We drove on for another few minutes, then Harry took the Qatif exit on the right. The town's perimeter, like some medieval city wall, stretched up and down the coast for miles: an uneven line of mud-colored concrete buildings, barely a crawl space between them, huddling together, keeping outsiders out.

Within, the town was poorer, even more down-at-heel than Khobar. For the first time I was glad that Harry was behind the wheel. The shabby buildings were indistinguishable one from the other. What would directions have meant here? The potholed streets were almost devoid of traffic and even pedestrians were rare: the occasional man or child in their flapping white *thobe*; the even rarer woman, a walking shadow in her black *abaya*. A town with all the life drained out.

"Christ," I said, "it's bleaker than hell."

"It's going to get bleaker. More arrests, more disappearances. Less government money. Hussain isn't stupid. No matter how much you love your community, if the ship's sinking, you'd better jump."

I was counting cars on the road. There weren't many. I asked, "Where is everyone?"

"I don't know. It's quieter than it should be. I wonder if something's up."

I wasn't really listening; it took a moment for the penny to drop. I said, "Like what?"

"Who knows? Maybe it's just too damn hot. I think this is it."

He turned into an uneven patch of sand that served as a parking lot. At the far end stood a low, rambling building with a painted sign in Arabic. Harry parked the car and we walked in.

The admitting room was bare except for rows of cheap plastic chairs on which a handful of the ill awaited their turn. There was no dirt—the place was obviously kept swept, maybe the linoleum was even polished—but everything was too old and too used to be really clean. Faded posters on the walls displayed in crude drawings the consequences of vice and virtue. Drugs: crooked men, grimacing, holding needles, submerged to a garish degeneracy. Devotion: upright men, smiling, in immaculate *thobes*, leading their upright children with pride toward a minaret. We walked past the silent patients, up to the counter. Harry asked in Arabic for Hussain. The attendant lifted a flap and escorted us down a hallway to a smaller waiting room. He knocked on a door and shouted something. Dr. Hussain Al Qatif opened his own office door.

He was a lean man in his sixties whose look of quiet authority was not diminished by clear signs of overwork. His shoulders were bent and his face deeply lined, but his eyes were alive. He shook Harry's hand warmly with both of his own, and called in a strong voice for tea. Harry introduced me, and the doctor ushered us into his office. It was typical of its type. A large desk dominated one end; in front were two sofas for supplicants. Unusually for the office of a man with favors to dispense, the sofas were empty. In that society it must have taken a rigorous discipline to keep them empty; it spoke of a man intent on getting work done.

I knew that Harry spoke some Arabic, but he always denigrated his proficiency, so I was surprised and finally irritated when the two of them started off immediately in a stream of Arabic, and stayed in that language for two or three minutes. The occasional greeting and pleasantry (the limit of my ability) greases the wheels, but I began to feel left out. Finally, the doctor woke up to the fact that I wasn't participating, and apologized in English.

"You have to understand," he told me, "we have not met for—how long, Harry?"

"Over ten years."

"Ten years! And we almost did not meet today. I tried to call—to warn you—but you'd already left your office."

"Warn me?" Harry said. "Of what?"

"Oh, another rumor . . . a police roundup. There have been many since our attempted coup."

"'Our' coup?"

The doctor smiled grimly. "It was a Shia coup, Harry. Almost the only sign of change, in ten years. Another failure. Like so many of our attempts at development. I am sure you saw, driving here, how little Qatif has changed."

"There's a huge new Aramco facility on the far edge of town."

"Yes, and how many of us, the Shia, work there? A few—as janitors. The world moves on. Here in Qatif, we stay stationary. We are like—what do you say?—a waterhole?"

Harry thought for a moment. "I think you mean 'backwater.'"

"Yes. Exactly. A backwater. We are petrified. Or preserved, like one of our anatomy exhibits. Even when the rest of the Arab world is changing. Here, look at this. . . ." He picked up an Arabic newspaper from his desk and showed us the front page. It meant nothing to me, of course. But Harry could obviously read, as well as speak, Arabic. "Yes," he said, "more elections in Palestine. Despite everything— themselves and the Israelis—they're moving ahead."

"The Palestinians achieve democracy, even if it did bring Hamas. Iran has had democracy of a kind for twenty years. Even Iraq now has elections. What do we have?"

Harry said, "The Palestinians had Israel. Iran had a beginning before the Shah. Iraq . . . well, Iraq has the U.S."

"And we have Al Saud."

They both laughed. Harry with mirth; the doctor, I thought, with a sliver of bitterness.

Harry said, "You had municipal elections last year—a first."

"I know you are better informed than that. Not one Shia was elected. All Sunnis. All Islamists. Does that sound like an 'election' to you?"

"We figured it was rigged."

"Of course. A little show for the Americans. Riyadh is very good at arranging these shows. And Washington claps." The doctor brought his hands together silently. "What we need," he said, "is a leader."

"Hussain, that's what all Arabs say."

"I don't mean another caliph. Those days are gone, if they ever existed. I am not a fundamentalist. I mean a real leader." He lowered his voice. "An Arab Ataturk."

"The father of modern Turkey was a secularist. You're the only Saudi I've known to have anything good to say about Ataturk."

"But isn't it true? Some say a leader has finally come."

Harry's pugilistic face widened in a grin. "Ali?"

"They think he's here."

"Here?"

"Yes. Why do you think the police are so interested in Qatif?"

"Excuse me," I interrupted, "you mean the police think he's here?" My mind, which had been slouching at ease, snapped to attention. I scanned the office: the book-covered walls, the dusty, framed diplomas, the worn sofas, the crumbling hospital behind the door. It looked a plausible place for the Arab academic "leader" in his rumpled suit.

The doctor laughed loudly. "No, Mr. Kemp. He is not here in my hospital. I can assure you, I am not that brave."

Harry said, "Or that foolish."

"Or that foolish. I have my family, my patients, to consider." He leaned back in his chair. "But there comes a time when we all have to think beyond the family, those we love—to the greater community. The greater good."

"Aren't we here today," Harry said, "because of your family—their financial security?"

Hussain sat up. "Yes. You are right. I am sorry, Mr. Kemp. I have talked politics, and neglected our business. Perhaps we should start."

It was not a standard introduction to investments. But at least we had gotten to the point. I opened my briefcase and took out my papers. But I barely had time to explain, even briefly, some of the more suitable funds and plans my company had to offer a man in what I calculated to be his financial position, when his secretary knocked on the door and entered, gabbling something in Arabic.

Hussain gave an order and the man departed. The doctor's shoulders slumped; he stared down at his desk. Harry said, *"Askari?"*

"Yes." He looked up. "I'm afraid the rumor was accurate. They are not our police, of course. Not Qatifis. They haven't reached the hospital . . . but we must prepare. They may want to search. There may be casualties."

He rose and walked out from behind his desk. "I am sorry, Harry. You must both leave immediately. I will give you a guide."

"We don't need a guide. We know our way out of town. The police won't bother us."

"Things have changed. It's not like the old days."

"They're not looking for Americans."

"No. But they don't expect them, either. Anyone who doesn't belong is suspicious. You don't want to spend a night in a cell. And . . . some of our young people are braver than they used to be. Or maybe they just have less hope. There could be trouble."

He passed us, gathering determination with every stride. We followed him through the door. In the hallway outside, his staff—men in white smocks and women in black head scarves—accosted him, shouting questions. He answered each without pausing, leading the way back to admitting.

Harry and I brought up the rear. We reached the waiting room with the plastic chairs and the posters on the walls, now crowded with staff and even a few patients; maybe they were looking for a place to hide. A tall young man in a doctor's white coat emerged from the group and made a beeline for us. He introduced himself as Dr. Ibrahim, Hussain's son, and told us he would take us out of the city.

Although still young he had a doctor's air of authority. We left the hospital with him. At our car he stripped off his white coat, bunched it up and handed it to Harry, telling him to hide it under the seat. He got in behind the wheel and ordered us both to sit in back. We obeyed without a word.

He pulled out of the sand lot onto the main road, but quickly turned off into side roads and back alleys, weaving generally south, taking what I supposed was evasive action, although evading what wasn't at first clear—the streets and alleys seemed even emptier than before. We were the only traffic and there wasn't a soul on the pavements: the town could have been deserted.

I'd had four months of peace and quiet. On my first outing to a Shia town, to see a client recommended by Harry, I was again in a dangerous situation. There wasn't any trouble in sight but I wouldn't have minded a cigarette. I said curtly, "What do you think's going on?"

Harry said, "You know as much as I do. They're probably looking for sympathizers."

"Sympathizers? How do they tell who's a sympathizer?"

"Tips. From people who turned themselves in because the cops arrested their families. From prisoners they interrogated."

"So what's going to happen? Hussain seemed to think we were in some kind of danger."

"He's exaggerating. We don't have anything to fear from a police roundup."

"Then what was he worried about?"

"I think he's worried about a shoot-out. Once these cops start shooting, it's like the Wild West. Bullets flying everywhere."

"Great. Do me a favor. If you get any more Shia clients, send them to someone else."

He didn't reply. Our driver was as mute as a well-trained chauffeur; he kept his attention on the job. Another minute passed. I began to think we were going to get back to Khobar without incident. Then, a couple blocks ahead, we saw a police vehicle with its lights flashing. I gripped the armrest as we swerved into a narrower side road. The next moment we almost barreled into a platoon of police. Everything seemed to happen at once: Ibrahim hit the brakes; Harry and I slammed into the seat backs; the cops rushed the car, pounding it with fists and rifle butts.

Ibrahim wound down his window. The cops shouted at him and he shouted right back, but not like a doctor. He'd assumed another persona. He was an Arab driver, a simple man convinced of his own innocence, innocent enough to be angry, as surprised and indignant at running into the police as the police were at being run into.

It didn't work. They yelled and gestured to us to get out of the car. Ibrahim shouted over his shoulder for our passports. We handed them over. The police pulled them from his hands.

My whole body seized. Americans were an officially protected species in Saudi Arabia, but it didn't look as if these guys had gotten the message. Maybe they were too far down the pecking order. I looked at Harry. He sat impassive, silent, displaying no emotion. I said, "What should we do?" He answered, flatly, "Let's see if he can handle it."

An officer's green uniform filled the window. He leafed through the pages of our passports with expert disdain, like a teller counting soiled banknotes. He barked orders to his men. They took up positions behind the car, and for the first time we could see what was going on.

Ahead of us to our right a group of police with pistols had three young men in white *thobes* on their knees, facing the wall of a dun-colored house; women in black *abayas* stood in a doorway under separate armed guard, expostulating. While we watched, more men were led out of a door farther on. One, younger than the others, in jeans, was arguing, hanging back, waving his arms, objecting.

Almost casually, one of the police raised his revolver and shot him in the head at point-blank range. He fell like a stone in a heap on the sidewalk.

I sat, openmouthed, staring out the window. I heard Harry say "Fuck."

The women sent up a wail; a couple of police pushed them at gunpoint back inside their house; the officer by the car yelled to his men. A cop with a rifle smashed its butt into one of the suspects still standing; he continued pounding him after he'd dropped to the ground.

The officer returned his attention to our car and its inhabitants: another problem to solve. He stared icily at the two of us in the back. Two Americans who shouldn't be there. Who might keep their mouths shut if he let them go. Who would be nothing but trouble if he didn't. He spat out an order to our driver and threw our papers into his face. Ibrahim started the engine and shoved the gears into reverse, winding up his window as he drove.

The police behind were in no hurry to get out of our way. We reversed in fits and starts. I don't know what I was looking at (not at the bodies in the street). Our driver was twisted in his seat, staring between our heads through the rear window. It was Harry who kept his eyes on the scene. It was Harry who saw the Saudi in a *thobe* walking down a side alley toward us, walking directly to our car, his hands in his pockets, walking too casually toward mayhem and gunfire.

"Ibrahim," Harry said, "get the hell out of here."

But a couple of soldiers were still standing behind us, insolent, obstructive.

Harry gripped the driver's arm. "Look," he said, pointing. "There."

The Saudi was still just hidden by the alley walls from the soldiers in front and behind. He was looking straight at our car, and for a moment I had the illusion of staring him straight in the eyes. Maybe I did. I don't think his expression changed. It was somber, but determined. I remembered that American soldier in the bar in Bahrain. This young man in his loose *thobe* looked like he'd got a grip on fear. He could have been a soldier himself, advancing to the front, holding his fear tight in his hand.

He was almost out of the alley.

Ibrahim gunned the engine and the car jolted as one of the cops bounced off the bumper. We swerved crazily in reverse and just turned into the safety of the street when the suicide bomber detonated.

The insurgency in Iraq has been sanitized for Americans. We never see the bodies of dead American soldiers arriving home; I don't recall seeing fatally wounded American soldiers on American television; I never saw men actually being blown up on American TV. But in my hotel room at the Al Wadi I had the British and Arab news channels, and they weren't so politically correct. Just clicking past them (as I often did at night, alone), I saw more than I ever had in LA.

One image in particular remains in memory. It was a long shot— a very long shot, from above—of a Humvee that drove directly over either a mine or some kind of remotely detonated device. The explosion was massive, far greater than the years of terse, detail-free, coalition announcements had led me to expect. One moment the jeep was driving along the road, the next, the vehicle, the road, the sand wastes on each side were gone, engulfed by an impenetrable cloud of smoke. Incredibly, the Humvee survived—it must have been armored. It careened out of the cloud and into a ditch. The driver's door swung open. A body, presumably that of an American soldier, fell out flat onto the ground.

Our bomb wasn't that big. Probably the Saudi had only a grenade— at the most, two.

We'd managed to make the street when the blast erupted from the alley like out the muzzle of a gun. The car rocked. Debris peppered the hood. The windshield cracked but didn't shatter; we were lucky. Luckier than the police. We didn't stick around to determine their condition, to offer help. Ibrahim drove through the cloud of smoke and swung off onto another road, heading north, zigzagging through side roads and alleys.

I don't know if there's a typical, or standard, response to that kind of situation. If one is able to think coherently, one probably realizes that one's safety, even life, is not in one's own hands, but in the hands of another—or in the hands of fate. In our case it was literally in the hands of our driver. The young doctor sat hunched over the wheel; whatever he was thinking, he didn't share it with us. Harry reached into a pocket and brought out a little prescription pill container; he took one out and popped it. His expression was impassive but his face was white as a sheet, and glistened with sweat. He started repeating like an obscene mantra his favorite word: "fuck." I don't remember what I said. I remember gripping my legs so hard the pain finally snapped me back to some level of mindfulness. I was scared to death we were going to run into or be stopped by more police. Over the rocking of the car the air was full of sirens. But the wailing grew dim and fell behind, then finally died in the warren of nameless streets.

We reached the outskirts of town. Sunken oases slipped by on each side—irregular patches of farm, rows of grayish date palms—clinging to a stunted life over a pumped-out and contaminated water table. We drove on through silence. Finally we turned back to the coast road. We reached it without incident and headed south, toward Al Khobar, toward the "safety" of Harry's consulate, of my hotel, of home.

I started to breathe again. I stretched, tried to relax. I became aware of wetness on my legs. Sweat from my palms had soaked through my thin cotton trousers. Dark stains stood out above my knees. I heard Harry say, "What a waste."

He was staring out at the featureless salt flats. His face, normally ruddy, had regained some color. He said, "Ibrahim, you're a doctor, an educated man: why did he do it?"

Our driver said, "He was Shia. One of us."

"But why?"

"I don't know. Maybe the police imprisoned his family. His parents, his brothers, his sisters. Maybe his wife. Maybe some were tortured—even killed. Or maybe he was political. The Shia are becoming political."

"But why suicide?"

"He saw no alternative. We have no organization. No organized resistance. You probably think it is like Hezbollah, or the Palestinians.

You are wrong. There is no Hezbollah, no Hamas here. No one instructed him to carry the grenades. He did it himself. I am sure. Because it was the only way he saw."

"The Shia—are they anti-American?"

From behind I thought I saw Ibrahim smile. He said, "Not my father's generation. They remember the old days. American scholarships and whiskey at the consulate. The young generation is different. They watch Al Jazeera. They know what went on in Abu Ghraib, at Guantánamo Bay, in Falluja. The world knows. For years my father told me: don't believe in our conspiracy theories, the Arab conspiracy theories. He told me they were dreams. He told me the only people holding us back were ourselves."

"He was right," Harry said.

"I used to think so. But what army defeated Ali? The Saudis? No. The Americans. You caught Ali—you had him in your jail. What did you do?"

For a minute Harry didn't answer. Then he said, "We had to get involved, Ibrahim. Ali was holding American hostages."

"I know, Mr. Laird. I know who they were holding. I do not blame you."

Harry leaned forward in his seat. "You know who they were holding?"

Ibrahim answered: "Yes."

"How?"

The driver's right hand left the wheel and sketched a question in the air. "I thought you knew Saudi, Mr. Laird. There are no secrets here. I don't blame the Americans for what they did. But, for all Shia, Ali is a hero. For a few days, he gave us hope. Why did you give him to the Mukharabat?"

Harry sank back and turned back to the window. The dun-colored walls of Qatif passed by at a safe distance. He said, "What difference does it make? You need more than an academic and a little hope. You need more than kids with grenades. It's a dead end."

"It is how the Algerians got rid of the French."

Harry didn't challenge the simple justification of bombs and suicide. I knew nothing of Algeria. Colonial wars had never interested me. Their investment opportunities were all in the past.

Ibrahim continued, "An Arab poet wrote: 'Arabs are used to swallowing hopelessness like water.' We are tired of that drink. Can you blame us? That young man needed to act. To do something. To avenge his family, or just to fight back. He did what he could. But, yes . . . I wish we were organized. I wish we had alternatives to suicide. Where shall I take you? The American consulate?"

"Yes." Harry looked at me. "How about it? I think we could both use a drink."

I said, "No thanks. I'll just catch a cab to the hotel." As soon as I said it I regretted it. I didn't want any more of his company, but I'd just passed up an opportunity to see Helen. I didn't have time to recant. Ibrahim said he'd take me to my hotel and then drop off the car and Harry at the consulate.

We reached the outskirts of town. A huge municipal dump—no different from any other stretch of desert, except for the amount of old machinery, of cast-off oil rigs and industrial junk—slid by on our right. It was a well-known landmark: the U.S. Consulate was just ahead. Harry told me, "I'm sorry for getting you into this. It didn't work out as planned."

The fake, tough-guy understatement exploded in my head like the grenade. My hands clenched. I wanted to take a swing at him. But I didn't want to give him the satisfaction of seeing he'd gotten under my skin. I tried to keep my voice steady, and said, "We saw a man murdered. Then a massacre by a suicide bomber. We narrowly escaped death. You're right: it didn't exactly work out as planned."

He replied, almost as if looking for sympathy, "I just wanted to do you a favor. Everything we try over here backfires. We're just shooting in the dark. Pissing in the wind." Then: "We should just get the hell out—pull everyone out."

I was fed up. I wanted to contradict. I said, "We're at least partly responsible for this mess. Shouldn't we try to help?"

"How? Find another Ali, give him enough rope to hang himself?"

"I'm just a businessman. But if you're on the board of directors of a company that's going down the drain, you don't sit around and do nothing. You make a recovery plan. Then you figure out how to mitigate risks."

"This is the Arab world. Not a business in California. Risk mitigation . . . people here riot because of an anti-Arab cartoon in Denmark."

"Maybe you've been here too long. A company without a plan goes bankrupt. You have to have hope."

He looked at me as if at a stranger. He said, "You sound like my wife."

"Maybe she's right."

Ibrahim said something in Arabic; it sounded almost like a chant. Harry asked him to repeat it. Harry thought for a moment, and asked, "It's a Hadith, right?"

Our driver assented.

I said, "What's a Hadith?"

Harry said, "A saying of the Prophet. This one's about jihad. Question and answer. I'm not good enough to translate it. Go ahead, Ibrahim. Give it a try."

Ibrahim cleared his throat, and said, "According to the Prophet: 'What deeds are good?' Mohammed replied, 'To feed the poor; to pray; and give freedom to those in darkness. And those who fight with the believers are allies. They will find forgiveness.'"

I thought it an obscure piece of scripture. I'm not interested in religious wars, and I had nothing current for which I wanted to be forgiven.

A few minutes later we pulled up outside the Al Wadi. I thanked the driver and got out. Harry leaned over and said, "Sure you won't have a drink?"

"Thanks, but no."

"I'm sorry. About everything. I'll try to make it up to you. We'll have you over soon. You and Helen—I hadn't realized you were an idealist, too. So long."

I walked straight through the lobby and took the stairs rather than wait for the elevator; Hartley sometimes haunted the ground-floor café. Upstairs I tried to calm down with a couple of cigarettes on the balcony. Then I lay down but couldn't relax, so I started smoking again with the air conditioner on and the balcony door open. There are no posttrauma counselors in Saudi. Coup attempts, suicide bombers— you had to deal with them yourself. Helen had been my way of dealing with the first, but now she wasn't available. Harry had to be traumatized as well; Helen would be ministering to him. I badly wanted a drink, but I never kept any in the hotel—too dangerous, in case the cleaners should find the bottle. Harry certainly had a bottle in front of him now. He prided himself on his grasp of the situation, but it was clear his judgment was gone. Driving into Qatif had been insane. Convincing Helen to leave him was more than an act of love; it was an act of responsibility. It's a proof of love to want to protect the loved one: to put their safety, even their life, before yours.

I sucked at my cigarettes until my throat was raw. Loneliness sucked at my insides so hard I could see despair like a cliff at the end of the road: there was still time to swerve, to avoid going over the edge, but it would take all my strength to turn the wheel. And like a hate that wouldn't let go, I kept wondering how Helen, that very minute, was helping Harry to relax.

CHAPTER NINE

My ex-wife would have said, sarcastically, that the stars were in alignment. I've never believed in any of that rubbish, but the Qatif debacle was followed by a marked and general deterioration of the security situation, although in Riyadh, not on the Gulf coast. In two days, two compounds were suicide bombed and there were several shoot-outs with police. We were as yet untouched (you could hardly drive a city block without running into another police checkpoint), but no one thought our luck would last.

It was more pressure on me to perform: to obtain more and better—especially better—clients. The disorder in Riyadh was a financial, as well as a security, setback. I hadn't yet secured even one client there, but Riyadh was a primary goal, for that was where the real money was: in the country's capital.

On top of that, I couldn't see Helen. She was in purdah, under pressure to remain on the consulate compound; the security types were picking up more "chatter." Not that you had to be a security type to figure out that things were going south. Every time I crossed the bridge, on every street I drove on in Khobar, I saw the surly look, the sullen stare. The local press played the bombings down, but we were making CNN and Al Jazeera—always a bad sign. It looked like time was running out.

I was counting the days—one week from our Qatif outing—until Harry was due in Riyadh, until I could see Helen again. How could one week seem so long? The day he was due to leave, Harry called to tell me he had another possible prospect. I didn't know whether to laugh or to scream. He said a potential client was talking about a big investment—Harry called it "very significant." Then he said the magic word: Riyadh. His voice was uncharacteristically grave: no irony, no manly bonhomie. It was as if real money had sobered him up. I asked him if we were talking about a Shia.

"There aren't any down there. This is nothing like that. I owe you a favor, remember? This is a big one, Steve. But the deal has to be wrapped up right away." He asked me to come over immediately. I wasn't eager to see him, but it would be foolish to pass up an opportunity. I telephoned to cancel an appointment with a small-fry businessman I'd been trying to hook since I'd arrived, and went down and got into my rental car.

Reaching his office was tedious. Two security walls, each with a full complement of concrete traffic barriers, ringed the consulate. The outer security force was Saudi National Guard: the king's private army, practically indistinguishable from Bedouin. The next group in were Indians, hired from a local contractor. U.S. Marines were stationed inside the consulate—safely away from the main gates, the usual detonation point for suicide bombers.

After the inspections there was a brief, peaceful walk up through an ancient grove of tall acacias, to the old stone consulate building, flying its flag at the top of the hill like a Foreign Legion post from another era.

Over half a century the consulate had been divided and subdivided and subdivided again into a warren of tiny offices and cubicles. Now it was almost empty. Every month there were fewer personnel left. Walking down the silent corridors I felt more than ever that we were near the end. It was like being on an inner deck of a sinking ship. Most of the passengers and crew had already taken to the lifeboats. Inside the lights still burned, but the bows were under water and the sea was lapping in through open hatches.

Harry rated his own office, small and crowded with a few sticks of cheap government furniture. There was a single framed picture of Helen on his desk. The bare minimum evidence of personal occupation. When the time came he would shred his papers and pick up the photograph and walk out, and there wouldn't be a thing left to show that he'd been there.

He stood up and shook my hand. He looked edgy, his usual amiability a little forced. I interpreted it as embarrassment—his last client hadn't worked out as advertised.

He said, "I'm pretty sure this is something good. The kind of thing you've probably been waiting for. And not a moment too soon."

"Not a moment too soon?"

"You know what's going on. Even the ambassador's not a complete fool. I'm trying like hell to get Helen to leave. We have less than a division in and around Riyadh, and it's not going to be enough. Our guys in the capital are hunkered down in the embassy like a foxhole, and the royals have begun to leave for Europe and America—at least, the smarter ones have. I only hope they'll pull us out before the rot reaches this far."

"That's more alarmist than the official embassy line."

He snorted. "You know what that's worth." He opened a drawer in his desk. "Here's your potential client. I've already vetted her. This is as good as it's going to get." He handed me the usual manila folder. I took it and opened it to the first page.

It was a standard Commerce Department vetting form. A Saudi national fifty-six years of age, resident in Riyadh, was cleared to invest eighteen million U.S. dollars in my company's mutual funds.

I stared at it, stunned. I did the math. My commission was three percent. I'd make a little over half a million on this one client alone. It was more than enough to get out, to set me back up. Maybe enough to convince Helen to come with me.

"A woman," I said, staring at the page. "Zainab al Badawi."

"*Doctor* Zainab al Badawi. She's part owner, with her brothers, of Al Badawi contracting group. Almost in the same league as the Bin Ladens. A woman like that hardly needs vetting, but I put her through the database for form's sake. She's clean, of course."

"Another doctor," I said.

He replied almost before it was out of my mouth. "Don't worry. She's in another class entirely. A Sunni. I don't think she's even a doctor of medicine. She's a businesswoman."

"A Saudi businesswoman?"

"Rare. Very rare in this league. But they exist."

I thought for a moment. "Why is she using me? She can't have any difficulty getting money to the States."

Harry sat back in his chair. "Badawi's not a small-town philanthropist like Hussain. She's been a high-profile reformer for years. Someone who's pushed for women's rights, tried to open up women's schools, get women appointed to chambers of commerce, that kind of thing. She's also not the average wealthy Saudi female. Her father had some kind of royal connection. That's how her brothers expanded the family business all over the Kingdom. Outside of business, I doubt she's accomplished much. But she's a pusher, probably stubborn as hell. Politically, she's likely to be an Arab nationalist—a Nasserite. The government's always hated her, but she's too connected for them to do much.

"My point's this: I don't think she's the type to have been salting her money away in the States. She's probably not a financial wheeler-dealer. I think she's interested in using you because she's never done this before. You're officially sanctioned and she's looking for an above-board solution."

It sounded credible. "How did you get her?" I asked. My referrals seldom came through his office directly; usually they came through third parties, like Joe.

An uncharacteristic expression settled on Harry's face, as if he had something to say he wasn't especially proud of. He said, "It was Helen's idea."

"Helen?"

"She met Badawi about six months ago at one of her consulate at-homes. She's got one on this afternoon. I'm banned from the house, of course: women only. Anyway, she remembered her going on about the U.S.-backed restrictions on sending money out—Badawi's not exactly a pro-government type. Or a pro-U.S. type, either, I expect.

"Helen wasn't too happy with the way Qatif turned out. She thinks we owe you something. I agree. Of course, I couldn't call Badawi direct. Helen did. A social call, but she mentioned your firm. It turns out, Badawi was interested."

I was still taking it in. "You mean, Helen pitched my company to Badawi?"

"That's about it. Of course, she said the consulate would vouch for you. I couriered a letter backing you up."

The irony of it made my head swim. Helen had gone to bat for me, and Harry was going along. Up to now, Helen and I had been conspirators only in love. Now we were conspirators in business. It gave me confidence. I was more familiar with finance than with love; it made love's foundations more secure.

"I don't know what to say."

"Yeah, well, it's not exactly standard operating procedure. These aren't standard times."

I looked down at Badawi's dossier. Here was my ticket out, back to LA—back to anywhere, with Helen—in a government-issue manila folder. "Is Badawi coming up here, or does she want me to go to Riyadh?"

"She wants you in Riyadh. It's part of the deal."

"Do you think she'll want the whole dog and pony show?"

"I doubt it. I don't think she would have gone this far, unless she was sure of what she wanted to do. But go prepared."

"Okay. Anything else?"

"Yes: keep this confidential. No one's to know you got this deal through Helen. No one here had anything to do with it, in any way. That's clear, isn't it?"

"Of course."

"Second, the Badawis aren't small-fry and they don't like their business public. I wouldn't tell anyone local about this client at all. You don't get far in this country by spreading news about where important business people are sending their money. Treat her like a VIP: make an appointment to see her as soon as possible. And be careful. Riyadh's going south. Don't stay longer than you have to." He added gloomily, "I'm heading down there this afternoon."

"What for?"

"A meeting at the embassy. Evacuation planning. If we have to evacuate. I'm coming back Friday."

It was my chance to see Helen. I stood up to leave, but before we could say good-bye the telephone rang. He picked it up. "Hello, honey," he said. "Yes, don't worry, I remember. Tell Flerida to bring my suitcase over, the small one. Guess who's here?" He sat back and glanced at me. "Steve. Yes, it has been a while." He put his hand over the mouthpiece and asked me, "What're you doing tonight?"

"I've got a party to go to at Joe's. He has a couple of clients he wants to introduce."

"Do you think it'd be fun for Helen? I mean, is it one hundred percent business, or social?"

"Oh, it'll be social. He told me he's invited half the town."

"Then why don't you take Helen along? She's going stir-crazy on the compound."

It was too good to be true, but I agreed hesitantly . . . I didn't want to appear too eager. After he hung up, I said, "Are you sure it's a good idea? Helen and I going together to Joe's party? You know how he is. He knows a lot of gossipy types."

For the first time Harry looked almost suspicious—but only as if wondering why I was so dense. "No one has to worry about gossip any longer in this flea-bitten town. The only thing we have to worry about is getting out."

I got up to go. I said, "I'll make an appointment with Badawi as soon as I can. And thank Helen for the client."

"Thank her yourself. Badawi's a better client than any you'll get at Joe's. I owed you one after Qatif."

I picked up Helen later that evening. I parked across the street and got out of the car just in time to see the last of her Saudi "at-home" ladies filing out. They'd slipped on their black *abayas* while still inside, but waited until they caught a moment of sun before they drew their veils. One spotted me, and before she hid her face, caught my eye. Her expression made me wonder if Helen had told them she was expecting a male guest. The look she gave was that of the sophisticated Saudi who views an element of Western culture of which they disapprove: severe, superior, almost courteous enough to hide the disdain.

I stayed by the car until their drivers drove them away, then crossed the street. Helen's daily maid, a middle-aged Filipina, opened the door. "Mr. Kemp," she said, in the same tone as "more rain" or "another sandstorm." "Mrs. Laird is still changing." After an initial glance she looked down and wouldn't meet my eyes. It was her usual greeting. Flerida didn't approve of me. Devoted to Helen, with a ferocious loyalty and Catholic virtue, she might suspect, but she'd never tell. But she was a disappointment. I'd hoped to find Helen alone.

I wandered into the living room. The detritus of the party was still there: cups of tea, trays of half-eaten cake, soiled napkins. I looked around for things more permanent, more personal. This was Helen's home; anything of hers interested me. We'd connected through crisis, through sex, and—on my part—through compassion, but I was always on the lookout for something else, even something pedestrian, something more normal, to cement the bond. Something not having to do with the expat life. A new book by Karen Armstrong with "God" in the title lay open on the sofa; my eyes shied away. A DVD lay on top of the silent TV; I recognized it at once. The morning after our first night in bed she'd put it on; she'd said she wanted to hear something familiar, something from home. Irish dance. One of the enthusiasms I'd learned to tolerate.

Then she appeared. Just the sight of her sent my blood racing. Her lips were parted and she smiled like a girl who'd just spied the present she'd been waiting for. Her eyes were slightly closed—like someone holding a secret, maybe a surprise. She glanced to the side and saw the maid darkening the wall like a shadow. "Come to the office," she told me, brightly, "there's something I want to show you."

She led me into the little room with a computer and a desk covered with papers in neat rectangular piles (I'd have preferred it if Harry hadn't shared my desire for an orderly workspace—I didn't want even something small to admire), and shut the door after her. She fell into my arms. I was hungry for every inch of her. It wasn't just sex (although I'd wanted her for days). It was her womanliness, her innocence, her purity. Even her guilt was a virtue. Her faults were minuscule: what did God and the tappers matter? I had one hand on her breast and another on her ass when she pushed gently away, and said, "Not here, not now."

"Why not?" I was almost panting.

"The maid. And Harry."

"Harry?" I took a step back. "He's here?"

"He's always here. Like a presence. Whiskey and rants—everything going to hell. He should never have taken you to Qatif. Never completely trust him, Steven."

I certainly distrusted his judgment. But. . . . "The Badawi lead," I said, "that's from you. I can trust that, can't I?"

"He told you."

"Yes."

"It's what you wanted, isn't it?" She looked like she was asking for reassurance for a questionable act. Even in business. Was it mortal, or just venial? I remembered the book in the living room. She had too many scruples.

"It's what I want for both of us. It's our one-way ticket. It's the best thing you could have done."

A smile fought the shadow over her eyes. She looked away and said, "Harry wanted to redeem himself. I only made a call. He thought. . . ."

I was tired of Harry's involvement. "It was your call that mattered. Don't worry: I'll close the deal. It's the contract I've been waiting for, our contract out."

The shadow lifted. "You know what he said about you?"

"No."

"He said you're an idealist, like me."

She was pleased, and I wasn't going to disabuse her. "You're a good influence on me," I said, which must have been true. She came to me again. After a long moment she pulled away and said, "Now let's go. I haven't been off this compound in weeks." Then she used one of her Irish expressions: "Let's see what the crack's like at Joe's."

———

I always met Joe at his office. This was my first visit to his home, although I'd been on his compound before. Hartley lived there, too. It was a small, private compound in a part of town full of them, full of Westerners working for British and American and Saudi contractors, Westerners hanging on, hoping to make their savings targets, but with their one-way tickets already booked and ready to hand. Next to the front gate was a dug-in, camouflaged machine-gun nest, manned by a bored-looking Saudi in a uniform several sizes too big. His own people were driving the car bombs, and if the incidents in Riyadh were any guide, in an attack he'd be the first to cut and run. He probably wouldn't make it.

We drove in, past the first courtyard ringed by narrow, two-story apartments, to the second courtyard, where the houses were larger, one home per floor. The curbs were lined with cars.

I'd called Hartley earlier. I wanted to drop in there first. I wasn't sure that Joe's party would be Helen's cup of tea, and I wanted to introduce her to Hartley's wife. Gina was Italian, short and compact and full of energy, and we'd got on well during my first visit. She had two small children, and spent all her time with them (her husband worked long hours and started drinking the moment he got home); it was as close to a family atmosphere as I'd seen in Khobar yet, and I thought it might be a change for Helen. She'd told me she'd spent a year, as a young girl, in Italy.

Gina met us at the door. She greeted Helen effusively and with the penetrating eye of one European woman checking out another in a country where they were both an endangered species. Her husband had changed out of his suit but still wore his tie for the occasion. He offered us both a drink—his bootlegged Johnny Walker. He and I sat down in adjoining chairs and Helen and Gina took the sofa, with the kids in front of them, like puppies trying to jump up on the elegant new visitor.

Hartley talked of Arab art (he was a collector of old wooden doors and plaster window frames, several of which, rectangular plaster excrescences, adorned his walls). It was not my subject, but I nodded attentively while observing Helen. She chatted happily, admiring the children. It was a domestic scene. I was glad I'd brought her. But inevitably the talk turned to the security situation, to the recent suicide bombing in Riyadh.

Helen told Gina, "You must have thought of leaving."

"Oh yes. Arthur asks me to leave. To take the children to the UK. Even the Italian Embassy—for years I hear nothing from them, nothing! Then, after the bomb in Riyadh, they send me an order to evacuate—now they want me to leave! But look around," and we did, at the walls, hung with plaster window frames, the tables, littered with framed photographs, the overfurnished room, the floor strewn with frayed afghan carpets and children's toys. "How can I pack all this? And how will Arthur live? He can barely boil a cup of tea." She cast a glance full of blame at her husband. He sighed and took another drink.

Helen asked, "Where is your home?"

Gina rolled her eyes. "It is here—you are sitting in it. Arthur, what do you have to say?"

Her husband cleared his throat. "Actually, we have every intention of settling in Sussex. I keep my eye on properties that come on the market in Rodmell. It's a lovely town, near the River Ouse. Of course, it's difficult to enter into serious negotiations from Dhahran . . . we've been gazumped more than once. But, soon, perhaps on our next holiday . . . I have a couple of new properties in mind. . . ."

Gina gave a sound between a cough and a sneeze; she bounced up and down on the sofa. "He has been looking at properties in this English town for years. He is what they call the long-stay expat. Now we are a family of long-stay expats. And now the Arabs cut our throats—they cut the throats of two Englishmen just across the street not two years ago—and the Italian Embassy orders me to evacuate! To where?"

Helen hadn't meant to spark a scene; I could see her mentally looking for oil to pour. She said, "We're in a similar boat. My husband's been an expat all his life. I imagine we'll settle down in Dublin or Limerick in the end, but we don't have a home in Ireland—not yet.

Our home's always been the local consulate or embassy. And you do have some security. The guard at your gate looks well armed."

"Security! He is my biggest fear. Every day I worry that he will pull his trigger finger, our guard at the gate. I worry every time a cab brings me back from the school with the children. You'd think he would know me. But always he points the gun!" Again she scowled at her husband. He slumped farther in his chair. I couldn't help but feel for him. What could he do about it?

Helen backpedaled: "At least you have only one guard; we have three sets of them."

"Useless! If they wish to strike, they will find a way. Arthur says the Arab guards are all—what do you say, Arthur?—infiltrated. And, you know, we have Arabs living here."

It was like lighting a fuse: her husband sat up, his eyes refocused. "Right above us," he said, "your next port of call. Yousef. Joe, as he prefers to be called. Our upstairs neighbor. I expect he passes himself off to you as American. In fact he's Iraqi. Born in Basra. Grew up like a Saudi in Jeddah, but I suspect he's Shia. On the wrong side of the tracks. Made it to the States years ago, when you were still letting in anyone, and got some kind of bogus degree. Bought it, most likely. Not that I have anything against your American universities—the best are as good as ours. But you know the kind of outfit I'm talking about.

"You should be careful of him. He's the worst kind of Arab: half Westernized. The kind who don't know what they are, and don't know the rules. Or don't give a damn. They think the rules don't apply. The kind of Arab who's on the fence. And, when push comes to shove, who knows which side they'll jump down on?" He looked up at the ceiling. "Thank God the floor's solid concrete."

Helen listened to him without expression. She said, "Isn't he an American citizen?"

Our host laughed. "He says he is. He probably even has a U.S. passport. Don't get me wrong, Mrs. Laird, America's a wonderful country. And I'm certainly not a bigot. But Arabs are different. You can take an Arab out of Arabia, but you can't take Arabia out of an Arab. No one knows it better than the Arabs themselves. They're all drinking his booze upstairs, and out at the pool—I bet it's Black Label, too—but do you think they respect him? Or even trust him? Not on your life."

Helen was poor at deceit (it was one of my worries); her face betrayed her. The conversation had taken a turn for the worse. It was time to go. "Nevertheless," I said, "we are expected. And we're late already. We ought to make an appearance. Helen?"

She stood up on cue.

Hartley said, "Already? I've found a new poem . . . I don't know whether Mrs. Laird. . . ." He held up his glass. "I may be wrong. He might be serving home brew."

"Thanks, but we really should be going."

We made our exit with the usual compliments. Helen was warm to Gina, and polite to her husband. Outside we started up the stairs to Joe's place. I asked her, "What did you think of them?"

"I liked Gina. And her children."

"And Arthur?"

"Oh, another English wanker." The expression surprised me, coming from her lips.

On the landing we heard the sound of the party through Joe's door; I rang the bell and he answered it wearing what I thought at first was fancy dress. My heart sank at how Helen and I would stand out, until I glanced at the crowd inside and realized it was Joe who stood out, not us. A shirt printed with psychedelic flowers fell straight from his narrow shoulders as if from a clothes hanger; his legs looked glued into a pair of skintight black slacks. I could only assume it was a party outfit he'd adopted from his wife's New York, working-class milieu. It would have been equally suitable for a Saudi fornication holiday.

He welcomed me effusively, as if I were his best friend in a world of doubtful acquaintances and potential enemies. Toward Helen he was more formal. He raised his eyebrows to me when she wasn't looking; I ignored it.

The apartment was roomy but crowded with guests. Joe introduced Helen to his wife. Her appearance was startling. She'd dyed her hair a vivid blond and her face shone with makeup like a halogen lamp.

But it was impossible to feel censorious at their vulgarity. They were both so clearly enjoying themselves.

Helen was an old hand at mixed, Arab-American parties, and I didn't have to shepherd her; she was soon chatting to a group of Lebanese ladies. I helped myself to the buffet and observed the crowd. Couples predominated. Westerners were a minority; their conversation identified them as ex–Royal Air Force or businessmen and their spouses. Most of the guests were Arab: Lebanese, Syrian, Iraqi, Palestinian. The men wore suits and sports jackets, their wives were dressed characteristically in the elegant dresses that Americans two generations ago would have appreciated but that now looked over-the-top. I saw no obvious Saudis.

A uniformed waiter, hired for the night, offered me a drink. I mingled. Security was the common topic. The ex-RAF contingent set the tone for the Brits: stiff upper lip. The Arabs needed no military training to support their equanimity. Insecurity was part of their life. Politics for its own sake didn't interest them. Government was like drought, famine, or sudden death: an act of God. What mattered was the family and the escape plan. The Arabs were professionals: doctors, engineers, academics, managers. Most would have either a Canadian or a British passport, or an American green card. They'd leave sober, in business class. The Brits who made it on would be boozing it up a class behind.

Everyone was there to relax. It wasn't the kind of party where you wanted to appear eager to sell your product or service. Nevertheless, within an hour, thanks to Joe's discreet introductions (more discreet than his outfit), I'd managed to quietly hand out two of my business cards to Arab managers of Saudi concerns, who promised to pass them on to the owners, with their recommendation.

The drinks were the real thing and I had just started my third and last when Joe steered me away from the Syrian doctor (trained in Edinburgh) to whom I was talking, and on the pretext of showing me the compound took me outside and down to the swimming pool. There I discovered the other, completely different party he was hosting at the same time.

The pool was half Olympic-size, and discreetly floodlit, with only a few of the lights turned on. Tables and chairs were arranged along the sides with another drinks waiter in attendance. The crowd was larger than the one inside, and consisted of singles—all Arabs. Here were the Saudis. The men all wore informal Western dress. They were handsome and well turned out, probably of good families, courteous and confident in their bearing. Several were in their thirties. The women belonged to a different category. I guessed them to be mainly Moroccan. They belonged to a class of women Americans never identified, because in public they were always behind a veil. Their profession was to run the shops—banks, beauty salons, and so on—that only Saudi women patronized. They were young and feminine and attractive, but not elegant as the women inside. They may have been in the marriage market, but I was pretty sure the men were looking for liaisons.

Joe guided me to a quiet corner at the far end and we sat down with our drinks. We talked business. The two men he'd introduced me to would probably bring two good Saudi clients, perhaps better than the type I'd been getting, but not much better. They were still small beer. I was grateful to him of course. He'd been a good source of referrals, probably my single largest source, and certainly the most Westernized of any of my go-betweens.

The expat life can be a lonely life. Before, in the carefree nineties, I'd had friends—even if only the temporary friends of a temporary expat—as well as a lover. I'd regained my lover, but Joe was the closest I had to a friend in Al Khobar. In the pervading doubt and anxiety, his American enthusiasm was refreshing. It was the enthusiasm of the successful emigrant. Dinosaurs like Hartley could not sympathize with that temperament. It summed up what they despised in American culture: too optimistic, too foreign, too insincere. To me it was a tonic: it reminded me of home.

But this life, everything around us tonight—the expat parties, the business deals—would probably soon be ending. Joe's enthusiasm could be a liability: he might need a reality check. And I wanted to share my good news.

I shared it carefully. I made it clear it was confidential. He listened attentively while I told him about my new referral. I didn't tell him the exact amount. But I let him know that it would set me up, let me buy a one-way ticket. I didn't mention Helen's role.

His expression took on an uncharacteristic sobriety. "So the Badawi are sending their money out," he said when I'd finished. "They have old ties with the regime, dating back to Abdul-Aziz. They're old money, as old as this country has." He cast a glance around the pool, then back at his apartment. "Maybe it is time to leave. Don't bother with those guys in there, Steve. Concentrate on al Badawi. Harry did you a good turn. *Inshallah,* he earned something in the process."

"What do you mean?"

"He didn't ask for a cut?"

"Of course not. He's a civil servant. He's just doing his job."

Joe shook his head. "What does he have to look forward to? A pension? I hope he got something out of it. If not from you, then out of al Badawi herself. She can afford it."

Joe was an immigrant. He'd always been scrupulously honest with me, but he had a third world attitude toward government employees. He didn't trust them as far as he could throw his arm, and assumed they were on the take. Harry belonged to a special category of government employee: he was also a business associate. In any business relationship, both members have to profit. Joe wouldn't begrudge Harry a commission. The man and the relationship were more important than the office. It was a technical illegality, best ignored.

Joe said, "Here's your companion." Helen had appeared by the pool gate. I stood and waved. "I'm glad you had someone to bring to the party," he said.

"She's a friend. And she was going stir-crazy, cooped up on that compound."

"She's a beautiful woman."

I looked down at him. "She's a friend, Joe. She's Harry's wife."

He said quietly, "There're plenty of women here, younger and even more beautiful, who I could introduce you to. There're some real ladies here, Steve, some from good families. I know their parents. They'd love to meet you."

I hadn't expected a proposition. The women around the pool

weren't prostitutes, but they certainly couldn't be more than casual companions, and "companion" was putting a gloss on it. In other circumstances I might have taken offense. But this was Saudi. It was a society where women were hard to come by, and sexual frustration was the norm. I wasn't interested in Joe's offer—I had Helen—but I appreciated it. I appreciated his thoughtfulness, one man—one American—to another. I thanked him, but couldn't say more before Helen came within earshot. I'd kept an eye on her advance. She was an object of attention: admiration from the men; curiosity from the women.

"Hello," she said when she reached us. "The two boyos together. It's a different party down here, isn't it?"

"The same party, Mrs. Laird, just different guests," Joe replied.

She said, "Yes, very different. How did you get all the girls past the religious police?"

"The *mutawas*? A couple of my Saudi guests are well connected."

"How convenient. For everyone."

He swept his hands out, palms open, in an innocent protest, smiling his toothy smile. "You know Saudi society, Mrs. Laird. This is just the equivalent of a local bar." He added, "A singles bar."

"Are they all single?"

"Most. The ladies all are."

She looked around. "So the women are all chancers. They don't have much of a choice, do they?"

Joe shrugged his shoulders. "'Chancers,'" he said. "An Irish expression? I like it. Here, we are all chancers. I'm sure your husband would agree. He knows the Arab world so well, so many insights. I always enjoy his conversation. I'm sorry he wasn't able to come."

"He's in Riyadh on business." Her ability—or desire—to mix had deserted her. Elegant, white, mature and Irish, she looked out of place. She said, "It's getting late, Steven. I think I'd better be heading back."

"Let me call you a cab," Joe offered. But I told him no, I'd drive her. The three of us went back upstairs. Helen and I said good night to our hostess, then took our leave.

Once in the car, I asked her where she wanted to go: to the consulate or my hotel.

"Oh, let's go home. I don't feel like spending a night at the Al Wadi. I suspect that's where most of those girls around the pool are going to wind up tonight: some Arab hotel room."

I looked at her. She stared straight ahead, but in the dark it was difficult to read her face. I drove out the compound gate, past the dug-in camouflaged machine-gun nest with the sleeping Saudi, and turned left toward the consulate. We drove in silence for a while, and then I said, "Joe's just a business associate."

"I don't like him. He's the kind of Arab Harry always talks about: unreliable. On the fence. And greasy: those Saudis downstairs—completely useless. Rich Sunnis. The ruling class. Never part of a solution. Except how and where to get laid."

She'd sunk into a mood. It was my fault. If I'd known what kind of party. . . . But I'd soon redeem myself. In her bed, we'd redeem each other.

Then, in a queue of cars at the consulate's first gate, we saw the driver of the car ahead waving back at us through his rearview mirror. "Who's that?" I asked.

"Christ, it's Bill. Our next-door neighbor. A great talker." Her voice fell like the end of hope. "He'll want to come out and chat as soon as we get in. Maybe you should just let me out."

It was a blow. I hadn't seen her for two weeks. "What about tomorrow?" I said.

"Harry's back tomorrow afternoon."

"I thought he wasn't back until Friday."

"He called me on my cell phone when you were downstairs with Joe. They canceled his meeting—he went down for nothing. But we're having the American businessmen party next Wednesday. We'll see each other then. I'm sorry."

With Bill in front, still waving to us like an idiot, we couldn't even kiss when she got out. I cursed him as I turned the car around. Then I thought: Stay focused. In a week I could have the Badawi deal wrapped up. That would be something to bring to the American businessmen's party.

———

Three days later the Interior Ministry in the capital came under attack in the broad light of day. The mujahideen—or whoever they were— shot the guards, then invaded the building. Inside were some high-profile Saudis and American "consultants."

One of the Americans inside managed to contact the U.S. Army base outside Riyadh. We had half a brigade in Al Kharj, an hour away in the desert; a sprinkling of support troops at compounds in town; and a small rapid-response force on the city's perimeter. Americans were at risk. Someone in the army gave the order to respond.

A platoon managed to get to the ministry before traffic ground to a halt. The building was on a major thoroughfare. It was a scene of chaos and confusion. Civilian drivers created a massive traffic jam. Some got out of their cars to take a closer look.

What happened next is disputed. The civilians and the Arab television crew filming the whole thing from the perimeter (they must have been tipped off) insisted that the only shooting came from inside the building. The U.S. Army insisted they were also taking fire from the crowd. They fired back. The insurgents reached the roof and fired down from there. The troops suffered casualties. The traffic delayed reinforcements.

The U.S. force was at a disadvantage. They were being picked off from above, while surrounded by a growing crowd of hostile locals. Maybe some were armed and shooting; it wouldn't surprise me. After a certain point the platoon was firing in every direction. There is no doubt about that because the TV crew were beaming pictures of the "massacre" live into Arab homes throughout the region.

Several women trapped in their cars were hit by stray bullets. One bullet penetrated the petrol tank of a school bus; some of the kids managed to get out, but not all. The mob turned homicidal. It came close to being another Mogadishu. Helicopters and APCs full of troops arrived just in time. But when it was over we'd lost four men and the streets were littered with Arab corpses.

The Saudi government issued statements. The insurgents were all either killed or arrested, and sweeping roundups were being made. It was not an attack on Americans or American interests, and Ameri-

cans in-country were safe, we could still rely on traditional Arab hospitality, etc., etc. On the other hand, the government condemned the
undisciplined behavior of the U.S. Army in the recent incident, and
insisted on explanations and monetary recompense for victims. They
were trying to have their cake and eat it, too.

I'd spent the day glued to the television and in the afternoon Harry
called to warn me against trying to cross over to Manama. Vigilantes
were rumored to be on the Saudi side of the causeway, looking for
Americans. I spent the night in the Al Wadi.

A near-miss from a Qatifi suicide bomber, two compound bombings in Riyadh, and now this. It was the kind of week one expected in
Iraq, not in Saudi.

No one I would consider normal would stay in a potential war zone
if they didn't have to. But Riyadh's a long way from the coast—all the
way to the center of the peninsula. Almost four hours by car. Half a
million dollars isn't as much as it used to be, but it's still a lot of money,
especially if you've been watching your dimes. It was more than
money: it meant a smooth-as-butter escape. It meant a new start. It
meant Helen.

I've been trained to assess risk. I thought about it all night, smoking cigarette after cigarette. Around 2 A.M. I decided to stick around—
just long enough to wrap up the Badawi contract. The next morning
when I walked out to my car, I found the windshield smashed. It was
a rental. I turned it in for another.

During the next couple of days security, already tight, constricted
even further; you literally couldn't drive a block without running into
a police checkpoint. They would have been more reassuring had the
police been less surly; one got the impression they were conflicted
regarding who the bad guys were. I began to notice something new:
young Saudis, catching sight of me on the street (there were few
Americans in public at that time), would start, as if surprised and
alarmed, and turn away or quicken their pace. I'm not a threatening
type. I just represented potential trouble. Something to avoid.

Business was disrupted and it was the middle of the week—
Wednesday—before I managed to get an appointment with Dr. Zainab

al Badawi. Her secretary arranged it for Saturday. I booked a flight down the day before; there was no point in spending more time in the capital than necessary. Wednesday night I had an early dinner at the hotel, and then drove to the consulate, to Harry's American businessmen party.

The party was an annual event, scheduled months before, for Americans involved in commerce at the executive level in the Eastern Province. Their parked cars lined the narrow road in front of Harry's house. The front door stood a few inches ajar; after so much security at the gate there was no reason to keep the house closed. A sign beckoned everyone to come in.

Guests jammed the living room. Nearly all were businessmen, with a sprinkling of U.S. Army and Air Force officers. The military were mixed in race and gender; the business contingent were white and male. Business in Saudi was a man's world, and almost to a man they were corporation men of a certain age and type.

The Saudi market had been in decline since I'd left a decade before. It wasn't the place where a global company sent its young, energetic MBAs eager to prove themselves. They went to the Asian, the South American, the emerging Eastern European markets. To Saudi, corporations sent their older men, men who had been expatriates for most of their working lives. They tended to be physically large, with spreading waistlines and red faces. Most had never spent enough time back home to change with the times, and their tastes were old-fashioned. On their vacations, they looked for a place where they could still order a whiskey and a porterhouse steak. (The party had an open bar and nearly everyone held a glass of hard liquor.) They were fossils. But they knew how to maintain a corporate office under unfavorable conditions. They would be among the last to go.

I stood out without a drink in my hand, and pushed my way to the bar. It was manned by a single Filipino serving nonstop. The queue was long; to avoid having to return too soon I ordered a double.

I made small talk with one or two people while scanning for Helen. A thick arm waved in a corner, bodies parted, and I caught sight of Harry.

"Steve!" he said, pushing his way through his guests. "Glad you made it. Been looking for you all night. I need to talk to you privately. About Helen."

"About Helen?"

"Yes. When can we get together?"

I made an effort to recover. "Whenever you like."

"Good. The party should end soon after eleven—these guys look pretty loud now, but they'll leave on cue. It'll be easier to talk when the place is quieter. Don't go before I've found you, okay?"

"You bet."

"I'm heading to the bar. Can I get you another one?"

"No thanks. This one's still fresh."

He barreled off back into the crowd.

I stood looking after him. He hadn't appeared angry or threatening. He looked as if he was enjoying himself. What could he want to talk to me about, concerning Helen?

The suits pressed in. A man on my right bellowed with laughter; someone behind jabbed his elbow into my back. A wave of irritation swept over me. I'd come to see Helen, not these examples of what I might have become, had I never gotten out, never left. Where was she? I wasn't far from her bedroom. I pushed my way to her door, and tried the knob. It wasn't locked. I opened the door just enough to slip inside, pulling it shut and pressing the lock behind me.

A single bedside lamp cast its glow on Helen, sitting with her back to me on the far edge of the bed. She jumped and turned.

"Steven."

I went to her. She was simple and elegant in a dark blue dress with a low-cut back. Her only jewelry was a slender silver necklace. For once she'd miscalculated: she was overdressed—too elegant for the crowd outside.

"What are you doing in here?" I asked.

"Hiding," she said. She put her arms around me. "Waiting for you."

The light was dim and the bedroom intimate. She held me tight, molding her body into mine, kissing hard, like a woman starved. Then she went down, unbuttoning me as she descended, her mouth pressed against me. On her knees, her hands on my hips, she performed the act.

My desire wasn't less than hers, but I was afraid of a knock at the door, of discovery. I whispered, "Harry's outside, and the others. . . ."

She withdrew, and panted, "No one's coming in."

Time was slipping out of our hands; we hadn't had each other for weeks. I pulled her to her feet, turned her around and unzipped her dress. She knelt forward onto the bed she shared with Harry. I stripped off her panties and she spread her legs. "Wait," she said, and slipped her dress over her arms. Then she bent over, accepting me. Her urgency fueled mine. I took like a man taking possession. Her breasts hung down, her long red hair swung forward, hiding her face. Doesn't love have a right to possess? How can't it? She was silent except for a moan when I entered, and a cry at the end. I hardly heard her over the din outside.

Afterward we lay together on the bed. I held her to me. She excited me so strongly I was again aroused. She asked, "Did you lock the door?"

"Yes."

She rolled away. "Then we were safe. Completely safe. No one could even hear us." She sounded flat, like someone used to disappointment. She got off the bed and began pulling on her clothes.

I lay alone on my elbows on the bed. I said, "Would you prefer it if I unlocked the door?"

"Don't be an idiot."

I got up and pulled her to me. "Maybe I should. If it turns you on. That was some of the best sex I ever had."

She said, "Sex, and hope. They go together, don't they?"

"I thought it was sex and love."

"That, too."

She gave me a kiss that was gone before I could respond, and turned around. She asked me to do up her dress. "I have guests. We should both make an appearance."

I zipped up my trousers and straightened my shirt. She was at the door, pressing her ear up against it. I joined her.

She whispered, "Listen. A room full of drunks telling each other how everything is going to hell."

"Harry's crowd."

"My crowd, too."

"Not yours. You're better than that."

"I wanted to try. I wanted to do something. Even Harry. . . ."

I put my hand on her ass, and slipped it down between her legs. "When can we see each other again?"

"Tomorrow. Harry's flying to Riyadh in the morning. He says it's for real this time: they're organizing the evacuation. You know he wants me to leave, too."

"When's his flight?"

"Noon. I'm not ready, Steven. Not yet. I don't want to go alone."

"Don't worry. As soon as I close the deal, we'll go together. When will I see you?"

"I'll take a cab to your hotel as soon as he leaves. Now let's get back to the party. You first. I'll follow in a minute."

I gave her a last kiss, picked up my jacket and squeezed out the door.

The party was in full swing. The sound hit me like a blow; I grimaced and leaned back against the closed bedroom door. I'd returned to a bad dream: a dream of vulgarity, shouting, drunken laughter. Reality was back in Helen's room: dim, quiet, with the scent of her sex and the feel of her skin against mine.

I'd lost my drink so I pushed through to the bar. The line was no shorter than before; the Filipino barman's white jacket was stained with sweat. By the time I got my whiskey I heard Helen's voice, high and from a distance. She and Harry stood together on the opposite side of the room, talking to some grinning, paunchy businessmen. Harry had his arm draped around her shoulders. I waved but she either didn't see or decided not to acknowledge; someone spoke and they all broke into laughter.

I was near the kitchen. I remembered it had a door to the back garden. I needed to get out. In a minute I escaped into the night air.

It was a summer night on the Gulf. The heat hit me like a wall; I pulled my jacket off and threw it over a lawn chair. The humidity dripped off the tropical plants overflowing the borders: the bougainvillea; the hibiscus; the wild orchids; the crown of thorns. Chinese lanterns hung from acacias, illuminating the guests scattered in isolated groups over the lawn. No one loitered near. I'd traded irritation for loneliness.

I ambled with my drink, heading nowhere. Then, passing by two figures under a paper lantern, I heard a voice that sounded different but at the same time familiar.

"In charge of what? His harem? That's all he's in charge of. How is he going to 'investigate' the U.S. Army? He can't walk out of his palace alive without an army of bodyguards. He's owned by the Americans."

It was Joe—an angry, possibly drunk Joe, talking politics, something I'd never known him to do. I stepped closer. The man with him was more than a foot taller, even stooped. It was Bill—Harry's next-door neighbor, the talkative young political officer. He still wore his jacket, and under the light his white shirt stuck wetly to his chest and stomach. His stoop must have been congenital; it couldn't have been to hear Joe. I heard him yards away.

He tried to say something but Joe interrupted. "How can you be so innocent? You work for them: you should know better. Let me tell you, for every massacre you see on CNN, there's ten that never make the news—the American news controlled by the U.S. Army, by the Jews. You're just a puppet, you're all puppets, like the king, with the Jews in Hollywood, in Washington, Tel Aviv, pulling your strings."

He began a pantomime, yanked by invisible strings: his right elbow and knee jerking up, then down, then his left side repeating the movement. He wore a white suit, and his mime beneath the lanterns and the full moon, among the bougainvillea and hibiscus, under the dripping acacias, looked like some weird tropical dance—maybe a Haitian voodoo. "Just a puppet," Joe repeated, his limbs jerking up and down, "dancing for the Jews." He stopped and leaned toward the stooping, sweating American. "You're here for the oil. Not to bring democracy to Saudis. It's bullshit. You're here for the oil, and screw the Arabs."

It was too much for Bill. He remonstrated in a polite, low voice that no one except Joe could hear to understand. He probably didn't want to draw attention to himself—it wasn't a diplomatic scene. But people were beginning to notice. I didn't want to get involved. I turned around, took a few steps, and almost ran into Harry.

I felt his approach before seeing him properly; he pushed a sort of atmospheric bow wave ahead of him through the gloom.

"Steve! Out getting some air? Don't blame you. Pretty thick inside." His attention flicked to the shouting nearby. "Who's making all the racket?"

"Just Joe," I told him. "He must be drunk. He's being anti-American to your next-door neighbor."

"Joe? Anti-American?" Now we heard him clearly. He could be heard across the lawn, his voice high with anger; he was one of those unfortunate men whose voices go squeaky when they lose control. Bill had retreated into the shadows. "Why didn't you stop him?" Harry asked me, and lumbered over to his guest.

Harry laid a hand like a raw steak on Joe's shoulder and greeted him effusively. He told him how happy he was that he'd come. He told him laughingly that he saw he'd been straightening out his neighbor, and suggested that it was a hell of a hot night for politics; maybe he'd like another drink.

Yousef deflated to Joe. It was like Mr. Hyde reverting to Dr. Jekyll. Harry glad-handed him for another minute, then walked him to the kitchen door. I stepped behind a dripping tree as they passed. Joe disappeared inside, and Harry rejoined me. "No harm done," he said. "He's okay—just a little too much to drink. You can't blame him. Everyone's upset. The climate," he said, obscurely, "has gone to hell."

"You mean the heat?"

He looked at me out of a boozy fog as if I were the one who was dense. "I mean the situation. Everyone's getting nervous. The Arabs are losing it. When Joe starts to go, you can bet the Saudis are already gone." He took another drink. "Never mind. He's a good guy. Better than most. You can't trust most Arab Americans in this country as far as you can throw your arm. They're on the fence, and you never know which side they're going to come down on."

I'd heard the phrase before . . . from Hartley? Suddenly the heat was too much. I wanted to get back inside. But Harry said, "I'm glad you're here. This is as good a time as any." His voice dropped, became conspiratorial. "I need to ask you a favor. It's about Helen."

I didn't know what he wanted, and I didn't want to talk to him about his wife. I said, "It's hot, Harry, maybe we'd better wait. . . ."

"This is important. Listen. I'm flying to Riyadh tomorrow. Saturday's mess woke up someone in Washington. You'll read the warden message in a couple of days. We're not calling it an evacuation—not diplomatic. But we're going to start pulling staff. Down to near zero. A level three." He waved his glass around the lawn. "This crowd's pretty tough, but they're smart. As soon as they find out there's no one to call the local hooch if they get into trouble, they'll be on a plane out."

He stepped closer. "You know Helen should have left a long time ago. We've been at a level two since Ali's attempted coup. She's only still here because I pulled some strings. She begged me, and I did."

I had nothing to say, so I said nothing.

"I can't tie her up and shovel her on a plane. I wish I could. I want her out before they start torching consulates."

"How long do we have?"

"Who knows? Maybe a week, maybe a couple of months. She'd just be getting things arranged for us in Ireland a little ahead of time, that's all."

"I don't understand where I come in."

"Dammit." He brought his glass up, but it was empty except for melted ice; he threw the water away. "I can't convince her," he said. "She says she won't leave without me. But she might listen to you. Hell, you saved her life. Tell her you're leaving as well. You will anyway, after you wrap up the Badawi contract. Tell her anything you like. But convince her. Convince her to go."

It was the last thing I expected him to ask me. It was almost as if he knew I had some hold over her, some real influence. He couldn't have known, he was just desperate. But it would do no harm to play along—as if I were doing him a favor. But if she were to leave immediately, I wanted her nearby, where we could make our plans together—not in Ireland. I'd tried to get her to move to Bahrain before. Now all the right cards were falling into my hands. "Maybe," I told him, "she'd agree to Manama. Just a temporary move. Until things blow over."

He thought about it. "Things aren't going to 'blow over.' But Manama is safer. It'd be a short-term solution." His face broke into a grin, and he laughed. "But what's long-term around here?" He clapped me on my shoulder like a football buddy. "It might work. I'll talk to her tonight. You'll back me up?"

"Of course. As soon as I can. Not tonight. Maybe tomorrow."

"Great. Let's get out of this heat and freshen up these drinks."

Inside, the party was still in full swing. I couldn't see Helen, and Harry disappeared into the crowd. The whole room looked drunk; it looked like a celebration of the last night in hell. I pushed my way to the front door and slipped out into the night.

CHAPTER TEN

I was too tired to drive the causeway back to Manama and I'd only have to return to Al Khobar the next morning for Helen; I spent the night in town at the hotel.

On Thursday mornings before breakfast I usually walked a couple of blocks up the street to pick up the *International Herald Tribune*. But this morning the little bookstore was closed. Another minor irritant. The big Jarir bookstore on the corniche would stay open until the noon prayer; I got into my car.

On the way back to the hotel I took a shortcut through the almost deserted streets of the old expat shopping district. It was the small part of a small town where previously the Aramco expats—Americans and Brits—would come to buy kitchen utensils and afghan carpets and Western jewelry: all the things a Western woman needed to settle in for a long stay. Since the bombings and the murders and the embassy warnings they no longer came. Except for a couple of banks and a handful of shops, the stores had closed and the district had shrunk to just a few streets. It was the beginning of August—the start of the summer storm season—and the day was unusually colorless even for Khobar; a flat white sky glared down on the crumbling white buildings.

At a stop sign I noticed someone waving on a corner. It was Harry. He stood outside a branch of one of the local banks, looking limp in the heat. I swore, but there was nothing to do but wind down the window and say hello. The smell of hot sand blew into the car. He ran across the street, opened the passenger door and swung heavily in.

"What luck," he said. "Where are you headed?"

"My hotel."

"Great. Mind dropping me off there? I've been waiting five minutes for a cab and haven't seen one yet."

"No problem." I let out the clutch and started carefully down the potholed road. Helen would be on her way to the hotel as soon as Harry left home. "I thought you were flying to Riyadh?"

"I am, but my flight's not till twelve. I had a little business to do in town. As long as I get to the airport by eleven I'll be all right. We've got time for a cup of coffee at the Al Wadi."

It was the last place I wanted him. Panicked, my mind froze; I was unable to think of a way to get rid of him. We got to the hotel and walked in.

Hartley had turned half the lobby into a coffee shop called Hanifa; it was popular in the early evenings with the better-off, lounging class of Saudi. Mornings were quiet. We took our seats at one of the little round glass-topped tables by the front window. There was no one else around. The waiter came and we ordered. I glanced at my watch. It was a quarter past ten. "Don't worry," Harry said, "it's only ten minutes to the airport." He settled back comfortably in his chair. There was an inward smile on his face as if he were thinking of something that pleased him. He looked a happy man.

I said, "I was just wondering if there'd be a line."

"Not for me. I'm flying business class."

Outside the window an eddy lifted a column of sand off the sidewalk. If Helen had left the consulate after Harry, she would arrive any minute.

He said, "You know what I was thinking, standing on the street outside the bank?"

"No."

"It'll sound funny to you."

"Funny?"

"I was taking in the scene. Helen says I'm not observant; I think we just see different things. Or see things differently. I was standing there, outside that crummy bank, with the empty street and a few beat-up, parked cars. I remember the sign for the translation bureau opposite was crooked—looked ready to fall off. There was some kind of black rot growing up the scabby walls. How it grows on concrete in this heat I don't know—must be the humidity. There was a smell of sand in the air and the sweat was dripping down my back. There wasn't a soul around. What a place.

"And then, you know, it suddenly struck me: I was happy! I could hardly believe it myself. Standing there, sweating like a pig, I was happy. I know it sounds crazy. But I felt like . . . well, I felt like it was home."

I took a sip of coffee. I said, "How long have you been in the Gulf, all in all?"

"Good question. I figure not more than five years. It's not much, really, is it? But before I married Helen, I spent most of my career in places like this. A lot like this. Third world shitholes." He stared into the distance, a thoughtful look on his face. He said, "It's a far cry from Ireland."

I stole another glance at my watch. Harry didn't look anxious to leave. I racked my brains for an explanation should Helen appear, out of the blue. I said, "Helen said she might want me to take her shopping this morning. She said she might take a cab to the hotel."

Harry looked abstracted. "Shopping? This morning?"

"Yes. She might drop in any time."

"In another hour everything will be closed for prayer. The shops won't open again until around four."

I mentally kicked myself for forgetting the noon prayer.

"Besides," he said, "she had a hangover this morning. I was going to tell her about your Manama idea, but she couldn't even get out of bed. She isn't normally much of a drinker—unlike most Irish."

Out of the corner of my eye I saw a besuited figure walking down the fake marble stairs. It was Hartley. He spotted us immediately and made a beeline to our table.

I introduced the two men and they shook hands. Hartley made the connection with Helen almost immediately: his double take was nearly imperceptible. He asked if we would mind if he joined us. I said of course not. He pulled up a nearby chair and sat down. The waiter came scurrying over but Hartley sent him back with a wave of his hand.

"It's not every day," he told Harry, "that Hanifa can boast of an American diplomat among its guests. We're very pleased to have you here."

Harry grunted something.

"Although, could we have hosted your wife? Perhaps at one of our ladies' luncheons?"

"It's possible," Harry said. "Did you ever escort her to one of those, Steve?"

"I can't recall. We may have had dinner here after one of our scuba lessons."

"That's probably it," Hartley said quickly. "We have so few guests of quality these days . . . they tend to stand out all the more."

"Business down?" asked Harry.

"Isn't it everywhere? So many of our old regulars have departed." His voice dropped, although there was no one around to hear. "I'm afraid most of our guests now are Arabs—with some exceptions." He nodded at me and sat back. "We attract the better class: you'll seldom find an Egyptian even in the lounge. Too pricey. But of course it's not the same."

I could almost see Harry's skin crawl. Most of us have a certain type, or types, who automatically repel us, often for no good reason. For Harry it was the Brits. "Don't much care for the locals?" he said, in a voice that should have raised a yellow flag.

Hartley's manner became confidential. "I depend on the better-off Sunnis. The Shia don't have the income for this kind of establishment—we're too sophisticated for them, in any case. Of course they're good workers. But I wouldn't trust them." He added, "Any of them."

"Must be tough, depending on Arabs for trade."

"The British have a long history with these people. We were financ-

ing Al Saud when their 'palaces' were made of mudbrick. We understand the Arab mentality." He finished, complacently, "We know how
they think."

Squat and powerful in his chair, Harry looked like a bouncer, a little past his prime, looking forward to manhandling an uninvited guest
to the door. But it wasn't his establishment. He said, evenly, "I think
I've heard of you. Maybe from my wife. You aren't a poet, by any
chance?"

An innocent smile rose on Hartley's face. "I'm afraid I can't claim
that honor. However, I am alive to poetry, as Steve here can attest.
It so happens that I've recently found a new one—new to me, that
is. Perhaps you know it?" He pulled a small volume from his jacket
pocket. "It's by Matthew Arnold, of whom I'm sure you've heard.
The subject is the decline of faith—Christian faith. The poet did not
approve. He thought Christianity a foundation of progress. In your
country faith is resurgent; the poem may speak to you directly. It's
called 'Dover Beach.'" He opened the book, held it some distance
away, and adjusted his glasses. "I'd be happy to read it for you. It's
not. . . ."

Harry stood up. "I'm an atheist. I've got a plane to catch. Have to
grab a cab. Nice meeting you."

Hartley, in mid-flow, took a moment to recover, but his professionalism reasserted itself. He stood up, called the desk clerk over, and said,
"Let me get you a taxi." Hartley and the clerk walked out the door
together.

"Sorry about that," I said.

"Forget it. Another Brit relic. He'll be the last one on the last flight
out—if he makes it. When are you flying down to see Badawi?"

"Tomorrow morning."

"Let's get together at the embassy there for a drink. Give me a call."

I didn't like to promise, but I said, "Sure."

Harry followed the manager out, and I sat back down. Now, as long
as Helen didn't show up in the next minute. . . . I watched anxiously
as a cab drew up to the curb. It was empty. Harry got in and it drove
off. We were safe. I slumped back in my chair.

I closed my eyes for only a few seconds—I hardly had time to breathe—when I heard Hartley's voice saying, "Come in, come in. Wonderful to see you. We just said good-bye to your husband."

My eyes snapped open. Helen stood inside the door, which the manager was holding open for her. I could see her staring up at him with her mouth slightly open. She said, "My husband?"

"Helen!" I called her name, waved, and rushed to join her.

She looked at me in surprise. She said, "Harry was here?"

"Yes. You just missed him. We were having a coffee together before he left for the airport."

Her expression said: Give me an answer, get me out of this.

"We're just going to have some lunch," I told Hartley, and then, before I could correct myself, "and then go shopping."

"Shopping?" he said, as if politely correcting a foreign tourist not yet aware of the local customs. "I'm afraid you don't have much time. Soon everything will be closed until four."

Helen recovered quickly. "You've forgotten, Steven—Peter and Sal have invited us over for a drink and a swim after lunch." She took my arm and steered me to the stairs. "Nice seeing you again, Arthur," she said over her shoulder. He was still holding the front door open when we started the climb up to the restaurant on the second floor.

We reached the top landing and the restaurant entrance when she took my hand, pulled me around the corner and pushed the elevator button. "I'm not hungry," she whispered. "Are you?"

I was, but I wasn't going to say so. We slipped into the elevator and she pressed the button marked seven.

She started laughing as soon as we made it to my room. She couldn't stop. Nerves and a hangover. She sat on the bed but didn't want to make love, she just asked me for a bottle of water. I got one from the room fridge. She immediately drank half of it down as if she'd been marooned on a desert island, and then lay back on the bed and closed her eyes. I drew the curtains shut and lay down beside her. We both had our clothes on; the air conditioner roared and clanked on the wall. She gave a chuckle which sounded half like a sob, but it was all right: her lips were smiling. She asked me to wake her before four.

I held her hand as we lay there like a middle-aged married couple (although I never felt middle-aged around her), while I kept half an eye open, like a dog sleeping by its mistress, on the alert. But all I had to be alert for was the passage of time, the change of color through the curtains as the sun moved down across the Gulf.

I must have dozed; when I opened my eyes the room was dark. I checked my watch: only five. It didn't make sense; I rolled gently off the bed and padded to the window. I pulled the curtains open and stared out at an impenetrable, dull yellow glow, uncomprehending.

Helen murmured something I didn't catch. I turned to her. She was lying on her side, staring at the window. She said, "It's a sandstorm."

"What does it mean?" I asked, stupidly.

"It means we aren't going anywhere for a while. Except to dinner. I'm hungry. Do you think the restaurant's open?"

"Yes."

So we went down to the second floor. We were the only diners. The waiter showed us to our table. It was like old times, during our scuba lessons, except for the yellow light pouring through the windows like sand through a trapdoor.

We ate hurriedly and went back upstairs. We stood together looking out at the storm. There was no sound; perhaps the sand deadened it. Helen asked me to open the balcony door a crack. A gust of wind hit me in the face like abrasive. I slid the door back shut.

"It's like a sign," she said.

"Of what?"

"I don't know. That we have to stay here; that we can't leave; that we don't have to worry about the future." Her eyes flashed and her long red hair shone like fire in the light.

The dingy room disappeared. The two of us alone had existence, and we existed only for each other. We made love. The room darkened and then glowed a dull gold when, through the clouds of sand, the Gulf caught the setting sun.

We lay I don't know how long afterward, until I got up and again tested the balcony; the wind had died. The air was clearing: I could pick out the streetlights along Pepsi Road almost to the corniche. I leaned on the railing and smoked a cigarette. When I stepped back in Helen was under the sheet. She could be modest after sex. I said, "Harry asked me to talk you into leaving."

"What did you tell him?"

"I said I'd try to convince you to move to Manama. He thought it was a good idea."

She laughed. "Both of you want me to go to Manama. For different reasons."

"Why not? It's just across the bridge. You could put up at a hotel there. Harry's right: Bahrain is safer than Saudi. And we'd see each other every night."

"And Harry?"

"He'd probably come across on weekends."

"You'd have more of me, then, wouldn't you? The ratio would be reversed. A bit like owning stock: you'd be the main shareholder."

"I want to be the sole owner," I replied, before I realized the offensiveness of the simile.

"How long would it last? A week, a month—until we're all evacuated?"

"Maybe sooner. I'm flying to Riyadh tomorrow morning. The next day I'm seeing al Badawi and flying back. This contract's our ticket out. If Harry's right, my firm won't want me here much longer, anyway. I can't vet clients without a working consulate."

"Where would we go? Los Angeles?"

"Why not?"

"And Harry?"

"Harry can go where he likes."

After a minute she said, quietly, "They've brought in divorce in Ireland. I imagine you know that."

My heart leapt. "I think I remember reading about it."

She slipped off the bed, pulled on my robe and joined me by the window.

"You mustn't think I'm a good Catholic, just because I'm Irish. I'm not. A good Catholic wouldn't live in a country where their religion is against the law."

"So you don't have . . . religious scruples?"

"Oh, I suppose I do . . . but I've broken so many rules already—large and small—what's one more?"

"Divorce is easy in the U.S."

"I know. Marriage vows don't mean much there, do they?"

She said it like an accusation, and for the first time I felt disappointed in her. It was as if she'd betrayed both of us by hitting me where I was vulnerable, where I'd failed. I said, "My vows were serious enough when I made them. Things don't always work out the way you plan. She wanted a divorce more than I did. It was she who was unfaithful—not me." I turned away. "I'm not saying it was all her fault. She was young. She probably thought she'd married someone exciting. I worked all the time. Then the crash came. I can't have been easy to live with. We both valued success."

Helen said, "I'm sorry, Steven. I didn't mean to be hurtful." She held me, then stepped out onto the balcony. "LA," she said, to the night air. "Cars and motorways."

"There are nice places. Santa Monica, Pacific Palisades. Places near the beach."

"At least *she* betrayed *you*."

"What do you mean?"

"It had to make it easier for you. To leave her. To divorce her." She turned to face me. "I'm the one betraying Harry. He's loyal. As loyal as they come. He wouldn't betray me in a thousand years. He'd never ask for a divorce."

"Do you still love him?"

"You know the difference between being in love and loving. And even love—does anything last? Does anything stay the same? For a long time I was still fond of him, maybe I even still loved him a little—when I didn't hate him. I hated his cynicism, his rants, his work—I think he hated it, too—and his drinking. Most of all I hated his lack of hope." She used the past tense for her hate, and I interpreted it to mean that she'd gone beyond even that. Hate's the opposite face of love: a truly dead relationship's too cold to keep something that strong alive. She leaned back against the balcony railing. "I've been half dead for so long. It's been like being—like being anesthetized. Without hope of waking up. Like this country." She pressed back farther, her body arching. "But I finally woke up. You woke me." She released the railing, holding out her hands. "There's some hope now, for us, for the future—isn't there?"

"Be careful," I said, grabbing her arms. "This balcony . . . it's as old as the hotel. It can't be that secure."

"I don't want things to be secure," but she swung forward against me. "You want us to be secure, don't you?"

She moved a little away. "What does it mean? For you?"

"Security?"

"Does it mean money? This big contract?"

"That's what makes it all happen."

"What else?"

I didn't understand her.

She said, "You want me . . . and money. What else do you want?"

Holding her, seven floors above that third world Arab town, I didn't have an answer.

"There must be more."

I felt like a candidate sitting an examination for which I hadn't pre-pared. I said, "Isn't that enough?"

She looked away. "I'm just a woman. And money, by itself, never meant that much. Even Harry, in his way . . . I think he wants some-thing more."

"Maybe you always had enough. Harry's spent his life on a govern-ment payroll. With a rock-solid pension at the end."

"What if you don't get the contract, if it doesn't work out? What do we have, then?"

I thought she meant finances, but that was one failure I wasn't going to face. I didn't blame myself for not having a backup plan. You can mitigate risk until the cows come home, but in business the bot-tom line is faith. You need to know, in your gut, that you'll sell your product. You need to know you'll close the deal. I said, "I'll have that contract signed, in my hand, Monday afternoon."

"Badawi didn't just come from me. Harry's involved."

"He had to vet her."

"Harry's deals don't always work out. It might be like fairy gold: it might disappear in the morning."

I smiled. She was superstitious. Banshees and fairy gold. "It's not going to disappear."

"You'll be careful? Riyadh's more dangerous than Khobar. More dangerous than Qatif."

"I'll be there less than two days. I'm staying at a good hotel, the Al Khozama. And I'll see Badawi alone, not with Harry." I held her closer. "You'll have to make a decision when I get back: about Manama, and me."

"Two days—it's not long."

"If this deal goes through, and the place goes south—as the embassy thinks it will—I'd be crazy to stick around."

She pulled away, and stepped back into the room. She said, "You left me once before, remember?"

I followed and slid the door closed. I protested, "I didn't mean I'd leave you."

"That's one thing Harry would never do." She sounded disappointed, as if she'd finally found one virtue of Harry's I couldn't live up to. "Come on," she said, "it's getting late, and you have a plane to catch tomorrow morning. You'd better take me home."

She insisted on leaving. She didn't want to talk anymore. In the car I tried again, unsuccessfully, to make her commit to Manama, and to accept my commitment to her. I was reckless. You should never try to sell something when you're desperate—especially yourself.

For some reason the religious police were out in force, and I had to detour to avoid their roadblocks. When I finally drove her into her consulate compound, and kissed her good night, it felt like a kiss good-bye, and I almost lost control of the car on the way back to the hotel, gunning too fast and too close past a car full of Saudi teenagers, shouting insults at me out of their windows.

CHAPTER ELEVEN

At eight the next morning, at the airport, I picked up the morning paper. Splashed on the front page was a photograph of Dr. Ali, dead.

Friday was the Arab Sabbath, and travel was light. The plane to Riyadh was more than half empty and I was the only Westerner on board. I finished reading the paper before we were airborne.

The *Arab News* is the country's English-language paper, and of course, under government editorial control. The story was that the security services, acting on a tip, had found Ali hiding in a village in the Eastern Province. They surrounded the house, and ordered him to come out. The usual shoot-out occurred.

Despite its being a close-up photograph, showing only the head and shoulders, I wouldn't have known it was Ali without the headline. The quality was poor. It had been taken at night, or in the dark, with an inadequate flash. There was little contrast or detail; even the focus was out. The face was that of a male corpse, bearded, the cheeks spread out, flaccid, the eyes half opened, dead.

It made for a thoughtful flight south. Although I felt no grief, there was something like a sense of personal loss. Not the kind one feels when a friend, or even an acquaintance, dies. Rather, the kind one might feel when a companion in shipwreck died—a shipwreck you had both survived. He'd been part of the picture—Helen's picture, too. A part of our shared experience. We didn't have enough yet to be able to afford losing any. Even Dr. Ali.

Politically, I wasn't sure what it meant. Other than that the Shia were farther up the creek than ever, and that the central government was still in some sort of control.

The aging Saudia jet made a bumpy landing in Riyadh. The country's major airport had been a regional marvel when built: hanging gardens, fountains, soaring roofs—the usual Arab dreamland overkill of the seventies, when oil was high and the population still low. Now the plants hung dusty and dry. A million feet had frayed the carpets, and the black spaces from the missing ceiling panels looked like the gaps between an old Bedu's teeth. The infrastructure, like so much else, was rotting.

Something was wrong with the air-conditioning; the air smelled stale. But at least it was cool. The moment I walked out of the airport, the automatic doors sliding shut behind me, the Nejdi heat hit. It was like being on a spit in a rotisserie: the sun radiating down from the sky and up from the concrete. The humidity was zero, the air dry as a fossilized bone.

Californians dislike taking taxis when they can drive themselves. I'd arranged to pick up a rental car at the airport and was pleased to see it was a fairly clean Honda. I turned the air conditioner on full and headed into town.

I'd visited the capital once before, back in '93. The airport in those days was marooned in the desert, twenty minutes from the edge of town. In the intervening years the city had grown to meet it. I drove past miles of Arab suburban sprawl: sand-colored strip malls and sand-colored concrete block villas, half of them half-finished, construction abandoned. New ruins surrounded by litter and broken walls.

The checkpoints started farther into town, and the traffic was almost as bad as LA; oil in the Kingdom was still as cheap as water. It was an hour before I pulled into the parking lot of the Swiss-built Al Khozama Hotel. The facade was unchanged, but one look at the lobby told me all I needed to know about the local business climate. Despite being in a still-fashionable business district, it was almost deserted. I checked in, turned up the room's air conditioner, took a shower, and pulled out al Badawi's file for one more review before meeting her the next morning.

After lunch I lay down to take a nap. I'd just fallen asleep when the phone rang. It was Harry.

"You're probably wondering how I knew you were at the Al Khozama."

"You're right. I am."

"Helen—who else? She just called. Wants me to make sure you're safe and sound. She saw the news about the latest bombing on CNN. You heard about it?"

"No."

"Happened this morning. The usual thing. Suicide car bomb in front of a Western compound. On the other side of town. Massive: they can't get as close in as they used to, so they're packing more explosive. A few Western casualties. I think we've gotten positives on four so far." He was as matter-of-fact as a coalition statement from Iraq: "A suicide bomber north of Baghdad killed seventeen Iraqis at a police recruitment station. In a separate incident, two American soldiers were killed and three wounded by an improvised explosive device." You had to let your imagination color in the blood. I told him, "I read about Ali in the paper."

There was a moment of silence on the line, then, "We can discuss that tonight. I'm heading back up tomorrow morning. Why don't you come over for dinner and see how the other half lives? The embassy compound's decent, and we've got real booze."

"Thanks, Harry, I appreciate the offer, but I'd planned to eat here. I've got some work to do tonight. . . ."

"Well, come over for a drink after. They won't have that at your hotel. We should talk. And I can fill you in a little more about your big client. The front desk can give you directions. Just ask for me at the gate. You'll be on the list."

He hung up before I could object further.

I had no desire to have a drink with Harry. On the other hand, he might have something useful to tell me about al Badawi. I tried to resume my nap, but it was hopeless, so I went over again the various funds I had to offer that were appropriate for someone in Badawi's financial position. After dinner I got directions for the embassy and drove there in my rented car.

The U.S. Embassy occupied a huge walled compound on the south side of town. The security was tighter than Dhahran, but I was on their list, and in a few minutes Harry was showing me around the well-tended grounds. He was staying in a government-issue guest suite about the size of my hotel room in Khobar, but modern, characterless and clean. It was on the ground floor and had a little fenced-in yard. He poured us both a drink (he had a head start) and then at his suggestion we sat down at a plastic table on the patio. On the table was a creased copy of that morning's *Arab News*.

"I like the heat," he told me. "Too many years in hot climates—I got used to it. I'll miss it in Ireland."

"So you still think we're going to evacuate?"

He grunted. "We'll evacuate all right. It just may be a little messier than planned." He nodded toward the paper. "You spent three days with Ali. Do you think that's him?"

I picked it up. The paper was already desiccated; it crackled like the wings of some insect. I looked at the blurred picture again. "I don't know," I said. "It could be almost anyone. It's certainly a corpse."

"Exactly. Almost anyone."

"What do you think?"

"The royals in charge don't want us to leave. We're propping them up. The photograph, the alleged shoot-out, the whole works: I'd lay money it's a put-up job. That corpse is no more Ali than I am. But it might work. At least, for a while."

"What do you mean, 'it might work'?"

"The government's pretty good at manipulating public opinion. Remember the cartoon craze, those Danish cartoons of the Prophet Mohammed? The reaction was hatched in Mecca. Arabs will believe almost anything—for a while. The locals might buy this Ali story. Washington's already buying it. At least, they're trying to convince themselves to buy it."

"But the evacuation's still on."

"The decision's been put off. When in doubt, delay. This has gone above the state department. The administration's beginning to realize what a collapse means: a Taliban government with oil money. There are only two scenarios on how to deal with that. Containment, which won't work, because of the oil, and an outright invasion, like Afghanistan. Both are so bad, they're trying to pretend our friendly royals will stay in power."

"Will they?"

He laughed sourly. "Hell, we can't even keep them in-country. Half the royal family are already gone, and the king has a fueled-up jet on standby at the airport."

That was Harry all over: Harry wearing the worst-case scenario on his sleeve, the Harry that Helen couldn't stand. I said, "There must be another option. Look at it from a business point of view. We're their market. They need us as much as we need them. There must be someone reasonable, some group, we could support. A third party."

"When I was young, we called it a 'third force.'"

"Whatever. There must be someone . . . from the business class, maybe, or the army."

"The business class is interested in business. The smarter ones are sending their money out. You know that, you're helping them. The army's worthless. Window dressing."

Politics has never been one of my main interests. I've always voted Republican in the same way I've always worn a tie to work; it's the thing to do in my profession. But Harry's pessimism, as usual, was getting to me—like the heat. I said, "Then what's next?"

"Another coup. Nature abhors a vacuum. The leaders might be the people directing the suicide bombs, the guys just back from Iraq. Or they might be the Wahhabis in Buraydah. For sure, one will try to co-opt the other."

He shifted in his chair, cradling his drink on his chest. "If Washington makes us dig in. . . . It won't be some UN peacekeeping mission. It'll be worse than Iraq. A lot worse. Any option's better, even splitting the country up."

It was an opportunity I couldn't resist. I said, "As Ali wanted to do."

"As he tried."

"What if he were still around? If that picture's fake?"

"He's probably somewhere," he said dismissively.

I wanted to see Harry squirm. I said, "So maybe we should have supported him."

"He never had a chance with his little crew and their popguns."

"We made sure of that, didn't we? With the U.S. Army and the Air Force. If he were around now, would you support him?"

"I'm commerce," he snapped. "Not state or the agency. You don't understand how things work. The people who provide that kind of support follow orders. It would have to be okayed by state, by the CIA, by the NSA—the whole alphabet soup and the administration. Everyone and their aunt would have to sign off. It would never happen. What the fuck's that?"

He sat up, staring toward a corner of the fence, then picked a coaster up off the table and threw it into the darkness. There was a thud as it hit a wooden plank.

"Thought I saw something move," he said. "Thought it might be a camel spider. Nasty things. Big as your hand. The hot concrete attracts them after dark. They probably don't spray the place enough." He slumped back in his chair and continued heavily, "Where was I? Oh, right. It would be the long shot of the century. Washington would never go for it."

I was tired of talking politics. It was like discussing the future of a company in a bear market after you'd unloaded their stock. You had to move on. I was about to bring up Badawi when he said, "Did you ask Helen if she'd leave?"

"Yes, I did. She refused."

He sighed, staring into the darkness. "This country's hard on women, harder on women than it is on men. They're restricted. They have to put up with a lot of crap that we don't. It gets most of them down. Helen's more of a fighter—or maybe just more of an idealist. She'd like to see us do something. Like you . . . find someone to support."

"Isn't that admirable?"

"Maybe. I don't know about realistic. Everyone would like to do something."

"Including you?"

"Sure, including me."

"What, Harry? What would you like to do?"

He gave a sudden, barking laugh. "Retire. That's what I'd like to do. Preferably someplace hot." He sat back, and his face settled into a thoughtful cast. "Or at least someplace warm." Was he thinking of Ireland? I'd always heard the Irish climate was cool, or cold. He continued, "Anyway, Helen's going, whether she wants to or not. We all are. That's the main reason I asked you over tonight. As soon as you get back, book a plane ticket out. When the crunch comes, it'll be a mass exodus. You might not be able to take the bridge. You need a fall-back."

"How long do you think we have?"

He shook his head. "Could happen anytime. Days, a couple of weeks, maybe a month. When it goes, it'll be fast. The inside's hollowed out. I spent an hour yesterday afternoon with a Colonel Ahmed in the Mukharabat. A private matter. You could call it an errand of mercy. Bailing out Joe."

I didn't get it. I said, "Bailing out Joe?"

"He's normally discreet . . . unless he's been drinking. He must have bad-mouthed the regime to the wrong potential client. The client was an informer—half this country's informing on the other half. Anyway, they threw him in jail. Didn't believe him when he said he was a Yank. Idiot was carrying his old Saudi ID."

"Is he okay?"

"He is now. He dropped a few names and they let him use his cell phone. Ahmed's an old pal of mine, so I got him sprung. The colonel and I had an interesting talk. He asked me if I could help him get a visa to the States. I said I'd do what I could. The point is, when someone like him asks someone like me for a visa, in their office. . . . It's another sign. It's the end."

He took a drink, then continued, "By the time they reopen the embassy, I'll be retired. In Limerick." He made it sound like just the next in an unbroken string of third world postings. Then he raised his glass, and his mouth rose with it in a crooked grin. "But we still have a concert to look forward to."

"I'm sorry?"

"In a long career I've been in a couple of countries where a friendly government was about to fall. We couldn't get our heads around it until it was too late. As a result, the machinery kept rolling up until the very end—no one bothered to stop it. That's what's happening here."

I thought I knew what he meant. "The American businessmen's party," I said.

"Exactly. What did we have to party about? But there's more coming. How do you like Schumann?"

"Schumann?"

"The International Concert Committee. Long-term, cultured expats, aided and abetted by their embassies. They organize concerts in Riyadh and Dhahran. They fly in performers from the UK, Germany and so on."

"You mean, professional concert artists?"

"That's right. Oh, not first tier. Little chamber groups just starting out, or guys that spend half their time teaching." He shook his head. "They're showing up next week, believe it or not. Two Brits. A singer and a pianist. We wasted an hour today discussing it. The British Embassy thinks it's important for morale to bring them in. They're asking us to provide security. The ambassador said no to Riyadh, but gave Dhahran the thumbs-up."

"They're coming to Dhahran to sing and play the piano?"

"We're talking lieder. Art. And the Brits. Stiff upper lip. Never," he said gloomily, "underestimate the Brits. It's next Thursday, and I can't go. I expect to be out of town. If you're both still here, would you take Helen? It'll be on the consulate compound, but she should have an escort—it'd make the security guys happier."

"Sure."

"Thanks. She's not really into classical music—more traditional Irish—but it'd be an outing for her. My first wife, she was into classical. I was divorced . . . you knew that?"

He'd never told me about his private life. I wondered how long he'd been drinking before I arrived.

"I think Helen mentioned it."

"My first wife was an American. New Yorker. Sharp, and beautiful, too, although not as good-looking as Helen. She thought that marrying a 'diplomat' was a great catch. She hadn't counted on the assignments in Colombia, in Pakistan, in all the shitholes of the earth. So one day she had an affair with someone she thought would get her out, take her someplace better." He gave a humorless chuckle. "I still send her alimony checks, but thank God inflation's taken the sting out of that."

So we'd both been cuckolded, and both divorced. We had that much more in common—more than his present wife.

He said, "I was single for years. But as soon as I met Helen, I knew. And, for some reason, she actually fell in love with me. So I went from a New Yorker to a girl from the back of beyond in Ireland. She's from a village the size of this patch of yard, outside of Limerick. You know she's Catholic. Irish Catholic. Loyal. They stick with you. Through thick and thin."

He spoke as if making a point, almost as if he knew about me and Helen. As if he wanted to deflate my hopes. I wanted to erode his certainty, if it was that—maybe he had only hope, too. I began deceptively, "You're a lucky man."

"You can say that again."

"And she's still a young woman."

"Fairly young. Younger than me."

"She's still in the prime of life. Lots of men your age would find it a challenge."

For a moment he didn't answer, and I wondered if I'd gone too far. He sank back further in his chair. "Sex," he said. "I had a lot of women before Helen, maybe too many. I took it where I could find it. I wasn't very, what's the word . . . fastidious. In the end, you can get beyond sex."

It sounded like a confidence. I wondered: Is this as close as he can get to saying he's incapable?

He said, "We were going to talk business. Zainab al Badawi. Can I freshen your drink?"

I was ready for another. I was ready to drink him under the table, if I had to. "Sure."

He came back and handed me my glass, and sat down carefully—he was beginning to look a little the worse for wear. But he focused. He said, "I've never met her, but Helen has, at her at-homes. Helen says she's impressive. A woman with authority. Rich and unmarried. So she's her own woman. I've met the type before. I advise you to avoid politics. She'll bend your ear for an hour with an anti-American rant."

"I usually stick to investments."

"Just as well. She has a reputation for being hardheaded, and I'm pretty sure she'll know the kind of deal she wants, and what it's worth. I wouldn't be surprised if, considering the size of her investment, she asked for a reduction in fees. You should try to meet her halfway. If I were you, I wouldn't try for a substantial off-contract commission."

It took a second to sink in. It was offensive, even for him. I said, "I've never asked for an off-contract commission. That's not the way I work."

"Really?" He shrugged his shoulders. "You must be offering the best deals in town, then. I've always believed when in Rome, do as the Romans do."

"I believe in the Foreign Corrupt Practices Act."

He stared at me for a moment, as if he couldn't believe what I'd just said. Then his face broke into a grin and he laughed.

"What's so funny?"

"Nothing, Steve. You've got an admirable attitude. It may just be a little too pure for this world. 'Corrupt practices'—it's a pretty fuzzy legal term. In a lot of places it's just greasing the wheels. It might even result in a positive outcome." He waved his arm around the little garden. "We're in the Middle East. That Act was written in Washington under Jimmy Carter, by people who didn't understand, and will never understand, how countries like this operate."

"It's how I operate. Legitimately. I follow the rules: the Corrupt

Practices Act, the Patriot Act, you name it. I'm here to make money, not break the law."

"Hell, you were selling mutual funds during the boom. Don't tell me you never gave a buy recommendation you wouldn't take yourself."

How much did he know? He was in commerce: it wouldn't be hard for him to discover that the SEC had investigated my old firm, if he were inclined to dig. But they hadn't investigated me, not yet—as far as I knew. My reply was as limp as my shirt: "A buy recommendation is just that: a recommendation. No one has to take it."

"Sure, I understand." He leaned closer, as if he knew he'd offended me by a misunderstanding, and wanted to correct it with another confidence. "Listen, corruption's part of this environment, like the oil that seeps up through the sand, or the heat. You don't have to be part of it. But you have to take it into account. You have to deal with it. Badawi's a businesswoman, but she's also a Saudi. My advice is: meet her halfway. Don't get offended if she makes some suggestion you don't like. She's not going to be in the mood for a self-righteous American."

I gulped down the rest of my drink—now warm—and stood up. "Thanks for the advice. I appreciate it. But my appointment with al Badawi's at ten in the morning. I'd better be heading off."

He walked me to the gate. As I got into my car, he leaned on the door and said, "Steve, you didn't mention the deal to Joe, did you?"

"No. Why?"

"Oh, they had him in long enough to get rough, if they wanted to. The Badawis like their business kept confidential."

His suggestion that the police might be interested in my investment contract struck me as ludicrous. I'd detected, at last, the result of one too many whiskeys. Real drunks can keep walking and talking long after they cease to make sense. I said, "If your assessment's correct, the police have bigger fish to fry than an investment contract."

"Just procedure. Need to know."

I couldn't resist one last dig: "I thought the ambassador said the police don't get rough."

"It was the Mukharabat, not the police. An outfit like that always has a few sadistic bastards." As I strapped on my seat belt, he said,

"Stick to the main roads tomorrow. Check out of the hotel as late as you can. After you see Badawi, head straight for the airport. It looks quiet out there, but there's no telling what's going to happen, or when."

I was on the road at half past nine the next morning. My appointment was at my client's home, in a residential district called Sulimaniyah, not far from the hotel. It was a good neighborhood, well kept up, the streets recently resurfaced. Her house was hidden from sight by a high wall extending the length of the block. I parked, got out and walked up to a heavy green gate. I wore a standard business suit and I felt as if I'd dressed for Antarctica. I pressed the button on a speakerphone. A voice squawked and I gave my name. An electric bolt shot back. I pushed the gate open.

A Filipina maid in uniform met me at the front door and ushered me through a hall to what I assumed was a living room, but on a massive scale. Pompous furniture—reproductions of fancy old-world European chairs, tables, sofas that would have filled two or three normal-size rooms—were just scattered objects here. I didn't want to take a seat before my client appeared, so I ambled around, inspecting the place. There were several heavy Oriental vases that must have cost money, and some original Arab paintings on the walls. The decor suggested wealth but a very mixed taste.

I was staring at one of the pictures when I heard someone enter. I turned around. A tall Arab woman in a Western-style business suit walked toward me, holding out her hand. I thought immediately of Harry's description: authoritative. "Mr. Kemp," she said. I met her halfway, and she introduced herself: Dr. Zainab al Badawi. Her handshake was firm. She had a purposeful walk like Helen's, but any resemblance ended there. She was strongly built with a heavy figure. Her face was large, long, and carried a shrewd and penetrating expression. The suit accentuated the manliness in her bearing and appearance. She emanated the confidence of someone used to command.

She called for tea, and we made small talk for a few minutes, but as soon as the tea arrived she was all business. We sat next to each other on a sofa, and I spread out my brochures on the table in front. I gave her a brief rundown of the various funds my company managed. She asked several questions, all cogent, in English that was fluent and correct but strongly accented. She was interested more in long-term growth than short-term capital gain, and was most interested in funds with conservative portfolios: blue-chip stocks. She wasn't interested in funds suitable for short-term trading on the part of the client.

Finally, she said, "Mr. Kemp, you were highly recommended. I shall make the investment I'd planned with your firm."

The deal was as good as done; I could have jumped with joy. Professionalism kept me on the couch. She continued, "I want to thank you for traveling to Riyadh to meet me. I am aware it's much safer in the Eastern Province."

Riyadh was her hometown; I'd seen little about it to compliment, but I could at least suggest that it wasn't worse than my part of the country. I said, "I'm not so sure of that. I had a run-in with a terrorist in Qatif."

She asked me to explain. I gave her a brief account, leaving Harry out of the picture. When I'd finished, she said, "I am very sorry you had that experience. A foreign businessman should be welcomed, not exposed to danger. The Shia have always been a problem in this country. It is not natural for us and the Shia to live together. I do not dislike them, personally. But of course their faith disgusts me. It is a corrupt form of Islam. Nothing in the Koran or the Hadith explains or condones their practices. But who can blame them if they wish to escape Al Saud? Who doesn't? You are a Christian, Mr. Kemp?"

I hadn't intended to have a conversation about religion. But it's always a good idea to form some kind of personal relationship with a major client. I knew that admitting to being an atheist was a sure way to shock and alienate a Saudi, so I said, "Yes. A Catholic."

"My roommate in college, in Illinois, was a Catholic. She believed that if she told her sins to her . . . imam?"

"Priest."

"Her priest, that Allah would forgive her. But it would only work if she intended not to sin again. I've forgotten the exact term she used, but that's what she meant, what she believed."

An ancient phrase from my childhood catechism surfaced on cue. I said, "I think she meant, 'a firm purpose of amendment.'"

Dr. al Badawi smiled; I think she warmed to me. "Yes, the intention must be firm. Of course she sinned again. We all do. But it was the resolution that counted.

"I think that faith, to be effective, must have a positive effect on the believer. On the spiritual life, and also on the practical life. I thought her religion strange, in some ways—you must excuse me, I am not a Christian—but it had a positive effect on her character. I respected it. We must all try, and try again, even when we fail, to do better. This holds true with all our activities. Have you ever heard of Gamal Abdel Nasser?"

I said, "The Egyptian leader?"

"Yes. He gave his country its independence from the British—like your George Washington—and invented Arab nationalism. If he had lived, the Arabs would be more developed than they are today. Many of us still work toward his goals. Like the sinner, we fail. But we continue the struggle. If the Shia wish to separate from the Al Saud, I wish them luck. They must follow their path to development, as we follow ours."

She leaned over and closed the pamphlets on the table. "Now, please come with me. I want to show you who this investment is for."

We got up and I followed her to a nearby table covered with several expensively framed photographs of Arab children, most of them in their early teens.

"These are my nephews and nieces," she said. "They were all born in America; they are all Saudi and American citizens. Soon their parents—my brothers—will take their families to your country. *Inshallah*, they will prosper. But no one can tell the future. My investment is their children's insurance. No matter what happens, when they grow up, they will have enough money to attend university. They will be able to buy a house. They will not be rich, but they will not be poor: they will have enough to develop their life. It is my gift to them."

I said, "That's very generous. And you? Will you also settle in America?"

A frown passed across her heavy features. "No. I will remain here. I have no children; I only have to take care of myself. I have been doing that most of my life. A change of government—in this case, the fall of the American puppet regime—is not a reason to desert my own country." She reached over to a low table and picked up a book. It was a coffee-table book, with a studio portrait from the fifties of a square-faced, determined-looking Arab on the cover. "When the British invaded Suez," she said, "Nasser did not hurry to find refuge in a foreign country. He stood and fought. That is what we must do now, in the way that Allah has given us."

"Whom do you expect to fight?"

"The Americans and the fundamentalists. Both are our enemies. The first to independence and national identity. The second to progress of any kind. Now, let us finish our business. My office is through here."

We walked through a tiled passage to a small office with a desk, bookshelves and a computer. She sat down at the desk and pulled out two documents and a large corporate checkbook. She said, "We have discussed the two funds I wish to invest in. There is no need, is there, for me to put those directions in writing?"

"No. I'll take care of that myself, dividing your investment equally in both. I'll give you a receipt now, and send you a complete contract with all the details from Manama."

"Good." She handed me one of the documents. "This letter contains instructions to add my two brothers, as the parents and guardians of their children, as co-owners with signature authority."

I took a look at it. It appeared very straightforward. "That will be no problem," I said.

She opened the checkbook. "I understand you require a check in U.S. dollars, drawn on a local bank, made out to Winston Investments?"

"Yes."

"Is the Saudi American Bank acceptable?"

"It's the bank I prefer." My heart was thumping in my chest; I surreptitiously wiped my palms on my trousers.

In front of me she wrote the check, for eighteen million U.S. dollars. Her signature was large, with an Arabic flourish. When she finished she laid down the pen, but kept her hand on the check. "How do you normally forward your clients' investments?" she asked.

"I deposit them in my firm's account in Manama, and from there wire them to my company in Los Angeles. The wire goes through a correspondent bank in New York, but it normally doesn't take more than a couple of days."

She nodded. "In this case, I must ask for a slight change in procedure."

"A change?"

"You may be aware that Islam requires us to donate a percentage of our income—it is called *zakat*—to charity. In Saudi, this is difficult. The government controls all charities within the country. It is not transparent, so it is impossible to know where your contribution has been sent or how it is being used. And now, thanks to American pressure, it is impossible to send money directly to Islamic charities outside the country.

"For many years I have had a small account in a bank in Kyrenia, in Turkish Cyprus. My father once thought of building a holiday home there. He was fond of the British, and respected the modern Turkish state. I intend to use that account to send my *zakat* directly to the charities I choose."

I knew nothing of Cyprus, and didn't get what any of this had to do with her investment. "I'm afraid I don't understand," I said.

"It is very simple. Instead of wiring the money from Manama to your correspondent bank in New York, you will wire it to my bank in Kyrenia. I will then send the manager my instructions to send all but nine hundred thousand to your company. That amount—five percent of my investment—will remain there, and eventually I will disburse it to charity."

I stared down at her. Intelligence types and most Arabs have one thing in common: they engage in conspiracy theories. Intelligence types because of political pressures and also because it's their job; Arabs because they have always believed in conspiracies and always will. But businessmen have to keep both feet on the ground. It's necessary for us to size up people, their interests and their motivations, realistically. Sober observation is more likely to lead to a correct assessment than politics or ingrained suspicion. I didn't think for a moment that Dr. Zainab al Badawi, the co-owner of a major construction and contracting group, was contemplating anything illicit.

Nevertheless, what she was suggesting was definitely against the spirit, and maybe the letter, of U.S. government regulations. Regulations designed to halt the hidden channeling of funds—especially from Saudi Arabia—to Islamic charities. Because of the size of this transaction, if the SEC or the Office of Homeland Security found out, there would probably be an investigation. My track record wasn't clean enough that I could look forward to that with equanimity. The first thing they'd suspect would be money laundering. I'd seen and talked to my client and I thought her credible. The feds would not have my advantages, and they would not be predisposed to my assessment. If there were an investigation, losing my job would be the most favorable outcome.

"I'm afraid," I said, "that's against the regulations."

"It is the condition for my investment."

We discussed it in a businesslike manner for a few minutes. This was a time for diplomacy and tact, not to dig in one's heels. I needed to convince her there would be serious repercussions, and I had to do it in a way that conveyed that a kickback would not solve the problem.

I brought up two practical points. The first was that so much money coming into the States from an Arab account in Cyprus would be bound to attract the attention of the authorities in Washington. The second followed: if the auditors checked the trail back, they would discover the five percent still in Kyrenia. That would be enough to trigger an investigation. It would turn up nothing, but her funds would be sequestered and I would probably end up under investigation. I didn't emphasize the last point, but we were developing a business relationship, and it was as well that she realized that we both had something to lose.

She was a woman used to finding solutions to operational problems. She solved mine on the spot. First, she would direct the bank manager in Kyrenia to add my name to her account, so that the transfer would not have, as she put it, an "Arab taint." Second, so that any audit would not find any money missing, she would keep the *zakat*—the five percent—in the account for three months. I argued for a year, and we compromised on six months. By that time I knew I'd been outmaneuvered. She'd won.

She handed me the check and I wrote her a receipt. She filed it away in a drawer and handed me the other document.

"Here are the details of my account with the Turkish Anatolian Bank in Girne. The Turkish government changed the town's name after the occupation." She stood up. "I am glad we came to agreement, Mr. Kemp. But it must remain confidential, between you, me, and your company. You understand that, of course."

"Of course."

"And now, before you go, perhaps you would care to see the youngest beneficiary?"

We walked through the house to a room set up for a children's party, complete with a huge birthday cake and favors. There were several small Arab children, all well behaved, in the care of their Filipina nannies. A wide, curving staircase led to an upper floor, and shortly after we arrived a uniformed Filipina nurse appeared on the landing, holding her small charge in her arms. "Noora, my youngest brother's youngest daughter," al Badawi said. "Normally Saudis do not celebrate birthdays, but there is no stricture against it, and we should not be afraid of adopting customs which cause no harm, and bring happiness."

It was a pretty scene, if somewhat extravagant—the children were all dressed in very elaborate party costumes—until the nurse reached halfway down the stairs. Perhaps the child had seen the cake and presents; for whatever reason, she became impatient at the nurse's slow progress, and began to slap the woman's face with her small hands. She slapped as hard as she could, with one hand and then the other, over and over again. The nurse continued down, smiling under the deliberate little blows.

My client appeared to notice nothing wrong. The nurse reached us and let the little girl loose. Dr. al Badawi took me back to the original room, where I picked up my papers and briefcase, and then showed me to the front door. We both stepped outside, and she shook my hand. "Thank you, Mr. Kemp. You are an honest businessman—an honest American. Some would have asked for something extra. You did not. I shall call the bank manager in Kyrenia today, instruct him to add your name to my account, and tell him to expect the transfer shortly."

"I'm not sure how fast the wire will be from Manama to Cyprus."

"To Turkish Cyprus. I am sure there will be no problem. Good-bye."

CHAPTER TWELVE

I had two hours before I had to be at the airport, but I was abstracted—I had a lot to think about—and somewhere I made a wrong turn. The street signs were useless; unlike Dhahran, the signs in Riyadh were all in Arabic. The rental car had come complete with a map, but once I was lost it was of little help. After thirty minutes I found myself in an older, residential part of the city. I hadn't heard the noon prayer call over the roar of the air-conditioning, but it must have been about that time, for the streets were nearly deserted.

I was pretty sure I was going in the wrong direction, but there was no place to make a U-turn, so I turned off into a one-way side street, hoping to find a way back. It was the wrong decision. The road surface was uneven and I had to reduce speed. My left front tire fell into a pothole so deep I was afraid the suspension might break. Near the end of the street a car was parked a foot away from the curb; I thought at first I'd be able to drive around it, but the road was too narrow. There wasn't even a sidewalk on that side to drive over. The driver was nowhere to be seen.

There was only one lane, the way ahead was blocked, and there was no space in which to turn around. The only way out was to reverse.

Looking into my rearview mirror, I saw that another car had just parked near the street's entrance. The street was deserted; I couldn't be certain, but I didn't think there was anyone behind the wheel.

When you've been in an Arab country for a few months (except, maybe, in Iraq), the first thing you think about in that kind of situation is not danger, but incompetence and inconsideration. It's an automatic response, like saying "*Assalamu alaikum,*" or switching on the air conditioner the moment you get home. I sat there for a few moments, fuming, then decided to get out. The car in front was closest. Maybe I could find the driver.

I walked up the street, hoping to spot a little store or a café. But it was all residential; narrow doorways led into narrow apartment buildings. There wasn't a soul in sight.

The intersection was only a few yards away. I could see a two-way road without a median: it was just what I'd been looking for. I was beginning to feel a little claustrophobic. A few people, a little traffic, would be an improvement. I stepped ahead over the broken sidewalk.

The road was deserted except for two Arabs in *thobe*s, a block off to my left, moving quickly away. I thought: It's just past noon in Riyadh, prayer time in the Saudi capital—everyone's at the mosque. But as the sun beat down on my suit and on the cracked concrete, as the silence lengthened, anxiety began to rise steadily, as steadily as the heat. It was too quiet, too empty. As empty as Qatif.

Then I heard the roar of an approaching vehicle. A Humvee painted in desert camouflage. As it neared it slowed, the driver seeming to hesitate—it was on the opposite side of the road—then it careered through a sharp U-turn and braked to a halt in front of me.

The driver's door swung open and the driver stepped out: a short, well-built, attractive young blonde. She wore khaki fatigues, a regulation floppy-brimmed hat and captain's bars on her shoulders. She couldn't have been out of her twenties.

"You American?" she asked. Her accent was Midwestern.

"Yes, I am." I still had on my jacket and tie.

"I thought so. It sticks out a mile. It's not safe to be wandering around here. Do you have a car?"

"It's right behind. But I'm stuck on a one-way street. I'm blocked in on both sides."

The captain slammed her door, scanned the road, and marched around the Humvee. She carried the standard army-issue rifle in her hand; in one fluid movement she hoisted it onto her shoulder on its strap. She asked me for some ID.

I pulled out my wallet and showed her my California driver's license. She was so pretty, but also so militarily competent, that I wasn't sure whether I felt attracted, or intimidated, or both.

"Just wanted to make sure," she said. "What are you doing here?"

"I'm trying to get to the airport. I got lost."

"How did you get blocked in?"

"I don't know. The car in the rear just parked."

"How long have you been here?"

"Five minutes, maybe less."

"Let's take a look at your car."

I led the way back. The silence was pervasive. There still wasn't a soul in sight. The captain quietly slipped her rifle off her shoulder, into her arms. She peered intently at the buildings on each side, boxing us in. "There's a Hala sticker on the windshield," she said. "Is it rented?"

"Yes."

"Then dump it. Do you have anything inside?"

"Just my suitcase, a briefcase. . . ."

"Grab them. Quick."

I grabbed them. We marched back to her Humvee, the captain scanning all the time. "Get in," she told me.

She threw the jeep into gear and accelerated to the next intersection. Traffic was nonexistent; she made a left against a red light. "No point in becoming a target," she said. "I'm heading to the airport to meet and greet. I'd better take you with me."

"Thanks. I appreciate it."

It was my first time in a modern U.S. military jeep. I expected a Humvee to be loud, and it was, but it was also air-conditioned. The captain was a good driver, but fast—I got the impression she'd be happy to drive as fast as she could, right out of town, right out of the whole Arabian peninsula.

Once on the freeway she relaxed. I asked her her name. "Captain Cathy Cathcart," she said, and the alliteration made me smile. It seemed to underline her young voice, her blue eyes and fresh skin, her youth. I said, "I thought you traveled in pairs."

"We do, most of the time. But we're short-manned, especially in town, and my sergeant's on morphine. A camel spider the size of my hand bit him last night. Anyway, this is just a pickup, and Riyadh's not an official combat zone—yet." She added, with a touch of bitterness, "Saudi's one of our big allies in the War on Terror." I asked her where she was from, and she cast me a suspicious look.

"We've got strict orders not to talk to journalists."

"I'm a businessman."

"That's what I figured. My father's a businessman." I thought, she's probably not older than twenty-five. To her, I'm a father figure. She said, "I'm from Kansas City. What about you?"

"Los Angeles. But I've visited Kansas City on business. I liked it."

"I don't see how you could do better. It sure beats this place."

"Are you stationed here?"

"Yes, but we're almost all TDY—temporary duty assignments. Most of us are out at Al Kharj, in the middle of nowhere. I'm lucky. I live in town at the Suwaiket compound. The army's taken it over. I actually volunteered—just wanted to see a little of the world." She gave me a self-deprecating smile. "I got a little more than I bargained for."

"It's not Kansas City."

"It sure isn't."

We drove on through the outer suburbs. I told her I worked in Al Khobar, and she asked me how life was there.

"It's pretty quiet. More relaxed. There haven't been any major incidents—not in town, at least—since the coup attempt last spring."

"You're lucky."

"How bad is it here?"

For a moment she didn't answer. "Like I said, we're under orders not to talk to journalists. But you're not a journalist—or a stringer—are you, sir?"

"I'm an investment counselor for Winston Investments, out of Los Angeles. And do me a favor: call me Steve."

"Okay. I believe you. There aren't any real reporters here, anyway; the government won't let them in. The Pentagon manages the news that gets back to the U.S. I don't think that anyone outside of the military really knows what's going on. Of course, locals like you know there's a bombing campaign, but you don't know how bad it is."

She paused. I said, "As far as I know, there hasn't been a single Western fatality in Khobar since the coup was put down."

"Our record here isn't as good."

I let her take her own time. Soon she continued, talking as she stared straight out in front of her at the road.

"We had almost daily drive-bys—drive-by shootings—even before that mess at the ministry. Now we have orders to stay off the streets. We just jump in and out of cars and compounds. That's why I was worried about you. You looked like a target, standing out there on the sidewalk, sticking out like a sign saying, 'American.'

"Last week we had two attacks. Someone tossed an IED—a home-made bomb—over the wall of a private compound where we had TDY quarters. Two men killed. We're not in that compound anymore. The other was some kind of mortar, set off remotely. One killed, two wounded."

"I'm sorry."

"We're under standing orders not to fraternize with the locals—the Arabs. It makes you wonder, doesn't it?"

"I don't think every Arab here's an enemy, Captain."

"Yeah. But how do you tell the good guys from the bad? We even have orders to consider uniformed Saudi security—the police and military—as potential threats. We're to deal with them, but we have to be armed and ready to respond. The intelligence guys tell us they have sympathizers in the ranks. Who is a terrorist, anyway, in this country? Who isn't?"

I wasn't sure of the answer. She let off steam all the way to the airport. She needed to. We led two very different lives in the same foreign country: my main problem was making money; hers was staying alive.

As we approached departures, she said, "I don't know what we're going to do if this place unwinds. There aren't many of us, and in town we're pretty exposed. I was never in Iraq, but I think this is going to be worse. People back home don't know what the situation is here."

"Can't you tell them?"

She looked at me. "Who should I tell? My chain of command? They're in the same boat I am. My representative in Congress? What should I say? This is a ball of mess ready to blow, and there're too few of us to make a difference? Who's going to listen?"

"People want to know what's going on."

"Do they? My CO says it was better in the old days, thirty years ago, when we had the draft. At least Americans knew what it meant, to be in the army. My old friends from college don't know the first thing about it. And they could care less."

She leaned over the steering wheel, weaving through the traffic. "There's another reason," she said. "Nobody wants to blow the whistle. The army's about loyalty. You know how it is: you've got to stick together. Isn't it the same in business?"

She looked at me with such an expression of sincerity—and innocence. I thought: What's this young woman doing here? The army had built her up, taught her how to do a job, given her self-confidence and some authority—but she was still a young girl from Kansas. Her blond hair pushed out from under her floppy, wide-brimmed hat. Her eyes were blue and clear and there wasn't a single line on her forehead.

"Yes," I told her. "Loyalty's important in business. But you've got to know when to cut your losses. In my business, accurate information is even more important than loyalty. You have to know when the company, or the sector, or sometimes even the whole market, is going south. And the sooner you know, the better. You have to know when to sell."

We reached the terminal and she pulled the Humvee over. I stepped down and lifted my luggage out. She leaned over and said, "Thanks for letting me sound off, sir—Steve. I'm sorry if I was out of line."

"You weren't, Captain. Thanks for the lift. I appreciate it." I reached into my jacket pocket. "Here's my business card. If you ever find yourself near Khobar, please give me a call. I'll take you to dinner in Manama."

"Thanks, that'd be great." I was about to close the door when she said, "You know what my CO told me the first week I was here?"

"No, what?"

"He said that in war, truth is the first casualty."

"Yes," I said, "I've heard that too." I slammed the door and waved as she drove off.

My plane was four hours late arriving in Riyadh, and it was early evening by the time I got "home." The places we live in, even temporarily, can become home faster than we expect, sometimes without us even being aware of it. As the plane touched down at the Dammam airport, outside Al Khobar, I was surprised at my sense of relief. And I was positively happy when I got out of the cab and walked into the Al Wadi. I'd only been gone for a day and a half, but the Jordanian desk clerk greeted me effusively, like a long-lost friend.

I felt like celebrating. I wanted to tell someone about the sale, and I felt like a drink. I wanted Helen. Harry was probably home by now as well, but I could put up with him for an hour or two. In my room I threw down my bag and picked up the telephone. I punched in the number and then, waiting for it to ring, was suddenly nervous, like a schoolboy afraid of being turned down for a date.

Helen answered.

"I just got back," I told her, "and I've got some good news—good business news. I thought I might come over. . . ."

"I'm sorry, Steven, but Harry's tired. He flew back early this morning and spent the rest of the day in the office." She was whispering, as if Harry were near enough to overhear. "We're going to spend a quiet evening in, probably turn in early." There was a pause. "I've got some news, too. He's convinced me that I should take some leave, just a week or two. To see if things calm down."

I was stunned. On reflex, I said, "Manama?"

"No, Antalya. Turkey. You remember Ayşen?"

For a moment the name meant nothing, then I recalled: the Turkish lady, a professor of architecture, who'd rented the apartment on the eleventh floor of Silver Towers. "Yes," I said, "I remember."

"She has an apartment there. I rang her up this afternoon. It's empty. I'm going to move in. She may join me later. A little reunion."

Antalya, instead of Manama; staying with an old acquaintance, a woman, instead of me. It was like a little punch to the gut, just enough to wind you, make you bend over and face the floor. I said, "When are you leaving?"

"Probably Friday."

"I hope I'll see you before you go."

"I'll call you." She hung up.

I walked to the window and stared out at the seedy, familiar town. This should have been my moment of triumph. Instead, I'd gotten the brush-off. The familiar anger and disappointment were boiling up—I recognized them the way a chronic depressive recognizes their familiar black cloud. I was tired of it, I didn't want to go there, I wanted to crush it before it took hold. But I didn't have a pill to pop. It wouldn't be enough just to lie on the bed and turn on satellite TV. I needed to be with someone, to talk—to have at least the semblance of a good time. Preferably with someone who knew enough to talk business. Someone who'd congratulate me on the deal.

I thought of Joe and Susan. I hesitated when I remembered his run-in with the police. But that was over; Harry had had him "sprung." Joe was the kind of man to get over it fast. He was probably having a party right now. I picked up the phone and dialed their number. He answered, and as soon as I told him I was just back from Riyadh, he ordered me to come over. He had a couple of people there he wanted me to meet.

I left the hotel without even changing, got into my car and drove to his compound.

The light was on at the Hartleys' but I avoided them; I wasn't in the mood for old poems. I went straight upstairs. Joe greeted me on the landing outside his door, smoking a cigarette. He looked in his usual high spirits, but I noticed that two fingers of his right hand were encased in a bandage. He didn't offer an explanation, other than to wave his hand and say, "A little accident," and I didn't ask for one. I looked through the screen and saw two Arab women sitting on the sofa, chatting. I asked him how he was and then asked after his wife. He gave me a wide, conspiratorial smile. "Susan's on vacation. Visiting her parents in Syracuse. I'm joining her in New York in a couple of weeks. I've got some old friends over, just watching TV and having a drink. Come in and let me introduce you."

We walked in. He introduced me as if I were his dearest, youngest brother. Then he introduced the ladies.

Fatima was tall and big-boned and heavily fleshed. She was voluptuous, half an inch in every direction from being fat. Only the natural firmness of youth saved her. She was Moroccan, Joe told me, an old friend (he'd known her since she was a child), and he'd assured her parents (also old family friends) that he would take care of her, keep an eye on her, in Al Khobar. She worked at a beauty salon in town. Joe explained all this to me because Fatima's English was rudimentary. From Joe's introduction, from his body language and from hers, and from her constant smile—which held a certain confident possession— it appeared they were on terms closer than those I associate with a family friend. I'm sometimes a little slow on the uptake. It was a few minutes before I realized she was his mistress.

At first I recoiled from the idea. He was a married man and I was, if not a friend, at least a friendly acquaintance of his wife's. The idea of Joe introducing me to his mistress in his own house rubbed me the wrong way. But everyone was so agreeable, the women so friendly, so vivacious. After the second drink (Joe still had a supply of real scotch), it was harder—it seemed priggish—to assume a judgmental attitude.

The other woman, Ofran, was a friend of Fatima's. Ofran was Lebanese, almost as full-figured but with a sharper face and temperament. Her English was fluent. Her attitude toward me fluctuated between attraction and caution, like a toy compass that won't settle down to true north. She was pretty and desirable and as the evening wore on I had the feeling we were each fishing for the other—it wasn't clear who had the reel and who was circling the hook.

The four of us drank and smoked and talked, the TV forgotten, murmuring in the background in Arabic. I told them about Los Angeles, and Ofran told me about Beirut. She was an educated woman: she worked in a local women's bank. When I told them I'd just returned from Riyadh, they wanted my impressions. To them it was the center of all that was corrupt and at the same time hopelessly backward in this, the most backward country in the Arab world.

Eventually Joe went into the kitchen and emerged holding a platter carrying four big T-bones. He suggested I accompany him out to the barbecue on the landing; he'd gotten the fire started just before I arrived. The girls, he said, had a lot to talk about between themselves.

He threw the steaks on the grill expertly. The night was dark and hot and as humid as a sauna. He'd grown up in Jeddah and it didn't bother him. He flashed me his wide, toothy grin, the rows of white, square teeth stretching from ear to ear, the lips drawn back in a rictus. "How do you like them?" he asked.

"Well done," I said.

He laughed. "I meant the ladies."

"They're very attractive."

"Ofran was interested in you the moment you walked in the door."

"Really? She's fun . . . I like her."

"Moroccan women are the sexiest in the Arab world. But the Lebanese have something special. They have brains. They have. . . ." He shrugged his shoulders and raised his hands.

"Temperament," I said.

"Yes, that's it: temperament. They're lively. But, as lovers . . ." His voice dropped to a whisper. "They are obliging. I think you know what I mean."

I've always been a bit fastidious, a little uneasy, about talking to other men about sex. I wanted to change the subject. Without thinking, I said, "I met Zainab al Badawi this morning in Riyadh."

It took a second to register, then, "Did she write the check?"

"Yes, she did."

"*Alhamdilillah!*" He waved his barbecue fork, did a pirouette, and clapped me on the shoulder, and suddenly I remembered his little dance under the dripping trees in Harry's garden at the consulate. But it's hard to resist someone who's sincerely happy at your own good fortune. Sincerity's a proof of trust. And what did Harry's pompous, "need to know" mean? Nine times out of ten it's a phony phrase, an indication of personal insecurity. Someone trying to convince themselves they really are important, they really are going to hold on to their job.

"Don't praise God yet," I said. "There's a hitch."

"A hitch? You have the check. What hitch?"

I told him about the five percent, and the bank in Kyrenia.

Joe thought for a few moments. I'd seldom seen him quietly thoughtful before. "Kyrenia's a Greek name," he finally said. "I thought you said the bank—the Turkish Anatolian Bank—was in Turkish Cyprus."

"That's right, it is. She said they'd changed the name. I have it written down."

"All the towns in the north have Turkish names. It's not important. But nothing about it makes sense. She said she wanted to use the five percent for *zakat?*"

"Yes."

"*Wallahi,* if Badawi's giving money to charity, it'll be a first for that family. They didn't make their money by giving it away. And Badawi's no Islamist. But maybe that's not important either."

"What is important," I said, "is that she wants her investment funneled through a Turkish Cypriot bank, and wants part of it to stay there. If it weren't for the fact that it's originating in Saudi it wouldn't be a problem. But it is."

"Hold on. The account's going to be in your name too, right?"

"Right."

"Then how will anyone know?"

My head was beginning to feel a little foggy—the Gulf sauna was turned on full—but even through the heat and the humidity I gaped in

amazement. What an innocent. "Joe, governments can find out anything they want. The only question is, will someone in some government office back in the States be suspicious enough to investigate?"

"Why should they? When are you wiring the money?"

"Tomorrow, in Manama—if she's gotten the account in Kyrenia set
up by that time, with my name on it."

He put his hand on my shoulder. "Take my advice. Don't worry
about it. You're covering your tracks. Take their money and run.
Maybe the five percent *is* for charity."

The ice in my drink had long melted; my shirt was dripping. I
blinked and tried to shake my head clear. I'm not as young as I used to
be and it had been a hell of a long day. I said something, and then the
cumulative effect of travel, of whiskey, of the Gulf, finally hit me. I hit
the wall. I went blank for a moment or two, then heard Joe say, as if
out of a steam haze: ". . . politics, a lover—maybe another woman.
Who knows?"

"What was that?" I said groggily.

"You asked, what else? You meant what else, other than *zakat*,
right? Hey, you okay?"

"I have to go in. This heat. . . ."

We stepped back inside. Joe was solicitous and got me a fresh drink;
Ofran looked at me with concern, wrapped ice cubes in a towel and
pressed it to my forehead, while giving Joe hell in Arabic. Bending over
me, her breasts were almost in my face. They were well covered—she
was, after all, an Arab—but they were also prominent. She had a heavy,
sweet perfume that made me think of sex.

I recovered quickly. But I didn't feel like eating a whole steak; I
gave half to Ofran, who polished it off with her own. She sat next to
me on the sofa during our meal, her leg resting lightly against mine.
After dinner we had one more scotch, and then I had to beg off: I had
to drive back to the hotel. Ofran said that she had to go too—she had
to work the next morning—would Joe call her a cab?

I can't remember which came first: my offer to drive her home, or
Joe asking me if I could. In any case, I did. We left together, Joe and
Fatima waving at the door.

Ofran lived in an Arab apartment house about halfway between Joe's compound and my hotel. As such things go, it wasn't bad: a new three-story building in a newish residential neighborhood. I parked, and thanked her for a fun evening.

She asked me if I'd care to come up for a drink, or a cup of tea.

Americans do not have affairs with Arab women in Saudi Arabia. But she wasn't Saudi; she was Lebanese. I hadn't even asked her her religion; for all I knew she was Christian. The bottom line was that she was as much a foreigner in that country as I was. I was keeping loneliness only just at bay. Bitterness and resentment toward Helen were out of sight, but ready to pounce the moment I was again alone. I didn't want to be alone, and Ofran was a very attractive woman.

I accepted her offer. At her suggestion I let her out and drove off, parking a couple of blocks away. I walked back and up the stairs to the second floor, and rang her doorbell. She answered it in the kind of robe that Arab women wear at home.

Neither of us needed anything more to drink. She showed me around her apartment—modest, but comfortable and clean—and by the time we were in her bedroom we both knew what the next step would be. She was one of those women who are sexy and forward during flirtation, and then surrender completely during the act. I took her like a man making a sexual statement. Ninety percent sexual relief, ten percent condoned aggression . . . the ratios aren't exact. She was well endowed, fleshy, and we were both sweating. As soon as it was over, as if a dead sense had awakened, I found her mix of perspiration, natural scent, and heavy perfume almost nauseating. I rolled off, already feeling the alcohol retreat. Maybe I'd sweated it out. After a few endearments she lay back, exhausted and half-drunk. In a minute she was asleep.

I slipped out of bed, picked up my clothes, and crept into the living room. I pulled them on. I stayed there a few minutes, making sure she was asleep, trying not to observe too closely the small evidences—the cheap framed photographs, the pillows hiding the worn-out furniture, the bright, fake-silk scarves—of poverty, femininity, hope. I didn't want her to become more of a person to me—someone to worry about—than she already was. I considered leaving some money on the table, but decided against it. She might misconstrue the gesture, and my disappearance was insult enough. I peered once more into the bedroom. She was sleeping on her side, her face to the wall. I snuck out of the apartment as softly as a thief.

Maybe I should have felt at least some tenderness. Maybe I did, but had it pushed down so deep I didn't recognize it. I was aware only of self-revulsion: I'd betrayed Helen—and myself.

I drove slowly and carefully back to my hotel. There was just one checkpoint. It was late; the officer saw my American face and waved me through. I parked and took the elevator to my room. The light next to my phone was blinking and the display showed two messages. I pressed the play button.

The first message was Helen's. Her voice was almost a whisper: "Steven, dear, it's me. You must be out somewhere, maybe at dinner. I'm sorry I was so rude, but Harry was tired and ill, and I couldn't leave him, although I wanted to. Listen, my dear, why don't you come over Tuesday night. Harry's leaving that morning for Kuwait—a regional commerce meeting. He won't be back until next week. I don't leave until Friday. That gives us plenty of time to catch up. We can even take in the concert at the Academy. It'll be just the two of us, and afterward we can go out for a late dinner, to the Wadi. Don't call me—I'll call you. I love you. Good night."

I felt stronger with every word she said. The second message was from Joe. He didn't speak in a whisper; his voice blared out from the speaker. "Hey pal, if I'm right you won't be getting this until tomorrow morning. I hope that's the way it worked out. I've just looked up Kyrenia. It's called Girne now. It looks like a flyspeck of a place, but it's the biggest town on the north coast. It probably makes Khobar look like Paris. Anyway, you'll need the name for your transfer tomorrow. Good luck, and if you need any help, give me a call."

I pressed the erase button, picked up a pen and wrote down the name of the town, just to confirm Badawi's instructions. Girne. A Turkish name.

I opened a bottle of nonalcoholic beer, pushed the sliding glass door open, and sat down on the balcony with a cigarette. Helen's message was a message of love: she wanted me. We'd see each other soon; we'd be able to spend several days—and nights—together. I felt a surge of relief. Yes, I'd made a mistake, but it wasn't fatal. There would be no consequences. Helen loved me, and I'd soon have enough money to get both of us out. Everything was back on track.

The cigarette tasted good after so much liquor. But as I sat there smoking, a competing scent, stronger, heavy and sweet, rose from my shirt. Ofran. Her scent clung to me like unshriven sin. I stank of her.

Faithfulness is as important in an affair as in a marriage. I'd disgraced myself, and worse, I'd let Helen down. I tried to switch my mind to the Badawi contract, to the check in my briefcase. But my self-respect—and my self-confidence—were shaken.

As I smoked and drank I thought again of my client's conditions. I thought of the Girne branch of that bank, probably not much larger than my hotel room, and of the town itself, probably no more than a village in Turkish Cyprus. Why would she want nine hundred thousand dollars parked in such a place? Charity? Nostalgia for her father? Joe had offered other reasons, while barbecuing those steaks—what had they been? Politics? Supporting a lover?

I had no interest in Badawi's politics or her love life, but I had to make sure that the five percent would stay put, as we'd agreed, for at least six months. Even more important, I had to make sure that her investment departed Cyprus for Los Angeles. There'd be no possibility of bank screwups in Manama or LA. The only place there could be a snag would be Girne. A bank the size of my bedroom in a third world village on the wrong side of a small island. How could I keep an eye on that from Manama? I didn't even know what kind of communications they had. And there'd be only one place to fix a problem, should it arise: on the spot.

I'd already made one mistake that night. I couldn't afford another. Harry was right: there wouldn't be another contract like this. He and the young captain from Kansas City both had the same message: I'd run out of time.

Managing risk has always, to me, been one of the activities that distinguish the professional from the amateur. I threw my clothes into the hamper, took a shower, and slipped on my robe. While the town slept below me I sat smoking and drinking nonalcoholic beer, planning contacts and strategies for an upcoming visit to the manager of the Turkish Anatolian Bank in Girne, formerly Kyrenia, northern Cyprus.

CHAPTER THIRTEEN

T he next morning I crossed the bridge to Bahrain.

My Manama office was a room at the Continental, an older hotel hanging on to its fourth star by its fingernails. An e-mail a couple of days old from head office was waiting for me. It was a form letter sent out to all sales staff, written in turgid legalese by the company's legal affairs department. Management was covering their ass by informing us of the requirement to comply with the latest SEC and Homeland Security reporting regulations, regarding investments by foreign nationals.

I was already in compliance. That's what Harry was for. I always forwarded his vetting forms on every client, as a matter of procedure. If the letter meant anything, it was probably that the company would now send those forms to some new office, or offices, in Washington— also as a matter of procedure. It was someone else's paperwork, not mine. But it underlined the need for due diligence on the bank in Girne.

It was time to get organized. Fortunately, Manama is a very small town.

I walked the five minutes to my bank to deposit Badawi's check. Because of the size of the deposit, the manager confirmed it over the phone with his opposite number in Riyadh. They agreed to clear it in twenty-four hours. Then the manager and I did a little research on the Turkish Anatolian Bank. It was large, privately owned, headquartered in Ankara and had branches all over Turkey and the eastern Mediterranean. About the branch in Girne we learned nothing, except its routing number.

After lunch I used the hotel's travel agency to book my flight to Girne. There was no direct route—Girne didn't even have an airport—but getting there was no problem. I reserved a round-trip ticket for Friday morning from Manama to Antalya on Turkey's south coast—Helen's destination—and then on to Ercan airport in northern Cyprus. From there I'd rent a car.

I'd never been to Cyprus, either to the Greek or the Turkish side. It was terra incognita. I didn't know a soul there. I needed an informant, an assistant, preferably a Turk or a Cypriot, who knew English, knew me and knew the lay of the land.

Helen was leaving for Antalya the same day, and staying in Dr. Ayşen Akyıldız's apartment. I had a dim memory that Ayşen had once had some connection with Cyprus.

The serendipity of it struck me as I made the booking. I went straight back to my apartment and called Helen. It was early enough for Harry to be still in his office.

She was alone. I told her my plan and suggested we fly out together to Antalya. She sounded distracted, and couldn't take in at first why I was visiting Cyprus. I explained it as simply as I could—Helen had no experience in finance—telling her it was sound business practice, especially with such a large transfer, to check out a correspondent bank in the middle of nowhere. After I'd gone over it she agreed that we should take the same flight out of Manama. I asked her to call Dr. Akyıldız in Istanbul that afternoon, to see if she had any contacts in Turkish Cyprus, and to give her my arrival date and time at Ercan. She said she would.

Then she asked, "When will the money be finally transferred—when will it get there?"

"I expect by the end of the week. Saturday at the latest. It ought to be in LA two or three days later. Then we're home free."

She was silent for a moment, then said, "Yes, free. . . . Steven, are you coming Tuesday night?"

"When's Harry leaving?"

"He'll leave for the airport around six."

"I'll be there by seven." I added, "I love you," before she hung up, and I thought: I haven't told her that, made that simple declaration, often enough. I'd been a long time without love; I'd gotten out of the habit.

The next morning, Monday, as soon as the bank opened, I confirmed the deposit had cleared, and made out the wire instructions for Cyprus. I arranged with the manager that instructions to proceed would come from me, from Girne, by phone, no later than close of business Saturday. Manama's a banking town; in the Arab fashion they close at noon and then reopen from five to eight. If all went well, I'd check out the Turkish bank on Friday afternoon, and call Manama to make the transfer either that night or the following morning.

I walked back to the hotel and wrote up Dr. Badawi's contract, with a cover letter stating that her investment was in my company's Bahrain account, and would shortly be wired to Girne. I sent the contract via courier and faxed the letter to her office, following it up with a phone call. She wasn't available, but I left a message with her secretary.

I'd been thinking about the bank in Girne and it concerned me; I doubted an operation that small would be used to transactions this size. I faxed them a heads-up, telling them to immediately follow Dr. Badawi's instructions to add my name to her account, in preparation for a sizeable wire deposit from Bahrain by the weekend. I gave them the details they needed to know and told them I expected to visit their bank on Friday afternoon, preliminary to authorizing the transfer.

All this took some time. It was late afternoon by the time I faxed a copy of the contract to my company with a note telling them the funds were already in Manama, and I'd be transferring them to LA shortly. I didn't say via Girne. Someone would notice such an obscure routing, but I'd answer those questions later, once the money was in the firm's LA deposit account. Eighteen million would put that kind of detail in perspective.

I spent the next day tidying up, getting rid of loose ends—I might soon be closing the office. After an early dinner I packed a small bag, turned everything off and headed downstairs. It was already six; it would take me an hour to cross the causeway. I stopped in the foyer to tell the desk clerk that I'd be gone for a few days, when he said, "Excuse me, Mr. Kemp, but are you thinking of crossing to Saudi?" He was a Bahraini and had probably gone to one of the better local schools. A faint British accent fought the native Arabic when he spoke.

"That's where I'm going right now."

"I'm sorry to tell you that we've just received word that the causeway's closed, from the Saudi side."

"Closed?" The causeway was never closed.

"Yes, I'm afraid so. We don't know whether the Saudis are trying to prevent someone leaving from their side, or trying to prevent someone arriving from ours. They've closed traffic in both directions."

"Do you know how long it will remain closed?"

"No. They have said nothing. However, I am almost sure it will reopen by Thursday." That was the first day of the Saudi weekend, the day that hundreds of Saudi men crossed the bridge to get drunk and whore in Manama. The Bahrainis despised them for it, but Bahraini business—or at least the hotel, bar, and prostitution trade—depended on it.

It was a struggle, but I kept my composure. Living in the Middle East teaches patience; it's a daily practice, necessary for the blood pressure. I thanked him and asked him to keep me informed. Then I headed for the hotel bar (hotels are wet in Bahrain) and had a drink to help the patience along. I went back to my room and called Helen to tell her I wouldn't be coming that night. The news depressed her. She told me she'd better make an alternate booking to Antalya, just in case the bridge remained closed. I wanted to cheer us both up, and asked for the telephone number of Ayşen's flat in Turkey—I suggested that we meet in Antalya after I wrapped up the business in Girne. She didn't have it, but gave me the address. It was full of diacriticals and customized Latin letters that only Turks use. It felt as if she was heading to a place far away, even more foreign than the one we were in now.

I spent a lonely night in my hotel room, channel surfing. There wasn't much to watch. After another couple of drinks I went to bed and awoke in the small hours to the swinging of a window blown open and a howling tropical gale outside. I got up and looked out into the black night. The warm, humid air slapped my face like someone trying to wake me up, and wind and rain lashed the palm trees below.

By morning the storm had cleared. The front desk had heard, as expected, that the bridge would be closed all day. After breakfast I decided to take a drive. There isn't much to see in Bahrain. Manama is tiny, and the suburbs are like any other Gulf Arab suburb: concrete houses with tiny windows and thick walls like eyeless slabs, designed to hide and protect, to wall up the family inside. I returned to the hotel along the corniche, and, gazing out across the tied-up dhows, was amazed to discover the Russian space shuttle, a craft that had flown only once, and then unpiloted, tied up on display on a concrete apron just beyond the boats, a fenced-in arm's length from traditional Arab technology. It was as lonely as I was, no gawkers, no group of school kids on a day trip to examine the twentieth-century wonder. Some kind of Russian goodwill gesture to a tiny corner of the Arab world, like a missionary's naive gifts to uncomprehending natives.

After lunch I went back up to my office to check e-mails. The telephone rang. I picked it up and said, "Winston Investments."

"Steve, is that you?" It was an Arab man's voice, but sounding thick—like the speaker had some kind of disability. I felt I knew him, but couldn't quite place him.

"Yes. Who's this?"

"Joe. I'm with the police, in Dammam. Where's Harry?"

I recognized him now. I said, "Harry's in Kuwait on business. I don't think he'll be back until next week. What do you mean, you're with the police?"

"They picked me up. I need Harry to bail me out."

The stress in his voice communicated across the line: I tried to think fast. I had to ramp up; it had been a slow morning. I said, "There might still be a consular guy in Khobar. Maybe he can help. Where exactly are you? How can he reach you? What happened?"

"I'm at the main Dammam jail. It's all a mistake—I keep telling them that. They picked me up at the airport, on my way out. Can you get Harry? Call him up? It's urgent."

"I'll try. Should he know why they picked you up? What the problem is?"

"They don't need a reason. I told you: it's a mistake."

My brain was slipping into gear; I remembered Harry saying that Joe still had his old Saudi ID. I asked, "Joe, which passport were you using?"

There was a silence on the line. Then, "My American one. It has the multiple exit-reentry. They must have put me on a list."

I saw the problem instantly. No wonder he was in jail. Like most countries, you need a visa to get into Saudi. Unlike almost any other country, you need another visa to get out. Joe had his in his American passport. But the Saudi government doesn't recognize dual nationalities. A lot of Saudi-Americans discovered that the hard way, but usually when they returned to Saudi, not when they tried to leave.

"Christ, Joe . . . can I help? I can vouch for you as a business associate."

"I need Harry, Steve. I need someone who can pull some strings."

"Okay, I'll try to reach him. I'll get on it right now. How can he reach you?"

"He'll know who to call. Tell him I'm sorry. Tell him—" I heard Arabic in the background, what sounded like a shout, or a command, and Joe answering, then with a click the line went dead.

I hung up the phone.

I sat there for a moment, trying to figure out what to do.

Joe was a problem I didn't need, one more thing on an overloaded plate, and my last experience with him was one I wanted to forget. But in an Arab country you do whatever you have to do to help a fellow American—even if he's an Arab-American. And one inclined to trouble.

The standard procedure was to notify the consulate. I called the consulate in Dhahran, and got a recording. Normal services were suspended; in an emergency you were instructed to call the embassy in

Riyadh. I called Riyadh and got another recording. Normal services were suspended. . . . Eventually I was able to talk to an actual human being, an Indian expat local-hire. I told her that an American citizen was being held by the police in Dammam. She took his name and told me she'd pass it on to a consular official. That was that, for official channels.

Then I tried calling Helen. Perhaps she'd have a number for Harry in Kuwait. But all I got was her answering machine. I left her a message, explained what had happened, and asked her to call her husband. I said it was urgent.

I'd done all I could. There was no point in worrying; I tried to put Joe out of my head. The rest of the afternoon passed slowly. I checked, but the causeway was still closed. The desk clerk reassured me again that it would be open the next day. After dinner I was desperate for some activity, and walked around the block to take in the club scene.

At night Manama's a pleasant enough town for the Gulf. The government keeps the religious types in check, and in any case the population is more tolerant than the Arabs on the mainland. Bahrain doesn't have oil, so they have to rely on more conventional ways to make money. There are clubs with Filipina singers, clubs with Egyptian dancers, and, of course, the clubs and hotels with Russian and Romanian prostitutes. It all depends on what you're looking for. Filipinas are great at mimicking singers from thirty years past; it's an act that starts to bore after a few numbers. The Egyptian dancers, large and fleshy, reminded me uncomfortably of Fatima and Ofran. The Romanians have a brutal sexuality—if you haven't a tie in the world and aren't too fastidious, they would probably provide an interesting night.

I had a tie and before nine I was virtuously back in my hotel's bar. When I finished my whiskey—the third of the night—I decided to pack it in. In the elevator I examined my slack expression in the polished steel door. I was drinking more heavily, and more hard liquor, than I used to in LA. I put it down to stress—to the environment.

As soon as I entered my room the telephone rang. I thought it must be Helen, and snatched it up. "Hello?"

"Mr. Kemp?"

It was a fresh, sober, young woman's voice. "Yes?" I said.

"This is Cathy Cathcart—Captain Cathcart. From Riyadh."

It took me a second; the alliteration as much as the whiskey confused me. "Captain Cathcart . . . how are you?"

"Fine. I'm sorry if I caught you at a bad time. I know it's late."

"No, no, that's all right."

"I'm in Khobar. I got a weekend's leave. We usually come up here, where it's a little safer, and you can see the sea. A lot of the guys cross the bridge to Bahrain. There's some nightlife there, I guess."

Yes, there certainly was. I doubted it would appeal to her. My brain was clearing and I remembered I'd asked her to give me a call if she was ever up in my territory.

"Listen, Captain—do you mind if I call you Cathy?"

She laughed. "I'd prefer it."

"Good. I'm actually crossing the bridge in the other direction tomorrow, if it's open. The next day I'm flying to Cyprus. But tomorrow night a friend and I are going to a concert at the American consulate, some kind of classical thing. Would you like to join us?"

"Sure. It sounds fun. I've never been to a classical concert before. When and where should we meet?"

She didn't have wheels—the army wanted its personnel off the streets unless they were on duty—so we arranged that she'd take a cab to the Al Wadi. I'd call her by noon if I couldn't make it. No news meant good news.

After we hung up I lay down and turned on the TV. The hotel movie channel was playing an old film with David Niven and a young Jean Seberg. It was called *Bonjour Tristesse* and was supposed to be about moral corruption, but by modern standards—by my standards—it looked more like a story of innocence than evil. I muted the volume and thought of the captain. She was more admirable than the character Seberg played; the captain was doing her duty in a difficult situation. She was innocent, too; innocent, I was sure, of personal corruption. She was a young woman whom I admired and liked, but I had twenty years' experience on her. I wasn't ready to trade my immorality for innocence. I wanted Helen. Along with as much legality as I could get.

———

Thursday morning I called down to the front desk as soon as I woke up. There were positive rumors, but they didn't have definite word yet. By the time I'd finished breakfast it was official: the causeway was open.

I didn't waste any time. I packed my bag for three days—my worst-case scenario for Cyprus—and drove back over the long bridge to Al Khobar. It was like reentering a prison as a visitor, a place you'd lived in for so long it felt like home, a place that still held the woman you loved—and were about to spring. I checked into the Al Wadi. I called Helen, had lunch in the near-empty hotel restaurant, spent the afternoon resting, then changed into a lightweight suit. I was down in the lobby by half past five. The captain was as punctual as a local cab could make her. A concert at the consulate must have seemed a very formal affair for the girl from Kansas City, and she wore the best outfit she had: her army dress uniform. For some reason the U.S. Army tailors them to show off a woman's figure. If I hadn't been old enough to be her father, and already committed, she would have been desirable. As it was I felt an added spring to my step, a sense of pride, escorting her, and her uniform helped grease our way a little with consulate security.

Helen was dressed formally in black. She greeted us with surprise; I'd called her earlier to say I was bringing an army captain, but I'd neglected to explain that the captain was female. She recovered quickly, but inside, mixing us a drink, I noticed she was sizing the younger woman up the way even the most secure women do, as if the world is bristling with potential competitors. Jealousy was just a few careless words—maybe just a hand on the wrong shoulder—away. I was happy to see it. I never needed reassurance in bed. But outside, it was sweet as honey on the tongue.

We had a little time to kill. I let the women chat while sipping my drink. The captain was an administrative officer with a medical unit; with Helen's former career as a nurse, that gave them something in common to talk about. The ice melted. Helen told the younger woman about her husband, and the recent meetings about evacuating the embassy staff. Cathcart listened soberly. As a civilian, I relied on the consulate, not only for business, but for assistance if I should need help with the authorities, or in my own emergency departure. The captain was in a different boat: the army was her backup, not the embassy. But no embassy meant one less lever for the army to pull; a little less security even for her.

I wanted a night away from politics; taking advantage of a pause, I asked Helen about the concert.

"It's the last one," she said. "They were supposed to play Riyadh, as well, but it's too unsafe. Harry thinks it's a mistake that they're here at all." She turned to the captain. "Are you into classical music?"

"I'm willing to give it a try."

"I always go. It's a night out, and it attracts a good crowd. Sometimes the music's good, too."

Then it was time to leave.

The venue was the auditorium of the International School. It was on the consulate grounds, enclosed within the compound's ancient stone wall. We took a shortcut, and as we approached saw a line of fellow Westerners streaming through the school gate and up the gentle hill to the hall. Professors at the local university, doctors, engineers, an architect or two, businessmen and oil engineers: all hanging on up to the last minute, trying to reach their savings goals. Wives were prominent. This was a social event, and there hadn't been many lately.

A couple of the wives hailed Helen, and at the same time we caught sight of the Hartleys on the crowd's periphery. Gina waved to us eagerly. Helen whispered in my ear, "Go say hello to Arthur, and tell Gina to join us." By "us," I assumed she meant the women (Irishwomen of her generation still have a segregated mentality). She steered the captain toward the wives, and, under orders, I walked over to join my hotel manager.

We said hello, and I suggested that Gina join Helen. She took off as if it were a natural suggestion, leaving me alone with her husband.

"Come to these often?" he asked.

"My first time."

"Possibly your last. There's a rumor that the Americans are going to evacuate."

"I've heard it's more than a rumor. Word seems to get around fast."

"Oh, nothing's a secret for long here, we're a very small community." He was looking in Helen's direction and I wondered if he was referring only to the consulate evacuation. I noticed he held two plastic cups in one hand; with the other he pulled a small metal flask out of a jacket pocket. He said, "The committee only serves punch. We don't have to descend to that level. Care for a whiskey?"

It would have been discourteous to refuse. We stood there, on the edge of the crowd, sipping our drinks, sweating into our jackets.

"Almost didn't come," he said. "Security situation and all that. But I noticed they've put on a Marine guard at the front gate and a two-man detachment down there, at the school entrance. After the concert we're going to dinner at the British consulate compound. They've imported a platoon of SAS. You don't get any better security than that." He drained his little plastic cup. "Like German lieder?"

"I'm not really a classical enthusiast."

"Think of it as poetry set to song. Makes it more accessible. Schubert and Brahms took all their lyrics from poems. The best poetry of their age." People were filing into the auditorium; the crowd was beginning to thin. It was a dark night. He said, "Some of it's pretty somber. But then, life here's getting pretty somber, too." Outside of his recitations, it was the most serious I'd heard him. "Come on," he said, "time to join the ladies."

The five of us walked into the little hall together. A piano and a music stand stood on the stage. Behind them hung a canvas backdrop, a painting probably done for the occasion, portraying a nineteenth-century romantic scene of heavily wooded mountains and lowering skies. The hall was packed. Most of the men wore suits but the wives outshone their husbands. I sat next to Helen, and as soon as the lights dimmed I pressed my hand against her thigh.

A spotlight blinked on, illuminating the stage. The performers appeared: a young English baritone and a woman accompanist. They took their initial bows, and the concert began.

German art song of the nineteenth century is, even for most Germans, an acquired taste. I don't know a word of German and I've never been particularly musical. The first song began with a bang: the pianist hammered out a series of loud, melodramatic chords. Helen handed me a program; I opened it and squinted to read the small print in the dark. The titles and lyrics were given in German and English. The lyrics, on the whole, were easy to understand (in English); they were mostly about unrequited love. For the first few pieces the accompaniment was so loud the singer with difficulty made himself heard over the piano. My attention lapsed. The music became so much background noise and my mind drifted. My chair was narrow and hard as a board; I shifted to ease the discomfort and my leg touched Helen's.

It was like a jolt of electricity. I pressed against her as far as I decently could and crushed her hand in mine. In that dim auditorium, with those dead songs, I felt like I alone was connected to life. She returned my pressure, but then a song ended and we all had to applaud. When the clapping died down she whispered in my ear the single word: "Later."

I took a deep breath and sat up straighter. I looked again at the program. The first half of the concert was near its end. The singer spoke the title of the last song: "Der Doppelgänger." The pianist began to play, but this time softly, the direction of the melody and the words as somber as Hartley had suggested. German has always seemed to me an unattractive language, but it sounded musical enough now. The baritone sang in a hushed tone, as if conveying a secret; the song was like a spell, drawing you in. I read the lyrics as he sang:

The night is quiet; the streets are still;
in this house my dear one used to live.
She has left the town long since,
but the house still stands in the same square.

Another man stands there too, and stares into the sky,
and wrings his hands for weight of his grief.
I am filled with horror when I see his face:
the moon shows me my own features.

It shook me, although I couldn't have said why. The audience gave it a good hand.

The lights came up; the five of us stood and followed the rest outside. Tables were set with punch and coffee and dry little cookies that no one touched. Hartley asked me how I'd liked the music; before I could answer, Helen said, "Steven's a finance man, or at least a part of him is. You can't expect him to take to lieder."

"I don't know," I said. "That last song . . . there was something about it."

Hartley said, "Lost love. It's about seeing the pain in another's face, and recognizing it as your own."

Helen said, "Another's face?"

"A husband, another lover, maybe even yourself, in another guise."

Helen turned away, her face hidden in shadow. The captain looked thoughtful. Gina said, "Italian songs are also about love, but are happier. Arthur, do you still have whiskey? I would like a drink. To cheer me up."

Her husband moved to the table to pick up some more empty cups. The crowd had dispersed into small, separate groups that didn't mingle; we were one of them. It was a quiet night, as well as dark. It must have been one of the consulate crew who'd brought the bottle of champagne. No one would want to transport it by car, in case they were stopped and searched by the police. The cork flew off with a loud pop, and a peal of laughter rang through the air; except for the captain, we didn't at first hear the echoing pop of rifle fire.

She stood by me, facing down the hill to the gate in the wall. People were beginning to look toward the sound of firing; conversation was dying fast. She asked me, "Where are the guards?"

"There'll be some at the gate. I don't know how many."

"Are there any arms up here?"

It seemed improbable. It was an international school. I said, "I doubt it."

Hartley stepped up. He'd left his whiskey behind. He said, "They might need help."

Already the crowd was beginning a ragged retreat farther up the

232 / JOHN LATHROP

gentle hill, back into the shadows of the consulate grounds. The captain asked Hartley, "Can you handle a rifle?"

"Did some shooting once. Country-house party. Some time ago."

She told me, "Go and alert the duty officer—whoever's on duty. Tell them there's a situation at the perimeter." Then she took off running in her army dress uniform downhill toward the gate. She was young and fit, and ran like the wind. Arthur hesitated. He gave me an apologetic look—as if to say, sorry, but I've got to do this—then he followed her, with a slow, swinging stride, his suit coat flapping behind him.

I stood there, irresolute. The captain had told me to alert the duty officer, but surely someone else was doing that. She was already halfway to the gate, Arthur following at a distance. I broke into a jog toward them—from solidarity, I suppose. I'd only just started down when I heard Gina scream, "Arthuurr," behind me, and Helen yelled my name, and I stopped and turned.

Then the bomb went off.

The car, as we learned later, managed to get within a few yards of the school gate. It must have been carefully planned. The two young Marines at the first gate were ambushed, maybe from the consulate side. The terrorists then shot the Pakistani guards at the second checkpoint. The Pakistanis were supposed to alert the Marines at the school gate of every vehicle passed and heading their way; when the Marines saw the car approach without notification, they followed orders and fired warning shots. It didn't stop, and at closer range they opened up with their rifles—all they had. But the car was armored. It was a sophisticated job. It had almost reached the gate when it detonated.

The blast wave slapped me to the ground. I don't remember hearing it—I remember seeing rather than hearing bits of stone and debris hitting the ground. I pushed myself up on my elbows and tried to focus my eyes down the hill.

A mushroom cloud was already rolling out of sight over what had been the parking lot. Most of the wall, over sixty years old and built massively of local sandstone, had held. But the gate was the weak point. The gate and the wall for yards on each side were gone.

I'd managed to struggle to my feet when Helen reached me. She was disheveled but in one piece; as she held me I saw Gina run past. Helen took my hand and we followed her, walking as quickly as my unsteady legs would allow.

Hartley was on his feet when we reached him. He was cut and bruised, and standing in his socks; he was trying to pull his jacket down from around his head. He'd gone deaf: he kept asking us what we were saying. When he saw the wall he interrupted his wife, and tried to say something about the captain.

Helen headed straight down to the hole where the gate had been. I followed.

It was clear we weren't going to find the Marines—or not much of them. Their position was obliterated: no gate, no wall—just rubble on the edge of a crater so deep the bottom was lost in darkness.

But the captain was still alive. We could hear her. She was screaming.

Helen stood by her. As I approached she knelt down.

The girl reminded me of what we'd seen on the thirteenth floor of Silver Towers, except that she wasn't yet dead. She lay on her side. Most of her uniform was blown off. One of her legs was half gone, the remainder a mangled mass of splintered bone and red muscle. The other leg jutted at an acute angle, burned black. The lower part of her back and her buttocks were flayed.

Helen looked up at me. Her face was white, horrified, the tears running down. But she was trying to hold it together. "Your jacket," she said, "give me your jacket to cover her." I tore it off and handed it over. Presently Hartley joined us, and we all three knelt together. Helen used Arthur's tie to apply a tourniquet to one of the girl's legs. After that she kept her finger on her neck, checking her pulse, and kept murmuring to her; soon she stopped screaming. That was a great relief. I'm sure she was feeling less pain. We heard the wail of ambulances in the distance, and I at least had begun to think she might make it, when she stopped breathing suddenly. Helen was performing CPR when the ambulances and the U.S. military arrived.

They took Helen and me and Arthur and Gina to the Aramco hospital as outpatients—my second time as an outpatient in that facility.

The nurses took the women first, leaving Arthur and me in the triage waiting room. He was silent. Neither of us had anything to say. They took him in, and then an American major showed up to ask me for details on Captain Cathcart. I gave them to him. He looked in his thirties, but he was in worse shape emotionally than I was—or maybe I'd been blown out of touch with mine. He looked on the verge of tears. He told me that she was the first American military casualty in the Eastern Province, and that she'd died in the line of duty. That was certainly true: she'd died going to the aid of her comrades.

After that they took me, and when I emerged—I only needed a couple of bandages and some pills—Helen was alone. She was pale and haggard, but composed. I could hardly see the captain's blood on her dress against the black. She told me the Hartleys had returned to their compound. I asked her what she wanted to do. Her voice, normally soft, was overlaid with a firm edge:

"I want you to take me back to the consulate, but only long enough to pack a bag and pick up my passport. After that I want you to drive me to Bahrain."

"What about Antalya?"

"I'm still going—we'll both fly out together. But I'm not coming back here, except maybe to pack a few things up. I'll come back to Manama. It's what you wanted, isn't it? What everyone wanted. I've had enough, Steven. I've had enough."

I said, "What about Harry?"

"What about him?"

"He'll be notified about the bombing. He'll be concerned."

"You didn't used to consider him."

I didn't want to consider him. But I said, "He's your husband."

She took my hand. "I'll leave a message at his hotel. Don't worry about Harry. Come on. Let's go."

So we drove across the bridge and spent the hours before dawn in bed at my hotel. Sex is a strange thing. We must have both been in shock, but we made love like we did the first time, after the coup—in a frenzy of passion. Or at least I did. Was it a reaction? Or an expression of release, of fulfillment, of possession . . . maybe of hope? I don't know.

We made the flight to Antalya the next morning together. Getting off the plane I noticed a fellow passenger, a skinny Arab with a toothy grin dressed in jeans and a loud shirt, and remembered Joe. I reminded Helen, and asked if she'd been able to reach Harry. She said she'd left a message on his cell phone, and asked me why Joe had been picked up. I didn't want to explain about passports, and said I didn't know. "Alcohol, probably, or pimping," she said contemptuously. "The kind of Arab Harry used to talk about, sitting on the fence." I regretted mentioning it. We'd left the Middle East behind. Even the air here was less oppressive; it was the Mediterranean, not the Gulf. She was here to forget.

I left her on the curb of the airport of that holiday town on Turkey's south coast. She looked tired and with a lot still ahead of her, the way I used to feel when arriving at a distant city, after a long and exhausting flight, with another client to see, more work to do. I gave her a kiss, but she returned it almost as if I were her husband—long married—rather than her lover. I thought: At least she'll be able to rest, but it's a hell of a way to start a vacation, alone, without me, in a strange country. I told her I'd join her soon, then they called my flight and I said good-bye.

PART THREE

CHAPTER FOURTEEN

A muffled voice was repeating there was nothing to worry about, but there was some confusion about whether it was Harry or I who shouldn't worry. I looked around to see who was speaking, and saw the hill leading down to the shattered wall, the captain at my feet, one of her legs half gone and the other at a wrong angle, with Helen on her knees, trying to breathe in life. Hartley stood across. He said something incomprehensible, in his British, upper-class accent, about another man with my face, then a jolt shook my spine and I blinked out at a straw-colored, empty plain slipping by below. The wing dipped into a bank and the sun exploded in a flash off the aluminum skin. I recoiled and squeezed my eyes shut. I gripped the armrests, my heart pounding. I opened my eyes again and stared at the seat in front. I was safe. I was on the plane to Cyprus.

My whole body ached and there was an empty place where breakfast should have been. I'd fallen asleep as soon as we'd taken off and was still strapped into my window seat; I hadn't been able to get an aisle. I looked out again, squinting against the sun, trying to distinguish a town or a village, but all I saw was a runway, a few buildings and stubbly fields. We were at least over land. It had to be the island.

The aircraft was small and the seats were just two abreast. I glanced at the young woman sitting beside me. Americans in foreign countries stand out, you can usually spot them at a distance with their back turned to you (I'm sure I'm no exception). She was a brunette, trim, petite, dressed in a skirt and blouse so conservative it might have been a business suit. She was immersed in a book. I could just read the title: *A History of Northern Cyprus.* She had the appearance of someone who prefers reading for instruction rather than pleasure. She reminded me of some of the younger of my former colleagues in LA: maybe a junior analyst, or an investment manager just starting out. Looking at her reassured me.

It was going to be a long day; the next step was a cab to Girne. I didn't even know how far it was from the airport. The rest of the passengers in the boarding line had looked mostly Turkish and German. I and the young woman sitting next to me might be the only two Americans on board. I said, "Reading up on the island?"

She closed the book carefully, with a finger marking the page. She replied, as if caught out in a minor secret, "Yes."

"Business or pleasure?"

She hesitated briefly. "Business."

My curiosity was piqued. "Really? Working for an American firm?"

"Yes." Her expression, not open, seemed to close a bit farther. This wasn't getting me very far. I said, "Tourism?"

"We're interested in prospects on the island."

I was beginning to feel like an interrogator faced with a suspect determined to reveal as little as possible. I decided to get to the point. "Do you know how far Girne is from the airport?"

"About forty-three miles." She looked back down at her book, and reopened it halfway.

I gave it up and tried to settle more comfortably in my seat. In any case we were on final approach.

Immigration was perfunctory and I'd checked no luggage. I left most of the other passengers behind and emerged from the seedy airport into a wall of heat. The Mediterranean sun burned down and radiated off the tarred parking lot in front of arrivals. I was looking around for a cab when I noticed an elderly, unshaven Cypriot standing in a small group of greeters, holding a scrawled sign: "Mister Cemp." I walked up and introduced myself. He nodded and replied in Turkish. I recognized exactly two words: "Akyıldız," and "Girne." Helen hadn't heard back from Ayşen, but apparently she'd made arrangements.

He led me to a van with an unlikely name on the door panel: St. Hilarion. We climbed in. I was the only passenger. The road was bumpy, the vehicle old and the seat thinly upholstered; the jolts hit my backside like the saddle of a horse. The Aramco nurse had given me some painkillers the night before; I managed to retrieve two and swallowed them dry. There was no air-conditioning and we were forced to drive with the windows open. I pulled off my jacket. Hot air and dust from the road blew in on my face; in five minutes my shirt was soaked and sticking to my back.

Cyprus is a long island east to west but short north to south. We turned north and were soon above the central plain, into the foothills and climbing steeply toward the peaks of what I learned later was the Besparmak range. As we gained altitude the temperature fell. Low brush and stunted trees gave way to pine.

We reached a pass and nosed downhill, winding down to the coast. The Mediterranean sparkled blue in the distance, like a holiday postcard.

On the coast road we turned west. It was the height of summer and, I imagined, of the tourist season, but the two-lane road was almost devoid of traffic. I was struck by the lack of population. Other than a few patches of olive and citrus groves, the coastal strip was uncultivated. Isolated homes dotted the landscape, many unfinished, roofless and windowless. They wore an air of abandonment.

We passed a sign with the single word, "Girne," and the driver turned inland, away from the sea, up a dirt road barely wide enough for the van. We lurched toward the base of the mountains. Then, on the right, rooftops and a sign in English announced our destination: the St. Hilarion Hotel.

The hotel—two rows of detached bungalows—nestled against the foot of the cliffs. At its back the peaks rose in an almost vertical wall. The dirt road simply ended; there was nowhere farther for it to go.

We climbed out. The driver insisted on carrying my single bag into the office, which also served as café and bar. It was empty but for a pale girl working behind the counter. She didn't look more than eighteen. She was dressed in shorts and a T-shirt. It was even hotter in the office than outside, and her shirt clung to her as if she had just climbed out of a pool. Under it she wore nothing. Her figure was undeveloped for her age. She spoke a few words in Turkish to the driver, and then smiled a friendly welcome.

"You must be Mr. Kemp." She had an English accent. I told her I was, and she said, "Dr. Akyıldız faxed us your reservation. Your room's ready, but I'm afraid the air conditioner's off—the electricity's been out all morning. This side of the island's only got one power station, and sometimes it goes down for a few hours. But it should be back up any time now. Would you like a drink? The first one's on the house. The beer and tonic's still cold—we've got ice in the freezer."

It was nearly noon. A drink seemed the thing to do, and it sounded refreshing. I sat down opposite her at the bar and ordered a gin and tonic. I saw no other guests and no other staff. The only other living being was a small bird in a cage hanging from the ceiling. The girl and I fell into conversation.

Her name was Kate and she was the manager, bartender, and occasional cook. She'd been born on the island. Her parents belonged to a small band of English expatriates who had lived on the northern coast since before the arrival of the Turkish army in '74, and who had never seen reason to leave. The more uncomfortable conditions got, the more determined they were to stick it out. The type of English expatriate nothing can dislodge. Kate, her T-shirt sticking unprovocatively to her undeveloped breasts, was happy to be among their number. I felt like an anthropologist who'd stumbled on a remote survival: the British colonial mentality. The stiff upper lip. In the stifling office, drinking the unaccustomed gin—I'd grown used to whiskey—I remembered Hartley. Hartley running down the hill to the aid of the captain. He was the fastest off the mark; I'd had to follow his lead. Arthur had shown more than just eccentricity.

The gin was cool going down; I ordered another. My appointment at the bank was not until late in the afternoon. As I always do when visiting a new town I asked about business; I like getting an idea of the local economy. Kate told me they had only two other guests, both Englishmen, but she'd sent the van to the airport to pick up another new American arrival. Business was down at the Hilarion, due to the recent deaths of two of their guests.

"Recent deaths?" I said. "What happened? What did they die of?"

"They killed themselves," she said simply. "They were an old English couple who'd been coming every year for a long time. We found out later they'd both been diagnosed with cancer. I guess they wanted to die together, in a place they'd always liked."

"I'm sorry." I felt a morbid curiosity. "How did they do it?"

"Poison."

The office-bar, empty but for Kate and myself, seemed suddenly lonely. I wondered who had found the bodies. I hated to think it had been this young girl. "Who discovered them?" I asked.

"Our handyman. The electricity went out for a whole day. Don't worry, it hardly ever happens. You'll see: it'll come on in an hour or two."

"You mean. . . ."

"Oh yes. The smell."

She said it as simply as she had spoken when telling me about her parents. I thought her a girl with either very little imagination or very deep equanimity.

I knocked back my drink and asked about renting a car. She said it would be no problem. I arranged to have one sent up to the hotel at five. Then I asked to be shown to my room.

Outside there was a terrace for dining, and nearby a small but deep pool, then the rows of bungalows. They were all identical: on the ground floor a small living room and bathroom, and upstairs—not a full upper story, but a loft beneath the roof—a bedroom, open to the room below. They were architecturally charming but primitive in execution. The heat was bad but not as bad as I'd feared. Kate made sure my air conditioner was turned on, ready for the imminent resumption of current, and then gave me the key.

I'd been traveling since early morning and the two gins were having an effect. My appointment was not until six and it was only just noon. I decided to take a nap. I stripped and tried to take a shower. But the shower was pump-fed, and with no electricity there was no water. Irritated, I climbed the stairs to the loft-bedroom, set my alarm clock, and lay down on the warm sheets, trying hard to relax.

Kate was right: I was half asleep when a crack and a roar startled me awake—it was the air conditioner shuddering into life. The sound was nothing like rifle fire or an explosion, but I was on edge. I got up and took a shower, but back on the bed sleep eluded me. I'd been on many an uncomfortable business trip; this was shaping up as among the worst. I had to get a grip; I'd have to be capable in just a few hours. I tried to concentrate on the questions I would ask the bank manager that afternoon. There were only a few, all formalities. I went over them so often they became a kind of soporific, like counting sheep. Eventually my eyes closed and I dozed off.

I awoke at five to the ring of the alarm clock, feeling stale and groggy. I took another shower, shaved and put on a clean shirt. It was time to pick up the rental car. I walked out to the office. By the pool I noticed a trim young woman in shorts with her head buried in a book. A wide-brimmed sun hat hid her face.

Inside, Kate was serving drinks to two men, one middle-aged and one quite young. She introduced them: George and Julian. The guests from England. There was a proprietorial ease between them which suggested a liaison. They offered to buy me a drink, but my car was already there and I explained that I had an appointment in town.

Kate handed me a letter as she walked me out. I was surprised: no one but Dr. Akyıldız, the bank manager, and Helen knew that I was in Girne. She told me it was from Yurdagül Kemal, and had just come. I asked her who Kemal was—I didn't know enough Turkish to even know if it was a man or a woman. She explained that Dr. Kemal was a Turkish academic, a friend of Dr. Akyıldız's, living and working on the island. I opened the letter. It was a brief note welcoming me to Cyprus, introducing herself as an old friend of Ayşen's, and suggesting dinner at the hotel that night at eight. I asked Kate if she thought a reply was required. She said that Dr. Kemal often dined at the hotel, and no reply would be an acceptance.

An elderly Cypriot from the rental agency was sitting smoking in the car he'd delivered. He got out and we sat at a table as I read the rental agreement. He was stooped and resigned; as I tried to read he insisted in broken English that the quality of the car (it was one of the company's best) and the high season justified the rate. I thought the rate absurdly low. I signed the papers and asked for the key. He handed it over as if giving away a cherished possession.

The car was a dusty and dented Fiat sedan. The man didn't ask for a ride back; presumably he had another method of returning to town. The Fiat had a manual transmission, with the steering wheel on the right. It's been difficult for years to even find a car with a manual transmission in California. I got in, put it in gear and jolted my way down the hill.

I turned left at the coast road and within a minute reached Girne. It looked quiet and down at heel, like a Greek coastal town off the tourist track, only poorer. Kate had given me instructions on how to reach the bank, but the size of the town deceived me—it was little more than a village—and I had driven right through it before I got my bearings. I turned around and drove haltingly back in, interpreting the directions in reverse. I identified the Turkish Anatolian Bank by its sign (in English for the tourists); the building itself was almost indistinguishable from the little shops sharing the street. I parked the Fiat nearby.

Inside was a dim, stuffy lobby with an exchange window doing business with a German tourist. Two other windows were unmanned. I stepped up to one and hailed a young woman working at a desk. She smiled and came up, but her English was poor and it took several tries to make her understand that I had an appointment with the manager. The lobby was airless—there was neither air-conditioning nor even a fan that I could see—and I was sweating when she finally lifted the hatch and directed me in behind the counter. She wrote down my name, knocked at the door of what I presumed was the manager's office and disappeared inside. After a moment she reappeared and ushered me in, closing the door behind me.

The manager was the picture of a big frog in a tiny puddle—but a welcoming frog. His fleshy face beamed as I walked in. An air-conditioning unit blew a current of cool air across the room, cool enough for the occupant to wear comfortably a three-piece suit. Its cut was extravagantly old-fashioned and the watch chain and pearl tiepin completed the obsolete look. He only lacked a wing collar. The compulsory framed photograph of Ataturk on the wall above the desk was a portrait of a more modern-looking man—less prosperous, and with more doubts. The manager stood up and offered me his hand.

"Welcome," he said, "welcome to Cyprus, Mr. Kemp. I am Mr. Rifat, the manager. Please sit down. Would you care for some tea?" He pressed a buzzer and barked a command into a box on his desk: "Tansü, *tschai*." He sat back down and held out a box of cigarettes. "Please take one."

We began with the usual pleasantries. He could have had few American businessmen call on him, especially with the intention of depositing eighteen million dollars in his bank (even for a very limited time), but his English was fluent. I made myself agreeable and he became expansive. He told me a little of his history. He was a Cypriot and had been born in Girne when it was still Kyrenia, but had been educated in Istanbul. He'd spent much of his career with the bank at various branches in Anatolia and finally Ankara. Missing his homeland, he'd asked for this posting to his hometown. I thought it a possible story but not one I should credit without more evidence. There was certainly little chance of advancement here—he must have had a very strong tie indeed to his native island.

I led the conversation to business. He had received Dr. Badawi's instructions to add my name to her account and had already done so. He had also received my fax. He'd taken the trouble to get in touch with both of his main correspondent banks, in Istanbul and New York, to double-check their procedures. The wire transfers would naturally take a circuitous route but he estimated that the entire transaction, from Manama, to Girne, to LA, would only take about five business days.

It looked good. Despite the appearance of Rifat and his branch, the arrangements looked efficient. I need not have come all this way, but I was glad I had. I'm sure I was smiling when he said, "And I have already prepared the corporate account for the remainder."

It took a moment for it to sink in. I stared at him, and said, "Corporate account?"

"Yes, the account for the funds that are to remain on deposit here."

"There is no corporate account."

He raised his eyebrows slightly. "Dr. Badawi's instructions were very clear."

"The *zakat* is to remain in the original joint account."

"'*Zakat*'?" He paused, with a puzzled expression, and then smiled. "Your Arabic is very good, Mr. Kemp. If Dr. Badawi intends to dispense this money as charity, that is of course her affair. She instructed me to transfer it to a separate corporate account." He pulled out a long sheet of paper from a neat stack on his desk—he seemed to have everything ready at hand—and perused it. "Yes. There is no doubt about her instructions. It is a corporate account with full privileges for both parties."

I have always disliked surprises. One of the main purposes of investment management is to avoid them. My mind raced. With that money in a different account, it would be invisible, gone, as good as vanished, to Homeland Security, to the SEC. But the solution was obvious.

I said, "For reasons of transparency, the money on deposit has to remain in the original account."

"I am afraid my instructions are clear. It must be transferred."

"Then it will have to be transferred right back."

"That can certainly be done. Either Dr. Badawi or the other signatory can transfer it back."

"The other signatory? You mean me."

"No. I'm afraid the corporate account is not in your name."

Something turned over inside me. Trust evaporated. It was a cramped and ugly office. I asked, "Who is the other signatory?"

Rifat smiled apologetically. "I am afraid my instructions are specific, Mr. Kemp. That is confidential information."

"Dr. Badawi is my client. I set up this entire transaction for her. There were conditions attached, one of which was that the funds be under my control. Hence the joint account."

"I can assure you that the money for her investment—a considerable investment—will immediately be wired to your firm. As for the remainder, a small percentage, I am sorry. There is nothing I can do."

"The remainder was to stay in the original account. With Dr. Badawi and myself as the sole co-owners."

"Perhaps there was some problem with communication. Between yourself and your client. She is an Arab."

I had only one card to play. I said, "The money is still in Manama. I wouldn't want this to jeopardize the investment."

"I can assure you, Mr. Kemp, we also would not wish to jeopardize your client's investment. But she is our client, as well. We must follow her instructions."

In LA, he would have been described as a passive-aggressive type. One of the most irritating and unprofitable types to deal with. I was losing this one, but only for the time being. I said, "I'll get in touch with Dr. Badawi and straighten this out."

"Excellent. In a transaction of this size, everyone should be"—he laid his hand again on his papers, as if to clarify his latest American slang—"on the same page. If you like, I too will try to contact her, to confirm."

He sat back, beaming.

I thought hard.

I didn't know why Badawi had decided to move her remaining deposit into a separate account, although it may have been, was probably, an innocent move, a result of miscommunication. I also didn't know why the account was joint, or who the other signatory was. She'd wanted her five percent held here, so that she could disburse her charity as she saw fit; had she delegated that responsibility to someone else? Why was the account corporate? Individuals generally use corporate accounts for tax purposes, but these funds were already far from the purview of any Arab tax authority. There was a lot I didn't know, but I did know one thing: as soon as those funds were moved out of the original transfer account—in my name and a Saudi Arab's—they would be an untraceable withdrawal to any auditor from the States. A significant and noticeable hole. I couldn't have that. I had to keep the trail clean.

I sat a little longer in the cool current of the air-conditioning, collecting my thoughts. Then I said, "Can you tell me the corporation's name?"

"Yes, I believe I can do that. It is Hanifa, Ltd."

The name rang a faint bell, but I couldn't place it. I said, "Is it a Turkish Cypriot, or Turkish, corporation?"

"That I am afraid I don't know. We normally do not check, or ask our clients, where their firms are incorporated."

I had reached a dead end with Mr. Rifat. We both stood up and he held out his hand.

"It was a pleasure to meet you, Mr. Kemp. I hope you will be able to begin the transfer tomorrow, as planned. If you want to come back for a further talk, please do. We stay open on Saturdays to accommodate the tourist trade. How long do you expect to stay on our island?"

"I'm not sure. Until early next week, maybe."

"And where are you staying?"

"The St. Hilarion."

"You could not do better. Their steaks are excellent."

I departed courteously, my facade intact. But back on the street I felt suddenly nauseous. The sidewalk and the signs in Turkish swam in front of me. I made it around the corner and then leaned against a wall and bent over, my hands on my knees. I made myself breathe deeply. I thought: I'm nearly fifty. I've traveled from Dhahran to Girne in one morning. Except for airplane food out of Manama, I haven't had anything to eat since last night. I've drunk two gins since noon, and I'm wearing a suit on Cyprus in the summer.

But I knew it was more than that. It was also a panic attack. I knew how the missing money—almost a million—would look to the U.S. authorities. It would look like money laundering. Money originating in Saudi: the main source of funds for worldwide terrorism. I had to find a way to transparently account for every cent. I had to find a way to keep it in that bank, and in the original account.

I straightened up, took off my jacket and loosened my tie. I decided to walk down to the sea. The air would refresh me. It couldn't be far. In fact, it was closer than I thought. In three minutes I was down through the little town, down a few blocks of uneven sidewalk, to the bay.

It was like Havana in micro-miniature: the crumbling ruins of a third world economy behind me, and on the waterfront the cafés and bars, the awnings with lanterns and lights already lit up, waiting for the international tourists. There was even a crusader castle, unadorned and squatting heavily at the far end. An ancient mole curved away, forming a breakwater for the smallest marina I'd ever seen. You could walk from one end to the other in less than a minute.

A second look revealed that two of the three waterfront hotels were roofless, their top floors unfinished and open to the wind. Beside a handful of tied-up yachts and dinghies on the quay, the mast of a sunken wreck leaned out of the sea like the flagpole of a defeated army. The bay was almost as much a ruin as its crumbling castle. The fairy lights and lanterns were like a new coat of paint on a rusted-out car.

But it was a working ruin and a tourist draw. A German party was laughing and drinking at a table set up near a moored yacht, and small groups of Brits and Germans sat scattered under the café awnings. It was a holiday scene, and I needed a lift. I ambled from one bollard to the next, taking in the boats and the diners. Then I saw the young woman from the plane.

She was sitting alone at a table for two in a patch of shadow, on the edge of one of the tavernas. With a drink in front of her instead of a book, she was gazing out to sea. She'd changed into a pair of slacks, but somehow she still looked almost as businesslike as she had on the plane. She could have been a clean young graduate of one of the better MBA schools, on a solitary holiday, or at least a night off. She hadn't been forthcoming before, but I felt like some American company. I walked over.

"Hello," I said, "mind if I join you?"

She smiled up at me guardedly, as if I were a potential client, but one without a recommendation. "No," she said.

I sat down and introduced myself. We could have been in LA in one of the more serious singles bars, where you identify yourself by your occupation. Steven Kemp: investment manager; temporary expat; cuckolder. I only gave her the first two.

"My name's Jones," she said, and, as if self-conscious of the formality, volunteered, "I'm an expat too, I suppose . . . based in Bahrain, temporarily."

"Really? What business?"

"Import-export," she said promptly. She dipped into a small purse and handed me a card. It was difficult to read in the shadow; I could just make out the two words she'd given me, and the name of a firm I didn't recognize.

I said, "I'm from LA."

"I'm from Shakopee. It's a little town outside of Minneapolis." The smile this time came easier; her face opened halfway.

"We're a long way from the Midwest."

She looked at the crooked mast leaning out of the water and gave a little, disappointed laugh. "I always wanted to travel."

"It's not much of a town."

"It could use a cleanup."

"Here long?"

"I don't think so. I'm looking for someone—" she corrected herself promptly: "I mean, something."

"Which one?"

"Both." She drained her glass—I think it was water—and looked about to go, when we heard a fracas in English to our right, among the awnings.

Two Western men stood by a table, shouting at a waiter. Something about their bearing and voices suggested they were gay. The waiter stood stolidly, taking the abuse. A group of Arab men at a nearby table looked on impassively. They were leaner and less prosperous than the Saudis at Joe's party, but were after the same thing: they wore the clothes of the Arab male on a fornication holiday. Their loud shirts hung on them incongruously. Girne was cheap. It attracted a lower class of Arab than Istanbul or Beirut.

Finally the waiter raised his hand in some sign—probably the Cypriot fuck-off—and turned on his heel. The two gays abandoned the fight. They walked toward us. I recognized my fellow guests at the St. Hilarion: George and Julian.

I'm not homophobic. On the other hand I wasn't interested in getting involved with whatever problem George and Julian had or were developing in Girne. But they hailed me, and came up bristling with righteous indignation.

Apparently the waiter, a Cypriot, had ignored them, serving the Arabs at the neighboring table first, even though they'd arrived later. The waiter had kept giving my fellow guests excuses, not even giving them a glass of water or a menu.

"Inexcusable behavior," the older man, George, said. "And those blacks just sat there. Arabs, didn't you say, Jules?"

"Aye. We had some as lodgers once. Bloody arrogant bastards. You can tell them a mile off."

"Sitting there, superior, not saying a word. As if they disapprove of buggery. Ha!"

"I told you we should have gone to Greece. To Lesbos."

"Greece perhaps, Jules. But not Lesbos."

I glanced at Jones. She was trying unsuccessfully not to look uncomfortable. Neither life in Shakopee nor her finance and marketing classes in business school had prepared her for the gay Brit abroad. But she was trying not to be rude. She was young. She just had a few things to learn.

I said, "Look, I'm just driving back to the hotel. I have a dinner date there. Can I give you two a lift?"

I could and I did. I said good-bye to Miss Jones and told her I hoped we'd meet again. She said she hoped so too, and held on a little long when we shook hands—almost as if she didn't want to let go. Maybe she was beginning to see as much reassurance in me, a middle-aged American businessman, as I did in her. We were both a long way from home. Then George and Julian and I walked back to my car. They were funny and a distraction, but I preferred the company of Jones.

We arrived at the St. Hilarion shortly before eight. The terrace in front of the office was set with tables and there were several diners. I said good-bye to my passengers and found Kate, as usual, behind the bar. She slipped out and told me my dinner guest was already at our table. I hurriedly pulled my tie straight, and she walked me out to perform the introductions.

Dr. Yurdagül Kemal rose from her table to greet me. She was stunning. She was as tall as me, and slender, with a model's bone structure. She wore a backless white dress cut with the kind of elegant simplicity only money can buy. She must have been in her forties, but she could easily have represented a fashion house that wanted a look combining breeding and intelligence with an ethnic flavor. Her face was strongly aquiline. She smiled and her wide red lips stretched back, revealing even rows of long, white teeth.

We shook hands and sat down. She told me what a pleasure it was to meet an old friend of Dr. Akyıldız's. I figured she must know that I was no more than an old acquaintance, and if she wanted to pretend we were old friends, I wouldn't object. I asked her about her connection. She and Ayşen had been schoolmates in college; Dr. Kemal had even, briefly, worked in Saudi—before my time. Like Dr. Akyıldız, she too was a doctor of architecture, a department head at a new, private school outside of Girne. "The academic environment here is a challenge," she said, "but it is good to try and build something new, and one feels, in Cyprus, that one is engaged in development work. It is satisfying." She spoke with a formality that matched her looks. But when I addressed her by her title, she placed her hand lightly on mine—her fingers, in that humid environment, were dry—and said, "Please, call me Gül."

Our steaks arrived—the famous St. Hilarion steaks. They weren't bad, they were certainly superior to a British cut, but they wouldn't have rated a mention in the States. The wine, however, was good: dark and rich and tasty, without much of a bite.

She talked about Cyprus, its history and politics. I let her talk, just asking a few questions, and making the occasional comment. She was an agreeable, if exotic, woman to have dinner with, and I wondered how useful she might be.

Dessert was followed by brandy and a Turkish coffee. I decided to sound her out, see how much she knew.

"My business here," I said, "is concerned with the local branch of the Turkish Anatolian Bank."

"Yes, I am aware of that. Ayşen told me. I believe you have already seen Mr. Rifat."

"You know him?"

She smiled. "This is, as I'm sure you have seen, a very small community. I know Mr. Rifat well. He is a trustee of our school. I hope you found him . . . complaisant?"

It was not a word I would have used to describe any bank manager, certainly not the manager of the local branch of the Turkish Anatolian Bank. I wondered for a moment exactly what she meant. "I have a small problem," I said, "small to him, that is, not to me. It concerns a third-party account."

She interrupted me. "Steven, you are not here for long, are you?"

"I don't plan to be, no."

"Then may I suggest we save business for a little later? It is nearly dusk. Although we are a poor island, we have some exceptional sights. I would like to show you one. Let us have a drink together on the belvedere of St. Hilarion." She looked past my shoulder, at the mountain behind us. "Our crusader castle. This hotel is named after it. We can discuss business there."

It wasn't the moment for discourtesy. A short delay meant nothing. I acquiesced.

She'd brought her own car, one of the smaller Mercedes sedans. It matched her persona. She drove us at breakneck speed back down the little road, leaving a cloud of dust behind. We skirted the town and turned onto a road that led straight up, past the olive groves, into the mountains.

In minutes we were among the pines. A wooden sign almost hidden in the trees pointed to a path just wide enough for the car, leading off to the right; it ended in a clearing and an open gate in a low stone wall. The wall climbed crookedly up the treeless peak.

We left the car and walked through the corroded gateway. The castle of St. Hilarion was not a beautifully preserved, listed monument. It was a shattered, overgrown ruin. Its broken walls wandered up and down the mountainside. Above, fragments of buildings littered the tumbled ground; below, bits of gray masonry and small mounds protruded from the slopes like old bones and disturbed graves. St. Hilarion had been constructed over three hundred years, and ruined over even more centuries.

Dr. Kemal led me along a narrow path ending in the remains of a second, inner gatehouse. The setting sun picked out the stone head of a woman projecting from a bracket on the wall. She wore the horned headdress of a lady dead six hundred years.

We entered a passage cut through the rock. Enough light filtered through to see, but we had to watch our step on the uneven floor. At the end we stooped through a low doorway into a surprise: a vaulted hall, high and long, with an open platform—the belvedere—overlooking the whole of the northern coast. Electric lights hung from the vault's groins and a bar lit with candles ran along one wall. The Mediterranean sparkled to the horizon. Dr. Kemal said, "It is enchanting, isn't it?" I agreed.

I gathered she was a guest of local prestige; the barman came and showed us to a table on the belvedere's edge. We both ordered a drink. She told me about the castle's history, and I admired the view. Then I broached the subject of my business.

"I have a client in Saudi Arabia. I hope to make a deposit for her in the Girne branch of Mr. Rifat's bank."

"I know," she said, smiling.

I was taken aback. "It was," I continued, "for a very considerable amount."

"For eighteen million U.S. dollars." She sat there grinning like the cat that caught the canary. I asked her, "How do you know that?"

She stretched out her hand. Her long dry fingers rested like a piece of paper on mine. "Steven, when Ayşen told me you were interested in the bank, I made it my business to discover yours. I was sure you would wish me to be informed."

I stared at her. "Naturally. How did you go about it?"

"As I said, this is a small community. You are not the only one with an account at that bank."

"You just asked Rifat? It's a confidential transaction. He won't even tell me everything I need to know."

She looked out to the sea and down the mountain. "You can see Girne from here. Look . . . do you see it? Do you see how small it is?" It was true: Girne was just a smudge on the coastline. "In a town this size," she said, "no one has any secrets—or at least, not local secrets; certainly not important ones. The people who live here know almost everything about one another. They certainly know everyone's business, because business is news." She turned back to me. "Eighteen million U.S. dollars is news. I know everything about your business with Mr. Rifat. Just tell me what you need."

She asked me to get to the point; I did. "Most of the money I'm depositing will be transferred to the States, but five percent is to remain here. It was supposed to remain in the original account, but my client—against the terms of our agreement—has opened a separate, corporate account. There are two signatories: my client and someone else, I don't know who. She has instructed Rifat to move the five percent on deposit into this new account."

"Yes. I follow you."

There were different ways to approach this. Dr. Kemal would know nothing of Badawi, but she obviously knew Girne, and the Girne business community. I said, "I need to know if the other signatory is someone local. If it's someone in Girne, or in Cyprus, I need to know who they are."

Dr. Kemal said, "This corporation—it is your client's?"

"I don't know."

"What is it called?"

"Hanifa, Ltd. Have you heard of it?"

She shook her head. "It is an Arabic, not a Turkish, name. It is not a local firm. But it is a corporation?" She made the word sound like a talisman: a synonym for legitimacy.

I said, "That doesn't mean much. Anyone, anyone at all, can open a corporate account."

She thought for a moment. "Mr. Rifat did mention another man involved in this transaction."

"Do you know him?"

She shook her head. "No. He is not a Cypriot. Mr. Rifat was told to expect an Arab-American, but with an American name. I cannot remember it, it is very—*tanımlanamaz*." She concentrated, then smiled as she dredged up the obscure word. "Nondescript. But he is here. He called Mr. Rifat, to tell him how he can be reached. He is staying on the coast, at the home of a friend, or an associate."

"An associate?"

"I believe a private developer. We are beginning to attract them. You know, prices are expected to go up. The northern coast is completely unbuilt. The only problem is the Greek Cypriots. They owned much of the north before '74, and there is still some disagreement about land titles. Sooner or later there will be a settlement. You are no doubt aware of last year's vote on the UN's plan for union."

I didn't remember the UN vote, and wasn't interested in the validity of Cypriot land titles. I said, "Could this whole thing be about real estate?"

"Why not? It is one explanation."

I tried to imagine a connection between Badawi's *zakat* and coastal real estate. It seemed tenuous. But how much did I really know about her intentions? I had to admit: nothing. As for the Arab-American . . . Badawi was using me to arrange her American investments; was she using someone in Girne to purchase local property? The more I thought it over, the more Dr. Kemal's information began to resemble the data sent back to earth from an unmanned, interplanetary mission: each answer raised another question.

"Look," I said, "I don't know what this guy's connection to my client is, or what he intends to do with that money. All I know is, it has to stop. The remainder of the funds cannot leave the original account. They have to stay there for at least six months. Those are the terms of my client's investment."

Dr. Kemal sat a little straighter, if possible, in her chair. She said, "How can I help you?"

"Can you get me in touch with him?"

"If he is still here, I can certainly get a message to him, yes. I am sure he has a cell phone."

"Do cell phones work in Turkish Cyprus?"

"The EU funded a network for the northern half of the island. It works, most of the time. If necessary, I will send a messenger."

My strategy was simple. It was dictated partly by time. My transfer instructions in Manama expired at eight the following evening. Badawi was a businesswoman, and I felt fairly confident that I could convince her to move her deposit back to our account. I could keep the eighteen million in Cyprus for a day or two, however long it took me to get in touch with her and straighten things out. But the Arab-American was the unknown factor. If I was going to okay the first transfer, to Girne, I had to neutralize him immediately. I had to get him out of the picture before tomorrow night.

I said, "Fine. Send him this message: he has to instruct the bank to withdraw his name from the corporate account by tomorrow afternoon, or I'm canceling the client's investment. Tell him that."

Was I bluffing? Would I have the guts to follow through, to not put through the call to Manama? I wasn't sure. But I was tired of being jerked around. I wasn't going to face an investigation back in the States because of some dodgy property investment—or whatever it might be. I had to take a strong line.

Dr. Kemal said, "Tomorrow afternoon may be too soon, Steven. I can get a message to him, certainly, if he is still here, but when he'll be able to reply. . . ."

"He'll have to manage it. Tell him his name has to be withdrawn before the bank closes. I need it confirmed by Rifat. Otherwise I cancel the deal."

"I will do my best. I'll call you at your hotel. Now, it's getting late, and I have one more thing to show you. I hope you have not forgotten that I am an architect?"

"No. . . ."

"Come with me. St. Hilarion has a beautiful example of Byzantine architecture. There is just enough light left."

We rose and I went to pay the barman. She led the way, back through the same passage, now in deep shadow. Before we'd gone far she turned left up a short, uneven flight of stairs I hadn't noticed on the way in. It was pitch-black and I had to wrench my mind off business to follow her. The stairs led out to a cloister and then into a small, separate building, like a tiny hall. The walls still stood but the roof was long gone; it was open to the darkening sky.

She turned to me and said, "This is the chapel. Originally it was domed. Two of the columns survive." She pointed them out in the gloom. "Over there is the apse. The east window is still intact." We walked through the narrow nave to the rounded east end. The apse couldn't have been more than three yards wide. In the center of the wall three narrow columns supported two round arches. Long unglazed, the windows stared, empty sockets, into the void.

As we peered out, the last sliver of sun sank beneath the waves. The broken walls seemed to merge into the night. A cooler breeze blew through the window. Dr. Kemal stepped silently closer. We were almost touching. Her perfume was heavy on the air. I wondered why she had brought me. To admire the Byzantine window? In the dark? It seemed unlikely, but so did a lot else. I was uncertain how I was expected to proceed. A tentative, or perhaps a confident, pass?

Before I could try either we both jumped as a sharp cry broke the silence: it sounded near, just outside on the wind. It sounded like a cry of pain. I thought it must be some strange Mediterranean bird. "What's that?" I said.

Dr. Kemal had retreated, her back against the wall. In the darkness her face was indistinct, but I thought her characteristic expression of poise had been replaced by something else. "The *hayalet*," she whispered.

"It's a hell of a sound for a bird."

"It is not a bird." She turned and stooped, slipping off her shoes, then hurried down the nave, like a bride fleeing the groom at the last minute. She called over her shoulder, "Come. We must go. The sun has set." I ran to catch up, tripped on a flagstone and fell to my knees. I swore and called her name, but she was already through the cloister.

She flitted down the hill like a bat. I stumbled after her, down to the main gate and to her car.

On the way back to the hotel, Dr. Kemal apologized for her "haste." She regained her composure as we descended. As I got out, she told me it had been a pleasure to meet me, and hoped I would visit the island again. She would call the next day.

Out of habit, or maybe for the comfort of a familiar face, I walked into the office-bar. The generator must have gone again; two gas pressure lamps glowed on the counter. Kate stood behind, making drinks for George and Julian and one or two others I could hear, still on the terrace. I sat down and asked for a glass of water. I'd had enough alcohol for one day. Looking out, I thought I spotted Jones in the shadows, but it seemed a doubtful identification: whoever it was gave a peal of girlish laughter. It reminded me of Helen during one of her better days, and I thought: This is the first time I've remembered her in hours. I was used to her being a constant obsession, always in my mind, as present as a wound that wouldn't heal, sewn open with love, lust, compassion. I was in Cyprus because of her. I'd taken this deal, potentially illegal as it was, because the commission would allow us to make a new start. I had never forgotten her for so long before, as if she were any other woman. Or as if my obsession depended in part on the environment in which it was born.

I dismissed the idea. I put down my glass and got up to go. I asked Kate to give me a ring around nine. Walking out, I noticed the bird in its cage. The light from the pressure lamps had kept it awake, and at my movement it gave a thin, hesitant tweet. The comparison with the bird at the chapel window made me smile. I asked Kate if she knew what a *hayalet* was.

She repeated the word, searched her memory a moment, then said, "Yes, I remember. My mum told me. She was Irish. It's the Turkish word for banshee. They say if you hear it, it means someone's going to die."

CHAPTER FIFTEEN

The telephone woke me the next morning. I fumbled on the night-stand for the receiver, until I remembered there was no extension to the bedroom loft. I groaned and swung out of bed. My head felt thick and heavy. I rose shakily to my feet and descended the wooden stairs one by one, holding tight to the banister. It was Kate. Breakfast was ready to be served on the terrace. I thanked her and hung up.

I shuffled to the window and opened the shutters. The day was already sharp and bright. I opened the door. The air was fragrant with flowers but held the threat of heat, like a boxer saving his best punch for later.

I took a shower, put on fresh clothes and ate a late breakfast on the terrace. Over coffee I planned the morning. I doubted that I'd hear anything from Dr. Kemal before noon; the most profitable use of time would be to try and fix my problem at its source: Dr. Badawi. It was Saturday, the first day of the workweek in Saudi. I returned to my air-conditioned bungalow, and after several tries, I reached her secretary in Riyadh. Dr. Badawi was in meetings. Could I leave a message? I didn't think I should leave the details with her secretary; I just left a message asking her to give me a call in Girne. I directed her secretary to say it was urgent. After that I paced the miniature living room, wait-ing for the telephone to ring. It remained silent. I paced for more than an hour, until I could no longer stand the sight of the place, then called Kate and told her I was expecting a call and would be in the swimming pool.

To my surprise, Jones was in the shallow end, resting on her elbows on the lip. She wore a modest one-piece suit. Her legs and arms were firm and shapely, and white as her native snow. I said hello and joined her.

"What a coincidence," I said. "Staying here?"

"Yes. Thought I'd do a few laps before it got too hot."

"Did I see you on the terrace last night, with George and his friend?"

She blushed. "They're fun," she said. She was like a young woman who'd discovered that a sexual act she'd thought revolting in theory was pleasurable in practice. "Maybe a little unconventional," she went on. "But this isn't really a conventional place, is it?"

"No. Have you found who, or what, you were looking for?"

"Not yet." Her face and her eyes closed. She slipped farther in, up to her chin. I waded to the other side and did the same.

The pump—if there was a pump—was off, and the water was still and already lukewarm. I closed my eyes and considered how the rest of the day might develop. I might hear from the Arab-American, saying that he'd go ahead with my demand. In that case I'd have to drive down again to the bank later, to confirm with Rifat. Or he might object, insisting on a conference with Badawi first. Or I might not hear from him at all. Yurdagül may have been right: there might not be time for him to get a message back today. There'd been some doubt about cell phone service in the north of the island. My transfer instructions in Manama expired tonight. I'd have to return to Bahrain and sort things out from there.

The scenarios went round and round in my mind, like a carousel. The warmth of the water and the sun's heat lulled me almost into a dream; the carousel's rotation slowed, became fainter, and I imagined Jones, a newly experimental and confident Jones, brushing her body against me as soft as an anemone, and gently pressing her lips against mine.

I knew that kiss. I thought at first I must still be dreaming, until I opened my eyes. It was Helen. Helen in her two-piece bathing suit, her breasts breaking the surface of the water as she floated away. Helen smiling as if she didn't have a care in the world. As if everything she wanted was right here, in this pool under the sunny sky.

She laughed, and said, "You should see your face."

I was too astonished to say anything.

"Aren't you glad to see me?"

"Of course I am. When did you get here? How did you find me?"

"Oh, Steven, you're still asleep. Finding you was easy. I simply called Ayşen. I arrived an hour ago and took a cab here. What a wonderful little place! I checked in and told the girl I'd be staying with you. She didn't give me any trouble at all. I moved into your little holiday home and changed—I wanted to give you a little surprise. Did it work?"

I couldn't remember when I'd last seen her this carefree: treading water and laughing and talking a mile a minute. Her gaiety was infectious and I laughed, too. I swam to her and we embraced.

I said, "You look terrific."

"I feel terrific."

We kissed again, and then I thought to check for Jones—I didn't want to embarrass her. She was just getting out from the deep end. "Hey, you," Helen said, regaining my attention, "so . . . did everything go according to plan?"

I couldn't bear to stop her laughter, to wipe away her smile. I was wondering how to answer, where to begin, when I heard Kate calling me from the terrace.

"Dr. Kemal's on the telephone for you," she said. "You can take it in the office."

"Damn. It's business. I have to take it."

"I'll come with you."

We waded out. I slung a towel over my shoulders and Helen slipped on a robe. Jones had already disappeared in the direction of her bungalow.

Inside the office, Kate handed me the phone. "Hello," I said, "Kemp here."

"Hello Mr. Kemp. It is Yurdagül. I hope you are well."

"Fine, thanks. Any news?"

"Yes. That is why I am calling. Before dawn I sent a messenger north. He has just returned. He found the gentleman I mentioned, the other signatory—he is still here—and brought back a note. Shall I send it to you, or would you like me to read it?

"Please go ahead and read it."

There was a pause, then:

> Dear Mr. Kemp,
>
> The bank has explicit instructions to transfer your client's investment, complete, to your firm. On behalf of your client, please on no account cancel or delay the transfer to Girne. I cannot come to Girne today, due to business here, but can meet you there tomorrow. Hoping you enjoy your stay in Cyprus.

She said, "It is signed, 'Smith.'"

"That's it?"

"That is the message."

"Do you have his phone number?"

"Yes, but I could not reach him earlier. Would you like it?"

"Please." I motioned for a pen and paper, and wrote it down. "Can you tell me exactly where he's staying?"

"Yes. The house is on the coast to the east, between Yali and Mersinlik. They are very small villages. It is not hard to find."

"Thank you, Yurdagül."

"It was my pleasure. I hope now everything will be satisfactory." A couple more pleasantries and we hung up.

I thought. Smith's reply did not begin to address my concerns. In fact, it showed a disregard—or an ignorance—of them. I'd made a mistake letting Dr. Kemal handle it. I should have tried to contact him myself, directly. I asked Kate if she had a wireless or cell phone I could use, and she gave me one; I told Helen to wait a moment, and went out onto the terrace to dial Smith's number.

The number rang, but there was no answer.

I went back inside and asked Kate, "If I had to drive to someplace right on the coast between Yali and Mersinlik, how long would it take to get there?"

She stared at me as if I'd announced an interest in driving to Tasmania. She said, "Yali's less than a hundred kilometers up the coast, but as soon as you leave Girne the road turns into a one-lane dirt track. It would take a couple of hours, maybe longer."

Two hours. I looked at my watch. It was almost one. I needed to talk to Smith today. I could wait around and continue calling—or go for a direct approach. Have it out, face-to-face.

I told Helen, "I'm afraid I have to take a trip up the coast. To a place called Yali. It's connected with the Badawi contract."

The familiar shadow of care, of the steady, background tension that hangs over every expat, or behind every expat's eyes, in the Middle East, drifted across her face. She asked, "Who's in Yali?"

"An Arab-American named Smith. He's only involved on the sidelines of the deal, but I have to talk to him."

Kate said, "Smith's a funny name for an Arab-American, isn't it?"

"I assume the Arab half came from his mother."

Helen said, "I'll go with you. We're on holiday, remember? We'll check out the coast together. Don't worry. I won't be around when you talk business. I'll tour the town or take a walk on the beach."

I didn't have time to object before Kate added, "There's nothing to see in Yali. There's nothing out there but a few shepherds and a few sheep. Plenty of good beaches, though. Take your swimsuits. I can pack you a picnic lunch. There's nowhere on the coast to buy anything decent to eat. There's really nothing there at all."

I told Helen not to worry, the contract was okay, and I'd fill her in on the details on the road. We got into some clothes, picked up a picnic lunch from Kate, and headed east on the coast, up the Karpas peninsula.

Kate was right: within half a mile the road turned to dirt and narrowed to one lane. I could see why driving such a short distance could take so long. The coastline was eroded and irregular. The road followed its every twist and turn. It was potholed and washboard in stretches. Impossible to keep up any speed. Driving the beat-up stick shift took concentration and physical effort. Helen seemed thoughtful and didn't talk much; it would have been difficult to, in any case, above the noise of the suspension. The scenery was worth a look, when I could spare a glance. The Mediterranean was nearly always in sight, and sometimes we'd catch a view of a short, sandy beach—always deserted. But mostly the sea broke in gentle waves over a gravel spit, or in foam against a bluff's rocky base.

The Fiat had no air-conditioning. We rolled down both the front windows but there was little breeze. The kilometers crept by, but we passed no villages, no houses, no sign of habitation. There was only the sun, the deserted road, the occasional glimpses of a deserted shore. It seemed to go on forever. Finally the road descended to a sandy beach, with a couple of cars in sight and a hut offering refreshments. I slipped the car into neutral and coasted down with relief, passing a sign pointing inland with the name of a village—Esentepe.

I pulled up at the edge of the sand and we got out. There was a map in the glove compartment; we unfolded it over the hood. I checked my watch. In over an hour of driving we were less than halfway to Yali.

"Let's have our picnic here," Helen said. Our shirts were sticking to our backs. There was a faint breeze blowing in from the sea. We stripped and changed into our bathing suits behind the car, then carried the basket Kate had given us to a sandy hillock covered with coarse grass.

As impromptu picnics go, it wasn't bad: beef and cheese sandwiches and two bottles of beer. We ate beside each other, facing the sea. We were so far from Harry and from "home"—Dhahran—that there seemed nothing surreptitious about us being together. We were so far away, we were no longer illicit. We'd escaped.

Over the lunch I filled her in. I left out nothing important, but tried to make it as straightforward as I could, a kind of précis. In a few minutes she knew as much as I did. My only omission was my own doubt that I'd have enough guts to cancel the deal, if Smith didn't withdraw.

After I finished, Helen remained silent, thinking. Below, across the beach, two middle-aged couples cavorted unsteadily in the shallow waves. Gray sand crabs emerged tentatively from their holes in the sand, darting for food at the base of our little dune. They reminded me of the crab I'd seen in the cockpit of the sunken Iraqi plane, deep in the Gulf. The day I'd deserted Helen, out of duty, for Harry.

Then Helen said, "I know what's going on, Steven. There's nothing for you to worry about. You have to trust me. And you can't tell anyone. Ever."

She leaned closer to me; her face was as damp with sweat as if we'd been making love, but her eyes were wide open, staring into mine. Appearing to confide something to build trust is a cheap confidence trick; I've seen them all, from the cheapest to the most expensive. In her eyes I saw only what I'd always seen: pure honesty. Looking back, I don't think she ever lied to me, except through omission and through kindness. The lies of kindness she believed—or wanted to believe.

She told me: "Harry's not what you think. His job's not what you think. His job's a cover. He really works for the CIA."

I remember thinking for a split second: What a time for a joke. It was like automatically throwing out a hand for a life preserver. But the ship hadn't carried the mandated number, or the sea was too high. She was serious. She continued, "His whole career's been in the agency. First as a case officer, then chief of station. There's no one left to be chief of, now. He's a one-man band. He told me before we were married—he wanted to give me the option of backing out. I thought it just made him romantic. Of course, there's nothing romantic about it . . . or even very dangerous. Just paying people to give you information, most of the time."

How banal she made it sound. Almost as banal as an investment manager.

"Money keeps the whole thing going," she said. "Almost no one does anything, even talks, for free. But Harry can't go around just handing it out. It would be incriminating. It comes from various banks, various accounts. It's set up to be hard to trace. The CIA must be the biggest money launderer in the world. I'm sure that's what this is, Steven. It's another one of Harry's operations. God knows what for. It means you have nothing to worry about. Nothing."

Flexibility has always been a problem for me. It doesn't come naturally, and it's when I've been most flexible that I've run into the most problems. But like everyone I'm susceptible to influences: money, profit, love; I could accept Harry being a spook if Helen said so. It meant readjusting my idea of him. But the more I thought, the smaller a readjustment it seemed. To me the CIA meant men in trench coats, bumbling men on government payrolls getting things wrong for years—wasn't the CIA often, or usually, wrong, caught off guard? (Hadn't Harry gotten both of us nearly blown up, in Qatif?) Thirty billion dollars a year, or something like that, and what did we get? A lot of surprises. The collapse of the Soviet Union. Missiles and bombs in North Korea. And nothing—no missiles, no anthrax, no WMD—in Iraq. So Harry led a double life. In retrospect he fit the profile: whiskey, politics, and clandestine meetings. Only the trench coat was missing. It was the wrong climate.

Yes, I could believe it. But Badawi—where did she fit in? Helen had an answer for that, too.

"She's probably one of his agents," Helen told me. "I never know who they are, although sometimes I can guess. Badawi's not in it for the money, she has plenty already. She probably needed a visa, for herself or for someone else. Or maybe she has political convictions. Harry can make almost anyone believe he's on their side, if he wants to. We'll never know."

I said, "Didn't she come from you? Wasn't she your idea? Didn't you talk to her, set her up for me?"

Helen looked away for a moment. "Yes, I did. I thought it could be your big contract, the one you needed to get out. I never thought that Harry would get involved—this involved."

"But you think he did."

"I'm sure of it."

"I don't see how this lets me off the hook."

"No one audits the CIA. No one, anywhere, is going to look into this. You're safe. We're safe. We might as well turn around, get back, get off this awful road and spend the rest of the afternoon in the pool at the St. Hilarion."

"And Smith? The Arab-American? Who's he?"

"Probably a local agent. A go-between. Someone to handle a transfer."

She'd solved my mysteries and fixed my problems; she was the fix for my life. But it seemed too easy, like a knot I'd been trying hopelessly to untie and that Helen with one tug had pulled free. I couldn't just accept it. I needed to be sure.

I said, "I still have to see him, Helen. I have to be certain."

"How?"

So I told her, thinking, deciding as I talked. We'd drive up, and I'd go in, leaving her in the car, or in the town—if there was a town. I'd act as if Harry (a close friend and colleague) had put me in the picture. A morning telephone call. I'd just come up to reassure Smith. I'd have to mention the agency, of course, and that should break the ice: the shared secret to create a bond, instill trust. I'd probably walk out knowing more than when I'd walked in. I'd certainly know if Helen was right.

She agreed, reluctantly. I told her: "I can telephone Bahrain to okay the transfer before we ever get back to Girne. We can fly back together to Manama tomorrow."

"I still think we should head back now. Let well enough alone."

I reached out and held her arms. "I can't. I have to do it this way."

She nodded, then looked at her watch. "Right, then. Let's get it over with. Let's go."

We carried our basket to the car and changed back into our clothes. I got the car on the road. I was distracted, thinking of how I was going to handle Smith; Helen was lost in her own thoughts. The scenery, as far as I noticed, did not change. On our right the narrow plain ended at the wall of the coastal range; on our left the Mediterranean stretched away beyond the bluffs. The one-lane dirt road wound on.

Almost two hours later I was in a daze of heat and fatigue, and

Helen was half asleep, swaying in her seat with the turns, when I spotted a lonely signpost pointing inland to Yali. I swerved the Fiat onto the narrow shoulder and stopped the engine. It was past five. We struggled out of the cramped car and spread out the map. Yali and Mersenlik were such tiny dots it was hard to believe they'd been marked accurately. But the next town couldn't be far. Our destination lay midway. We had to be near.

After a few more miles of potholes and washboard, we rounded a bend and almost drove straight into a herd of sheep, shambling toward us on the road. I hit the brakes but missed the clutch. The car shuddered to a halt.

The advance line hesitated, then stumbled forward, pushed by those behind. The herd resumed its unhurried progress south. The car windows were wide open. Outside there wasn't a sound. The silence of the afternoon was complete. The sheep shuffled by, the herd parting and pressing close on each side of the car, as if Helen and I and the vehicle were a tree stump or a rock, just another inert obstacle to get over or around. We could have reached out the window and touched their dusty coats. Then we heard a tinkling—it sounded loud, alone in the silence. Some of the sheep had bells. I looked for a shepherd, but even the sheep were alone. Kate had been right: there was nothing on the coast.

As soon as the animals passed, Helen said, "It could be Connemara: sheep but not a living soul. What's the time?"

I checked my watch; it was just past six. She said, "Let's get out."

I parked on the roadside and Helen led me down to the beach, only a few yards below. It was as deserted as the road. Helen started unbuttoning her shirt.

"What are you doing?"

"Going for a swim. Come on."

In seconds she was stripped to the waist. I hesitated, took another look around, and then kicked off my shoes. She had a head start and was already up to the water's edge, completely naked, before I had my pants off.

I ran and caught up with her in the surf. She laughed, striding forward, like a maenad returning to the sea. She grabbed my hand and we dove into a wave, and came up treading water.

We swam out a little farther than I thought prudent, then turned back to the beach. The sand was hot under our feet; we ran up to the grass below the road and she pulled me down. She was passionate, giving everything a man could want, and taking everything I could give. Afterward, as we lay beside each other, I thought: I'm safe. She'll never go back to Harry.

We let the sun dry us out, then dressed and walked back to the car.

In less than a minute, as we rounded the next bend, the house came into view.

A low bluff had hidden it from sight; it stood in a field a little back from the right side of the road, as alone as the sheep. It was small, with two stories, and looked complete except for the windows on the upper floor. They gaped empty of frames, shutters or glass. A Turkish flag hung limply from a pole on the roof. A sedan was parked off the road nearby, and a bicycle leaned against a wall. Despite the heat a thin sliver of gray smoke rose from a chimney. The house was inhabited.

I put the car in reverse and backed up just far enough to be out of sight. I said, "I hope this won't take long. If it's not Smith I'll be right back. If it is, I'll finish it as soon as I can. You'd better stay here."

"Don't tell him too much."

"He has to know I'm in the picture."

"I just mean be careful."

"I'm always careful." I kissed her, picked up my briefcase from the backseat, and left the car.

I walked around the bend and up to the house. A short stretch of crazy paving led to the front door. I let the brass knocker fall twice. The dusty road was empty, the sea too far away to hear, and no sound came from inside. Silence enveloped me. Then the knob squeaked and turned, and the door swung open.

It was Harry.

A welcoming smile creased his pugilistic face. He wore a clean white shirt without a tie, a blue blazer, and a pair of tan trousers, like a guy on holiday who'd dressed up a little for dinner. He said, "Hello,

Steve. I'm glad you made it." He looked behind me. "Good. You left your friend behind. Come on in."

I stood fixed to the mat; the mention of my "friend" fixed me more rigidly still. He opened the door wider and pulled me gently inside.

I took in my surroundings with the detachment of a dream: the kind you have when you're half awake and know you only have to open your eyes. The living room was furnished. A sofa did double duty as a bed; a pile of sheets lay draped over its arm. An open suitcase was pushed against a wall. Stairs led up to a landing. A simple arch in the back wall led to what looked like a small kitchen and dining area beyond. Across from the sofa a low fire smoldered in a stone fireplace. Green branches tumbled half off the hearth onto the carpet. A bottle of scotch and two glasses stood on a table.

I asked him, "How d'you know I'm with someone?"

"There's a local kid I use sometimes for a lookout. He said you two were having quite a time. Let me guess. A Brit tourist? Something on the side?"

"I'm single. There isn't any side."

"Right, I see." An edge fell into his voice, like the point of a knife slipping out of a sleeve. "Just another piece of tail."

I was barely in the door and we were already wildly off-message. I said, "Let's leave her out of it. What are you doing here?"

Fast as a flick, the edge retracted. "It's a long story, Steve. You've had a helluva drive. Why don't you sit down and have a drink. You look like you could use one."

"I don't want a drink. What's going on? I'm looking for an American named Smith."

"Smith couldn't make it. An unexpected hitch. I had to step in at the last minute."

"I got a letter from him this morning."

"It was from me. I got here last night."

"You're impersonating him?"

"Acting for him. He was supposed to be acting for me." His eyes evaded mine. He looked close to embarrassment, like a man within sight of being caught out. "Look around," he said, turning and sweeping the house with an outstretched arm. "What do you think of it? It's going to be our holiday home, Helen's and mine. She doesn't know it yet. She doesn't know it exists. It's going to be a surprise. I like Ireland, but I won't be able to stand that climate year-round. Hell, I don't think she can, any longer."

He led me on a guided tour. It was a small house and it didn't take long. He took me through the whitewashed kitchen and dining area, and out a sliding glass door to a little patio and an excavation in progress beyond: "Our swimming pool," he said, "when the sea's too rough. The contractor's behind schedule—they're all behind." Then up the stairs to a couple of bedrooms, plastered but not yet painted, with their unglazed windows gaping to the sea. Finally he took me up another narrow flight to the roof. "It's going to be a sundeck," he explained, "and an observation point. You can see up and down the coast for miles." He leaned over the parapet, facing the Mediterranean. The sun, low on the horizon, picked him out clearly, like a photograph you'd want to keep: Harry: the happy homeowner, in the middle of nowhere, Turkish Cyprus.

I glanced surreptitiously down and to the left, but I could see only the top of my car, half hidden behind the bluff. Helen, I assumed, was still in it. Harry said, "Come on, let's go downstairs. I've got to fill you in."

In the living room I sat on the sofa. When he again offered me a drink, I accepted. He poured one for himself. "Normally I wouldn't," he said, "before an operation. But this is an exceptional case."

I said, "Operation?"

He pulled over a chair. "What I'm about to tell you is top secret. You can't tell a living soul. Agreed?"

"Agreed."

He sat hunched toward me. He said, "I'm afraid you're part of it, Steve, whether you like it or not. I wish you weren't. You weren't supposed to be. There wasn't any reason for you to come here, to check things out." He paused, as if aware he was getting sidetracked. He continued, "My job isn't exactly what you think. The Commerce Department is a cover. Always has been. I work for the agency."

I said nothing.

"It's just intelligence work, really, trying to find out what's going on. We're all under cover of some kind. Mine's always been commerce. Has been for thirty years." Perhaps he took my silence for disapproval. He shrugged his shoulders like a man making a joke. "It's a dirty job, but someone's got to do it."

"What's this got to do with Badawi's account?"

"Everything. You were with Helen at the consulate, just two nights ago. You saw it happen?"

"We saw the whole thing."

"How is she?"

"She's okay."

"I'm sorry it took that to get her to move. But at least she'll be safe in Manama. We'll both be joining her soon. If you've any sense, you'll head straight there. Forget about Al Khobar."

Suddenly I wanted a cigarette. I pulled one out and lit it.

He said, "Saudi's imploding. We don't have anyone left to work with. When the royals go, the national guard and the army will go. The government will fall apart. The Saudi jihadists in Iraq are already flooding back. Most Saudis admire them. Whoever tries to take over will have to bring them in. Imagine the Taliban, with oil. Do you think that Washington is going to let that happen? We'll invade. It'll make Iraq look like a birthday party.

"We need another power center. I think I've found one. That's what Badawi's money's for—she hates the jihadists as much as we do, maybe more. Certainly more than she hates the Shia. We're using her money to fund him."

"Fund who?"

"Dr. Abdullatif Ali. Who else?" Harry'd gotten up to pace; now he stopped. "Ali," he said, "represents a chance. He doesn't have to take over the country. All he has to do is take over the Eastern Province. It's where the oil is, and it's where the Shia—his own people—are. The rest of the country can go to hell. It's not important."

So Harry had his dream world. A world dreamed up by a cuckolded spy too incompetent to know that his wife was sitting in a rental car around the corner. A world where Helen would be happy in the middle of nothing and nowhere. A world where a revolutionary manqué in a three-piece suit was going to save Saudi oil for America. I wanted to get out. To leave him to it. Helen was right: I had nothing to worry about. Just one little confirmation and I'd be out of that half-built holiday home, out of Harry's illusions, delusions, back to her.

I said, "So you're giving, somehow, the five percent of the investment to Dr. Ali?"

"That's the plan."

"I'm assuming that, since you're CIA, you'll be able to square the deal with the authorities back in the States—Homeland Security, for example."

He looked at me for a moment as if his mental eye were somewhere else. He glanced at his watch. He said, "I'm afraid it's not that simple."

"Why not?"

"How's your drink?"

"I'm doing fine."

"I'll just have a little top-up." He poured himself some more and switched on a lamp; there wasn't much light coming through the windows.

"It's not that simple," he said, "because this is off-mission."

"What do you mean?"

"It means, Steve, I'm doing it on my own. Hell, they don't even know I'm here. They think I'm massaging some agent in Kuwait." He added, irrelevantly, "I don't even have an agent in Kuwait."

He continued, "The agency's had thirteen directors since I joined. Nowadays the administration listens to the Pentagon, the NSA, even the American Enterprise Institute, before us. There's no way I could get this passed."

We sat silently for a few moments, like two business partners with a divisive problem between us, a conflict of interests. Normally in those situations I always tried hard to stay under complete control. Now I could feel my blood pressure rising. I said, "You can't square things in the States?"

"I'm afraid not. I wish I could."

"Do you realize what you're asking me to do?"

"I'm not asking you to do anything except sit tight and stay mum."

"You're asking me to risk my career, maybe more . . . for this hare-brained scheme. The NSA and God knows who else is automatically monitoring all this stuff. The bank in LA is legally obligated to report the transfer. Someone is going to look at it. It'll be red-flagged. How often do amounts like that—eighteen million—arrive from Girne? It won't take much digging to trace it back to Bahrain. Then they're going to do simple subtraction and wonder where your money went."

"Take it easy. If that's all you're worried about, I'll just bribe Rifat to cook the books a little."

"And the books in Manama, Harry, at Citibank: can you bribe someone there, too?"

"You're overestimating Washington. They're inundated with this stuff. Buried. There's almost no chance of your transfer surfacing."

"Any chance is high risk for me. It'd mean the end of my job. It could mean jail. I'm not willing to risk it."

"What are you going to do?"

"Nothing. All I have to do is not make a telephone call. I'm killing the deal."

He asked, quietly, "Can you afford that?"

"I've still got Badawi's money in Manama. I'll tell her Girne didn't work out. I'll tell her something. I don't think she'll withdraw, just because of this."

We'd reached an impasse. Then I jumped as the doorbell rang.

"Stay put," he said, unnecessarily—where was I going to go?—and went to answer the door. He half opened it. The late-afternoon sun picked out a young boy, maybe thirteen or fourteen years old. They talked together; I couldn't make out what the kid was saying, but I could hear Harry thanking him and telling him to go home. He reached into his pocket, gave him a handful of lira, and closed the door behind him.

"What was that about?" I said.

"He's the lookout. From Mersinlik, up the coast. There's a ship to the west, heading in our direction. There's no port, but the water's deep. They'll anchor close to and land a dinghy. There's a good beach across the road." He started stuffing the fireplace with the pile of green branches.

"What are they landing?"

"This is a pickup, not a drop-off." The branches were beginning to smoke. "Come on," he said, "let's go up to the roof. We'll be able to see it from there."

I followed him back up the stairs. The sun was getting low. It illuminated the ship clearly: a little freighter, the kind of tramp steamer you can still see in Turkish ports, making for shore.

"What part of the plan is this?" I asked.

"You don't make an omelet," Harry said, using one of his hackneyed phrases, "without breaking a few eggs. Ali needs something more serious than the rusty popguns the Shia have under their beds in Qatif."

"You're smuggling arms?"

"Old Soviet stuff from Adjaria, on the Black Sea. It only takes a day to get through the Bosphorus, down the Sea of Marmara, into the Med. There aren't any customs, any tolls, any checks. Nine hundred thousand buys a lot in that part of the world. It's just another cargo for them. From here it'll go through Suez, down past Aden, up through Hormuz. They'll land it at night around Ras Al Gar, near Qatif."

"That's just up the coast from Khobar."

"So it is." He squinted down the coast. "Can you see a car down the road? My eyesight's not what it used to be."

I looked but all I saw was the roof of my own car and the irregular coastline meandering south. Then, out from behind a bluff, I saw a car heading in our direction. It disappeared around a bend. I said, "Yes, there's a car coming."

"It should be Ali."

It took a second for it to register. "Ali's here?"

"They're picking him up."

"Without the money?"

"You don't carry money bags these days, Steve. He'll make the last transfer from his own account, from his cell phone, before they reach Suez."

"If it's that simple, what are you here for?"

"To give him the account name and number. But basically just to make sure. Anyone could do it."

Anyone . . . any Arab-American. I said, "It was Joe, wasn't it, who was supposed to show up?"

He sighed. "My mistake. He's not really an operational type. Even as an informant he never had anything important, or something I didn't already know."

"So he's still in jail?"

"I'll try to spring him again when I get back, but it'll be harder. They'll make him talk—they always do. A guy like Joe always has some dirt to hide. But he doesn't know anything about Badawi. There's nothing important for him to blow."

The sun was nearing the horizon. It was that point in the late afternoon when everything is still. The Turkish flag on the pole hung limp; the smoke from the chimney rose straight up into the air. The sea was calm. The freighter made slow, steady progress toward the coast below.

Harry broke the silence. "I've done this more times than I can remember. Thirty years at the game. This is the first time I ever did anything—at least, anything important—off-mission.

"In my line of work, you create situations, you enable groups. Parties more aligned to our interests than others. You don't always wind up backing the people you'd like. Early on you realize you've got to make a choice. Either you get out, and save your principles, or you stay in. If you stay in, it's because you hope you'll be able to do more good than bad along the way. To even out the scorecard." He stopped and looked down the road. "Do you see him?"

"No," I said. "He's probably around one of the bends."

"My night vision . . . anyway, I totted up the scorecard not long ago. It didn't look too good. If we have to invade Saudi we're going to have a lot of dead soldiers. But if we only have to help secure the east. . . . I think Ali's the one chance we've got. He may not be much, but I don't see any other. So that's what I'm doing. Trying to add something to the plus side."

We could see the car clearly now. It was nearing my own. I said, "I'm sorry, Harry. I wish I could help."

"Would you do it for Helen?"

I didn't understand.

He said, "She's an idealist. She'd back me up."

"She's not part of this."

"All you have to do is make a phone call."

I shook my head. I thought: He can't force me. Then I saw his boxer's hands clenched on the parapet. After a moment they relaxed. Despite his appearance—and his job—I don't think he was really the violent type. Or maybe he was just getting old. He said heavily, "Come on then. Let's go and get it over."

Downstairs he got another glass from the kitchen, then refilled ours. I said, "I thought you didn't drink before an operation."

"I don't. Having second thoughts?"

"No."

"Then there isn't any operation. Bottoms up."

"You have to understand my position."

"I understand your position better than you think. You're straight—in business."

I was about to ask him what he meant, but the doorbell rang.

Before he could reach the door it swung open, and Dr. Ali stumbled in as if pushed. A sense of déjà vu gripped me: he looked almost as he had when I'd first seen him, when he'd walked into our apartment on the eleventh floor of Silver Towers. He even wore a suit and tie, although the jacket hung over his arm. But his air of authority was compromised. He blinked with confusion, as if he'd gotten off on the right floor but walked into the wrong flat.

Helen strode in behind him. She pulled the door closed and turned around. She looked strung-up, almost high. Then she saw Harry. Shock, disappointment, anger chased across her face. She said, "Harry," and the name sounded like the last person on a long list she never wanted to find.

I don't think Ali recognized me at first. He turned to Harry and said, "Mr. Laird? Your wife didn't tell me . . . I'm pleased to meet you."

He peered at me, but recognition brought more confusion, not less. "Mr. Kemp?"

Harry looked nearly as stunned. He asked Helen, "You're supposed to be in Antalya. What are you doing here?"

"Making sure. That everything works. That nothing happens—to Ali."

Harry let this sink in before saying, "Nothing's going to happen to him. Just what we both planned."

"Then why are you here?"

"I had to step in. My agent couldn't make it. A last-minute hitch." Helen's suspicion was unmistakable; it irradiated the room. Harry gave a short, mirthless laugh, and said, "What did you think I was doing? A setup?"

I couldn't stop hearing what Harry had said: "What we both planned." It was like an echo in my head. The implication was there, staring me in the face. She had known about the operation: they'd planned it together. Had she known it was theirs alone? Off-mission?

Nearly all love affairs are challenged by betrayals, major or minor, but usually only after years of habit have anesthetized, or semi-anesthetized, the perpetrator—and the victim. Our affair had barely started. My nerves were still raw.

No one said anything; then Harry broke the silence. He told me: "Steve, you'd better get back to your friend." I hardly heard him. I was trying to figure out how far back the lies of omission went. "Steve," he said, but Helen told him to leave me alone. He gave her a long look, then asked Ali, "Did you drive here alone?"

"Of course. I followed Mrs. Laird's instructions."

Harry turned to his wife. "It was you in his car. You on the beach, wasn't it?"

Her one idea had been confrontation. I don't think she'd thought as far ahead as explaining herself. Her lips opened, then closed. Her confidence seeped away.

Harry said, "Of course it was."

I'd sometimes thought about how I would break the news to him, the news that she'd left him for me. It wasn't a job a man would leave to his mistress. I was always the one to initiate it. I looked at Helen. The color had drained from her face. I said stupidly, as if denial were an option, "What are you talking about?"

I think he finally came close, then, to throwing a punch. I think he gave it some thought. Instead he just said: "Your affair with my wife."

It was a tableau I won't forget: myself, Helen, Dr. Ali—all of us wondering what came next. There was a lot in common with the beginning of the story. Only Harry was new, the odd man out.

Helen whispered, "How long . . ."

Harry sat down heavily on the sofa and reached for his glass. "How long have I known?"

"Yes."

"I don't know. Probably from the beginning."

"How did you . . ."

"How did I figure it out? You're amateurs. You married an older man, remember?" He cradled his drink. "Thirty years on the job." Then, almost consolingly, like she'd failed a test he never expected her to pass, "You lacked experience."

Ali said, "Harry, I am sorry, but the ship. It must be time for me to go."

"You aren't going anywhere. The deal's off. Mr. Kemp won't make the transfer." In the deepening confusion one thing was clear: I was the spoiler.

Ali looked at me accusingly. He asked Harry, "What do you mean?"

"He won't transfer the money."

"Why not?"

"Ask him."

The doctor addressed me as if I were a slow student undergoing an oral examination. "Mr. Kemp, do you understand the purpose, the intended outcome, of these funds?"

It was his pompous phraseology all over again. I said, "Yes, I do. I'm sorry. I can't do it. It's too risky."

Helen interrupted us. "Steven, I explained—there's nothing to worry about."

"Harry explained more thoroughly than you did."

"Don't waste your breath," Harry told her. "I already filled him in."

Ali hadn't yet got the message. He said, "Mr. Kemp, Mr. Laird is doing me and my movement a great service. His motivation is to save lives, American and Arab. He is being of great assistance to my cause." It sounded like a small part of a much longer speech: the founding father acknowledging his gratitude to his foreign comrade-in-arms.

Harry told him, "It's over. You'd better call your contact on the ship. Tell them not to land."

Helen stepped toward me. "Wait. Do you know why we're doing this?"

"Like he said: he filled me in."

"Harry, tell him again. Make him understand."

He sat hunched over, with his elbows on his knees, speaking to the floor: "I just wanted to even things out a little, before I'm finished. I don't know if Ali has a chance or not."

No one had anything to say to that. I hadn't been swayed; I'd stuck to my guns. No one was taking me for any ride. I'd done what I knew was right, what was the correct and the legal thing to do. But it didn't feel that way.

Helen said, quietly, "Steven, you have to make that transfer."

There's a word for what I felt: whipsawed.

She said, "It's not about you. Not any longer."

"It could put everything at risk."

"Everything?"

"You and me."

"Are we that important?"

I've gone over it a hundred times since then. Had I just come to the end of my resistance? Professional interrogators say that everyone does, sooner or later, although this wasn't exactly an interrogation. Did I do it for Helen, because I was afraid of losing her? Or because it was, somehow—despite the illegality, despite all my doubts—the "right" thing to do? I still don't know. Certainly if I'd known the consequences—for everyone—I wouldn't have done it. But it's impossible to foresee all the consequences of any action. All you can do is hope for the best.

I pulled out my cell phone, and dialed the bank manager's number in Manama. When he answered I identified myself, told him I wanted to make the transfer, and gave him the code word we'd agreed upon. I asked if he could guarantee it would go out that night. He said it would. I thanked him and hung up.

Helen stood silent. Harry only said, "I'm damned." It was Dr. Ali who walked over, shook my hand and thanked me.

"And now," he said, "I must leave you. Mr. Laird, don't you think it's time?"

"Yes. Do you need help getting down to the beach?"

"No. I am taking only one small bag. I know how much I owe you. I hope to see you again, either in Washington, or Qatif."

Harry cracked a smile, perhaps at the unlikely juxtaposition of the two cities. He got up and took a slip of paper out of his wallet and handed it to Ali. I suppose it was the information he needed to access the Girne account. Then Ali embraced him and kissed him on both cheeks in the Arab way: without the lips actually touching the skin.

Ali nodded at me, but avoided Helen. I don't think he was being rude. He was just unsure of how to handle the situation. He walked out with dignity and shut the door.

After a moment, Helen went to the window and drew the drape. "He's climbing down the bluff."

I said, "Congratulations, to both of you."

Harry was back in his chair. He said, "Your commission's as good as in the bank."

"It won't be much use if I wind up in jail."

"Pin it on me. I'm through anyway."

Helen left the window and walked over to him. I thought I saw shame in her eyes. She said, gently, "We thought we were cleverer than we were. I didn't want you to know. I never wanted to hurt you."

He looked up. His face showed pain, an expression I'd never seen there before. I suddenly wanted out, if only for a few minutes. I retreated into the kitchen. The sliding glass door to the patio and pool was open; I stepped through and in the gloom almost walked into Miss Jones.

I only got out half an expletive before her hand clamped over my mouth. "Quiet," she whispered. I stood still, and her hand dropped a little.

I whispered back, "What are you doing here?"

"Is it just the Lairds inside?"

"Yes. You know them?"

"I've been listening," she said. Like so many of her replies, it was only a partial answer. She said, "We'd better go in." She didn't sound enthusiastic and she didn't make a move, so I went first. She followed.

I interrupted them with an introduction: "Harry, Helen . . . Miss Jones." They looked up blankly at the new arrival.

Harry said, "Skrypnek."

"Hello, Harry."

"What the hell are you doing here?"

She stepped past me. "Can we talk—alone?" She added, "I don't think there's much time."

"Why not?"

"I think there's a team. I'm not sure they're friendly."

A shadow of what must have been his old professional self returned: he sat straighter and said, steadily, "Start with why you're here."

She glanced at Helen and me, as if to reassure herself we were bona fide. She said, "Langley's suspicious. They have been for a while. They're not sure you're keeping them in the loop."

"So they sent you?"

"Yes."

I said, "'Jones'?"

She looked almost apologetic. "Common. One syllable. Easy for us to memorize; easy for them to forget." It sounded like an early lesson. I was certain she had them all memorized.

Harry asked, "How did you find me?"

"I decided to follow your wife, but she and Mr. Kemp left the hotel suddenly. By the time I picked up their trail they were already being followed."

"By Ali."

"By two cars."

"Two?"

"I picked up the second near Esentepe."

"Who's in it?"

"Saudis. Four of them. I saw them in town last night. It's the same car. They look like a team."

Harry stood up. "Did they see you?"

"I don't think so. They had to drive like hell to catch up and left a cloud of dust. I kept well back."

"Where are they now?"

"Their car's about half a mile away, parked off the road. They climbed down to the beach. I found their tracks. They were heading in this direction, keeping close in to the dunes." She looked at her watch. "They've had about twenty minutes. They're in sand and they'll have to climb back up to the road. But I still don't think we have more than five or ten minutes. I think this is a good time to leave."

Helen said, "We have to warn Ali."

Harry pulled out his cell, and punched in some numbers. He held it to his ear for a few moments, then slipped it back into his jacket. "Either it's off or his battery's dead. Come on, let's go."

She said, "We have to do something."

"It's too late. He's on the beach by this time. He'll make it or he won't. There's nothing we can do. We'll take my car." He started out, but Helen grabbed him.

"Harry, he saved our lives—mine and Steven's—we can't just leave him."

He caressed her shoulder with one of his big, fat hands. "Honey, it's over. I did as much as I could. We have to cut our losses. Don't make me manhandle you into the car."

He had a good grip on her arm and dragged her with him through the door. Jones—somehow I still can't think of her as Skrypnek—and I followed.

Harry made for his car with Helen, while Jones cased the road; I walked across and looked out to sea. The sun was about to touch the horizon. The freighter was plainly visible, riding at anchor. I didn't see a dinghy. I did see a small, solitary figure, standing erect, out in the distance, by the shore. No one else was in sight.

I wasn't thinking: he saved my and Helen's life. I was just taking in who and what was visible, and who and what wasn't. I heard Jones say, "The road looks clear."

It was now or never. I said, "I'm going to warn him."

Harry spun round. "What?"

"I'm going to warn him. It's not too late."

"You're out of your fucking mind."

"He's in sight. There's no one else. I don't see a dinghy, do you?"

They crossed the road and we peered at the waves. Jones had the youngest eyes. It was she who answered, "No."

Harry said, "We don't have time for heroics."

"I can get there and back in five minutes, maybe less."

"With Ali?"

"That'll be up to him."

I started down the bluff. Harry yelled, "Wait." He asked Jones, "Do you have a firearm?"

"Yes. Do you?"

"No." And then, as if he had to explain himself, "Never had to use one." He looked out at the figure on the shore. "God dammit."

Helen tried to say something, but Harry cut her off. He turned back to Jones. "Do you object to hanging around for five minutes?"

"He's important to you?"

"Yes."

"Okay."

Harry told me, "This is the stupidest thing I've done in thirty years. Think twice."

"I've thought twice."

"Then get going. I'll be down the bluff, keeping a lookout. Skrypnek will be up here with Helen. When you see him, if the dinghy's there, tell him to get in and shove off. If it isn't, tell him to drop everything and get back. If you hear a shot, forget him. Just get back yourself. As fast as you can. Got it?"

"Got it." I started down the narrow path to the beach.

It wasn't a characteristic decision.

I might have turned back if I'd had time to think about it. The grassy bluff dropped off suddenly, not steeply enough to hurt yourself badly if you fell, but steep enough to make you want to watch your step. It must have taken the doctor of comparative religion some time; he didn't look fit, and I'm sure he was wearing the wrong shoes. I didn't have time for caution. I just ran down, trying not to pitch headlong.

When I reached the sand I spotted the figure right away, out near the surf. He looked farther away than he had from above—a trick of the light, maybe, or maybe just my nerves. I scanned the beach. It looked deserted, except for him. I was already winded but couldn't stop to catch my breath; I started a steady jog to the sea.

The salt smell reminded me of LA and how I'd jogged on the beach in Santa Monica in my better days. Anything to keep my mind off the Arabs up the coast. Jones had suggested that marching in sand would slow them down, but weren't Arabs used to sandy conditions? Unless they were urban-bred. But weren't most of the national guard, at least, Bedouin? I sucked in air and the sand sucked at my shoes. On the beach in LA I'd be barefoot. This time of day the pretty young blondes and the surfer boys would be gone, back on the road. It would be nearly as deserted as it was now. But something was missing. The lifeguard huts. There were no lifeguards on Turkish Cyprus.

I was near enough to identify him now, even in the failing light, even with his back to me. He had one arm over his head, although I couldn't pick out to whom or what he was signaling. I'd got to within easy shouting distance but I had to stop and bend over, my hands on my knees, rasping (it was the cigarettes), trying to catch some breath. I straightened up and yelled, "Ali. It's me, Kemp."

He swiveled as if I'd pressed a button.

I waved, caught some more breath and hollered, "Steve Kemp. We've got to get out. Now. Forget the boat. We've got to leave."

We stood there, staring at each other over the length of sand. Probably he wondered what on earth I was up to. He cast a quick glance back over his shoulder and then started walking toward me. That's when I finally saw the dinghy, floating low but not far out, as it crested a wave. I thought he could wade out to meet it and was about to tell him to stop, when he doubled over as if someone had punched him in the gut. I heard a pop, like a toy gun, then two more, from up the beach. He fell over on his side, curled up. I stood there a moment or two, but I didn't see him move after he went down.

I turned and ran like hell. I don't know where my wind came from. I thought I heard more shots, but couldn't be sure—I was pounding the sand too hard. I reached the bluff and started scrambling. Halfway up I stopped—I hadn't a breath left—and heard Harry: "Keep going but keep your head down. They might be on the road." He was crouching in the grass, keeping a lookout.

I gasped, "Thanks for covering me."

"Skrypnek hasn't fired a shot. They're out of range and you can't see shit. Did they get him?"

"Yes."

"We've got to get back to the car. You first."

I made it to the top with my head swimming. Jones was there, on the edge of the road, holding her revolver in both hands. Helen crouched behind her.

Jones asked, "He didn't make it?"

I said, "No."

Helen whispered, as if we were on a bluff in County Limerick instead of Turkish Cyprus, and the sea was the river Shannon instead of the Mediterranean: "God have mercy on his soul."

Harry clambered up behind me. "The shots came from the west."

Jones looked down the coast. "I think they're near the end of that cliff. I doubt they've made it back to the road yet."

"So you think we should try to get past them?"

"If we head east, we'll be running from them all night. There's nothing up there. I checked the map. At least Girne's west. And the road to the airport."

"They might have sent someone back to the car."

"I didn't see anyone. But you're right, we don't know for sure."

"Okay, it's west to Girne. Come on."

It sounded reasonable at the time.

We ran across the road. Harry got in the driver's seat with Jones beside him; Helen sat next to me, behind her husband. I don't think we got more than a hundred yards. Harry had to take the first turn slowly, and as soon as my rental came into view we heard shots and metallic thuds on the car's body; a starburst exploded on the windshield, and the car swerved sharp left. He must have hit the brakes: we went off the road and stopped hard, but we didn't hit anything. There was nothing but low brush to hit.

Jones yelled, "Keep down," flung open her door and rolled out like a parachutist hitting the ground. Harry opened his door and fell out. I think Helen called his name.

We heard more shots. I thought that the car would afford as much protection with us outside it as it did with us in, and at least we could run, if we had to. Then we heard another thud as a bullet hit a panel. I thought of the gas tank and that decided me. I opened my door and grabbed Helen's hand, telling her to keep low. We clambered out and crouched in the grass. Harry had crept around and knelt beside us. I didn't see Jones.

The shooting from the Arabs' side of the road was sporadic and aimed at the car, if it was aimed at all. I didn't hear any from us. I asked Harry where Jones was.

"She's trying for their flank. Get ready to run when I tell you. Take Helen. Head for the fields beyond the car. Wait until I give the word."

I waited. After a minute another volley of bullets whizzed in our direction, a couple hitting the car. We crouched lower. It was getting dark now, and I was wondering if I should just go ahead, take advantage of the next lull and make a run for it with Helen, when Jones opened up.

She must have crawled down through the grass, and then crossed the road without them seeing her. We could tell it was her from the way she shot: carefully and methodically. I heard a scream for God in Arabic, and then from another voice only a scream. I raised my head and peered over the hood.

It was dark enough to see the flame spurt from her barrel. She advanced on them, holding her revolver with both hands straight out in front. I expect it looked like one of the exercises she'd gone through in training in Langley. I'm sure she scored high during those sessions; she scored very high on the Karpas peninsula in Cyprus. But she wasn't properly equipped for night fighting.

The first bullet hit her foot. She stumbled and dropped one hand, then raised it again to steady her aim, and went down on one knee. I think she was waiting for the flash to see where to aim. Another shot rang out from their side of the road and she returned fire twice, with deliberation. There was silence for several moments. She stood up. Then the last Arab shot her from the grass verge behind.

He must have been hiding, and let her pass him as she advanced to the car. Biding his time. His tactic didn't do his companions any good: they were all dead or dying.

The bullet struck one of her ribs, just below her arm. It spun her around and dropped her. She lay on the road by my car. The Arab rose from the grass and walked toward her; as he got closer he started shooting at her prone figure. But he was a poor shot, or maybe by that time too panicked to aim. She managed to fire once more, and he crumpled to the ground.

Harry ran out to her. Helen and I followed. Jones was leaning on her elbow, trying to get up. Her face was contorted, but she told Harry to take her gun and check the Arabs. Helen asked her where she was wounded, and went into nurse mode. She asked for my shirt for a bandage and compress and folded it and tied it around Jones's chest; then she removed the shoe from the injured foot as carefully as she could, and used one of her own socks for a tourniquet above the ankle. The girl whimpered but never complained; Harry on the other hand swore steadily as he stumbled through the grass and the gloom, looking for bodies and firearms.

Helen insisted on driving Jones to Girne herself. We carried her to my car, and got her as comfortable as we could in the backseat, lying on her good side. I gave Helen my keys and she drove off.

Harry and I got back into his car, but he asked me to drive. I was so high on adrenaline I didn't notice at first how exhausted he looked. I reversed onto the road and headed west after Helen.

I hadn't gone far when I heard him moaning. I asked him if he was okay, and he said, "No, I'm not." I stopped the car. The passenger seat was forward and Harry sat with his knees up, his head back on the headrest, his face in a grimace of pain. He held his left hand over his chest. I reached down between his knees for the lever and shifted the seat as far to the rear as it would go, then switched on the overhead light.

Beneath his blazer, under the dim bulb, his shirt was black with blood. He'd been hit in the chest, I think by one of the first shots. I never learned much first aid but I knew that pressure has to be applied to a bleeding wound. But I was shirtless and there was nothing available. I told him to keep his hand pressed as tight as he could to his jacket. To make him more comfortable I pulled the recline lever, but the seat only tilted a few degrees; it was a cheap car. He seemed to breathe a little easier, and said something I didn't understand about "ducking the angina." I started the engine again and put my foot on the accelerator. Helen was long gone—I couldn't even see her taillights.

After a few miles I remembered my cell phone and pulled it out and dialed 911, as if I were in LA, but there was no ring. I asked him the local number for emergencies, but he said, weakly, "I don't think they've got that far yet."

"There's bound to be a hospital in Girne." It was hours away.

I wheeled around the twists and turns until he gasped, "Slow down. You don't want to go over the edge." So I slowed down. We drove on in silence. I was worried about the bleeding, but I didn't know what else I could do.

After a while I heard him say something about a commission. I said, "What, Harry? What did you say?"

"Don't worry about the money. You're safe. It won't leave the bank now."

I began picking up a little speed again, but gently, trying not to rock the car. I thought he was breathing easier. When he spoke again, it wasn't more than a whisper, and I had to lean over to hear him. His mind must have been wandering: he said, "Get Helen out of there. I told her she had to move to Manama. I want her there when I get back. Make sure she goes."

"Sure. We'll all be there, Harry."

"You got her out once . . . from Silver Towers. You've got to do it again."

"Don't worry, I'll get her out."

He said something else, but I didn't catch it. I thought I heard him say something about "the bastards," and then I heard one word: "Fuck." After a couple more miles of twists and turns, and I hadn't heard anything, I switched off the ignition and let the car coast in neutral. It rolled gently to a halt.

The hand holding the jacket had slipped and hung down by his side. His head was back, his eyes half closed. His breathing was shallow but rapid, like someone running a race with only half a lung. I thought for some reason I should check his pulse, and groped for his wrist under the dim overhead light. I felt nothing, but then I've never had any training and have never consistently been able to find my own. In any case, he was still alive. I started the car and drove on to Girne.

CHAPTER SIXTEEN

Harry didn't make it.

I got to Girne more than an hour behind Helen, due to a flat tire about twenty kilometers out of town. I don't think the delay made any difference. I met Helen at the hospital. Fortunately she had already called the U.S. Embassy in Ankara to inform them of Jones's injuries. She collapsed when I told her that her husband was dead. The doctors sedated her and insisted she remain the night in the hospital. I spent the night alone at the St. Hilarion, after agreeing with the local police not to leave town until they'd finished their investigation. I phoned Ankara and told them about Harry.

It was another complication for the embassy; they probably wondered what was coming next. But Harry's "diplomatic" status saved me a lot of trouble. The Turkish authorities, including their representatives in Cyprus, were wonderfully cooperative. There's a lot to be said for a country like Turkey, with strong political, military, and intelligence ties to the U.S., and a government apparatus that can take charge of such things in a directive way, without worrying too much about judicial oversight, local procedures, or the press. I hope Turkey achieves its ambition to join the European Union, although, given the characteristics I found so helpful, I don't expect it to happen for many years yet.

I managed to visit the hospital the next morning. Helen was still on medication and was not talkative. She did insist that she wanted to return to Manama. From there she could supervise the disposition and removal of hers and Harry's household effects. Also, I think the Gulf was still home for her; she wanted to go home. The doctor told me that Jones would recover, but she was in a morphine sleep, pale, with a couple of IVs in her arms. I didn't get to talk to her. I never saw her again.

They were flown to Ankara that afternoon in a chartered jet sent by the embassy (or maybe the CIA). Harry went with them, in the cargo hold.

I never found out what happened to Ali or the Arabs we left on the road.

On the second day an American diplomat flew over from the mainland to have a talk. We met in my miniature living room at the St. Hilarion; I was under a kind of unofficial house arrest that extended to Girne. (Kate handled the situation with as much aplomb as she had the double suicide.) He was a young man in a neat gray suit, very clean-cut and respectful, like one of my firm's domestic account managers who had gotten on the wrong plane and landed on the wrong island. Over a can of Coca-Cola he gave me a friendly "debriefing."

I told him the whole story. He nodded seriously as I related it, taking the occasional note on a yellow legal pad from his briefcase, as if I were analyzing a major sale the firm had thought locked up, but which due to unforeseen circumstances had fallen through. Later he even asked me to sign a document—some kind of official secrets thing. But I dug in my heels. I told him I intended to resume my job on the Gulf. As long as I was able to do that, as long as my company stayed in the dark, and Badawi's investment was cleared, I'd keep my mouth shut. I thought Harry would have been proud of me. The "diplomat" resigned himself. He said we had a deal. He may have been relieved: I wasn't really important, and I wasn't asking for much.

After that there was nothing to hold me for. The embassy in Ankara told me Helen had already left for Manama; I flew to Istanbul the next day and caught a connecting flight to Bahrain.

I arrived late at night and took a taxi from the airport straight to my hotel. From there I called the embassy switchboard and got patched through to Helen's guesthouse. Her voice on the phone sounded distant, as if she were still sedated. She said it was too late to meet, but asked if I could pick her up from church the next morning, after the nine o'clock Mass.

At nine-thirty I parked my car on a dusty side street outside the Sacred Heart Catholic church. One of the few churches in the Arab Gulf, it's a humble, stuccoed building dating back to British administration, before the country discovered oil. The tin roof was replaced with tiles during the affluent '70s, but then the oil dried up and improvements stopped. I walked through the gate and up to the west porch. The service was still going on. I quietly opened the door and slipped in.

The interior is a simple, hall-like nave, without aisles or side chapels. The walls are whitewashed and devoid of ornamentation, except for carved stations of the cross. A baptismal font stands at your left as you walk in; an old-fashioned dark confessional, complete with doors for the confessor and penitents, stands against the wall on your right.

It was a third world version of my childhood Catholicism, even to the odor of stale sweat overlaid with incense. I almost, from a forgotten habit, dipped my fingers into the holy water to make a sign of the cross. The nave was more than half empty, the congregation standing. I edged over to the confessional, stepping into its shadow.

In front of the altar a stout, pale priest, maybe an Irish missionary, had almost finished bestowing communion to a row of Filipinos and Sri Lankans kneeling at the rail. The dark faces stood out against the stark white of the walls. The effect—the heavy, white priest, the slight, dark communicants—was anachronistic, colonial.

Helen was easy to pick out, tall and white as the priest. She was toward the front. I had no wish to disturb the service, for her or anyone else. I slipped back out. The heat and humidity were already intense. I sat in my car with the air-conditioning on, waiting for the service to end.

After a few minutes the doors opened and the congregation filed out into the road. They were happy; for most of them, their sins had been forgiven. Their voices rose in a happy babble. Through the mystery of transubstantiation they had shared in the body and blood of their beloved savior. Even as a boy I'd found it difficult to comprehend; as a teenager I'd jettisoned it. I was only interested in one body: Helen's.

I got out and stood by the car. She spotted me almost as soon as she emerged, her hand to her eyes, shielding them from the glare. She looked thinner. She walked over and greeted me with a modest kiss to the cheek. Bahrain's a looser country than Saudi but the whole Gulf's tightening up; I refrained from embracing her. I held her door open while she got in. I offered to drive her back to the embassy but she wanted instead to go to my hotel. She said she wanted a cool drink in the lobby. We'd be able to talk.

We found two chairs at some distance from the rest, and I ordered us both drinks. She'd spoken little in the car; now she asked me to tell her again about Harry's death. It didn't take long.

After I finished we sat for a while in silence. She sat facing me, her shoulders hunched. When she spoke, it was as if she were already distant, already on the wing, but with a message to give, something serious she had to work out with me, before departing.

She said, "I was married to Harry for ten years, and I feel as if I'm just now really beginning to understand him, to appreciate him. I wonder if that's normal for widows to feel, soon after they've lost their husbands."

I said, carefully, "You're grieving. It's normal."

"He was always so negative, especially here, in the Arab world. Despite the fact that it was his world, really, certainly more his world than Ireland. I doubt he would have been happy there." She added, inconsequently, "I'll have to sell that ridiculous house in Cyprus."

"You don't have to do anything for a while."

She continued as if she hadn't heard me. "It was his idea to use some of Badawi's money to fund Ali, he said he'd never get the okay from the agency. I didn't know whether he was doing it for me—maybe an attempt to regain my affection, my respect—or for himself.

My job was to meet Ali in Antalya—we'd recognize each other—to brief him, give him the passport he'd need. But Harry was always so secretive. It was part of his job. Secrecy breeds distrust: it's like an infection. It infected me. I began to distrust him. That's why I flew to Cyprus. But it was you I should have distrusted. You with your certainties, your fear of consequences."

For days the memory of what she'd told me on the coast had lain like something badly buried, something I wanted to keep underground. Now it was disinterred, with one turn of the shovel, in the bright light of day. She'd told me I had nothing to worry about, that Harry would fix everything. She'd been willing to betray me to protect their operation—or at least, to betray my interests, which I'd thought were hers. But wasn't it, most of it, just lies of omission? And maybe she'd believed the rest. It didn't matter. I still wanted her. There wasn't even anything to forgive.

She put her hand on mine. "You see things in black and white, Steven—right and wrong. I thought of you this morning, when I was listening to the sermon in church. It wasn't a very good sermon—the priest wasn't very articulate. It must be a difficult mission. Perhaps he even drinks, like Harry. He tried to talk about giving to Caesar what's Caesar's. How not breaking our laws was as important as not breaking God's. It was a sermon for children. Like the catechism.

"I don't think life's black and white. Harry didn't think so. He tried to do the right thing, or work toward the right end, but the method, the means. . . . We're taught, aren't we, that the end never justifies the means. But they were flexible, for him. I think it depended on how important the end was, the objective. There were only a few rules he wouldn't break. Certainly not the rules of governments. There wasn't much sacred for him there. People were what counted. Not the arbitrary rules of states, of agencies, of whoever might be making them up, might be in power at the time.

"You don't see things that way. You see life more like that priest does: black and white. You were always afraid of breaking the rules. Even the rules of accounting."

"You'd be surprised," I said, "how flexible accounting can be."

"Well, then, like the financial regulations you always talked about. But life isn't like that. Harry was willing to break the rules—some man at the embassy even accused him of being corrupt; what a silly word to describe Harry—if he thought it might lead to a greater good."

I couldn't protest that I'd transferred the money. I'd done it too clearly under duress. Instead, I said: "We both broke the rules. You and I. With our affair."

"Yes. The one that Harry wouldn't break. He didn't have many absolute loyalties. He broke rules for others. We did it for ourselves. And he let us. He loved me that much."

"He was sure you'd stay with him."

"Was he? Do you think he would have wanted me to?"

"Love's selfish, Helen. That's part of it."

"You can accuse him of love. Can you accuse him of selfishness?"

A waiter came over and asked if we wanted fresh drinks; Helen shook her head. After he left she said, "You and I both hated the secretiveness, the lies, the deceptions. But don't you feel that what we had depended on it? Don't you feel that now, it's over? Everything: my marriage, our life in Dhahran, our affair?"

I tried to choose my words carefully. "I never thought of it as temporary—as an 'affair.' I loved you. I still love you. I hope you love me."

"I feel as if it was all wrapped up together—almost as if we needed Harry to make it work."

"I didn't fall in love with you because you were married. Harry was an impediment. Now he's gone. The impediment's gone."

"He was what brought us together. Remember, that first day? You were calling him, not me."

He was like a ghost that wouldn't be laid to rest, the breaker of rules held up as a virtuous example. I was suddenly weary. I'd reached the point where all I could do was repeat myself. But how many different ways are there to say, "I love you, I know you love me"? And she wasn't in a receptive mood. I wanted to hold her, but couldn't in the hotel lobby. She was withdrawn, and withdrawing further. Like someone slowly dying and fading slowly, and I could do nothing but sit there, watching her, both of us, die.

She stood and said she had to get back to the embassy. I offered to drive her but she insisted on a taxi. It was like a small cruelty. I said, "I don't even know how long you're staying."

"Neither do I."

"When will I see you again?"

"I don't know."

"At least you won't leave without telling me?"

"No, of course not, Steven."

It was something. I said, "I'll give you a call." But she had already turned, walking alone out the foyer.

My ex-wife always used to tell me that I was out of touch with my emotions, and it's true that sometimes they creep up on me unawares. I could feel tears coming. I didn't want to make a fool of myself in public, and walked into an empty elevator and pressed the button. Before the door slid closed, one of the Indian girls the hotel employs to meet and greet looked at me with surprise and compassion. I broke down upstairs. I hate losing control. It never lasts long.

I spent the rest of the day thinking about how to get her back. She'd return to Ireland, but what she was going through would pass. I had to make sure I wouldn't pass with it.

I knew from experience that if I went back to the States I'd probably never see her again. Los Angeles is its own world; if people there look outside of the city, it's usually not farther than the borders of the state. Hollywood's a good paradigm of LA: it's been feeding on itself for the past half century.

My best chance was to stay in Bahrain. I could work the Saudi market from there. The regime in Riyadh was still standing (is still standing), if shakier—Harry had been premature in that judgment. Maybe Arab regimes are more durable than the ones he'd dealt with in the past. Their very sclerosis lends rigidity, keeps them standing longer, after their supports have rotted away. There'd still be flight capital looking for somewhere to fly: with the price of oil, probably more than before. I still had contacts in Dhahran. And after Badawi's investment, the firm in LA wasn't going to object to keeping the business going. Just the opposite.

Ireland's only six hours from Manama. You can weekend there. So, this time, I decided to stay on in the Gulf.

I cross the causeway most mornings for business. I get my investors vetted by our commerce officer in Manama—they closed the consulate in Dhahran. I've made a few new acquaintances, but no new friends. Joe disappeared. I haven't seen him since before Cyprus, although Hartley says he thinks he saw him on Pepsi Road a few months ago, looking even thinner and wearing a *thobe*. Maybe he finally came down on the Arab side of the fence. Maybe he's managing one of those small Saudi businesses I still occasionally sell an investment to. Or maybe Arthur's tentative identification was mistaken, and Joe's at the bottom of a special hole—somewhere, in some police facility—reserved for Saudi-Americans of Iraqi origin who talk too much, to the wrong people.

Arthur and Gina are still here. They come over to Manama now and then for dinner and drinks. Gina says they'll never evacuate as long as Arthur can spend a weekend or two every month in Bahrain—still a civilized Arab country. With them, I sometimes feel that I've started down the road of the permanent expat myself, although of course I haven't. The security situation across the bridge fluctuates, and I've given up my Khobar office. I drive back here every evening.

I still haven't visited Ireland. Helen and I are in touch, although not regularly. I think of her every day. The nights are long and I probably drink too much, but a few whiskies take the edge off the heat. I stay clear of the local girls—almost always. They don't mean anything.

Bahrain doesn't have sandstorms, but sometimes a storm comes in from the sea. A few weeks ago I went to sleep with the rain lashing the windows, and dreamed.

I was wading out of the Gulf at Jana Island—the same island that Harry and I had landed on before. I pulled off my mask and undid the releases of the buoyancy compensator, and the tank and hoses slipped off me onto the sand. I walked up the beach to the low gray scrub. Harry sat there on a deck chair, his back to me, facing away.

I said, "I'm sorry, Harry. I should have tried to find you, to follow you up. I stayed with Helen. I know the rule, but I had to break it. She needed my help. She was more important."

He said, "Don't worry about it. You did the right thing." Then he turned, and I saw his face. It was pale and wet and glistening from the sea. I saw my own features. His face was mine.

ACKNOWLEDGMENT

For her help in reading drafts and suggesting improvements, for her confidence, support, and from the inspiration I gained from her, I will always be grateful to my late wife, Mariann Befus.

Printed in the United States
By Bookmasters